Sheever's Journal, Diary of a Poison Master

Sheever's Journal, Diary of a Poison Master

by

K. Ritz

Strategic Book Publishing and Rights Co.

This is a work of fiction. Names, characters, places, and incidents either are a product of the author's imagination or are used fictitiously, and any resemblance to actual persons, living or dead, business establishments, events, or locales is entirely coincidental.

Copyright © 2019 K. Ritz. All rights reserved.

No part of this book may be reproduced or transmitted in any form or by any means, graphic, electronic, or mechanical, including photocopying, recording, taping, or by any information storage retrieval system, without the permission, in writing, of the publisher. For more information, email support@sbpra.net, Attention: Subsidiary Rights.

Strategic Book Publishing & Rights Co., LLC
USA | Singapore
www.sbpra.net

For information about special discounts for bulk purchases, please contact Strategic Book Publishing and Rights Co. Special Sales, at bookorder@sbpra.net.

ISBN: 978-1-950015-32-0

I would like to thank Toni Dietkus for the aid and encouragement she's given me, and for being my friend. I'd also like to thank my husband for enduring my insanity.

Some time ago, while I was traveling, a herald caught up with my party claiming to have an urgent message. I expected to hear of a crisis at home and listened in disbelief as he recited a simple request for me to stop by the Riverview Inn in Tiarn. "Soon as possible," he stressed, as if he, too, realized the inanity of the message and hoped to add import with force of breath.

"Sir," he addressed me when I asked who had hired him, "she'd not give a name. Said this would do." He held out a brooch shaped like a hawk, a ruby clutched in its talons.

"She?" I mumbled, then took the brooch, needing to feel its weight. It was the first evidence in years that Me'acca Mysuth Sheever was yet alive. The last firm report I'd gotten on him had also placed him in Tiarn where he'd purchased a bakery. I had been skeptical, but sent men to inquire. The signature on the deed was genuine. Sheever, though, had gone. A wench ran the bakery in his absence.

I flipped the herald a gold piece to whet his memory. "The wench who hired you, a baker's wife was she?"

"No, sir." Grinning, he winked. "She weren't no baker's wife."

One of my guards bent to my ear and whispered, "Don't go racing off to Tiarn. It's a trick, is all."

"Aye, a trick," I agreed, but doubted it was one crafted by an enemy. I altered my plans and headed for Tiarn, a good sixtnight's ride.

I arrived in late summer. Despite extensive reconstruction, the city was abundantly familiar, hot as Blazes and swarming with people. It was past noon ere I reached the Riverview Inn, an old clapboard building on Bridge Street where shops boast their wares in five languages. I hesitated in the foyer, unsure what name Sheever might be using. Ere I uttered a word, the innkeep nodded to the stairs, "Top floor, last on the left."

Two of my guards sped up the steps. Moments later they plodded down. "Nobody."

I refused to cede hope. I went up myself and, ordering my men to stay in the hall, I entered the room alone. Shutters on the window blocked a portion of the day's heat, but sunshine burning between the slats provided ample light to see the crude furnishings. A table, bowed under the weight of a wine keg, seemed worthy of a kindling pile. Coarse linen covered a bed unfit for a hound. A vanity, obviously Mearan-made, was rough even by the lowest standards, brass mirror flecked with green, drawers askew.

Clutter on its top drew me to the vanity. Strands of glass beads, the sort a street brothid might wear, sprawled over a pewter comb and countless hairpins. I wiggled a drawer ajar. A strong lily scent wafted up from the clothing inside.

I surveyed the room again. Nothing suggested Sheever's presence except, knowing his propensity for drink, the keg. A clay cup already positioned to be filled invited me to twist the tap. Dark red wine splashed into the cup. Aroma alone labeled the vintage as imported from Drayfed. The mellow taste proved it to be well-aged and too expensive for a wench who wore glass beads. I checked the keg's side. Charred into the wood were a ram's head and a date: 521, the year Sheever and I had met.

I decided to wait. Sipping his wine, I strolled to the window. The sill, broad as a dinner plate, held a tin box the size and shape of a taxman's ledger. Dirt jammed in the welds promoted the idea of a defiled grave.

The box resisted my attempt to open it. Rust had weakened the tin and more force, I knew, would cause damage. I imagined Sheever scolding, *You have a cat's curiosity and a gnat's patience!* I returned the box to the sill and spread the shutters, hoping for a bit of breeze.

Sunlight mustered a sweat as I squinted at the new steel bridge spanning the River Tyrne. I scanned the trees on the far bank. I'd been told the natal compounds had been toppled, but the impact of not seeing them rising above Royal Wood hit harder than secondhand news. It was as though the past itself were gone, swallowed by a sea of trees.

Movement dropped my attention to the dirt alley between the inn and the city's protective wall. Three boys plodded barefoot amid weeds and the glitter of broken bottles. They halted by a clump of buckbrush near the wall, then, one by one, fell onto their bellies and disappeared into a hole behind the brush. The city's defenses were as lax as ever.

I leaned out of the window to assess my own security. A ladder clung like ivy to the side of the inn. Had Sheever plotted to climb up and startle me? Or would he call from the alley, urge me to go down and escape my guards for an evening of risky freedom? I envied his ability to blend into the common weave, yet it was annoying when he'd vanish and not show up again until he wanted to be found. This time he'd been gone too long.

I endured the sun's glare and sat on the sill to keep watch on the alley. The tin box beside me teased my curiosity. He'd put it there, I was sure, to torment me.

Sweat had soaked my shirt when I spied a wench hurrying through the alley. As she passed under the window, her round face tilted up and I caught a whiff of lily scent ere she fled from view. I assumed I was in her room and wondered about her relationship with Sheever. I'd never get a straight answer from him. He'd say, *Someone I bumped into,* or *Someone who owed me a favor.* Half the world owed him favors. The other half wanted him dead.

I picked dirt from the tin box as I mused over where he might be. His fascination with Tiarn puzzled me. My dislike of the city paled beside his hatred of it and yet, like a wound that still itches after it's healed, the city pulled him back again and again to scratch old hurts. Why? The longer I'd known Sheever, the more I realized how much I didn't know about him. He guarded his privacy as if it were treasure.

The boys returned from their swim in the river, emerging from the hole wet and filthy and infinitely cooler than I. My patience waned. The box began to remind me of Sheever himself, smug with secrets. Why had he waited so long to contact me? I'd missed his friendship. Had he not missed mine? The obvious answer stung.

The sun set, a burst of blood on the sky. Shadows rooted in the alley. I replenished my cup and, weary of sitting, stood by the window. The tin box lay like a corpse on the sill. Irritated, I seized it. The metal warped as I pried up the lid to reveal a corked ink bottle, a pen, and a leather-bound book. A Haesyl Crescent on the cover didn't amaze me. Sheever had been close to Evald's Royal House and it would be like him to cherish a journal kept by a family that no longer exists.

I lifted the cover. Even in the poor light I recognized the fluid style of Sheever's hand. This wasn't a diary of the Royal House. I read the year of the first recorded date, 516, then gazed out at the dimming sky as I understood why I'd been summoned.

A rap on the door didn't turn me, nor the creak of it opening. "Sir, want food sent up?"

I spoke over my shoulder. "We'll eat on the road. I want to leave the city tonight."

"Tonight? What ..." He seemed about to question my decision, but must have thought it better to hint, "They'll be closing the gates soon."

Sheever's Journal, Diary of a Poison Master

"They'll open them again for us."

"Aye, sir. Whenever you're ready then."

I heard the door ease shut. The breeze I'd wanted earlier gusted in, cool on my face and thick with smells of the river. Watchmen lit lanterns on the bridge. I tucked Sheever's journal under my arm and started for the door, then paused and, knowing Sheever would approve, I left my coin purse for the wench.

*****

The following journal was penned in secret by Me'acca Mysuth Sheever, Poison Master, and my friend.

*****

Year 516 Post Cyntic War, Month 9, Day 3. Why did I buy this journal? The desire to stain these pure pages is too great to resist. I should throw the damn thing away while I still can. Already it has seduced me into committing a crime. I stole pen and ink.

    Five years. I have been here five long years.

516, 9/5. I was born 477 years post Cyntic War, in the 2nd month, on the 16th day. I am thirty-nine. My hair was dark when I was young. It's grey now. My eyes are also grey. I'm five foot and a half span tall. Weigh between nine and ten stone. Small for a man by most standards.

    I live in Tiarn, capital city of Meara. Actually, the city is across the river. The River Tyrne, that is. I am not Mearan. Mearans are the most inaccurate people in the world. I am not one of them. But I pretend to be.

    I work in the base kitchens of High Lord Fesha Trivak. As a cook. I'm clean-shaven. All the base cooks are. Shaving is required. Bathing is not. I earn 6 coppers and 14 hopence a month. I've been here five years. 384 days in a year. I've been here 1,920 days. Actually 1,922. I go by the name Sheever. It was my father's name.

    What am I doing with this journal? If it becomes known I can write, questions will arise. Gossip flies through the kitchens. If Cyril caught wind of it, he might consider me a threat. And writing about myself is insanity. Worse. It's suicide. I loathe these people. I loathe this place.

516, 9/6. Royal Park is about 3 leagues in length, and half as wide. Residents say the park is hilly, but few have seen a true hill. Only a bird knows how it appears from above. I picture it in the shape of a fat man's boot print. The kind High Lord Trivak would leave if he stepped in muck. Royal Wood covers the greater portions of the park though roads slice it into sections. Mearans must have devised the overall plan. The symmetry is off-center.

Coming from the bridge, the road splits three ways. To the right and left is Perimeter Road, which circles the park. Straight ahead is Natal Way, one of four Natal Ways, none of which has a signpost. All four lead to the arena.

Other than the legal aspects set down by the Cyntic Treaty and the Seto Pact, I don't know much about natals. Basically, each of the Four States sends a royal army to live and spend coin in Tiarn. Natal legions are trained for war and vowed to peace. They must be frustrated.

Every four years people from all over flock to Tiarn to watch the Games – and spend coin. Any damn fool can enter the Prelims held at the arena. Champions from each state join the natals for a final battle, which is held in private for the pleasure of the lords. All of this is done to honor the god Eshra who is viewed by lowlanders as a god of peace.

About the roads. If from the bridge one goes right on Perimeter Road, eventually Cemetery Lane breaks off near the eastern toe of the park. There's no signpost there either. Anyone residing in the park who happens to die can be buried in Park Cemetery. Except maybe natals. I'm not sure where they hide their dead. There are cemeteries scattered throughout the city and beyond its gates. In Tiarn disposing of the dead is a profitable business.

If from the bridge one goes straight on Natal Way, the first spur, to the right, leads to the compound of the Mearan natals.

It and the other compounds can be seen from a distance, poking above the trees like up-ended sewer pipes.

Continue on Natal Way and the arena is impossible to miss. It's the largest structure in the park. Natals don't cross blades in the arena, but at the end of the Preliminary Games they ride in and parade about, or so I've been told. I've never attended the Prelims. Nor have I been inside the arena. Iron-clad doors bar the curious during off years.

A rotary circles the arena. Staying right, the next Natal Way leads, again eastward, to Drayfed's Compound. The nation of Drayfed lies to the east of Meara, which could be why their natals were placed here, though I doubt it. Too logical. Drayfed is famous for its beautiful women and fine wines. A ram is the state symbol. If I recall correctly, Tavian, the Dray sun god, disguised himself as a snow-white ram to seduce Ophena, goddess of the night, and from their union, the Royal House of Sarum was born. Mearans claim Drays have magical powers and are inherently evil. This might better explain why the Rams were given the compound most distant from the High Lord's Palace. Royal Wood provides a comfortable buffer between the Dray natals and Park Cemetery – the sexton may think differently.

Continue on the rotary. The next Natal Way goes almost due north to Somer's Compound, which proves direction wasn't a factor in deciding which natals would live where since the nation of Somer is east of Drayfed. The best sailors in the world supposedly come from Somer, but the state symbol is a bull. Why? I have no idea. Soms are believed to be gifted mathematicians and thus, to Mearans, unworthy of trust.

On the rotary again. Take the next Natal Way, west toward the park's boot heel, and one finds something stupid. Verdina's Compound sits smack in the middle of the road. The road does split, rounding both sides of the compound, then joins itself, to again go west, but why didn't the fools kick the compound to one side or the other and build the road straight? Plus this Natal Way leads directly to the palace. If the Verdi natals ever decide to break their vows and march against the High Lord, nothing blocks their path. Did the park's designers have no sense of history?

Verdina is north of Meara. A white stag is the state symbol, an odd choice for people who worship a battle god. Before the Cyntic War united the lowland states against Uttebedt, Verdi armies invaded Meara and razed Tiarn. Had I been Meara's lord when the park's design was crafted, I would've insisted that my own natals be placed between me and those from Verdina. But I must admit, during the past five hundred years Verdi natals have not once broken their vows. Maybe a deer is an appropriate emblem.

Back to roads. If from the bridge one goes west, the first branch off Perimeter is Main. Unlike most of Perimeter, this section – from the bridge to Main – endures more traffic and is paved. Main is also paved. Taking Main, the western boundary of Royal Wood is to one's right. On the left is Valley Green, a field a wildflowers and clover, which isn't really a valley though it does slope downward. Near the bottom, where Perimeter arcs to form the southwestern corner of the park's boot heel, the bee keeper's thatched hut sits among his flock of royal hives.

Moving on. When Natal Way emerges from Royal Wood to intersect Main, the Church-Palace Complex is on one's left. A barberry hedge serves as a border between the wild beauty of Valley Green and the manicured sod and paving in front of the Church of Eshra. Next is a network of herb beds. Few, if any, are harvested. Behind the herbs, crouched between the Church and Trivak's Palace, is the Saeween where natals release their frustrations in the Finals.

A line of dwarf pear trees edges the palace side of the herb beds. As with the Church, paving leads to the main steps. The rest of the front orchard, on the other side of the pavement, is a mix of peach, standard pear and a few pampered citrus trees. Gardeners don't pick the fruit and most of it rots. If nobles care to taste bounty from the front orchard, so be it. Should a commoner do the same, the penalty is death. Or so Cyril says. He also says the fruit, especially the citrus, is bitter. I asked him how he knew. "I were tolt," he gruffed, and stomped away.

Trivak's Palace was built of quarried stone. The style is Post War with little thought put toward defense. Potted hippit vines spill red flowers over balconies where the highborn can enjoy sunshine or night breezes without soiling their slippers. I've heard rumors of a secret passage through which the High Lord smuggles brothids in without his wife's knowledge. I don't know if the passage exists. Thirty-six steps lead to the front entrance where royal troops stand guard, when the weather suits them.

The rear of the palace extends down the western slope to meet the troopers' barracks. Guards don't eat in our dining hall, but we supplement their rations. They show up in the afternoons and cart off bread, kettles of stew and whatever else they fancy. The Eshra Church, as I've stated or at least implied, stands south of the palace. We don't feed the priests; acolytes tend to their unholy needs.

The north side of the palace, the side I see daily, has a few narrow windows. I've never spotted anyone looking out. From this side sprout the base kitchens, a one-storied, rectangular structure where a stinking mob of men and women live and work.

The kitchens' east wall is flush with the upper embankment. Sod covers the roof. From Main Road, we're invisible. Only smoke from our ovens, rising behind the front orchard, gives us away. Like a bastard child of a royal house, we're hidden from public view.

The back orchard grows on the terraced slope in front of the kitchens. These trees, mostly apple, are harvested, and provide more than enough for our use. There are steps between the terraces, but more often than not people scramble over the banks, eroding them little by little.

To roads again. Past the front orchard, Main Road changes its name. North Main continues to border Royal Wood and connects with the far stretch of Perimeter. Lower Main swings around the front orchard, goes by the north door of the kitchens and down the slope, skirting the back orchard, then runs past the stockyards to the stables.

Between the stockyards and the northwestern curve of Perimeter is a cluster of shacks called Fieldtown, where stockmen and other common laborers live. These people don't dine with us – except for Jenner, the stable master. He and Cyril are friends. They're an odd-looking pair, Cyril plump and balding, Jenner scrawny and bowlegged. I met Jenner through Cyril and because of Jenner I sit at Cyril's table during evening meal. Thus I hear all the latest gossip.

Seen from the stables, the kitchens are attractive; the red-shuttered windows against the white brick seem pleasant from afar, especially in spring when the fruit trees form tiers of pink and white blossoms. But inside, in any season, the kitchens are dark and stuffy.

The oven rooms, on the western side, have windows, as does the dining hall. But the sleeping rooms are on the eastern side and if the walls did have windows, we'd have a fine view of dirt. During rainy seasons, a musty odor seeps into the rooms and the bricks become damp. Someday they'll collapse and smother us all. Tobb, my roommate, has a great fear of this. He mounted ashwood planking over the bricks to reinforce the walls. I doubt it will help, but I haven't told him. Why strain his mind?

Tobb is a meat cook. He's worked here less than a year. He's usually assigned to the outside spit, a job needing a minimum of skill. Cyril constantly nags him to shave and every few days Tobb complies. His chin is the only spot on his body touched by soap.

Except for Cyril, the cooks sleep two to four in a room. Before Tobb came, I shared this room with a man who habitually spat on the floor. Cyril fired him last spring. All the women sleep in a single large room. I assume it's large. I don't go in there. Boys ten years or older share another room. Ten is an approximate age. No one here keeps an accurate record of births.

So this is where I live. What else can I say? A door at the end of the hallway leads to the palace. House staff cart the food we prepare to wherever it will be eaten. I don't know how much of it, if any, reaches the High Lord's table. Somewhere in the palace are kitchens the private cooks use. Coal, being less expensive than wood, is our primary fuel. Boys shuttle it from a shed by the north door to the oven rooms. Girls earn their keep in the scullery.

Candles to light our rooms are free. Food is free. Cyril charges for ale and wine. Clothing is washed by a grotesque woman, Baz, and her idiot daughter. Prolonged viewing of Baz could make one pray for blindness. She eats enough to feed five men, and drinks as much ale as she can lay hands on. Can't blame her for that.

516, 9/8. Why did I buy this journal? To write of Trivak's kitchens? Not hardly. To record secrets? Here's something few people know. I swore an oath of celibacy.

That's enough. No more secrets.

516, 9/22. I banned myself from writing again until I was ready to record why I bought this journal. I'm ready. The reason? Because I pitied the woman selling it. That's a lie. Must I lie even to myself? I didn't pity the woman. That's the truth. I'll explain. The 3rd day of this month ended my 5th year in Trivak's kitchens. Also, it was wages day. Cyril, while tidying the stores, had come across an unmarked wine bottle and wanted to sell it to me unopened.

"Could be a Dray red," he tempted.

I countered, "Could be vinegar," which is what he thought the bottle contained. I convinced him to part with it for a mere hopence. He wanted me to pop the cork immediately so he could mock me for wasting my coin.

I told him I wanted to savor the mystery of it and took the bottle to my room, hoping to sample it in private, but Tobb was there – with one of his women. My presence would not have bothered Tobb. I doubt it would've bothered the woman either. I swear, these people breed like rats and no one minds the hordes of filthy children.

Tobb's presence bothered me. I went out.

Instead of taking the short route to the city, I went down Natal Way, around the Verdi Compound and past the arena. It was still light when I reached the bridge. I sat in weeds under the planking and put my back against the wall that blocked my view of the river.

The entire Royal Park is encircled by a wall. The only way in or out of the park is to cross the bridge. Have I already mentioned this? The park's wall is meticulously maintained. I'm not sure if its purpose is to keep people out – or to keep the natal legions in. Beyond the wall are the royal fields and pastures. If they built another gate, produce could be sent directly to the kitchens. As it is, livestock and other supplies are ferried across the river to Portsgate, then herded or carted through Tiarn and across Park Bridge. It's stupid really.

The city is also enclosed by a wall. Maintenance of it is lax, but this wall has several gates and a clear purpose. People living within the wall pay a higher tax than those in the shanties beyond. Enough about walls!

The mystery bottle held neither vinegar nor a fine Dray red. The wine inside was Mearan, a heavy, sweet variety, best served in a stew. I considered dumping it. Mearans don't decant wine. They drink it dregs and all. Savages. A group of riders cantered overhead. Dirt sifted through the slats of the bridge. I drank the wine. Dregs and all.

At dusk, I crossed the bridge, my wages clinking in my pocket. I usually go to the markets. The beggars know me by sight though not by name. I give them half my wages. It isn't kindness on my part. The beggars disgust me. I give them coin to atone my sins. Bribery to escape damnation.

For some reason, perhaps the wine, I was drawn to what people here refer to as Snake Street. As in any large city, some areas are less safe than others. Water Street, for instance, is considered unsafe for a lone man at night. Slavers, so I've been told, will rap a man's head and carry him off to wield oars on their ships. Size is my protection there. Slavers want big brutes like Tobb who will wake undamaged from a blow to the head.

The section of Tiarn reserved for the natals' pleasure is no doubt unsafe, perhaps even to those who work there. Those streets do have signposts, plus natal crests are painted on the corner curbs, warning even the illiterate of the risk. I've yet to find an adequate reason to go there though I've heard natals are foolish gamblers and fortunes can be won by lucky dicers. But do they live to spend it?

I seldom go to Brothid's Row. And Feaker's Knob is an area of high-priced homes I haven't explored in years. At the foot of the Knob is a debtor's prison. I wonder if the inmates pray for coins to roll down into their pockets.

I'm delaying my explanation. Snake Street is an area I should avoid. Yet that night I was drawn there as surely as if I had an appointment.

The Snake House is shabby on the outside to hide the wealth within. Everyone knows of the wealth, but facades, like the park's wall, must be maintained. A lantern hung from the porch eaves. A sign, written in Utte, read 'Kinship of the Serpent'. I stared at that sign, at that porch, at the door with its twisted handle, and wondered what the people inside would do if I entered. Would they remember me? Greet me as Kin? Or drive me out and curse me for faking my death? Worse, would they expect me to redon the life I've shed? Staring at that sign, I pissed in the street like the Mearan savage I've become.

As I started to leave, I saw a woman sitting in the gutter. Her lamp attracted me. A memsa's lamp, three tiny flames to signify the Holy Trinity of Faith, Purity, and Knowledge. The woman wasn't a memsa. Her young face was bruised and a gash on her throat had bloodied her clothing. Had she not been calmly assessing me, I would have believed the wound to be mortal. I offered her a copper.

She refused, "I take naught for naught," and began to remove trinkets from a cloth bag, displaying them for sale.

Her Utte accent had been enough to earn my coin. But to assuage her pride I commented on each of her worthless treasures, fighting the urge to speak Utte. (I spoke Universal with the accent of an upper class Mearan though I wondered if she had seen me wetting the cobblestones like a shameless commoner.) After she had arranged her wares, she looked up at me. "What do you desire, O Noble Born?"

I laughed, certain now that she had seen my act in front of the Snake House and, letting my accent match the coarseness of my dress, I again offered the copper.

"Nay, Noble One. You must choose." She lifted a strand of red beads. "These to adorn your lady's bosom?"

I shook my head. I wanted her lamp. But to steal the light from this woman ... I couldn't ask for it. She reached into her bag once more and withdrew a book, leather-bound, the pages gilded on the edges. "Be this worthy of desire, Noble Born?"

I stood stunned a moment, then touched the crescent stamped into the leather and asked if she'd stolen the book. She denied it. I've had the Training; she spoke truth. Yet how could she have come by a book bearing the Royal Seal of the Haesyl Line? I opened it. The pages were blank.

"Take it," she urged. "Record your deeds for study. Lo, the steps of your life mark the journey of your soul."

I told her I couldn't afford the book, but she smiled as if poverty were a blessing and said, "The price be one copper. Tis a wee price for salvation, Noble One."

So I bought this journal. I hide it under my mattress. When I lie awake at night, I feel the journal beneath my back and think of the woman who sold it to me. Damn her. She plagues my soul. I promised to return the next night, but I didn't. I promised to record my deeds. But I can't. The price is too high.

516, 9/24. After work, I went to Snake Street. Couldn't find the woman. Should have gotten her name. Didn't even check her ears to see if she were a half-breed. Maybe I should look in the brothid houses. Maybe I should forget her.

516, 9/25. Went to Snake Street again. A caravan was being unloaded. Silks and perfumes from Uttebedt. The crowd was large enough and mixed enough that I wouldn't be noticed – everyone enjoys watching a Snake caravan being unloaded.

One crate fell from a wagon. It must have been a special order because Tarok snapped at the man who let it slip. "Damn thy soul!" His voice was unmistakable. "Use more care or lose thy hands!"

I so crave my mother's language even a threat from Tarok was music to my ears. He climbed the stairs to the porch. He was in official garb. I couldn't see his face.

I wonder. If I went into the Kinship House and asked for him, would he give me news of Evald without trapping me in the past? Do I want to be trapped? No. I just miss home. Ha. Never thought I'd ache for Evald. I hated that city so many years. When I was twelve, I applied for a passport to Uttebedt. My entry was denied. I applied again when I was fifteen, again at twenty, at twenty-three, twenty-six. I'm a slow learner.

On my fourth birthday, my father gave me a paddle-ball. Most children hold the paddle waist high and bat the ball a span or two into the air. Dynnae children, who have been quickened, bat the rock-hard balls over their heads. Courting disaster. That was how I wanted to do it. The first time I tried, I bloodied my nose. The second, I bloodied my lip. My father watched me toss the ball up, watched it plummet down, hit the paddle, and the paddle strike my face. Again and again I tossed the ball up. Time after time the ball smacked the paddle and the paddle smacked me. "Stupid," my father called me. "Fool," he named me. "Stop trying to be what you're not."

Sheever's Journal, Diary of a Poison Master

I am stupid. I'll never find that woman again so why go to Snake Street? Is courting disaster habitual with me?
Stupid or no, Father, you're dead – and I'm not.

516, 10/3. A peddler stopped by the kitchens this afternoon. He brings his wagon two or three times a year, always on a payday. The women here never go to the markets in Tiarn. And Baz never does laundry on a payday. I once thought she didn't trust Cyril to hold her wages, but I've come to believe she lies in wait for the peddler. As always, she announced his arrival – and led the stampede out the north door. As always, most of the men escaped out the west door and hid until the threat to their wages had passed. Cyril, as always, got badgered into buying bolts of cloth and whatnots for the women to share. He and the peddler fought over prices. Cyril called him a cheat. The peddler vowed never to return. As always.

516, 10/20. Rain has driven Tobb into our room with more frequency. He's added another layer of wood to the walls. The rain keeps me inside as well. I helped him nail the planking.
Tobb currently has four women. One, Liana, is so heavy with child she has difficulty rising from his bed. He has no difficulty tugging her onto it. When he brought her in here tonight, I went out and waited in the hall. Didn't take him long. "Goodnight, Sheever," she said to me as she waddled toward the women's room.
But it is not a good night. Tobb's snores keep me awake. He's lying there now, the filthy oaf, sprawled over his cot, mouth agape. How can one man emit such noise by simply breathing? It may be an error to write while he's in the room, but I need something to combat the impulse to smother him. Writing about him does not lessen the urge.

As with everywhere in the world, there's a hierarchy among the cooks. Filson, second under Cyril, runs the soup kitchen. He's the hairiest human I've ever seen, with more hair on his knuckles than Cyril has on his head. He sheds in hot weather. Summer is not a good time to dine on soup. Padder, third from the top, rides herd over the meat cooks and if strength were the only consideration, he'd be head cook, for he can heave half a steer onto his shoulders.

Old Wix used to rank fourth and was in charge of breads. His son, Young Wix, replaced him. Now Old Wix runs, more or less, the spare kitchen, which is where I work. And where Liana works as well. It's the least favorite of the oven rooms, partly because of Old Wix (he's nearly deaf and often confused) and partly because we're subject to Cyril's whims. Assignments vary. Meat pies, desserts, sauces. I do whatever Cyril orders, then add muffins or some sort of bread to please Old Wix and get along fine. I begin work before Tobb. I'm free by mid-afternoon. Tobb isn't done until evening meal.

The women work harder than the men. They do the plucking, scraping, peeling ... All the preparations and cleanup, but never the actual cooking. These Mearan idiots believe women don't have the wits to blend the ingredients. Why don't the women protest? They're idiots too.

The early women rise before I do. Their lamps splinter the gloom of the kitchens. They chatter in whispers as they brew tea for the cooks. Windows are open to counter the heat of the ovens. Outside, the sky is as black as my soul.

We have one free day a week. There's no written schedule. Everyone knows his day by who was off the day before. I prefer to work through, save my days, and take them during the full moon. Cyril doesn't object, yet every month I have to make trades to get the proper days. It would be easy for him to schedule my days (there's an almanac posted in the dining hall), but he refuses. Each evening, he goes to the almanac and scratches out the date, as if he, too, were counting his days here. It was from Cyril that I stole the pen and ink I'm using now.

Three to four evenings a month I help in the stables. Jenner, the stable master, must have gained his position by graft, for his knowledge of horses is moderate at best. As pay, he lends me a horse on my free days. I've told him I have a wife in Brithe. The lie spread and was accepted. A wife in the next town is easy for feeble minds to grasp. I do ride toward Brithe. Midway there, however, I leave the road and follow a trail to a secluded meadow. It's a good place to camp. The river provides water, but it's the view that attracts me. In fair weather I can see the Purnath Mountains. When I ride to the meadow, I can imagine I'm going home.

Tobb turned onto his side. The room's quiet for the moment. I should sleep while I can.

516, 10/22. Wet weather brought a mushroom rush in the back orchard. Cyril sent the women in the spare kitchen out to pick them. Even Liana. She shouldn't be out in the damp. She has a hacking cough and her child is due any day. The horehound tea she drinks does little to ease her discomfort.

Like a fool, I went up to the front herb beds to gather yssop roots to fix her a brew. Yssop grows by the Saeween. A marvel anything grows near such evil. The Saeween is where the Finals are held. The building's walls are glossy black with no windows and no apparent doors. Eshra's arena, people here call it, if they mention it at all. The Saeween is the heart of the Church's power. I feel it in my bones.

The sky was spitting rain when I went to gather the yssop. There were no guards on the palace steps. Clouds hid the spires of the Church. Like a dark mirror, the Saeween reflected my image. I dug quickly.

I was tamping dirt into the hole when I spied an Eshra priest walking toward me. The hood of his cloak covered his damned head. I knelt. How could I not? I didn't see his eyes, but I'm certain he was a true priest. Not one of the fakes they use on occasion. He was barefoot, and the dark triangle branded on his right foot was true. Brands of power are difficult to fake.

Mud soaked my pants as I waited for him to speak. Rain beat my back. I emptied my mind of thought. He took the roots I had dug, saying nothing, and walked away. I left as well. Liana will have to make do with horehound tea.

I now wonder if the priest recognized me. Priests in the Father Church rotate duty at the Church in Evald. Had this one seen me there? Years ago they actively sought me, but surely their search has ended. And who would expect me to be living near their stronghold? I must be a fool.

516, 11/16. Liana gave birth to a boy. Named him Tobbson. Clever.

516, 11/17. Tobb brags of his son, brags he has fathered more than twenty children. He doesn't know the exact number, doesn't know their names. I hate this man. Why do women love him?

Liana is ill and unable to nurse.

516, 11/18. Tobb brought a new woman to our room. She works in the scullery. Has red hair. Is fifteen at most.

Tobb sleeps with a carving knife jabbed into the wall above his bed. I could carve his chest with it. Like Tobb and his children, I don't know the exact number of men I've killed. I don't remember all of their names. One more wouldn't blacken my soul any more than it is.

Sheever's Journal, Diary of a Poison Master

516, 11/23. Went to the meadow. Clouds socked the view. The rain was constant. I was miserable, but stayed anyway, hoping the clouds would lift. I needed a glimpse of the mountains, a glimpse of home. No such luck.

I got back to the city well before they closed the gates, but Jenner scolded me for being late. As punishment, he wants me to train a newly purchased mare.

Liana died while I was gone. Tobb passed her son to a woman with a one-year-old girl. The boy refuses to suckle.

516, 11/27. I've spent my evenings in the stables with Jenner. The mare is a roan. She's a beauty. With the narrow hooves, arched neck and short muzzle of the highland breeds.

Jenner's had trouble controlling her and thinks she hasn't been trained. In truth, she was trained Kinship-style and responds to toe commands. It was a simple matter to adapt her to the standard rein signals.

I hope the High Lord doesn't plan to ride her himself. I've seen Fesha Trivak. He weighs more than the mare.

516, 11/28. Tobbson died this morning. Son of Tobb. Dead.

Eshra is the official god of all four lowland states, but most Mearans pray to Loric, slayer of demons. They bury their dead and believe in an afterlife where souls reside in a garden. In these kitchens, clay idols of Loric adorn doorways and bless each oven, but the people tend to be less devout than some Mearans I've known. Until there's a death.

There was much praying this morning as Tobb's women wrapped his dead son in linen. Usually a two-wheeled cart is used to transport a body, but the child was no bigger than a lamb haunch. They put him in a wicker basket.

After work Tobb and his mates, and a drove of women and children walked to the cemetery. I went with them. We took North Main to the back stretch of Perimeter. In summer it's a pleasant road. Royal Wood lines one side and on the other wild roses break the tedium of the park's wall. But today the trees were bare, the roses thorny snarls, and the road, dusty in summer, was mud. We turned onto Cemetery Lane about sunset.

The common graveyard begins shortly past the turn, on the western side of the lane, flowing up a small hill, not quite to its crest. Markers vary – rocks, rusty swords, wooden stakes, some with cross-pieces and names, most half-hidden by weeds. Trees hem the upper boundary. The lane hems the lower, cutting across the hill's base.

Gazing ahead, we could see the Temple of Loric, white bricks seeming to glow in the twilight. Beyond the temple a wrought-iron fence encloses a graveyard for the wealthy, an extra barrier to separate rich from poor. Noble families have marble crypts with fancy doors. Granite slabs mark the graves of lesser nobles. Lesser lesser nobles have slate markers. Even the dead are bound by hierocracy.

The sexton lives in a cottage made of field rock. It and a stable, also of field rock, are on the eastern side of the lane. Tobb went in to make the arrangements and pay the fee. The rest of us walked a few paces more and gathered by the temple. Smaller than the cottage, it's an oddly plain structure, considering it was built to honor a god. A carving on the wooden door depicts the Fiery Staff with which Loric banished demons from Meara.

Padder and Vraden lit lanterns while we waited. Women fussed with children. Crows perched on the bare limbs of a quince in the sexton's yard, lumps of black on grey.

Tobb joined us, carrying a spade and pail of lime. Liana's grave was at the upper edge of the common cemetery, almost in the trees. A stick served as a marker. Tobb dug a hole by the stick, dropped his son's body in with her and added a spadeful of lime. Rain drizzled as we chanted the Song of Death – a prayer that begs Loric to accept the spirit of the dead. My father taught me this dirge, so I chanted with the others and if my saying the words was sacrilege, so be it. I'm damned anyway.

After the ceremony, I lingered, telling Tobb I'd catch up with him and the others, then I took a shortcut through Royal Wood and arrived ahead of them so I had time to write. Tobb should be here any moment. I'd wager a month's pay he'll have the red-haired woman with him. A pity he wasn't buried today instead of his son.

516, 11/31. A special day. At least it was 23 years ago.

516, 11/32. Last day of the month. Uttes call this month Lassamout – Moon of the Wolf. The wolves have been well-fed indeed.

516, 12/3. The Beggar's Moon. There were beggars a-plenty at the market. They squabbled over my coins.

The women have been avoiding Tobb. Someone started a rumor he has the pox. Who could have done such a thing?

516, 12/6. Tobb drinks more every day. Ale mostly. It's cheaper than wine. Our room smells worse than the privy.

516, 12/7. Tobb bought a brass necklace. He mocks me for the cloth one I wear. If he knew the braiding covered a gold amulet given to me by the current Lord of Uttebedt ...

Jenner wants me transferred to the stables, but Cyril won't let me go. Just as well. I need to be where I am.

516, 12/8. After work I went out to the bridge and watched the river flow. A group of natals rode past. Soms, their black cloaks lined with orange. A person should be wary around natals – no matter from which of the states they hail. Vowed to peace or no, natals were raised for combat and it's said they'll kill a man for mere sport. Perhaps, perhaps not, but they will slay anyone who gets too close to their na-kom. They protect their own.

The natals I saw today were too hurried to stop and kill me. Their horses steamed as they clattered past. Sword hilts, blades tucked in saddle sheathes, shone by their knees.

I've never been to Somer. I've heard the best way to get there, rather than through Drayfed, is to sail the Chaderon Sea. I've never seen the sea. I've heard the water's salty. I have been to Drayfed. Once. Special assignment for the Kinship. I remember the man I was sent to 'meet,' a petty noble who surrounded himself with guards. Can't recall his crime against the Snakes. He died easily. Maybe he should have surrounded himself with natals.

516, 12/10. Caught Tobb with my journal. He can't read Universal, nor Mearan for that matter, but he's suspicious of me. He demanded two hopence to keep quiet. I paid him. The situation is bound to escalate. Do I kill him to ensure his silence? There would be too much pleasure in it.

516, 12/11. I went to an apothecary on Water Street. Ophren was the cheapest buy. Purchased a dram of gisek powder as well. Will I use them? If the chance arises, I must.

516, 12/13. I drugged Tobb, then took the little finger from his left hand. A tidy job. Gisek quelled the bleeding.

When he woke, I told him I had placed a hex on him and he had cut off his own finger. Warned him that if he spoke to anyone about my journal, or about the hex, the next time he woke, he'd be missing his tongue. He believed me.

This morning, he pretended to injure his hand while hacking a side of beef. The ruse was accepted. It isn't uncommon for a meat cook to lose a knuckle or two.

Jenner wanted me to exercise the roan mare, so I rode her to the cemetery. I buried Tobb's finger with Liana and her son. If she's in Loric's Garden, maybe the finger will remind her of the man who helped put her there.

516, 12/15. Tobb fears me now. At night, I sense him lying awake. He no longer keeps a knife in the wall above his bed. It's under the blanket, in his hand.

516, 12/18. Tobb looks ghastly. Everyone thinks he's dying of pox. Cyril told me that if Tobb dies, I can have the room to myself. He shouldn't tempt me.

516, 12/19. Tobb is unable to work. He truly is ill. No one dares enter the room to feed him and he'll take nothing from me.

516, 12/20. I bribed the red-haired woman to feed Tobb. I laced the broth with ophren. He's sleeping now. My hatred has turned to pity. Is this a part of the process, Sythene?

516, 12/21. The name I wrote in the last entry I should not have written. I should scratch it out. But I can't. I'll write it again. Sythene. And again in full. Sythene Ayriata Maedi Lonntem. The sight of her name makes me weep.

Sythene, why did I think of you last night? In the meadow I allow myself such liberties, but here in the kitchens I try to block you from my mind. Why do I think of you tonight?

Because of Tobb's red-haired woman? She came tonight, fed him the drugged broth, then left when he slept. Her hair is red, but not the same shade as yours. It has no luster like yours. No curl. Her face is flat and round, the face of a peasant. You bear the face of a god.

Tobb's woman treads with a heavy step. You walk with the grace of a dancer, silent as a ghost. She's fifteen, yet her shoulders sag. You were born with the world on your shoulders, yet your back is straight. Do you ever bend, Sythene? Do you ever twist the rules to suit your fancy? Do you ever think of me?

Twice I asked you to let me follow you into Uttebedt. More than twice if you count my written requests. Did you read my letters? Did they amuse you?

Sythene, you're the same as my father, the same as the Kinship. You want my services, then pay me with trinkets.

I recant. You're not the same. Gold spills from your hands. Promises spill from your mouth. "Speak and I shall listen," you said. "Ask and I shall answer." Well, I've spoken. I've asked. I've heard no reply.

"As my father be the Crescent," you said, "so I be the Moon Complete. Gaze upon its fullness, and I shall feel the touch of thy eyes. Weep beneath its light, and I shall taste thy tears."

I have gazed, Sythene. I have wept. Once, when you were a child, you wept in my arms. Do you ever weep now?

516, 12/22. I can't believe I wrote what I wrote yesterday. I must be losing my mind.

Tobb has improved. He's able to feed himself, but he had the red-haired woman do it. Then he coaxed her onto his bed. Stupid fool woman. She believes he has the pox, yet still coupled with him. At least she didn't stay the night.

Tobb is watching me now. He's asked me to teach him to read and write so he can be a head cook someday. I promised I would.

I'm losing my mind.

516, 12/27. Went to the meadow. No view. Cold.

I'm ashamed of what I've written about Sythene. I sound like a scorned lover. I never was, nor ever will be, her lover. When last I saw her, she was a child of six. That isn't exactly true. She wore the body of a six-year-old, but Sythene has never been a child.

516, 12/32. Shortest and last day of the year.

Mearans call next month Gurn. They celebrate a new year on Gurn 4, as if they need four days to be sure it's a new year. Dolts.

Uttes call next month Seimout. They celebrate a new year the evening before the first day of Seimout, as if afraid they won't live through the last night of an old year to see a new one dawn. Considering the fact we lost the war, is this significant?

517, 1/1. Drank too much last night. Stayed in the city too long. Tobb asked where I'd been. I reeked of mead and attar. Was late to work. Cyril had me prepare liquor cakes for Trivak's up-coming banquet. I almost heaved from the smell. Thought the day would never end. Slept as soon as I finished work. Now Tobb's snoring. And I can't sleep.

Last night I went to Snake Street. I didn't intend to stay, just walk past and hear the revelry. At the corner I paused by a three-storied house, holding my cape tight about me, hood up, a muffler masking my face. Lanterns shone from every porch. People filled the street. Laughing people. People who called to one another in Utte. I moved to the edge of the porch, to the edge of the crowd, then climbed the stairs to improve my view.

Mead casks, each with a knot of happy drinkers dipping their cups, were stationed four to five houses apart on both sides of the street. Mid-way down, a fire blazed, lighting a circle of singers, warming their bright faces. The strains of a lute wove through the crowd like tendrils of fog through a grove of young trees, blending them, uniting their voices into a single tune.

A door opened behind me. As I turned, a woman came from the house. She wore a quilted shirtcoat and wool leggings – and a sheathed knife strapped to her thigh. A cord bound her hair in a loose braid. She tipped her head and porchlight illuminated the snake tattoo on her cheek. She was a Kinswoman. "Be ye awaiting thy companions?"

"Nay," I whispered. In over five years, this was the first word I had spoken in Utte. Nay. I doubt she heard that word, spoken softly through my muffler. I'm sure she didn't know what it meant for me to speak it.

Suspicion flashed in her dark eyes. My clothing was obviously Mearan. I spoke louder. "My business be private." To Kin, private business can range from dealing for a new market to planning an assassination. Only the foolish, or the high-ranking, would probe further. Yet I didn't want to be rude, so I answered her question. "I've nay companions with me." I offered her my wrist for the traditional Kinship greeting. "Tis alone, I be."

She tapped her wrist on mine. "Ye be alone nay longer, Kinsman." She latched onto my arm and, before I could utter a protest, she drew me down the stairs and into the crowd.

We went to the nearest cask. Toasted bread floated in the mead, befitting the occasion. Cups hung from the rim. With furtive glances, I assessed the people around us. Most were young and none familiar. What harm in a brief stay?

Pressed by the crowd, the woman and I stood close. Her rose-scented hair perfumed the air I breathed. She told me her name was Kara. I asked if she knew it meant dream in the old tongue. She shook her head, laughed, and for the rest of the night called me Scholar.

She was born in a village to the west of Evald, in central Uttebedt. Her parents named her Kara, she told me, because she had been conceived during a trip to the blessed city of Karamorn. A memsa selected Brinta Dae for her (Far Traveler) and though Kara was the name that stuck, she lived up to the memsa's prediction, working on caravans the past seven years, traveling throughout Drayfed and Somer.

Kara bubbled with tales. She claimed she saw Lord Maisouff board a Som pleasure craft on the Chaderon Sea. Said he carries a staff made of a bull's member. She spread her arms wide, bumping two men, to show me the length of it. I thought she was stretching the truth and said so. Her laughter was as sweet as the mead. "Twas the bull who was stretched, Scholar! Least the part dearest to him!"

I smiled. Though I had detected no lie, I couldn't believe her. I drained my cup and hung it on the cask rim, preparing to leave. She must have thought she had offended me, for she begged my pardon and asked me to stay. "Will ye not have one sip more?" I let her refill my cup and, to be polite, asked if the Chaderon Sea is salty as I had heard.

"Yea, Scholar," she murmured into my ear. "Tis as salty as a lover's tears."

It was then I should have gone, for it was then I realized Kara was seeking a companion to share her bed. Men outnumbered women twenty to one at the gathering. She could have chosen any of them. She was pretty and good-humored. She was wasting her time on me. I should have gone. But a man beside her lifted his cup and yelled, "To Lord Sythene Lonntem! May she rule long!"

How could I shun such a salute? For an Utte, sipping on a toast is considered an insult. I gulped my mead and kissed the bottom of my cup, as did everyone else. I was starting to slide away from Kara when another man cried, "To Sythene's partner, Daemis Brandt!"

Cups splashed into the cask. As I dipped mine, I spoke to the man beside me. "I didn't know Sythene had chosen a partner. When did she sign the contract?"

The man pushed back a pace and eyed me. "She partnered with Brandt years past. Whither have ye been?"

Kara defended me. "His business be private, Jaro."

The man, Jaro, nodded in understanding and raised his cup. "To Sythene and Daemis! May an heir be conceived soon!" His words burned in my mind as I downed the mead. 'May an heir …' Sythene had no daughter. I wanted to ask if she had a son, but didn't dare bring more attention onto my ignorance. As it happened, I didn't need to.

A lively discussion arose concerning Sythene and Daemis Brandt. Apparently, the Memsa Tribunal had advised against their partnership. Opinions differed as to the reason.

"Brandt has nay seed," one man declared. "The memsen foresaw it and wished Sythene to choose another."

"They've had nay children thus far," another man added.

"Bah!" Jaro spat. "Brandt be Dynnae. That displeased the memsen, not his lack of seed. If lack he has! They wanted her to choose a memsa who would guide her. Bah, I say. Do they think Sythene has nay vision of her own? If she desires Brandt to share her throne, so be it. Who better at her side than the foster son of Dyn Luka Massu?"

A woman on the opposite side of the cask contested him. "If the Dyns goad Sythene to war, what then, my brother? Whither shall our caravans go with the world in flames?"

Among Snakes, nothing sparks a debate faster than politics and trade. Fresh arguments heated the discussion. The woman who had countered Jaro was quick-witted and sharp-tongued. She bore her Serpent on her chin. Most Kinswomen choose visible spots for the tattoo. Not due to pride, but for protection. Women in Uttebedt may be equal under the law, but everywhere else in the world they're treated as inferior. A woman raped in Meara must prove herself blameless to win a conviction. Rape, though frowned upon, is a common crime here. No lowlander, however, and no member of the Victor Class in Evald would dare assault a Kinswoman. Snakes don't use courts of law when they're wronged and, like natals, they defend their own.

Kara ended the disagreement by shouting, "To Daemis Brandt! May his seed be as potent as his blade!"

This spurred a rash of toasts – to the night, to the new year, to Tarok who had paid for the mead, to his partner (her name was never mentioned, and I didn't ask), to his house in Evald where he was wintering ... On and on, cup after cup, I drank until I thought I would burst.

Mead.
O sweet elixir,
Ye bless the lips and steal the wits.

When I found myself drinking to honor someone's boots, I knew it was time to go. I squirmed through the crowd. Kara, following me, lured me into her house. Lured is too strong. She invited me in. As we climbed to the porch, she staggered against me. This is an old trick. I expected the jab of her knife between my ribs. She was merely drunk.

Her room was on the third floor. Hot coals glowed in the hearth. She beckoned me to the bed. I was too drunk to resist.

She anointed my brow with attar of roses. I kissed the tattoo on her cheek, kissed her honeyed mouth, her throat, her perfumed hair. She wanted more from me. I was too drunk to oblige. My oath is still intact.

517, 1/3. All the cooks are complaining about the extra work preparing for Trivak's Gurn 4 banquet. This grumbling and talk of finding work in the city happens every year. As usual, our wages were delayed. I'm sure the paymaster believes we would spend our wages on drink and not finish cooking the feast. But what I fail to understand is why doesn't he pay us on the fourth of every month? Then no one would complain of the Gurn delay. I live among idiots.

517, 1/4. Mearans fast during the morning of Gurn 4. At noon they extinguish all hearth fires, then gorge themselves on food and drink. It's a religious practice. In theory, Loric relights the fires with his Staff at midnight. In reality whoever rises first does the deed, but the household is considered blessed by Loric's Fire anyway. I like Gurn 4. Cyril gives us free ale. He locks the wine stores.

By noon today, the ovens were cold. The banquet we'd been preparing for days had been carried off to wherever Trivak and his guests dine, and troopers had carted off their portion. The women were setting out our feast in the dining hall when Cyril ordered the cooks to don our uniforms – black pants and red tunics bearing the Hawk Crest. This struck me as odd. Many cooks wear uniforms every day, especially those who have been here long enough to own more than one, or those who have nothing else to wear. But Cyril never required us to wear them – until today.

Once we were all properly clad, he lined us up in the main hallway, near the door that leads to the palace. We could hear laughter from the dining room, but he wouldn't let us join in. He said we were awaiting the paymaster.

Vraden, one of the meat cooks, mumbled that we could wait just as easily in the dining hall. Cyril didn't hear him. Vraden has a pocked face and eyebrows so bushy birds could perch on them. He waggled those brows as he repeated his comment. Cyril pretended not to hear. So we waited.

Finally, the paymaster arrived with his steel box. As usual, two guards accompanied him. As if a palace thief would bother with such paltry sums. Another man was with them. His uniform was similar to ours, Black Hawk of Meara on his chest, but his was satin. A gold chain, links as large as Tobb's knuckles, lay about his shoulders, dipping mid-way to his belt. The paymaster introduced him as Hickten Jazuf, First Secretary to the Royal House.

Jazuf is a thin man and fidgety, like a mouse caught in daylight. He worked his hands as if kneading cheese while he lectured us on the honor of being employed by the High Lord, the prestige of wearing the Hawk, then asked if any of us thought there should be an adjustment in our wages.

Clearly, our usual holiday grumbling had leaked beyond the kitchens. Tobb was beside me, and I knew the thoughts running through his thick head, knew what each of the brutes in line with me was thinking: we would be awarded a raise in pay, if only we asked for it. Fools. A first sec's time is valuable. Trivak wouldn't send his here, not today of all days, merely to give us a raise in pay.

I sensed Tobb's intention to speak out and seized his arm to silence him. No one silenced Vraden. "Cooks at the inns fetch two coppers more a month," he said and, if he had stopped there, perhaps we would have gotten a raise, but he continued, "It's a Game Year, mate. Any cook worth his pepper could name his price in town, so why earn less just to sport the damn Hawk on my shirt."

In my opinion, Vraden committed three errors. Four, if you count his profanity. Five, if you count opening his mouth. But worse than his hint that he might ply his trade elsewhere, worse than his implication that wearing the royal crest was worth nothing, Vraden called the First Sec 'mate.' That alone would earn him a flogging. Or so I thought.

Instead of ordering the guards to arrest Vraden as I expected, Jazuf smiled. "Well," he said. His hands were deathly still, then he toyed with his gold chain. "I'm pleased you brought this disparity in wages to my attention. We wouldn't want to lose our cooks during a Game Year." His smile broadened, a pleasant smile, a first sec smile. It meant trouble. He motioned to Vraden. "If you would delay celebrating, perhaps we can discuss the matter privately."

Vraden, fool that he is, agreed to go and, after the paymaster had doled out our wages, he lumbered through the doorway to the connecting hall with Jazuf and the guards.

Tobb and the others cheered as they went into the dining hall. I felt compelled to record what happened before I'm witless from drink. I can't stop thinking about Vraden walking through that doorway.

517, 1/5. My mother is a memsa. Before I could read, she read the Word of Dynnas to me. She raised me in the faith. As a boy, I helped her train novices and for a while I, too, wore the white gown of a novice. I studied scriptures, recited the catechisms. I know, in part, the lore memsen use to attain power. I learned the controls of mind and body.

One such control is Dohlaru. Literally, the word means retreat, but it's a mental feat and has nothing to do with feet running from danger. Dohlaru is a state of mind.

A memsa aspiring to be a judge must be adept at Dohlaru. Facts must be weighed without emotion. "Caring without caring," is how my mother explained it. Thus a memsa can judge anyone – friend or stranger – and remain fair. They care without caring. Perhaps my mother, if she ever thinks of me, practices Dohlaru when I sneak into her thoughts. Here in Trivak's kitchens, I try to practice Dohlaru. Some days I succeed. Today I failed.

During yesterday's celebration, I got drunk early and went to bed. I woke in the middle of the night and got up, thinking it was dawn. My mistake was apparent when I opened the door. Head throbbing, I should've spun around and gone back to bed. But Cyril doesn't often give away ale. Filthy brew or no, I went to see if any was left in the kegs.

The dining hall was a shambles, food and drink spilled on the floor. Tobb, Padder, and Woset were in there. They were waiting for Vraden to return. I joined them, sharing a bench with Tobb. He served me a brew.

Gossip swung from one topic to another but circled back to Vraden. They wondered what had delayed him and created explanations, each more outrageous than the last. The suggestion that Trivak's wife fancied him in her bed earned the deepest laugh, but no need to record them all. Suffice to say the mood was high.

A ruckus outside hushed us. Tobb went to a window and yelled through the shutters for the merry-makers to identify themselves. A man shouted back that they were royal troops, had slain a boar and wanted to roast it on our spit.

Troopers poach game often enough that the request wasn't unusual, but this was Gurn 4 and no cooking fires were to be lit. Yet even a dolt like Tobb knew how drunken troopers would react if denied the spit. I assured him it was past midnight. He seemed relieved and called out permission. I heard the sarcastic reply. "We're so in your debt!" The troopers would have used the spit regardless.

Padder and Woset decided to go to bed. I stood to go as well. Tobb asked me to stay. Vraden was his dearest mate. He wanted to wait up for him, but not alone. "Gurn 5 is a free day," he argued. (Though it isn't officially, most people are ill from overindulgence on the 4th.) "Besides," he nagged after the other two had gone, "you promised me a reading lesson."

We went to my workbench for the lesson. The spare kitchen was freezing. The shutters were open – they're rarely shut in the oven rooms and can't be without going outside to unfasten them. We could hear troopers snickering around the spit. Neither of us wanted to go out. My head was still pounding. I wanted bidda and tea.

Tobb kindled a fire and set a kettle on to heat while I shook flour onto a kneading board. I don't know how long the lesson lasted. The room grew warm. Bidda eased my aching head, a blessing since I would not have been patient otherwise. I drew the Mearan alphabet into the flour. Tobb studied each letter, his three-fingered hand wrapped around a cup. He'd squint, sip tea, trace my lines, squint again, sip again, then copy a letter.

I printed his name. That delighted him. He was like a child with honeycomb. He wanted me to write Cassie, the name of his red-haired woman. Then Vraden's name, then my own. Seeing my name did not delight me. I halted the lesson and smoothed out the marks.

Tobb didn't object. Sniffing the air, he commented on the aroma wafting in from the spit. "Don't smell like no boar." When he went to a window, I thought nothing of it, but when he stayed, I went to look for myself.

Eight troopers squatted around the spit like the savages they are. A ninth hunched perilously close to the fire, head tipped as though he were drunk. Then I realized that a head was all he was – a head seated on a post, bushy brows shading the eyes. Vraden, if alive, could have watched his body sizzle, for Tobb's nose had been correct. The leg roasting on the skewer had never been attached to a boar.

Tobb moved from the window and sat on the floor by the grain bins, hugging his knees. "They're eating him! Them stinking Uttes! And I gave them permission!"

I stared at him, this man whose finger I had stolen, and I tried to capture Dohlaru, tried to retreat and weigh the situation. Tobb is neither friend nor stranger to me. Vraden was neither. It should have been easy.

"He chose his path," I said, though I knew my words would bring no comfort. Tobb wasn't raised in the faith.

"Vraden will haunt me," he wept.

Mearans are a superstitious lot. Most of their beliefs are odd, but none is more so than their view of cannibalism. Not only is a person who partakes of human flesh damned, the one eaten is damned as well. And damned for eternity, for the eaters have a chance to repent. The dead can't.

I should note that Tobb knew the men dining on Vraden were Mearan. The myth that Uttes are cannibals is a widely held notion in the lowlands. Labeling the troopers Uttes was his way of debasing them.

The insult to my mother's people didn't anger me. Confident I had achieved Dohlaru, I gazed outside and began to examine the facts. It was unlikely the First Sec ordered those men to roast Vraden – punish him for sure, but not eat him. Vraden had been a stupid fool. But had he deserved this? My grasp of Dohlaru vanished. Hatred welled up within me. I wanted to kill those men. Tobb and I were no match for them, but if we woke others to aid us ... My mind dashed through a plan to mete justice, yet I knew it would never happen. If even one trooper escaped to tell the tale, every man, woman and child in the kitchens would be slain.

To stand there though, listening to Tobb weep, and do nothing while those men finished their unholy meal ... I went to the kneading board and floured my face. "I'm going out," I stated. "They'll eat no more of him."

"Sheever!" Tobb hissed my name. "You can't go out!" He sprang from the floor. "You'll be next on the spit!"

His concern for my welfare amused me. I told him to fetch a broom. We tied rags around the bristles, greased them, set them afire, then I went out the north door.

Had it been any night except Gurn 4, my ruse would not have worked, but when I stepped around the side of the kitchens, my face white as a ghost's, those troopers leapt to their feet. I waved my flaming staff and shouted the chant Loric had used to drive out demons. The troopers fled, yelping like beaten hounds.

The rout brought no joy. I sent Tobb to wake Cyril and we gathered what was left of Vraden. He was buried today. Everyone in the kitchens went to the cemetery except me.

Sitting here on this cot I call my bed, writing these words, I realize my exile is far from over. The hatred I tasted today was as bitter as ever.

> Whither be the heart of Justice?
> Lo, in stone, child. Lo, in stone.
> Whither be the heart of Justice?
> Lo, tis fast in stone.

I remember a conversation with Sythene. We were in my suite in Lord Haesyl's Keep. We sat on the sunporch, my lute on the table between us. Moonlight poured through the glass walls, dusting her copper curls with silver. She was not quite three years old. Jamin blooms scented the air.

I had been trying to convince her to overthrow the Vic government and reclaim Evald for Uttebedt. She sat there, legs drawn up so all of her was on the chair seat. She had balanced a teacup on one bent knee and though, as we talked, she waved her arms and rapped the table with her small knuckles, that cup remained perfectly balanced on her knee. (I recall this so clearly because she was lecturing me about balance in politics.) "When ye be a tad older," she said in her little-girl-lisp, "ye shall understand the illusion of government. Perhaps then, we can discuss the matter fully."

I smile as I write this, remembering her, a sea of wisdom in the guise of a child. At the time, however, her words annoyed me. It was she, I thought, who failed to understand. I asked her to go with me to the windows and as we stood there, gazing down at the lights of the city, I told her of the misery of the Uttes and half-breeds who walked those streets. They were Evald's Lost, I told her, descendants of Uttes left behind after the war. They deserved justice, I argued, and accused her of not caring.

No taller than my waist, she tilted her face up and smiled her god-like smile. "Dearest Me'acca," she said, calling me by my first name, "if I did not care for this world, I would not have come."

Sythene had mastered Dohlaru before her birth.

517, 1/6. Today the kitchens were as busy as ever. We churned out food for the innocent and the damned alike. I watched as the troopers came for their bread and stew. It would be so easy to poison the lot of them.

517, 1/7. If Vraden's death was intended to scare the cooks into behaving, First Sec Jazuf failed. There's talk of quitting and finding jobs in the city. Cyril won't go. Tobb might. He asked me what it's like during a Game Year. I told him it's no different than any other year, which isn't true, but if too many cooks leave, Cyril will catch the blame.

People seem to be treating me oddly. I'm not sure how to explain. It isn't anything explicit, just a feeling. Perhaps it's my imagination. Or maybe they're put off because I didn't attend Vraden's burial.

517, 1/8. Cooks were issued new uniforms. We weren't measured by a tailor. The uniforms were simply doled out according to general size. My tunic is too long in the sleeves. I can't say we didn't need or deserve new clothes, but the timing makes me wonder. Are the uniforms a bribe?

517, 1/9. Fesha Trivak left for Dartsport. He goes there each year to visit his first wife and eldest son. We were forced up into the front orchard to watch him go. Few of the women and none of the children had capes. They stood shivering until Trivak finally waddled down the palace steps and into his carriage. All of us cheered. Good riddance!

517, 1/10. Yesterday, one of the meat cooks spent his free day in Tiarn. He hasn't returned. Cyril is worried. Everyone believes the spit is haunted by Vraden's ghost. It hasn't been used since he died. I suggested to Tobb that he build another spit and bless the old one with a burial ceremony.

517, 1/12. Two more cooks have fled, both of them from the spare kitchen, which leaves only three of us in there – me, Old Wix and Lanerd who used to work soups until he and Filson clashed years ago. The spare kitchen is the smallest of the oven rooms, too small, in my opinion, for five cooks and seven women. I'm pleased with the extra space. I moved to the workbench nearest the door where I can keep an eye on the hall and have more air as well.

Lanerd is also pleased. He had bunked with the two cooks who ran off. Now he has a four-bed room to himself.

Cyril, however, is frantic. He wants to cancel my free days this month, thinks if I leave, I won't return. I told him my wife was with child and I had to go. The clear weather we've had won't last. If I don't get to the meadow this month, I'll lose my chance to view the mountains before the rains. But he's determined to keep me here.

517, 1/13. Another cook gone, this one from soups. Yet Cyril told me I could take my free days. "I'd not want you ignoring your wife," he said, pausing ever so slightly before wife.

Something's up. I think he knows I'm not married. Plus people are definitely acting odd. They seem to be afraid of me. Why? Have they discovered my past? How? Has Tobb told them about this journal? He's sleeping now, but I intend to ask him tomorrow. I hope I don't have to make good my threat of taking his tongue.

517, 1/14. Everything is as clear as the sky. The quick glances. Cyril's change of heart. Tobb cleared everything.

A rumor has spread that on occasion I can transform myself into a demon. I have to laugh at the insanity of it. The rumor began when Tobb's son died and I lingered at the cemetery. When Tobb brought Cassie to our room that night and found me already here, the woman deduced I must have flown back, literally sprouted wings and flown! (The idea I had taken a path through Royal Wood didn't occur to her.) Couple this with the fact that I prefer my free days during the full moon (a most auspicious time for demons), and we have the makings of a fable fit for simple minds.

Tobb added the final spice. He's been busy embellishing the tale of how we saved Vraden's remains. According to his version,

I grew twice the height of a man and spat fire at the guards to frighten them away.

He's here now, lying on his bed as I write this. "Cassie's yet scared of you," he's saying. "But I says to her, so long as you got that necklace on, you don't change into no demon. That necklace protects you, don't it, mate?"

I think Tobb actually believes the demon fantasy he helped create. I ran my fingers down the braid covering the gold chain I wear, fondled the swirl of tiny braids hiding the disk. I wish I could cut the cloth and gaze on the god's face etched in the gold, but I resist the urge.

Tobb wants an answer on the necklace. I told him it does protect me and maybe it's true.

"Are you writing what I'm saying?" he asked.

I told him, "Yes," and we both laughed.

Hearing him speak in one language and writing his words in another reminds me of when my mother taught me cross-recording. Poor Ry'aenne. She so wanted me to become a first sec. I used to practice constantly, hoping to please her. She spoke Universal a tad slower than Utte, making it easier to get an accurate translation, but compared to her, Tobb talks like a turtle walks. He pauses to scratch the stubble on his chin and sniff the air, as if his thoughts slip past his tongue and need to be located elsewhere.

He asked where I was born. I told him Eastland. He's sniffing. Does he smell my lie?

"Where's Eastland?" he asked.

"West of Brithe," I said. "Near the Uttebedt border."

"If it's west of Brithe," he's saying, "and west of here, why's it called Eastland?"

Dolt. He doesn't have the sense to realize the city was named by Uttes. I told him I didn't know why. He's scratching his belly.

Probably has fleas. He wants me to ask where he was born, but I'm not going to. I don't care where he entered this world.

He asked if I had been a head cook in Eastland before a wizard cursed me and turned me into a kor-man (a part-time demon of sorts.) I said, "Yes." What harm in the lie?

He asked what I had done to deserve the curse. I don't have a good answer for this one. He asked if the wizard sent me here to work off the curse. I told him, "Yes," and in part that's true, though a memsa sent me here.

Tobb asked me ... Can I put his words on paper? They stab my heart. My humor has fled. He asked if I would be free of the curse when I had written on every page of this journal. I wish it were true. If it were, I would write day and night to save my soul. "Yes," I said, and asked if he had kept his promise to me about the journal.

"I've not tolt nobody. Swear to Loric! And you've no need to worry of nobody finding it when you're off moon-howling. I'll watch over that book for you. On account of what you done for Vraden." He's scratching his head. Maybe he doesn't have fleas. Maybe scratching stimulates his mind. "Kor-man or no, Sheever, you're my best mate."

"You're a fool, Tobb," I said.

He laughed as he snuffed his candle. When I snuff mine, our room will be black.

517, 1/15. Cyril went into Tiarn to hire more cooks. He returned alone, but stated that he had "spread the word."

This evening Tobb reinforced the woodwork in our room. Preparing for the rains, I assumed, but he added shelves and built a hidden nook for my journal.

Any sane person would think he'd hate me for taking his finger. When I asked him about it, he stopped hammering and looked at his left hand, as if he had forgotten he had one less digit, then said, "I never did use that one nohow." He also admitted, somewhat shyly, that Cassie had told him of my paying her to feed him when he was 'ailing.' Then he went back to pounding. Tobb missed his calling; he should have been a carpenter. His head is made of wood.

He's snoring now, but before he fell into bed, he made me promise to write at least one page. "So you won't be no kor-man no more," he said.

In keeping with my promise, I'll continue to write, but thus far I have avoided what has truly been on my mind – namely my exile and the memsa who suggested it.

I met her by chance. I was going to Eastland on private business for the Kinship and stopped at a way station a half league or so from town. She was sitting cross-legged by the roadside, head bowed, shoulders hunched beneath a faded cloak. Other travelers had thought her a beggar for coins lay in the dirt beside her and, with her in common dress, I almost made the same error. But as I rode past, I sensed the power in her. After hitching my horse to the station post, I walked back to where she sat.

On second look, I wondered if she were truly a memsa. I'd never seen one in the lowlands. I remember thinking perhaps I'd been mistaken. But I addressed her as I would my mother. "Memsa, do ye speak?"

A shudder rippled through her as she raised her head. "I speak, Believer," she said without opening her eyes. Her ancient face had the pallor of a corpse. "What do ye wish?"

I dropped to my knees. It had been so long since I'd heard those dear phrases. I begged for the Rite of Grace. She refused. No surprise. My mother refused me the rite when I was younger, and time had only darkened my soul.

This memsa didn't shun me completely. Her eyes remained closed as she gazed upon my future, and she told me it would be possible for me to receive the rite. In fact, it would be offered to me without my asking for it – if I followed her guidelines.

Memsen usually encase their predictions in riddles. She was no exception. I won't record everything she told me, but I can recall each word. I've been trying to decipher them these past years. Some parts were clear.

"Don thy father's name if ye seek salvation. Serve the highest in the land and give half thy wages to the lowest. Thus the bread formed by thy hands shall feed all living."

I'm sure this meant I should work in Trivak's kitchens, using the name Sheever, and give half my pay to beggars.

"Appropriate timing be essential," she warned, then said I would know my exile was over when I saw my death in ink. I assumed she meant one day I would see my own death warrant, but what if there is a simpler solution? What if I can end my exile – myself – by writing of my death?

This idea has plagued me since last night and I must credit Tobb, for his notion of finishing the journal to overcome my 'curse' planted the idea in my head. If I can end my exile merely by inking my death on this page, should I do it now?

If I want to be cleansed with the Rite of Grace, I'll have to return to Evald to receive it. And the memsa cautioned I may not live long enough to do so. "Thy days shall be likened unto a Vetteth," she said. Vetteth has many meanings, numerical and otherwise. As a number, it can be the sum of three threes, nine. Or ten, a complete whole. Either way, nine or ten, once I've seen my death in ink, there'll be no scratching it out. Once it's on the page, I might be dead in little over a week. Do I do it now?

I'm giddy with the thought of ending the torment of this world. So much power in a pen. A few strokes, and a life is ended. When my father was Vic Chairman, he ended countless lives with the stroke of his pen. Suddenly, I'm heir to his power of commanding death, a dab of ink the ultimate poison. Do I want such a legacy?

Appropriate timing. There's snow in the high country for certain. The passes could be blocked. If I do it now, I may not reach Evald in time for the rite, and to die without being cleansed ... Also ... (I add this with hesitation because I have yet to understand it.) The memsa stated that before I began my return to Evald, my life would be spared by "a man who shall rule thy home." An impossible situation. No ruler in Evald, Vic or Utte, would spare the life of a man already believed to be dead. And if I scrawl my death on this page, who other than myself will know?

My hope of release is dashed by the rocks of reality. I'm too weary to think and I've completed more than my promised page. Another day of life and servitude awaits me.

517, 1/32. For the past two evenings, Tobb has nagged me to write. He's nagging me now. Says I should record my "moon-howling" while it's fresh in my mind. I ache when I think of it.

Jenner lent me the roan mare. Riding her along the river road was sheer joy. I wanted to keep going. Past Brithe. Past Eastland. Up into Crossover Pass. I stopped at the meadow as usual. The ground was frozen, the sky clear. By day, the Purnath Mountains shone like a vision. By night, the full moon ... I can't write more of this.

It has been raining steadily since I returned.

"That weren't enough," Tobb said when I closed the journal, so I opened it again. Why do I let him bully me?

He's sitting, half-dressed, on his bed. A short while ago, Cassie was in here. They coupled. They don't bother to snuff the candles, don't bother to undress fully. Tobb is as gentle as an ox with her. I didn't want to watch, yet I didn't leave, nor did they ask me to. After he sated his appetite, he chased her out. So I could write. Damn him.

Seven cooks have left. Twelve new ones have been hired. We're overstaffed, but Cyril hopes to keep them all. "It's a Game Year," he says to defend his position. "Them lords like their fancies and they don't bring their own cooks. We'll be busy as fresh-bought brothids."

Maybe so, but we aren't busy now. He put two of the new hires, Rebic and Grutin, in the spare kitchen. Both are bunking in Lanerd's room, and he's qualified to settle them both in. But Cyril ordered me to help. Lanerd's been here longer than I and got first pick. He chose Rebic, a freckled-faced young man who seems pleasant enough.

I got Grutin. He's an ugly brute, big as Tobb, but with fewer social attributes. The first thing he asked was which of the women were mine. I told him the women were assigned to a kitchen, not to a specific cook. This wasn't what he meant. He repeated the question in a more crude fashion. I told him none of the women were mine.

He sneered. "Catamite," he called me.

I've never coupled with a man and have no desire to, but I let his opinion stand. Few comprehend celibacy. When I worked with the Kinship, there were those who thought my tastes varied and as many men as women tried to gain access to my bed. It wasn't a matter of love. Or of lust. They wanted my attention. I don't bear the Snake tattoo on my skin, but during my years with the Kinship, I acquired a title that made me the equal of a Soehn Nager, a Snake Master. My title was Soehn Biehr – Poison Master.

In those days, friends called me Me'acca. Peers called me Soehn Mysuth. Associates called me Soehn Biehr. And at Kinship gatherings, Snakes who had merely heard of me referred to me as the Serpent's Tooth. "The Serpent's Tooth be hither tonight," they'd breathe into my ear. "Have ye seen him?" Even Snakes were wary of saying my name too loudly. In those days. These days, Grutin calls me "Catamite."

I'm sure he intends it as an insult. I have, however, known highly educated men who happened to prefer the company of other men. Far better to be classified with them than with oafs such as Grutin. And yet, if his insult failed to prick me, why do I rattle on like a common gossip? Why did I boast, if only to myself, that I had been a soehn biehr?

Do I fear his insult may be true? Why did I watch Tobb and Cassie tonight? Was I hoping for a spark of desire to prove Grutin wrong? I felt no spark. There is no desire left in me. Watching them, I felt nothing. Is it lack of desire, not Grutin's insult, I fear? Do I hide behind my oath of celibacy? Use scriptures as my shield? Lie even to myself? On New Year's, did mead halt my attempt to pleasure Kara? Or is my body incapable of performing an act of love? Have I chosen celibacy? Or has it has chosen me?

Tobb is snoring now, satisfied. A stupid smile adorns his face. I envy him for it, sure he's dreaming of Cassie. I lie awake. I know which dream will overtake me tonight. The same one that tormented me last night. The same one that haunts me whenever the rains come and the smell of a damp cellar invades this room. I fear sleep.

Once I had a partner. I can't write her name. I can't speak it even in my mind. She was young like Cassie when we penned the contract. I thought I could protect her. Like Liana, my partner bore a son, and when she and my child died, my heart died with them. A woman who shares my bed has Death as a lover.

517, 2/1. There is no full moon this month. Uttes call this type of month a lue-mout, a month with a hungry moon.

Cyril likes lue-mouts. He gets extra days from me. Though I could take the last four days of the month as free and the first four of the next, I usually take two and two. Hungry moon or no, four days of fasting is enough. Besides, if I had an entire week away from here, I might not return.

517, 2/3. Wages day. Cooks were paid two coppers more. I'm sure Vraden's ghost is pleased. A runner who arrived with the paymaster delivered a speech from First Sec Jazuf. Any cook who remains in the High Lord's employ through Gurn 4 of next year will be given a daekah as a reward. The First Sec has regained his wits. The promise of a gold piece works better than shackles. No more cooks will slip away.

Before I came here, I feigned poverty when it suited my purpose, but I never really lived it. I owned eight houses and had a suite in the Royal Keep. I stored my clothes in cedar closets and lacquered dressers with framed mirrors. A single daekah was next to nothing. Now I store clothing in an apple crate that slides beneath my bed. I have one pair of boots and one pair of low shoes with wooden buckles. And a single daekah seems like wealth.

517, 2/5. Tobb wants me to write, "Cassie is with child." So I've written it.

517, 2/8. I'm sick of rain. Haven't slept well. I've asked the early women to add more silth to my tea. Silth keeps me on my feet, but it frays my nerves. I've been reluctant to gain rest by trance induction. Cyril noticed my lethargy and gave me a vial of ophren. If I'm not rested tomorrow, he'll wonder why. A pity ophren has no effect on me.

517, 2/10. Due to my nightly trances, I've been more alert than I cared to be the last two days. A groggy mind is an asset in the kitchens. There isn't enough to do.

Tobb bribed Old Wix to get Cassie transferred from the scullery to the spare kitchen. He offered me a hopence to keep an eye on her. I told him I'd do it as a favor. The work's easier and it's a raise in status if not pay, but the shift doesn't agree with her. She's ill in the mornings.

Grutin has taken up with one of the early women, Mira, who has a do-nothing son and a young daughter. Mira's a big-boned, dark-haired woman. Her children were fathered by a cook who left. Since he and Mira were not married, nobody thinks less of him for abandoning her.

Grutin swatted her son today. Called the boy a bastard. Actually, he said, "Sakweth," as he was speaking Mearan, but in Universal it translates into bastard.

I find it odd that Mearans are insulted if called a bastard, yet they see nothing wrong in creating bastards. This isn't true for the upper classes. The wealthy and titled go to great lengths to avoid fathering children 'out of wedlock.' By law, a woman can bring suit against the father of her child. Or rather, her family can bring suit – her father can, to be exact. Of course, it must be proven that she hasn't been accessed by any man other than the accused, but if taken to court, sirehood suits can be expensive. Thus a man of property is more careful with his seed.

Poorer men, those who own a spot of land or a small business, usually marry after a son has been born. A man can divorce a woman, but a divorced woman is entitled to one tenth of a former husband's earnings, and a sirehood suit is rarely brought against a man of meager means. It's to a poor man's advantage to postpone his wedding. If he tires of a woman, he can discard her without legal responsibility.

I know this is why Tobb hasn't married. On a cook's wage he certainly couldn't support the children he claims he has fathered, but does he ever wonder what's happened to the women who shared his bed? How do they support his children?

Women here earn eight hopence a month. Eight hopence! Cyril provides them cloth on occasion, but never enough for every woman to craft a new dress, let alone have any left over for their children. Clothes are handed from child to child until the cloth rots on their backs. The peddler offers wooden buttons and bits of ribbon at low cost, but unless a woman can squeeze a few coins from a man, luxuries such as used shoes are beyond her reach.

Mira, I assume, hopes Grutin will help support her bastard children. But already it's rumored she's with child again and this morning I saw her retching in the pail with Cassie. I'm sure Grutin will deny being the father of Mira's newest bastard, and maybe he isn't, but if he stays here long enough, he'll give her another.

So why do I care? I don't. It's the unfairness that annoys me. I asked Cyril why he doesn't pay women enough to clothe their children. He laughed as if my question were a joke. "Them stinking bastards gets by easy," he said.

I'm not sure if he meant the women or the children, for the women are probably bastards, too. (I wouldn't be surprised if I'm the only one in the kitchens who isn't.) But if he did mean the children, some of those 'stinking bastards' are his own. Yet I can't expect him to change.

It's a difference in customs. A difference in law.

There is no word in the Utte language that corresponds to bastard. Proopru is the closest and it means orphan. An Utte daughter inherits the name of her mother's line. A son, if his mother has chosen to partner, inherits the name of his father's line. If a woman chooses not to partner and gives birth to a son, she can name him whatever she pleases and thus begin a new line. There's no dishonor to her or the child. If anyone's dishonored, it's the father.

Unfortunately, laws in Evald are written and enforced by the Victor Class. By Vic law, men own not only their wives, but also children under the age of seventeen. This stems from a similar law in Drayfed and because of this law, Vics, even poor ones, tend to marry. Children are assets, like spare houses, which can be sold if the need for coin arises.

There are laws unique to Evald. For example, it is illegal for people of pure lowland descent to be used as brothids in Evald. I assume the reason was too many Vics were selling their children to list masters, and since brothids are rendered sterile, Vic seed was going to waste.

Another unique law is the Racial Purity Act. Historians such as Theenan Shurth claim the RPA was passed to entice lowland families to settle in Evald. Most historians, including Shurth who was born a good century after the war, record hearsay as fact. If Shurth had checked the old files, he would've known that settlers had arrived before the RPA had been conceived. Perhaps the act drew more lowlanders into Evald, but I doubt it was forged for that purpose.

Consider this: the RPA was enacted four hundred and eighty-seven years ago. Vics, mostly soldiers, had been in Evald about thirty years. Only a fool would believe they had slept alone, and the women in Evald were Utte. Add an influx of Vic settlers shocked by the interbreeding, plus a growing fear of an Utte takeover and a growing pride of belonging to a superior race. Suddenly there's a demand for a law like the Racial Purity Act.

Under the RPA, it is legal for a Vic male to marry an Utte woman – they couldn't punish all those soldiers. So where did they aim the law? Toward the offspring. Being born a half-breed is a crime against the State of Evald. Half-breeds are registered as Mules, forbidden to have their own children, and 'earmarked' for easy identification.

Had my father not been Juboe Sheever, Vic Chairman, my ears would have been clipped. "Power," Juboe often said, "is being above the law." I owe him for my intact ears. I owe him for my being able to pose as a Mearan. Were it not for him, I would not be where I am today. No Mule would be permitted to knead dough for the High Lord. Legally, all lowlanders are Vics. Thus Tobb and Cassie are Vics. Cyril, even Grutin, is a Vic. They are of superior blood. Were it not for the power of my father's hand, I would have missed living among these superior people who can neither read nor write. People who breed without thought.

I should close this journal, shut it now, before rage possesses me and I do what I would regret. Tobb and Cassie are not to blame for the injustice in the world. Nor are Cyril and Grutin. These people are poor stupid bastards. I doubt they know the laws. I'm sure they didn't pass them. It was I who bribed the Vic Council to pass the Marriage Equivalent Agreement so partnership contracts would be viewed as legal forms of union. At the time, I saw it as a victory. Fool. Though I don't have the vision of a memsa, I should have guessed what the future held.

I should not have signed a contract with a woman. Due to the amendment, the contract held me responsible, under Vic law, for my partner's child. Perhaps if my ears had been clipped, I would have remembered my place as a Mule. But other Mules had paid a simple fine as punishment for breeding more of their kind. I should have guessed my father's intent. I should not have trusted my mother.

According to Juboe, I was guilty on all counts. Stupidity included. My partner was a full-blood Utte. Without the amendment, our contract would have been invalid in the eyes of the State and if I had disclaimed her and our son, no law would have been broken.

Odd that of all the crimes I have committed, I was arrested for fathering a child. Odd that Mearans abandon their women and children without punishment, yet because I loved mine, they had to die. Odd I should think it odd. I should have known.

517, 2/12. Yesterday I read my last entry and wouldn't permit myself to write. Putting my anger on paper doesn't lighten my soul. I hesitated before wetting my pen tonight, but I'm not tired and there's little else to pass the time.

This is the worst part of the year for me. The days are damp and gloomy. With the High Lord gone, there's less work. We finish early and there's nothing to do. Men gather by the windows to drink ale and smoke foul weeds in their pipes. Older boys hover near them, stealing sips from untended cups. Women cluster around the ovens. Children cling to their skirts, dull eyes drifting from one speaker to another as the same worn gossip passes around and around.

Outside, the rain pours, grey sheets blown this way and that by the wind. The dining hall is thick with mud.

When Jenner came up, I asked if anything needed doing in the stables, but like Cyril, he went on a hiring spree. There are more hands in the stables than work.

I should put this time to good use, record my many sins, and repent. My lack of repentance is why memsen have refused to bless me with the Rite of Grace. I wasn't sorry enough. I'm still not. I'll record my sins another day.

I miss snow. Not the meager flakes that dust Tiarn and melt the next day. I miss deep snow. Snow that blankets the world in pristine beauty. Snow that dazzles the eye.

I miss bathing. The custom here is to wash in stages. The upper body is bared and rinsed, then recovered before baring the lower half. Squatting, half-dressed, in a pan of tepid water is hardly a bath.

I miss my lute. There is no music in these kitchens. Oh, ditties are sung on occasion, but nothing that frees the senses and lets one's heart soar.

I miss intelligent conversation. I drank with Tobb and the others for a while. The men are less boring than the women, but not by much. Tonight – again – the topic was Vraden's ghost, who has seen him, who hasn't, who isn't sure. Tobb swore he saw Vraden in the back orchard, searching for his missing parts.

I have never understood the Mearan Netherworld. If nether means under, and it does, one would assume the Netherworld is under this world, but if that's true, why do Mearans bury their dead? Isn't that putting them in the Netherworld? And if Vraden is in the Netherworld, how could he be seen above ground? If Tobb had poked his head into a hole and saw Vraden's ghost, it would be easier to believe.

I remember my father trying to explain the Netherworld to me. I was fairly young, but it was one of the few times Juboe carried me up to bed, and it stuck in my memory.

"Is the Netherworld the same as Pheto?" I asked.

My mother had described Pheto as a place with no sun, no moon, no stars. Cold and dark, like a liar's heart. If Juboe had said, "Yes, the Netherworld is Pheto," I would have understood, but "No," he said as he tucked me under the covers, "they aren't the same."

"Eshra is the god of Pheto," he told me, as if I didn't know. "Krich is the god of the Netherworld."

"Where is it?" I persisted.

"It's where bad boys go," he told me. "Good boys go to Loric's Garden. Bad boys become ghosts in the Netherworld."

Since I also had difficulty understanding the difference between a ghost and my mother going out-of-body, his explanation didn't enlighten me.

I understand that being damned, even for a Mearan, isn't good. And to be haunted by the dead ... That I understand. But to this day, I don't have a clear image of where Mearans go if they're damned. Mearans don't believe in being reborn, so where do they go when Loric won't accept them in his Garden? And does it get crowded there?

Religion is an odd thing. Either you believe, or you don't. In Evald, I was exposed to most of the world's faiths and there were times when I toyed with the idea of rejecting mine for another. But which one?

The Dray religion confused me with its host of gods. Of the Dray Vics I knew, no two prayed to the same god. They have several fertility gods, a sun god, a moon goddess, gods who live in rocks, others who live in trees. On and on. For all I know they have a god of shoes.

I have attended several Dray weddings. Most of the service is spent appeasing this god or that goddess. After the appeasing, the Holy Man blesses the people who have come, blesses the couple who are to be joined, the house they will live in, the carriage that will take them to that house, the children who shall be born, food that shall be eaten, wine that shall be drunk, and just about anything else he can think of to bless. I enjoy Dray weddings. They are blessed events. But could I believe in their faith?

Drays are a superstitious people, as much if not more than Mearans. Every cloud in the sky, every stir of the wind or song of a bird, is an omen of fortune or doom. Like Mearans, Drays fear ghosts, but they often try to summon a spirit, hoping to force it to do their bidding. I never saw one succeed though. I couldn't believe.

Visher, the ancient god of Somer, is a god of love. One would think Visher would be easy enough to believe in, but even the slightest scrutiny reveals that he is mostly concerned with the physical aspects of love. I couldn't pray to a god who spends all his time in bed. Nor would it have been prudent politically. Soms were the smallest faction of the Vic population. On close votes they were of import, however, for they tended to vote as a bloc. The key to winning them was the Metreek family, which could trace their lineage to a Som officer who fought in the war.

The Metreeks were an odd bunch, eccentric, to put it kindly, and none more so than Ebe. Gentlemen abound in this world, but there are few gentle men. Ebe Metreek was one. That alone made him odd. Slight of build, he had a nose the size of Mount Ahsett. He owned a pair of Dynnae lenses. Paid a fortune for them. "Vanity glasses," my father called them, which may have been true, for I never saw Ebe look through the lenses. He'd wear them on the tip of his great nose and peer over the gold frames, even when reading.

I vaguely remember calling Ebe "Uncle." Actually, I remember Juboe telling me not to call him that. "People might get the wrong idea," he cautioned. I didn't understand until I was older. Ebe, as Grutin would say, was a catamite. His family blamed his preference on his four sisters. Ebe blamed no one. Not for his inclination, that is. He blamed many people for criminal activity. As Primary State Advocate, casting blame and proving guilt was his profession. He rarely lost a case.

Catamite or no, Ebe frequently visited our house. Juboe needed the Som votes. Only death or impeachment could oust a Vic Chairman from office. Juboe feared neither, but a chairman lacks the power of a lord. Juboe couldn't rule by decree. To pass legislation, he needed a three-fourths vote in the Vic Council. Six of the eight members had to agree with him. Sounds easy enough, and he often won that way, but councilmen could be bribed by wealthy opponents.

A defeat in the V.C. left Juboe two options. He could bump a bill to the Church and try to get it woven into the Seto Pact or Cyntic Treaty, which formed the bedrock of Vic rule. To my knowledge, Juboe never did this. He despised the Eshra priests. Indeed, he won his office by swearing to lessen their influence in government affairs.

His other option was to hold a general vote. General makes it seem everyone could vote. Not so. Only Vic men over the age of seventeen had that privilege. The entire Vic population was, after all, a minority in Evald, and they'd never chance being out-voted by the Utte majority. (After I turned seventeen, Juboe pushed through a bill that granted male Mules the right to vote and hold office. It was the most contentious act in his career.)

In general elections, Mearans invariably sided with Juboe. Ebe brought in the Som votes. He was madly in love with my father and denied him nothing. I doubt his passion was ever consummated, but Ebe didn't sleep alone. True to his faith, he had more lovers than hairs on his head. And he was not bald. Thinking twice, maybe his passion was consummated at some point, before Juboe was elected Chairman. Ebe helped more than one man achieve political office and my father would have done anything to gain power.

Som and Mearan votes together weren't enough to ensure victory in a general election. Drays weren't reliable. Their votes changed with the weather. To win, Juboe had to secure a portion of the Verdi vote, which meant he had to sway the most powerful Vic family in Evald – the Howyls. There are no royal houses among Evald's Vics, but the Howyls act as if they were. The first Vic Chairman was a Howyl and through the centuries so many Howyls had held that office, the family believed they owned it. They were not happy when Juboe stole it from them.

My father courted the Howyl family like a hound at a dinner party performing tricks for scraps of food. He attended every Howyl function and, when I was young, I went with him. Thus I came to know Leister Howyl.

Leister had unruly brown hair; a shock of it always drooped over his left eye. He was my elder by a year or two, but when the men settled into their dry discussions, he and I would sneak out and search for ways to soil our clothes. He was a devout follower of Briss and tried relentlessly to convert me. "Loric is a stupid god," he'd say. Since Juboe went to the temple, Leister assumed I did also. I never told him I prayed to Dynnas. When I was with him, I was ashamed of my faith, ashamed of being half Utte.

Leister claimed his father possessed the Sword of Briss, a holy relic. He said if I converted, he'd let me see the Sword. Said we could make a blood sacrifice. This idea captured the deviant side of me and he knew it, for every time we were together, he'd describe the latest occasion when his family slew animals to honor Briss. He said they drank blood at those rites, and he'd go on and on about the taste of it. At the time, I had not endured the training of a sensitive and couldn't tell if he spoke the truth. Not only did I believe him, I was awed. The only blood I had ever tasted was my own.

My awe faded one autumn evening when we were rooting about in a neighbor's yard. We had crawled through a hole in the fencing and, on our way back, a nail caught my shoulder. It was little more than a scratch, but it bled profusely, soaking my sleeve and dripping from my fingers. Leister swooned from the sight of it. Blood-drinker indeed!

My awe diminished further when a Howyl from Verdina, Leister's cousin, paid a visit. The three of us were out walking. Leister was boasting of his father and the Sword.

"Lord D'brae has the original," his cousin declared with such confidence Leister didn't attempt to refute him. He went on to say hundreds of copies of Briss' Sword had been made and swore the Verdi natals had one of solid gold.

Do they? I don't know. I could walk to the Verdi Compound and ask the natals if they have a gold copy of the Sword, but since I'm not entirely sure they don't make blood sacrifices, I'd rather not annoy them with stupid questions.

After his cousin returned to Verdina, Leister renewed his efforts to convert me. One day while strolling along Lake Boulevard, we happened upon an Utte funeral. The pyre had been lit; emmod oil perfumed the air. Leister wrinkled his nose. Verdi, as do all lowlanders, bury their dead. "If you don't convert," he said, motioning to the pyre, "you'll go to Blazes like that Utte." A breeze stirred his hair; the front shock flapped on and off his left eye. "You'll be damned, Sheever. You'll burn forever."

My mother didn't like the Howyls. "They be prideful," she'd say and scold me when I spent time with Leister. "Ye be full of pride, Me'acca. Tis thy greatest flaw."

In a perverse way, I was proud of that flaw, but after I became a novice, Leister and I went separate ways. Maybe he was prideful, but he had good reason to be. He was the youngest man to gain a seat on the Vic Council and after my father died, Leister became Vic Chairman.

When I abandoned my hope of finding justice in the courts and turned to murder, I spared Leister Howyl. I'd like to think it was because of our childhood friendship, but, in truth, I believe his pride stayed my hand. Pride was something I could understand.

I remember chatting with Sythene. Unlike my mother, she saw nothing wrong with pride – as long as it was kept in balance. For Sythene, balance was the key to everything.

During a period of about a year (after her second birthday to when Praechall, her mother, died) Sythene often came to my suite in the Keep. Always at night, and without so much as a single guard. There was a passage behind a wall mirror in my bedroom. She'd rap on the back of the mirror and I'd let her in. The first time she came I was startled to say the least.

I don't know why she visited me. She said she came because I was a novice, but I doubt she blessed every novice with private visits. She said she liked the view from my sunporch, though the view from the royal suite was better. She said she wanted me to teach her the lute, but any number of people could have taught her, and she learned so quickly, there was little teaching on my part. She told me she feared the darkness in her bedroom and my suite was better lit, but that wasn't true, and she may have feigned her fear of the dark. More than once, I woke at night to find her alone on the darkened sunporch.

I stopped asking why she came. Perhaps my suite held fond memories for her of a past life and she didn't want to tell me of it. I'd heard memsen complain of her reluctance to divulge her past lives. She spoke the old tongue better than modern Utte, and historical facts she mentioned kept both Dyns and memsen busy arguing over which centuries she had lived. I resisted the temptation to question her on it. She was alive now. Nothing else mattered.

Yet one night she did set me to wondering. I had unlatched the mirror and gone to bed. I'm not sure what woke me, but I donned a robe and went out to the sunporch.

Sythene was pacing in the moonlight. Back and forth in front of the glass wall, she paced the length of the room. She moved with such grace she would've been a joy to watch if she hadn't appeared to be so driven. Suddenly, she turned to where I was on the steps, stared at me as though trying to decide who I was, then spoke in a tongue I have never heard another human speak. In a blink, she switched to Utte. "Novice Mysuth, would ye fetch me a cup of milk?"

Sythene was a god in the flesh one moment, heir to Uttebedt's throne the next, a child wanting milk the next.

One night she brought honey cakes. As usual, we went to the sunporch. She giggled as she slid the sticky cakes onto the table for us to share. Praechall had forbidden her to eat sweets. Sythene put her hands on her small hips and in an imitation of Praechall's voice, said, "Ye cannot thrive on sweets, my daughter! Eat thy porridge!"

I pitied her at times. She was born with too much knowledge, was heir to too much power. No one cultivated the child in her, yet that part did exist, if only in brief flashes. I tried to use that to my advantage. Like Juboe with the Howyls, I wooed the child in her.

My gift of a wooden puppet delighted her. She stood on a stool to be tall enough to work the wires. The puppet was a ploy. Though she did not yet wear Uttebedt's crown, if she ordered the Dyns to overthrow the Vics, they would obey, and I wanted the Vics out of Evald more than ... more than I wanted to please a child. I compared the puppet to Katre Haesyl, and her to the Vics, pulling his wires. "You can free your father," I told her. "With a single command, you can cut his wires."

"Tis true," she agreed, making the puppet dance. "But Katre follows the path of his father, and his father afore him, and the one afore him. He desires nay other path." Then she stopped in her play and smiled at me. "If I cut the wires of this puppet, Me'acca, how would it stand? How would it tread its path?" Sythene was not a simple child.

I tried using religion to convince her. I told her of my father's faith and how he wanted me to pray to Loric. "Half-breeds often pray to foreign gods," I said, hoping to appeal to her sense of spiritual duty. She listened while I ranted, until I stated, "Their souls shall be lost."

At this she straightened in her seat. "Lost?" she queried. "Lost in what way, Me'acca?"

"They pray to the wrong god," I said. "A person who prays to Eshra cannot reach Bahdala after death." I chose Eshra to make my point, sure it would horrify her.

"Novice Mysuth," she said sweetly, and I knew she would skew the topic, "have ye ever wondered why the practices of the Church be so akin to our own?"

In fact, I had wondered on this. Both priests and memsen tap the same sort of inner power. Both release that power through brands. Both have the exact same ranks. (Natals use the same ranking system also, but I don't know if they have brands of power.) The main difference between the two faiths is priests view Pheto as the goal to attain. This would be akin to Leister praying to be damned to Blazes.

Before I could respond to her first question, she posed another, "To which god, Me'acca, do ye think Eshra prays?"

Her jest annoyed me. "I suppose," I said, "Eshra prays to himself. But what of those people, thy people, Sythene, who pray to Eshra. Will their souls not be lost?"

"'Tis true," she conceded, "many who vow their souls to Eshra shall perish because of it. A pity to be sure, but how many of my people have sought shelter in his Church?"

She had cornered me. The Church would be the last refuge an Utte would choose. "I don't know," I hedged, "but many attend services at the temple. And if, after they die, they go to Loric's Garden, their souls shall be lost." I was deep into the study of scripture at the time and rattled off a few about the 'true path' to strengthen my argument.

"I know naught of Loric," she murmured, "nor have I seen his garden. But many paths be true. Worlds of spirit be as numerous as worlds of flesh. And if his garden be as ye say, I'd not consider those thither to be lost."

She said this so casually, yet sitting here now, wrapped in a blanket for warmth, I recall the shiver that swept me that night long ago. I totally forgot the reason I had initiated the topic and breathed a question I have rued asking. "Sythene, be there such a place as Pheto?"

She replied, "Pheto be as real as thy hands."

As the years passed and my soul grew heavier with each new sin, I've tried to turn away from the faith. I'd seen memsen wield power, but memsa lore is different than the scriptures. There is no proof of Pheto or Bahdala. And yet ... When I asked Sythene that fatal question, if she had paused to muse over the possibility of Pheto, I would not be here today. But she had no doubts. She spoke not from faith, but knowledge. And though I have ignored the beliefs from time to time, always I remember that night and the chill that swept my soul. It was that chill which made me obey the memsa by the way station.

I will endure the boredom of these kitchens. I will tolerate living among these savages. I will shed my pride. And if I fail to earn the Rite of Grace ... I can't deny I deserve damnation. I deserve to roam Pheto's dark plain. But I'd do almost anything to shorten my stay there.

If Vraden is damned and his soul forced to dwell in the orchard near the spit, I envy him. I would choose such a Netherworld to Pheto. Yet it's too late for me to choose.

Damnation isn't final for an Utte. When my soul departs this mortal world, the weight of my sins shall pin me to Pheto's cold ground. In the distance, the soothing waters of Bahdala will shine, offering salvation and rebirth – if I can reach them. Burdened with my sins, I may be able to crawl toward the light, but it shall take an eternity to get there. I don't want to believe

Sheever's Journal, Diary of a Poison Master

it. I try not to. Yet tonight as I pen these words, I know Pheto is as real as my hands.

517, 2/16. Today I am 40 years old. Utte children receive First Blessings at birth and every ten years thereafter they are formally blessed again. I received no such blessing today.

The morning fog refused to lift and grew thicker as the day progressed, hiding the barren fruit trees and everything else from sight. After work, I came to this room and sat in the dark, thinking. I wanted to be alone.

Tobb rushed in and lit candles. Cassie was with him. They coupled quickly, as if the act were a requirement of the day, then he hurried out, leaving her behind.

I watched her tidy her clothing. The women here take pride in their bonnets. That statement may be misleading. I don't mean their bonnets are special – or maybe I do. It's a cultural nuance I haven't totally deciphered. Most women I've known, regardless of race, sometimes wore hats and sometimes they didn't. It's the same among women in Tiarn and in other Mearan cities, so far as I can tell. To be honest, I never placed much import on hats. But here the women never walk about bare-headed. The kitchen women, I mean. I've seen Fieldtown women without hats.

The bonnets can't be a uniform. They vary in shape from great puffy things that look like mushrooms, to simple scraps of cloth pinned to the hair. Cassie's is a swatch of undyed linen, probably a remnant of an apron. It crosses her head from ear to ear like a saddle. Her red hair streams out behind the thing and down her back nearly to her waist. What possible purpose could it serve?

Men here, even those such as Tobb and Grutin who weren't raised in the kitchens, seem to understand the significance of the bonnets. To reveal my ignorance might be unwise. It's a conundrum I don't need to solve.

Damn Tobb for asking me to keep an eye on Cassie. I wouldn't be puzzling over bonnets if he had left me out of his romantic affairs. Nor would I notice how rarely Cassie smiles. Or that the old shoes he gave her are too big for her feet. She scuffs when she walks. I hear. I see. When I should be deaf and blind.

Today, as she fussed with her bonnet, I wondered how she felt about him running out and leaving her with me. She caught me staring. Uncomfortable, I asked her to fetch me a pot of tea. She obeyed though she didn't want to. The women sass each other, but they're obedient to the cooks. I gave her a hopence for her trouble. She's no less poor than Tiarn's beggars and the smile that hopence released from Cassie's mouth was the closest thing to a blessing I'll receive today.

And so I enter the fourth decade of my life. To Uttes, forty begins the Age of Wisdom. I feel no wiser.

My mother told me I was born in the Keep. "On free ground," she told me and, in her mind, thought it important.

By law, Katre Haesyl is Lord of Evald. In truth, his realm is limited to the Keep. Had I lived my life within those walls, I would've been free of Vic rule. Had my mother not married Juboe, she could have denied he sired me, and I would've been free to live as a full-blood Utte.

I never found the courage to ask why she had adopted the Vic customs she detested and married Juboe. Did she love him? Or had the Memsa Tribunal ordered her to unite with him? And if so, why did she wed him? Was a marriage vow less real to her than a partnership contract? If I ever see Ry'aenne again, I'll ask.

My grandmother, so I was told, gave me First Blessings. Dear Thylla. She spoiled me. I am her only grandchild.

Ry'aenne herself performed the Rite of Vision and named me Me'acca Waen Tronaruth Yen Mysuth – Goat Who Dares The Storm To Witness Glory. Whatever that means.

When I was quite young, Ry'aenne shuttled me back and forth between the Keep and the house she shared with Juboe. For a while, I thought Katre was my father. My confusion amused everyone except Juboe. I think he truly loved my mother, before he grew to hate her. He always competed with her. Because she taught me to speak Utte as well as Universal, he insisted I learn Mearan though he spoke the tongue poorly. He hired a lowlander to tutor me.

An Utte's tenth birthday marks the end of the Age of Innocence. The Age of Choice begins. After blessing me, my mother explained how my life's path was now mine to choose. She then told me I'd become a novice, would – after testing – join the Order of Memsen and eventually become the Utte First Sec to Katre Haesyl. She had arranged for me to study under Loehl Ohmswreith, a young memsa who had studied under her. Since I agreed with her plan, I suppose I chose it.

Juboe was not pleased. "Utte First Sec," he hissed when I told him. "Not hardly!" He put an arm about me. "You'll be Vic Chairman! Like father like son, eh?"

When I informed him that I was old enough to decide for myself, his mood worsened. By law, he stated, I belonged to him until I was seventeen. I was his son, his property, and if I didn't do as he told me, he'd sell me. "And you, wife," he added, pointing at Ry'aenne. "I own you till the day you die! How much would a memsa fetch on the block?"

Ry'aenne had a face that was beautiful one moment and could scare the dead the next. "Me'acca," she said to me, her gaze on Juboe. Light flickered from her branded right palm, trapped power, like a caged beast, itching to get out. "Thy father and I shall discuss this in private."

My parents' house was large, yet from my room that night I heard their raised voices. I remember wondering if she would kill him. As it turned out, the next day she killed herself. I knew her death was a ruse, her method of divorce. But to the Vics she was dead and Juboe's friends showered me with sympathy. I gladly accepted their gifts.

Worried about my father's threat of selling me, I asked him how much it would cost to buy myself. "700 daekahs," he replied, an outrageous sum. "And you can't borrow it from your mother." He, too, knew she was alive.

I borrowed the sum from my grandmother. Juboe was amused, maybe even proud, when I gave it to him. We drew up the papers together. "You're a man now," he said when I penned my name. "The world's yours for the taking."

I accepted the Vic tutors he hired. I studied hard under them. I also studied under Loehl. Within a year, I shed my last name and, though Vics persisted in calling me Sheever, by law I became simply Me'acca Mysuth, Glorious Goat. Juboe failed to see the humor in my new name. In hindsight, I think my act of autonomy started the breach between us. But I didn't know then where it would lead.

As for my mother, she went to Uttebedt. We developed a written code and communicated with letters only we could read. So far as I know, she and Juboe never spoke to each other again. I was the chain that bound them. They used me to hurt each other and I used them to gain my own ends. Each gave me an allowance (should I call it a bribe?) and if I wanted more, I'd hint that one was outdoing the other.

I spent most of the coin at the flesh markets, buying half-breeds and Uttes. I thought I could end slavery by buying all the slaves. A childish notion. I didn't expect Juboe to approve, but he taught me how to haggle for lower prices. "If you're going to do this, do it well." In time, he persuaded the Vic Council to issue me a list master's license so I could own brothids as well as house servants.

It was my mother who didn't approve. In her opinion, I was wasting my time. "Concentrate on thy studies, Me'acca!" Perhaps when she walked among the poor, she could see beyond their immediate misery to future lives when they would be wealthy. But I never had her vision, never had her faith.

Ry'aenne and Juboe were a perfect couple. He slew the sinners and she saved their souls.

The twentieth year begins the Age of Passion. Loehl blessed me when I turned twenty, then counseled me on the abuses of passion. Too late. I was in love. Her name was Murtah. Her eyes were as blue as the sapphire brooch I gave her, her embrace warm as a summer's night. We explored the pleasures of flesh, flirted with the idea of partnership. And I did to her what my parents tried to do to me.

Oddly enough, I met Murtah through her parents – they'd been arrested for theft and I was assigned the paperwork. Murtah's father, a Vic, was fined. Her mother, an Utte, was executed. Juboe signed the order. Ry'aenne wasn't available to do the soul-saving. So be it.

When I heard Murtah's father planned to sell her to pay his fine, I went to the sale. She was merely a name on a roster – Murtah Rugman, female Mule, sixteen – one more half-breed whose freedom I'd buy. But when I saw her ...

Most people put up for auction are a sorry lot. Murtah was a treasure. Her father led her onto the platform. She was shackled according to procedure, her dark hair brushed back to expose her clipped ears. "She can read and write in two tongues," he

65

announced, as if he intended to pass her off as a clerk. He had dressed her in a snug-fitting gown and when someone yelled for a better view of the goods, he ripped open the front to oblige. She stared over the heads of the crowd as if we didn't exist. Such pride in her eyes.

Twenty daekahs was the starting bid – higher than the final price of most sales. I knew these men, list masters all, knew the price would creep up daekah by daekah while Murtah shivered in the chill air. How long could her pride last? I didn't wait to find out. When the bid hit thirty, I shouted, "One hundred daekahs!" And Murtah was mine.

Shackles are part of the sale and usually left on to prevent the flight of a newly-bought slave. I ordered hers removed, put my cloak about her, took her by the hand, and we walked around the corner where I bought her a fresh gown.

The same day, on impulse, I bought her a house in the Utte Quarter. I can still recall that house. It was late in the day when we made the purchase. The rooms were cold, dark and empty. We placed the bundles of food, drink and whatnots we had bought on the floor. I kindled a fire in the hearth while she changed clothing. She was modest as well as proud; she went into another room to dress.

I remember her coming back with two cups she had found. The gown we had selected was of pale blue silk with a dark blue sash, but when she entered the room, I saw the gown as white, the sash black, and her a novice. At that moment, with the fire crackling behind me and a bottle of mead in my grasp, I knew she would become the memsa I couldn't be.

That first night, I didn't mention my plans for her. We sat on the floor and sipped mead as I wrote a fresh bill of sale. Murtah had no idea who I was, couldn't comprehend why I would pay so much for her then let her buy back her freedom for a copper which I lent her. Since I spoke Utte, she asked me if I were Dynnae. I shook my head.

"Be ye of the Kinship?"

"Nay," I replied. How could I tell her I was the son of the man who had ordered her mother's death? From the beginning, I lied to her, said my parents were dead, said I had inherited a little wealth, said I preferred privacy in my affairs. She asked one last question – my age. "Eighteen," I answered. Eighteen. So long ago.

According to scripture, people choose their own paths, but I wonder if it's true. Murtah had no dreams of power. She wanted children. Mule or no, she wanted to be a mother. To please her, I told her of ways to get around the laws and have a child with a minimum of punishment. It wasn't necessary. For all our lovemaking, she never conceived. She wept over this, prayed for just one child, and worried the Vics had, on the sly, given her claetona to render her sterile. Perhaps they had, but there was no record of it.

To please me, she studied lore. "The Order shan't accept me," she'd say when weary of the lessons. "They'll not want a Mule in their ranks." She was correct. She wouldn't have been accepted for training. I taught her in secret, visited her in secret, loved her in secret. It wasn't difficult. Both of my parents had, at one point or another, hired spies to follow me. At an early age, I learned how to slip from sight and resurface elsewhere. Murtah accepted my sudden comings and goings; the spies expected me to disappear.

It was difficult not to speak of her, especially to Sythene, but somehow I refrained and when Sythene went to Uttebedt to be crowned, I devoted myself to teaching Murtah.

Those years sped by. When she was ready, I asked Loehl to test her. He refused, as did every other memsa in Evald. Murtah swore she didn't care, one of the few times she lied to me. She no longer spoke of children. I'd given her a new dream. But she was too proud to admit how much it meant to her. Her false indifference fueled my determination. I besieged my mother with letters until she agreed to meet us outside the city. "If the woman appears worthy," Ry'aenne wrote, "I shall test her, my son, but if ye ever again divulge lore to another without the Order's approval ..."

My mother's threat didn't worry me. I did dread her meeting Murtah. Once they became acquainted, it was only a matter of time before Murtah would discover I was Juboe's son. Yet I chose to arrange the meeting.

After Murtah earned her brand, I went to her home less often, then not at all. I was glad we had no children. I could not have left her if we had, and with the lies – my lies – between us, I could not have stayed.

It does little good to regret a choice. So often people say, "If only I had known," implying they would've acted differently in a given situation. It is true that desires of the moment can blind one's sight of the future. Revenge is not as sweet as the adage claims. Yet who could pass a chance to taste it? And if the chance were allowed to slip by, would the fool regret his lack of action?

At forty, I wonder ... If people could see the outcome of their choices, would any of us choose a different path? I think we would not.

517, 3/10. Sunshine!

Tobb, damn him, was outside all day, tending the new spit. Soon as I finished work, I grabbed my cape and went to the bridge. I stood by the rail, facing west, a favorite spot. Walls may imprison the park and city, but the river flows free and gazing upon it frees me as well.

Sheever's Journal, Diary of a Poison Master

Today the river was high from the rains, challenging its banks. Weeds, tall in summer, were brown and matted, but slips of green peeked through in places. New life. Snow geese muttered among themselves as they patrolled the waterline. Rosy finches, perched on bridge supports, chattered beneath me. Many highland birds winter here. I imagined myself one of them, here for the mild climate, soon to be winging home. My soul felt light as the breeze.

Grey chimney smoke hovering over the city blushed pink as the sun set. At the docks by Portsgate, tethered skiffs rocked against each other, softly thumping. Lanterns hung from the mooring posts and waves tossed the yellow light. Such beauty in this world. I ached for my lute.

Grutin caught me humming. "What you doing, Sheever?" He rammed me with his shoulder. "Waiting for a lost boy?" It was a perfect chance to kill him. He laughed and sauntered across the bridge. I stayed by the railing and tried to recapture the song I'd been composing.

A cargo ship plowed upstream, oars splashing in a gentle rhythm. As the ship passed under the bridge, finches poured from their roosts, a swelling mass of pink and grey, a living reflection of the sky. The song within me was almost on my lips. The ship's prow – adorned with the ram's head of Drayfed – emerged into view. Lamps lit the men on deck. Foreign words drifted up. Then I heard the crack of a whip. The cargo within that wooden hull was people. A slaver's ship. I left, my song forgotten.

Twilight had settled over Tiarn's narrow streets. I went straight to the common markets. Mild climate or no, winter had claimed its toll – there were fewer beggars. On my return, I hurried across the bridge. The Dray ship was still being unloaded at Portsgate, new prisoners for the walled city of Tiarn. Misery abounds.

517, 3/11. I've been pondering my finances. I'll continue to dole half my wages to beggars, but the rest I intend to save for my journey home. If I want the Rite of Grace, far better to buy a horse than steal one for the ride to Evald. Is it possible the memsa's predictions won't be set in motion until I have the funds for passage home? I should've been saving coin all along. It'll take more than a year to have enough to buy a peddler's nag. I'll earn a daekah next Gurn Four. Maybe by next spring ... Can I endure another year?

Tobb just burst in. He's alone, but he startled me. He plopped onto his bed and is tugging off his boots. His face is flushed. "Should've come out," he's saying. "Grutin were telling us of Drayfed. Was there two years back, he was." Tobb's grinning like a silly ox. He, Grutin, and a few others have been drinking and gossiping around the spit. He wants me to record the tale. "Tossing dice, Grutin were, with a pack of Drays, and he were winning a tidy sum, when they ups and calls him for cheating. For cheating, mate." Tobb's rambling. It will take an eternity to get the entire story. Since my pen's moving, he thinks I'm writing his words.

Grutin has become a favorite here. It's no secret he hits Mira, yet no one, not even Mira, thinks worse of him. He's traveled a lot and his stories break the boredom of the kitchens. I hear most of the tales secondhand from Tobb, so I don't know if they're true. Tobb believes them all. According to him, Grutin comes to Tiarn every four years for the Games. This may be true. The Games draw the best and worst of the lowlands. I doubt, however, that Grutin was nearly selected Mearan Champion in the last set of Prelims. He doesn't move like a swordsman. He lies like one though. Maybe if I focus on that aspect of him, I could hate him less. For the sake of my soul, I must learn not to hate.

"So he ups and runs," Tobb's saying, "and runs smack into Drayfed's Barrens. Into the Barrens, mate!" Tobb's eyes are huge.

The tale grows wilder by the moment. "This wizard sends up an army of winged demons ..."

I've heard (and read for that matter) many tales about Drayfed's Barrens. It seems everyone living there is a witch, a wizard, or a demon. I doubt the place exists.

"So Grutin dives into the river and them demons ..."

I broke in and asked how he could believe such a tale. "It's true," he insisted. "You being a kor-man, you should know it's true." He's pouting. Won't finish the story.

A few weeks ago, he asked me to print his name above his bed, then he carved the letters into the wood. His name is the only word he wants to be able to write. Every night he fingers those letters. He's fingering them now.

"It's true," he said once more, then stretched out on his bed. He'll be asleep in a moment. I envy his ability to sleep for great lengths. On his free days, he sleeps until I finish work and come in to wake him. I have never required much sleep. When my life was full, it was a blessing. Now it's a curse.

Tobb's name shines in the candlelight. I know grease from his hands is the cause of the shine and yet the letters seem eager to shout that the man sleeping beneath them is TOBB. He carved those letters with such care. They give him such pleasure. They remind me of a grave marker.

517, 3/12. High Lord Trivak returned today with his eldest son. More mouths to feed. More horses to groom. I expected Jenner to ask me to go the stables after work. He did. He hasn't needed me lately yet still loaned me a horse on my free days. I couldn't refuse his request.

When I got there, he led me to a stall that held the meanest-looking animal I've ever seen. A stallion. White except for a black patch on his left haunch. Stiff mane and stocky legs, the type of horse Mearans prize for parading and such. This one was a gift from a Dray Jarl.

I stared over the gate. I wasn't about to open it. "Does Trivak want him merely for stud?" I prayed it was so.

"Loric's Fire," Jenner cursed. "He's for the boy." By boy, he meant Trivak's eldest, Prissen, who is twelve – maybe thirteen – years old. Jenner asked me if I had ever seen Prissen ride. I admitted I hadn't. He invoked Loric more rudely this time and spat at the gate. "Prissen is as gainly on a horse as a hog on wheels. Why the Jarl gave him this demon ..."

I laughed, imagining a hog scooting along on wheels and, without thought, said, "Clever way to assassinate an heir."

Jenner took my comment as a jest. After a brief laugh, he sent one of his stable hands for a pitcher. I knew what he would ask. He let me down two cups of ale before he voiced it. "Train him for me, Sheever." He refilled my cup. "Train him, and you'll have a horse saddled and ready whenever you want." Implying that if I didn't train the beast, I would no longer be given a mount on my free days.

I was irritated. But also intrigued. I waved a hand over the gate. The beast snapped at my fingers and I got a glimpse of his teeth. He's a good seven years old. Set in his ways. "Don't have the time to train him," I said. "But I'll break him for you." Jenner accepted the compromise. We're to start tomorrow.

517, 3/13. I'm bruised head to foot. I ate bidda before going to the stables, ate more when I returned, and still ache in every bone. That damned beast kicked me a dozen times just while I slapped a saddle on. It took five of us to force him into a paddock, where he tossed me into the mud more times than I'd care to count. To make matters worse, most of the cooks came down to watch. "You're a tough cut of meat," Grutin told me as I staggered up to the kitchens, "I'd never have guessed it." By week's end, I'll be pounded tender.

517, 3/14. I was stiff and sore this morning. I asked Cassie to soak bidda in my tea. After eating six leaves, I felt mildly better. Most of the day passed normally enough. But after work, things began to border on strange.

I went to my room to change into old clothes before going to the stables. I had just stripped, when Cyril came in. He eyed me in a way that made me wish I were dressed, then whistled. "Bruised right good, you are."

I climbed into my pants and donned a shirt. The frayed front laces broke as I tied them.

"Headed to the stables?" he asked. He knew I was. "Stop by my room before you go."

Cyril's room is also his office. Where a second cot could be, there's a desk. A chair had its back to a wall, a stool nearby. There was a ledger, cloth-bound, on the desk. An inkwell. Pen. And nothing else. Cyril's a tidy man.

When I entered, he told me to sit on the chair. He left for a moment, returned with a bottle of wine and two cups, and sat on the stool, facing me, uncomfortably close, his knees touching mine. The door was shut. He held the bottle on his lap and twisted out the cork. "This's between me and you," he said. "Me and you. Nobody else."

A thousand thoughts littered my mind. I tried to sweep them away so I could get a better read on him, but he was as blank as the bricks on his walls.

He talked about how long I'd been in his kitchens. He had the bottle in one hand, cork in the other. Still hadn't poured. He abruptly changed topics. "Jenner says you're good with horses. Not many cooks have a knack with horses."

"My father was a smithy," I lied.

Cyril grunted. "When you came rapping at my door …" He cocked his head northward. "Looking for work, you was. Can cook, says you. I didn't ask where you'd been cooking. Proof's in the pot, says I." He drizzled wine into my cup, poured even less into his own, then set the bottle on the floor. "You'd the hands of a gentleman, you did."

I glanced at our hands. His fingers are thick as sausages. I have my mother's hands, in shape anyway – minor burns and flour under my nails declare my present trade.

"First day I seen you," he went on, "I knowed you weren't no common cook. And with them fancy sauces you make, I knowed you could go in private service. Or be a head cook somewheres. Used to worry, I did, that you'd find work in Brithe where your wife were living." He leaned forward. His face no more than a span from mine, I nearly gagged on his foul breath. "Then I find you're a kor-man." He squinted, as if the sight of me hurt his eyes. "What do you do them days you're gone? Dance naked under the moon?"

"Loric's Fire," I grumbled. I shoved him out of my face and shot down my wine. There was barely enough to wet my tongue. When I bent for the bottle, he snagged my shirt, tearing the front open. My first thought was to smash the bottle and slit his throat. I'm not sure why I didn't. "Cyril." I spoke his name in a whisper. "Don't try it."

He hopped up as if the stool had stabbed his rear. Moving to sit on his bed, he pointed at my chest. "That thing," he said, indicating my necklace by scratching at his throat, "do it keep you from changing into a demon? I mean, if you was to stay here during a full moon …"

"You plan on changing my free days?" I asked. "Is that what this's to do?"

Instead of resolving the matter with a simple response, he prolonged my confusion by rambling about himself, how difficult his life had been. "Worked dawn to dark. Sal, he were head cook then and beat me sore. Flogging stick, he had." He lifted his shirt to show scars. "Now I'm head cook. Now this place is mine. And I run it square."

"Who says you don't?" I asked.

"Nobody says it. Not yet nohow."

There was no rushing Cyril. He drummed his fingers on his knees, tugged on both ears, tugged on what hair he has left on his head. I filled my cup and sipped wine while I waited for him to explain. Finally, with his gaze on my chest, he asked, "Sheever, can you read and write?"

"A little," I hedged.

From under his bed, he dragged out a crate full of neatly stacked papers. He handed me a receipt for lamp oil, his initial boldly printed on the bottom. "Can you decipher this?" I read it to him. He next handed me an unopened letter that had a posting seal from Eastland.

I broke the seal. The letter, dated a sixtnight ago, was from a cook at the Double Ox, the best inn in Eastland. He had heard Cyril was hiring, and wanted a position held until he and his family arrived. "Don't need more cooks," Cyril mumbled and, at last, I understood. He can't read a blessed word.

"Since they haven't come," I said, "maybe his wife cussed him out of it. But if he shows, you may want to try him. The D.O. has some good cooks." I put the letter on his desk, then asked how he kept track of supplies.

"Up here." He tapped his forehead. "It's all up here. Didn't used to be no trouble, but the First Sec has his eye on us now, he does. Says we have to watch costs. Wants this year's costs writ down proper." He stroked the ledger before opening it. The pages were blank.

"When's Jazuf planning to check it?" I asked.

"End of the month," Cyril groaned. "He'll turn me out if it's not done proper."

When I frowned at the crate, he offered to pay me extra, but if Jazuf is watching costs, the coin would doubtless come from Cyril's own pocket. I told him I'd do it as a favor, then drank the wine I'd poured and suggested we eat before starting the ledger.

Jenner was waiting for me in the dining hall, probably wondering what had delayed me, but before he could utter a word, Cyril grumped, "Sheever's got kitchen duties tonight!"

They bickered throughout the meal, arguing over my time. Jenner cursed Prissen's stallion, then stated, "It'll take a kor-man to drive them demons out of him."

"Shouldn't take no gifts from Drays," Cyril retorted.

"Tell it to Jazuf!" Jenner spat.

If I remember correctly, it was here Jenner mentioned the First Sec had said the stallion was tame when presented to Trivak. On the trip back to Tiarn, the horse had grown wilder by the day. My mind stuck on this curious bit of information. I heard little more of their chatter. It was sunset when I stood. Cyril thought he had won. "Can't tame a horse in the dark," he crowed. But I didn't feel like balancing sums tonight. Nor getting kicked by Prissen's beast. I complained of being tired and came to my room. Both of them can stew in their problems.

Cyril views the ledger as an impossible task. In truth, it's nothing compared to the stallion. I can't believe the beast is possessed. There's a different solution. I'm sure of it. But I can't puzzle it out. Another puzzle torments me. For five years, I did my work, kept my distance. I buy this damn journal and in less than a year I'm more involved with these people than I care to be. Why? And does it bring me closer to release?

Sheever's Journal, Diary of a Poison Master

As for Cyril knowing I can write ... He could turn me in, saying he thinks I committed a crime before I came here. I doubt he will. Nothing in it for him. Even if he does and I'm given truth drug, they'll learn nothing. This journal is the only thing that can convict me. And if it's found or Tobb gives me away ... So be it.

517, 3/15. Jenner was frantic this morning. He'd been warned Jazuf intended to drop by and observe him taming the stallion. As it happened, I had solved his puzzle. The answer came to me during the night – panix salt. I told Jenner to send a runner to the Snake House to buy it. They won't sell less than a half-stone apoth's weight. "Cost you a silver or so," I said.

Jenner hadn't heard of the salt. Can't blame him. Panix isn't common in Meara. In Evald, wealthy Vic women buy it through the Kinship (imported from Drayfed) and toss the crystals into their baths. They claim it keeps them "fresh." As for its connection with Prissen's beast: a former friend of mine, Ayros to be exact, once told me of a Dray who fed his horses panix to improve the sheen of their coats. Two problems developed. It reduced the man's stallions to geldings. And he discovered that panix, when ingested (at least by horses), is highly addictive. Prissen's beast was suffering from withdrawal.

I should note that I doubt the Jarl intended to harm young Prissen by giving him an addicted horse. In my opinion, the Jarl didn't want the stallion mated.

At noon I slipped out and went to the stables. The stallion, when I glanced into his stall, puffed through his nostrils and rolled his eyes. He did look possessed.

Jenner and I dissolved a few crystals in hot water – they won't melt in cold. We added the potion to a bucket of cool. The beast bared his teeth when I opened the gate. But he slurped every drop from the pail and afterward actually nuzzled my cheek without nipping off my ear.

Jenner was astounded. "Magic," he whispered, then made the sign lowlanders use to ward off evil. I'm not sure if he meant it for me or the horse.

I left before Jazuf came, so Jenner will take full credit for the "taming." Fine with me. But I'll hold him to his promise of lending me a horse whenever I want one.

Before, during, and after evening meal, Cyril and I worked on the ledger. (We ate in his room.) The task was even easier than I thought it would be. Cyril had kept every slip of paper in order. He's uneducated, but not stupid. And his memory is a wonderment. I read aloud as I transferred the figures. He repeated them. When we had finished the first month, he recited every entry. With no errors! I did consider that if the ledger fell to the wrong person, my hand might be recognized. A remote possibility. I printed crudely, in a style suitable for a head cook.

We were partway through the second month when Jenner peeked in. "Thought you should know, mate," he said, "all's well." Then he left, shutting the door behind him.

Cyril and I completed the ledger. I promised to help him keep up on it, but said it would be better if he did it himself. "I can't write no more than my mark," he insisted, jabbing at his initial on one of the slips.

"You can learn the rest," I argued. "I won't be here forever." It felt good to say that.

Cyril believes himself to be stupid. Yet he can juggle sums in his head faster than I can with paper and pen. He'll soon be tending the ledger without my aid.

517, 3/19. Cyril pulled me from work. Wouldn't say why. Just led me down the hall. A woman and two boys waited by the north door. Cyril chuckled, "Guess who they was."

The woman wore a dress of brown wool, with a tailored waist, hip pleats, and a flat lace collar. The hem fell to mid-calf, a length seen commonly enough, but shorter than the style in the kitchens, exposing her black stockings. Mud glazed her leather shoes. She clutched an embroidered handbag. A brass marriage bracelet circled her wrist. Her hair, a shade darker than the dress, was combed into a bun at her nape. She looked like a working-class woman who had dressed up for an occasion – and had cleaned up after a bit of trouble. Bruises marred her face.

The older boy – I'd judge his age as eight – seemed ready to swoon, swaying slightly. Blood had soaked through his shirt. The younger boy, a four-year-old at most, sat on the floor, sucking his thumb. Both boys wore shoes.

I noticed these details mainly due to Cyril's guessing game. For a moment I thought he planned to tease me by declaring that the woman was my non-existent wife. I was about to tell him I had no idea who these people were, then the answer struck me. "They're from the D.O."

"The Double Ox Inn," Cyril said, as if to correct me. "They was waylaid this side of Brithe. The cook, he were killed, and she were had for certain." He motioned to the woman's bare head, as if her lack of a bonnet proved she'd been raped. "Now they comes to us. We don't need no girl. Don't need no cook neither, but sure don't need no girl." He said all this in front of the woman, not caring that the dead man had been her husband. Would he have shoved her and her boys out to fend for themselves? Perhaps.

"Could use another girl in the spare kitchen," I lied.

Cyril grunted. "Jazuf's watching costs."

"I'll pay her wages," I said, and he readily agreed.

We took them into the dining hall. She wanted a healer for her older boy. Cyril laughed. Healers aren't cheap in Tiarn. In these kitchens a person heals on his own or dies. The boy had numerous bruises, plus a gash on his shoulder and a scrape on his side. I cleaned his wounds with vinegar. He didn't shed a tear. I asked Cassie to feed the three of them and settle them in.

I realize why Cyril chose me. He knew I'd offer a part of my wages to cover her pay. Damn him. Eight hopence is nothing though. I'll deduct it from the beggars' share. The woman does qualify as a beggar. Her name is Damut.

517, 3/20. Damut was up early. I told her she could take the day free, but she insisted on working. Old Wix assigned Helsa to assist me. She's an innocuous woman who rarely speaks above a whisper, not a good teacher. Cassie was assigned to Lanerd. I told Damut to stick near her, and asked Cassie to instruct Damut on the dos and don'ts of the kitchens.

The day didn't go well. My bench faces the hall so I'm not sure what instigated the conflict. Grutin either said or did something to Damut and she shouted loud enough for even Old Wix to hear, "I am not a brothid!" Grutin smacked her. Then I stepped in.

I said something to the effect that since I was paying Damut's wages, he could keep his stinking hands off her. He called me a catamite, grabbed his crotch and asked if I wanted some. I said he didn't have enough to fill a pocket pie. Childish. Yet the incident could've escalated into a brawl if Cyril hadn't entered.

He shifted Damut to my bench. I had assumed she'd be rotated as the other women are and would need to learn the habits of all the cooks in the spare kitchen. Not so, Cyril decreed. "You're paying her. She works for you."

I didn't want Damut to attach herself to me and it's unlikely she will, after hearing Grutin's remarks. He did me a favor there.

But I don't want to feel responsible for her and would have preferred to place her with another cook. Why did I ever agree to pay her wages?

517, 3/25. Cyril and I were in his office this evening, working on his ledger, when he asked how Damut was doing. I told him, "Fine," though she's doing better than fine. She knows most of the recipes and anticipates my needs. And not only does she clean up when I'm finished for the day, she restocks my station after the scullery women are done, so we get a quick start the next morning.

"There's been talk about her working only with you."

"What sort of talk?" I asked.

Instead of a direct answer, he told me he had decided to reorganize the spare kitchen. Said he'd been thinking of replacing Old Wix and asked if I wanted to be in charge.

It's true that age and partial deafness have made Wix somewhat incompetent. Cyril's been carrying him for years. Yet replacing him would send ripples of conflict beyond the spare kitchen and into breads. Young Wix wouldn't be happy to see his father deposed. I mentioned this to Cyril and he nodded, then repeated the offer. So I allowed myself to muse on it. I could have a bench by a window. Plus Grutin would rank beneath me. Tempting.

Daydreaming of ordering Grutin about, I rinsed Cyril's pen (I'd completed the day's entries) and I realized the rise in position was probably meant as a reward for doing the ledger. "If you bump Old Wix," I said, "Lanerd should get his spot. He's more senior." Window bench or no, I'd rather keep Cyril in my debt.

His comment about 'talk' concerned me enough that I sought Cassie's opinion of how Damut is doing. I cornered her, literally, in the dining hall. It was after evening meal so the room wasn't crowded, yet we both whispered.

"Damut don't fit," Cassie said cryptically. When I pressed her to explain, she broadened her review to include Damut's sons, "They don't fit. Waiting by the door all day. They too good to mix with the other boys?"

Damut's sons do loiter outside the spare kitchen while she's working. It's as though they're afraid to lose sight her, or she's afraid to lose sight of them.

"They need time to feel safe," I told Cassie, then slipped her a hopence. "Be their friend." I can't, in good conscience, deduct the bribe from the beggar's share. I've done fairly well saving coin this month though. Spending nothing at all is too high a goal to attain, and if the hopence –

Tobb came in. I wish the oaf would learn how to knock! He's drunk. Flung himself onto his bed. I asked him if he'd heard talk about Damut, more to torment him, keep him awake, than to get an answer. He's taking his time responding. Is he already asleep? No. He's saying, "Everybody were talking about you and Damut." His head lifted. He's squinting at me. "Bonnet her, mate." Head's down again. He's out. What did he mean?

517, 3/26. An awkward day. Damut worked as efficiently as ever. Thoughts about her not fitting in distracted me.

The women often share clothing, especially among their children. They haven't shared a thread with Damut. She wears the same brown dress every day. I noticed her older boy, Malison, out in the hall, quietly amusing his bother. Malison's shirt still bears blood stains. Will I have to bribe Baz to get her to wash it? I haven't enough coin to bribe every person in these kitchens. Would Damut be accepted if she wore a bonnet? The question simmered in my mind. But when we pulled out the last tray of raisin tarts, I had yet to raise the topic with her.

This evening I spied her in the back orchard. I decided to sacrifice one of my better old shirts and carried it out to her. The weather's been warm of late. Buds on the apple trees are ready to burst. Usually by this time of the year, at that time of day, the back orchard is full of screaming children. Damut's boys were the only two. They were on the terrace below her, running through the slanted sunlight, chasing each other around tree trunks. She stood above them, like a merlin watching rabbits play.

She frowned when I offered the shirt. "We're not beggars, Sheever." But she called Malison up. He's an average-looking boy. Dark hair and eyes. My shirt is too big for him, but he must have been glad to don it. He sent me a hint of a smile as he rolled the sleeves.

"What do you say?" Damut demanded.

"Thanks," the boy uttered, then dashed back down the terrace steps to rejoin his brother.

I had hoped my giving the shirt would provide an opening to ask Damut about wearing a bonnet, but I still felt inept discussing the matter. I complimented her on the tailoring of her dress. "You're a fine seamstress."

"My sister-by-law made it," she confessed. "I can't sew good. Guess I need to learn."

Afraid the conversation would turn astray, I plunged to the point. "The women here all wear bonnets."

Anger flamed her cheeks. "I'm a widow!" she declared, as if that exempted her. "You telling me to cover my head?"

"No," I said. Was this an error? My insight on bonnets is as scanty as it was this morning. They can't be a sign of marriage. None of the women here are married. Besides, Damut hasn't removed her bracelet and that, I know, is a symbol of marriage. I've no doubt both her and her husband's names are engraved on the cuff's underside, and possibly the date of their wedding. Are bonnets a sign of obedience? Of modesty?

I'm weary of thinking about bonnets. Damut is Mearan. Even if she is from Eastland, she should know better than I whether to cover her head or not. It seems she does know. And there's the difference between us. When I came here, I observed those around me and copied them. I wanted to be as invisible as possible. I wanted to blend. Damut does not.

517, 3/32. Cyril took his ledger to the palace for Jazuf to inspect. He returned, beaming. The last entry was in his own hand which, remarkably, resembles what I forged for him. Confidence soaring, he revealed his scheme to improve the spare kitchen. The plan was far less ambitious than the one he leaked to me. Only the women's schedule has altered. In short, there are eight women in there. He assigned five to work specific benches. The three left over – "floaters," he called them – would go where needed or fill in when any of the "regulars" had a free day.

Nothing changed for the cooks. Especially for me, since Damut was assigned to my bench. It did, however, prompt a discussion between her and me about free days. I told her I take mine all at once.

"So you can visit your wife," she said. "I've heard." That may be what she'd heard, but I could tell by her tone she didn't believe it. Not that it matters.

I asked her what days she wanted free. She asked if she took no free days, would I pay her extra if she worked even though I wasn't here. I told her I would, thinking just of the one hopence more it would cost me. I didn't consider the hassle of fixing things so she wouldn't be a floater and end up under Grutin's thumb.

Cyril had put Cassie with Old Wix. I bribed her to trade with Damut and be a floater herself on the days I'd be gone.

Then I cleared the deal with Cyril and Old Wix. The only one unhappy with the arrangement was Damut. Wix's bench doesn't face the hall, so she won't be able to keep an eye on her boys. "Can't I work with Rebic while you're gone?" she asked.

"No," I told her. That woman is impossible to please.

517, 4/3. Wages day. We were paid, as usual, at the noon break. I gave Damut the four hopence she'd earned, then halved the rest of my pay, a more honest division, I've resolved, than subtracting her wages from the beggars' share. I may think differently next month when her bit jumps to nine hopence.

Jenner stopped by this afternoon to ask if I wanted a horse tonight or tomorrow. He's never done this before. I assume his courtesy was a show of gratitude – Prissen rode the stallion yesterday without mishap. "Daybreak tomorrow," I told him. I wanted to go to the markets tonight. Lighten my soul before traveling.

Grutin and I finished work at the same time. He invited me to toss dice with him and Rebic, who had been free today. I declined, but tagged along to watch. (I don't walk into Tiarn before dusk and had time to waste.) Except for three children catching sod beetles in a corner, the dining hall was vacant. Grutin chose a table away from the windows. The game was high pair. As I suspected, he has a set of weighted dice. He let Rebic win a few rounds before making the swap. After winning slightly more than he'd lost, he switched sets again. He's clever with his hands. I barely saw the exchanges. Rebic did not.

Perhaps I should have exposed the sham, but I've been practicing Dohlaru of late. I was not born to judge Grutin. Nor was I born to advise Rebic on the hazards of gambling. I did go out to the spit where Tobb was roasting a calf and mentioned that Grutin and Rebic were dicing.

Tobb paused in laying wet cherrywood chips on the coals. "Grutin has the luck of Loric," he said. "Only a fool would toss dice with him."

'Tobb,' I thought, 'you ARE a fool.' But I took his response to mean he and his wages would not be parted.

Once outside I was reluctant to go back in and since chatting with Tobb has its limitations, I ambled up to Main. Guards were lolling about on the palace steps. I crossed the road to put distance between them and me. I hadn't intended to enter Royal Wood. Indeed, I was wearing my low shoes. But finding a trail, I ducked into the trees.

Cyril has lived here all his life yet has never gone into the Wood. He cautions everyone about the dangers of getting lost or stumbling into a natal hunting party. "Stay on the roads!"

The trails do twist this way and that. I've walked many of them enough to know where they lead, but there are plenty more that still provide the illusion of being lost.

Today I wasn't seeking adventure, just a pleasant stroll. Most of the trees are hardwoods and spring has cast a green flush on their branches. Purple trilliums and scarlet adder's tongues colored the leaf litter. The scent of bluebells freshened the air. I wasn't looking for mischief. But when I spied a bevy of ink-veiled mushrooms, my mouth watered as I recalled the first time I had eaten them. I'd been staying with Ayros at the Blue Falcon and fried them as a jest. Their subtle flavor surprised me. I became so fond of them, Ayros reserved a skillet for my use. (They taste rather foul raw.) Pity he couldn't eat them.

Today I would have given anything for a skillet and a tad of butter. As I wondered where I could prepare my imagined feast, the idea struck to borrow a pan from the sexton. I gathered the mushrooms with zeal, using my cape as a sack. Tonight,

I thought as I strode along an eastern path, I would dine on something other than the usual fare.

I came out of the trees above the common graveyard and couldn't help but notice the sunken ground of Liana's grave. Not a single weed nor blade of grass had sprouted from her eternal abode. To a Mearan, this would signify she had not been accepted in Loric's Garden.

I slid down the slope toward Cemetery Lane. Smoke was curling up from the chimney of the sexton's residence. I rapped on his door, waited, rapped again. He finally opened the damned thing. His felt shoes were muddy. Blood dotted his sleeves. The sexton is a frail man, about as capable of murder as Old Wix. But he isn't above poaching and that's what I figured he'd been up to. I identified myself as one of Trivak's cooks and asked to borrow a pot. He asked why I wanted it. I had little choice except to show him the mushrooms stowed in my cape. He shook them out, stomped them flat, then lectured me on poisonous plants. He thought he had saved me from certain death.

I thanked him for his 'good deed,' though in my heart I cursed him for ruining a fine meal. To prevent my walk from being a total loss, I asked for a spade. This he lent. I went back up the slope, dug bluebells and violets from the Wood and planted them in Liana's grave. While searching for a rock as a marker, I found a clump of widow's tears, ferny leaves just beginning to unfurl, and transplanted them as well. Daylight was fading as I scratched 'Liana' on the rock.

When I returned the spade, I could smell the old man's dinner – boiled cabbage and rabbit. He invited me to join him. He was starved for company. Few people visit him, I suppose, unless they have a dead friend they want to cover with dirt. I was starved for warmth and, with a walk into Tiarn ahead of me, the chance to snuggle up to a fire had appeal.

His name is Calec Wessel. He is more than a sexton. He's a reverend, as he informed me when I entered his home. "I don't expect no special treatment though," he added, so I didn't give him any. He chatted endlessly while we dined on the blandest meal I have ever eaten.

Calec's father had also been a reverend, and his grandfather, great grandfather and on back to the start of time, each of them, in his turn, tending the park's temple. He said both the temple and the kitchens were built before the Cyntic War, after a battle with Verdina. The bones of the dead, he claimed, were ground up and made into bricks. It's true both buildings are made of white brick. It's also true the natural clay here is red in color. But the tale seemed more legend than fact. Most of what he told me though had the ring of truth.

During his grandfather's watch, he said, the Trivaks decided to plant their dead by the Grand Temple in Tiarn. Other nobles followed, and by the time Calec took over only common remains were being buried in the park. He prays for the chance to take part in a royal funeral. "Just once." But, as with special treatment, he doesn't expect it.

Calec bemoaned the fact he has no sons. His wife and daughters ran off long ago, and he never remarried. Now he worries no one will tend the temple after he dies.

"It's the end of an Age," he told me. "Five centuries of peace robbed us of our teeth." (He had none so far as I could tell.) "War is coming," he predicted as he gummed his rabbit, "and we won't be ready. We've grown lazy. Playing at war in the Games. When the real thing strikes, we won't know what to do. Uttes will swarm down and kill us all."

I nearly laughed aloud. What would the old man say, I wondered, if he knew he'd invited a Mule to his table?

My mood is high tonight. Maybe it's because I'll be riding out of here in the morning. I know it isn't because I paid off the beggars, though I'm glad that chore is done. I think Calec deserves credit for my humor. Tomorrow, when I'm reciting prayers to Dynnas, I must remember him – and pray his predictions come true.

517, 4/7. Got back mid-afternoon. A bit early. Weather turned damp. Plus I was concerned for Damut. While in the meadow, I sensed an ominous cloud around her – which goes to show why I wouldn't have made an able memsa, for Damut is well. Indeed, she's been gleefully plotting. Somehow she convinced Old Wix to allow her boys in the spare kitchen. Quite a feat. Letting children dawdle in the oven rooms during work hours is forbidden – or was.

Wix had one condition. He wanted Damut on his bench. Of course, he didn't want saddled with paying her. And that was the hitch they had fretted over. Would I continue paying her if he received the benefit of working with her?

"Have you cleared this with Cyril?" I shouted into his good ear. Would have been simpler to ask Cyril himself. But Wix stated the deal had Cyril's approval. So I agreed to take Cassie and let him have Damut. To be honest, I'm relieved. Now he can be responsible for her.

517, 4/15. Spring is my favorite season here. Evenings are chilly enough to wear a cape, yet the markets remain open well past dark. Flower peddlers brighten the streets with their scented wares. Shopkeepers sweep walks and tidy their storefronts. A youthful glamour excites the air.

This spring, prices on everything from muffins to shoes have risen. More weapons are offered, as are masses of good luck tokens in abundant varieties. Game Year wares.

I usually don't enter the shops. Tonight was an exception. I was strolling along Wayward Street, remarking to myself that I had never seen a pane of glass in Meara. Lumps of glass are sold as weights. Glass bottles and jars are as common as crockery. Women wear glass beads. Why don't homes have glass windows? It wasn't the first time I'd noticed this deficiency, but tonight I had nothing else to ponder, so glass filled my mind.

Anyway, I was walking along, wondering whom I could ask without sounding foreign, when I passed a shop with a sign on the door. Fresh in – Uttebedt silk.

The instant I stepped over the threshold, the owner bustled from behind his counting table. He was a squat, balding man with more rings than fingers. From the look in his eyes, I assumed he intended to toss me out. I flipped my cape over my shoulder to show the Hawk Crest on my tunic. He hesitated, then asked in Universal, "Fancy anything in particular?" He was testing me. Most lower-class Mearans speak Universal poorly, if at all. He smiled, sure my tongue would expose my place.

"I haven't had time to inspect your goods," I replied in the flat accent of a Vic, "so how could I fancy them?"

He arched an eyebrow. "Just arrived from Evald?"

I ignored his question and went straight for the bolts of silk stacked along the back wall. He tailed me. Lamps overhead did scant justice to the cloth. A bolt of green with gold squares leaned against the others. A popular pattern in Evald, gold squares on green. I fondled the edge. "Double weave," I mumbled, more to myself than him.

"None finer outside the Snake House," he said, then qualified his boast, "not in Meara, that is." He must have thought I was a Vic buyer retained by the High Lord.

A customer entered, a thin man in a ruffled doublet. His guard came in, too, and glanced at me, then rested a hand on his sword hilt, as if to say he'd use it. The customer murmured to him in Dray. I like hearing Dray, a soft, purring language. I can't speak a word of it.

The shop owner rushed to assist him. "Fancy anything in particular on this fine evening?"

"Laetris," the man said, dabbing his nose with a scarf.

The owner slipped behind his counter and, from shelves beneath it, brought out lacquered mediboxes. He had every shade of the expensive powder, from yellow to green to brown to black. "Kinship quality," he swore, "none finer outside the Snake House." Color has nothing to do with potency, but sellers often claim otherwise. He recommended the brown.

I snooped about as the sale transpired. Vanity mirrors were displayed in one corner. Most were polished bronze – to give the viewer a healthy appearance. A few were silver. None were glass. Why this Mearan aversion of glass?

After the Drays had gone, I went to the counter. The owner was putting away his boxes – laetris is not a servant's drug. Since he had assumed I was from Evald and thus already thought me a foreigner, I asked him about windowpanes and mirrors. He called panes "sheet glass."

"Don't sell sheets," he said. "Nor glass mirrors neither." He seemed baffled when I asked why. "They break," he said, then asked why I would want to hang glass in a window where it was sure to be broken. "Shutters keep out the cold. Or put cloth over your windows."

"But cloth keeps out the light as well," I argued.

"If you want light," he said, "I've a fine supply of lamps."

And so it went. I finally left, more puzzled than ever. In Evald, Vic homes have glass windows. Why not here? It can't be a matter of expense, for surely the High Lord could afford glass panes, yet the palace has none. So far as I know it isn't a matter of religion. Tradition? Perhaps. Or perhaps something in the water here makes people stupid. I'm certainly more stupid now than I've ever been. Why am I wondering about windowpanes?

517, 4/21. Chatted with Cassie this evening. After Tobb finished with her. Gave her a hopence. She reported the latest rumors flying among the women. I feel as though I've hired her as a spy. Maybe I have. She gives me another view of what's going on. For example, I thought Damut's sons had created a minimum of fuss in the spare kitchen. Wix made a point of telling me how handy Malison was. (So handy he suggested I pay the boy an apprentice's wage. I suggested he pay the boy.) And Basal, the younger boy, knows enough to at least stay out of the way.

The women see things differently. Mira in particular, according to Cassie, is angry about Wix teaching Malison the trade. Her son Nulan, who is older, hasn't been accepted as an apprentice. Nulan hasn't completed an hour of work in his life. Nor, I suspect, does he want to. I should add that Cassie's assessment is skewed. She has, as promised, been friendly with Damut. However, both Cassie and Mira are with child, and the two of them spend a fair amount of time together, so she hears Mira's complaints. The other women may not dislike Damut as much.

"Tobb don't like her neither," Cassie told me.

Tobb doesn't like Damut because he's afraid she'll put ideas into Cassie's head. He isn't a worry though. And really, none of this is my concern. Why can't I just leave it alone? Damut's a smart woman. She'll survive.

517, 4/26. Mira swooned this morning. I confess I thought about making her ill. I swear I didn't act on the notion.

517, 4/32. Mira lost the child she had been carrying. She wasn't that far along, so there couldn't have been much to bury, but this evening Baz and a few other women walked to the cemetery with her. Tobb refused to let Cassie go. Good for him. She was on her feet too long today.

517, 5/3. Wages day. I received 8 coppers and 14 hopence. Nine hopence went to Damut. I gave Malison 5. Beggars claimed 4 coppers. That left me 4. Minus whatever I decide to slip to Cassie. Giving her that first coin was a stupid mistake. She's begun to expect rewards.

I haven't bought a brew for so long I can't recall how foul the stuff tastes. Why am I denying myself? Saving coin is a hopeless task.

517, 5/10. Ended a needed stay in the meadow. Fasting helped me focus. I must think beyond the moment. I must not lose sight of my goal – the Rite of Grace. When the time is ripe, I will need transport to Evald. I will need coin. My resolve is strong now. How long will it last?

517, 5/18. First Sec Jazuf blessed us with a visit. I was making bread pudding when Cyril shouted from the hall, "All cooks into the dining room!" Jazuf was in there with four guards. We were permitted to sit while he delivered a speech.

"In a few months," he began, "we shall have the honor of being host to the lords of our brother states." He rambled on and on. Stripped of the rhetoric, his basic message was: let's give these nobles food they like to eat. I don't recall a similar speech four years ago and I'm not sure why we earned one today. Perhaps when the lords came for the last set of Games, they complained about the food. Or perhaps Jazuf wasn't First Sec then. Who knows.

He wants us to create new and exciting dishes. "Start now," he said, "so they can be tested." To guide us, he had a list of foods designed to please foreign tongues.

"Lord Macon D'brae of Verdina!" he announced as if D'brae were about to step through the doorway, crown in hand, and sit in our kitchens. "Lord D'brae prefers rabbit over chicken. Honey over maple syrup." And so on.

When Jazuf finished with D'brae, he cried out, "Lord Banuri Sarum of Drayfed!" Then he told us how to steam river clams, as though none of us had done it before.

Cyril bobbed his head, an agreeable loon, the whole time. I kept thinking the eggs I'd whipped were going flat. So raptly was I thinking of those eggs, I nearly hopped from my seat when Jazuf sang, "Lord Crey Maisouff of Somer!"

He glared at me as he stated Maisouff fancies bull cod simmered in a cream sauce, and I got the impression that if I didn't pay more attention, MY cod simmered in cream sauce would grace the Som Lord's table. I can appreciate Jazuf. Not as a person. As a first sec. He ended his talk with a maxim: "Lords rule the world, but stomachs rule the lords."

Before leaving, he and Cyril assigned us lords for whom we're to create new dishes. I was given the task of devising a dessert that is "unusual yet distinctly Verdi" for Lord D'brae.

When I returned to my bench, I could've kissed Cassie. She had folded the eggs into the pudding during my absence. "I seen how you done it," she whined, hunching with one arm raised to ward off a blow, "and they was going flat."

The other women stood around like ghouls, waiting for me to hit her. Whether she had saved my pudding or no, she had forgotten her place. Damut was the only one who defended her. "You would've had to start fresh," she muttered.

Cassie is a waif of a girl and Tobb's child within her is already so huge ... If she had ruined the pudding, I wouldn't have struck her. But I spoke crossly to satisfy the customs here, then whispered as we filled the pans, "If Tobb wants you tonight, bring needle and thread."

A smile bloomed. "I done good?"

"You done good," I said in the same gutter-Mearan she speaks. We ladled the extra pudding into bowls. Usually I slip this portion to the children. The bowls bake faster than the pans so I always set them in front. As I put them in the oven today, I was thinking about Jazuf and what sort of Verdi dessert I could create to keep myself off the menu.

Leister Howyl entered my mind – easier to imagine what to prepare for a man I knew than one I'll never meet – and I resented having to cook for him, or D'brae, or any other Verdi. Damn them all to Blazes, I thought. The oven blazed merrily as if to grant my wish.

Pudding slopped onto my hand as I shoved the last bowl in, and I remembered how Leister hated bread pudding. "It's common food." I also recalled the time he pinched a bottle of his father's dari. Dari is distinctly Verdi. Green in color, minty in taste, it's the most repulsive concoction I have ever had the misfortune to ingest. The night I drank it with Leister, it burned going down. And burned again when I heaved it up. What better treat for a Verdi Lord?

I asked Cassie to keep an eye on the oven while I got Cyril to unlock the wine stores. We had to search for dari. Cyril had never ordered the stuff, but Sal, the head cook before him, had. We found a case of it tucked into a corner. By then, the bowls were cooling.

Cyril grimaced as I flooded a bowl. A browned peak of pudding jutted from the green pool. It looked disgusting. I tipped in a little more dari, then set the damn thing afire. "Blazing Pudding," I named it. To my surprise, he clapped his hands, delighted! He didn't care to taste it though. Nor did I. Jazuf can have that honor.

Tobb did want Cassie this evening. He was drunk and after coupling, fell asleep, which left me free to give her the hopence I had alluded to. As she stitched the coin into the hem of her skirt, I asked what she was saving for.

"I want me a velvet bonnet." Her brown eyes seemed to shine. "For my wedding."

This was the first I'd heard they planned to marry. I was lying on my bed and sat up to congratulate her.

"Tobb don't know yet," she murmured, "so don't tell him nothing. But he don't have no girl but me and after his son's borned lucky," she patted her belly, "he'll wed me."

There's a belief in the lowlands that male children born during a Game Year are lucky. I was born in a Game Year and I can't say I've been lucky. Since I was born in Evald, maybe I don't count, but – I'm tired. My mind's drifting. I asked Cassie if she knew why Tobb "don't have no girl but her."

She finished her stitching and cut the thread with her teeth. "They think he's poxed. I'm not about to tell them different neither. Tobb's mine, he is."

When I asked if she loved Tobb, she shrugged. "He don't beat me much." She straightened her skirt and stared at me. "You don't beat nobody. Damut says you was refined, but Mira says ..." She lowered her gaze. "I heard what Grutin calls you. Don't believe it though. I seen you eyeing me and Tobb and it weren't Tobb you're aching for."

I'm not easily embarrassed, but she had succeeded. I apologized and promised to leave when she visited Tobb.

"Don't have to go." She smoothed the lumps in her hem, and I wondered if she thought I paid her for the privilege of watching her and Tobb. "Don't mind you staying." She stared at me again, a probing stare, as if she were a Court Sensitive. "How come you don't have no girl, Kor-man? You feared a girl might birth demons if you have her?"

It seemed as good an explanation as any, so I nodded.

"When you're rid of the curse, you'll get you a girl?"

"Maybe," I said. "If I can find one good as you."

She laughed. "You won't have no trouble, Kor-man. After you're rid of that curse, girls'll come begging. Damut has eyes for you as is."

"Damut is best off without a man," I said.

"Every girl needs a man," she stated. "Even old Baz has herself a man."

'Old' Baz is younger than I am. Or maybe not. Hard to tell. The woman is immense, weighing at least 20 stone. Mearan men prefer women with large hips, which could be why many of the women here layer skirts over their dresses (or under, depending on the age of the dress) to gain broader shapes. Fashion isn't bound by reason or logic, however. Baz often wears an extra skirt and she hardly needs wider hips. I've heard she was once the pet of the kitchens and for a while enjoyed sole access to Cyril's bed. Hard to imagine. Her hands are red as boiled crayfish. Blisters pock her face. Time changes us all, I suppose.

When I got here, she and Filson were a pair and she still visits him at night on occasion. He's the man Cassie was referring to. Rumor has it Baz and Cyril parted when she gave birth to a half-wit girl. Rumor also has it she and Cyril share the same father. But I'm digressing again.

Cassie said, "Even old Baz has herself a man."

I asked, "What has she gotten from it?" What I meant was Baz does the laundry, not a desirable task. She and her daughter Izzy tote our clothes down to Fieldtown, which is a stupid place for a laundry, behind the stockpens and slaughterhouse. Little wonder our clothes often smell worse after they've been washed. But my point, which I thought obvious, confused her.

She gaped at me a moment, then said, "Baz were our – "Cassie didn't pause here, but an exact translation of the title she gave Baz – Hammer Keeper – makes no sense, and I'm trying to think of an apt denotation for the higher rank her tone awarded Baz. Matron will do.

"I know," I said, for I knew Baz wielded some influence over the women, though I hadn't heard anyone refer to her by a title before. "But she still has to do the laundry."

"That's cause of Izzy. If Baz had birthed a lucky son instead of Izzy, Cyril, he'd not have done her wrong."

Cassie might be right. Izzy's birth may have affected Cyril. After he's favored a woman, he insists she go to another man's bed. It could be a sensible plan. On occasion, he claims most of the children here are his. When they're underfoot, he denies them all. The truth, no doubt, lies in the middle. But he always denies he fathered Izzy. Cooks leave the girl alone. The boys, however, lure her away from Baz whenever possible. Izzy, following her mother's path as a social pet, adores the attention. I once caught a group of boys with her in the coal shed and, though I don't approve of such behavior, I didn't put a stop to it. The girl is older than Cassie.

Anyway, I agreed with Cassie, mostly to humor her, that a lucky son would have improved Baz's life. Her smile returned. "Don't you tell Tobb about my wedding bonnet," she warned as she wiggled her feet into her shoes and scuffed to the door. "I'll have your tea steeping when you wake," she said before she left.

I'm glad she's saving coin, but I'm sorry she intends to buy a new bonnet. She needs a decent pair of shoes.

517, 6/3. Wages day. The peddler came this afternoon. Mira snared Grutin before he could escape and begged him to go out to the wagon with her. I asked Cassie to take Damut and her boys. (Tobb, I knew, was long gone.) Old Wix and I tended the ovens while everyone was away.

Mira returned, crowing about a red ribbon Grutin bought her. She wore it around her wrist like a marriage cuff.

I heard Cyril cussing in the hall. Saw Baz march past the doorway, her arms loaded with two bolts of linen, one undyed and the other red. Unlike the red in the cooks' tunics, the dye in the peddler's cloth isn't fixed and doesn't hold up in the wash. Dresses made from it fade into various shades of pink. Sometimes Cyril buys bolts of blue or yellow. Those colors fade, too.

Soon after I saw Baz, Damut passed by, her sons skipping on either side of her. She carried a bundle of grey cloth. Then Cassie entered, a pained expression on her face. I helped her onto our stool. (The stools – there's one for each work station – are supposed to be used by the cooks, but Cassie has needed to sit more than I of late.)

She fanned herself with a hand, nodded when I asked if she were all right, then whispered, "I knowed you wanted Damut to buy herself a new dress. And I knowed she can't sew good, so I taked her to the ready-mades. There were a blue dress she fancied. Cotton, it were. Soft as silk. But she'd not buy it. Said her boys needed pants. Bought them cloth, she did. Said she'd learn to sew."

Cassie hushed when Damut came in (sweating in her brown wool dress, her boys in tow) then nagged me like a botfly. "Needs a cooler dress, she do, Kor-man, and that peddler, he'd be down by the yards now." And so forth.

Did the two women plot this? Perhaps. But since Cassie swore she'd watch my batch of rolls, I walked down Lower Main and caught the peddler by the stockyards, selling his trash to the Fieldtown women. Cyril's right. The man is a thief. He tried to justify his price for the dress by saying its color proved it was Dray cotton and claiming he'd paid an import tax on it.

There is both a state and city tax placed on imported goods. But cotton (which will never feel soft as silk) is grown in Meara as well, and color alone proves nothing. Besides, the dress, like all his ready-made clothes, was a cast-off, and I doubt the former owner taxed him. I told him his records could and should be audited. He knocked his price down to 19 hopence. I gave him a copper. Got a hopence and the dress in return. The coin went to Cassie, the dress to Damut. Who's the fool here?

517, 6/32. I haven't written much this month. It's hot. Stuffy in the sleeping rooms. Unbearable near the ovens. Grutin torments me less, but he's merciless to Old Wix. His latest prank is moving his mouth, pretending to speak, making Wix believe his hearing is worse than it is. This sort of humor may ease tempers stretched taut by heat. It certainly burnishes Grutin's repute as a 'funny man.' But it doesn't amuse me. Last week he broke Mira's nose. Funny man, indeed.

After the sun finally sets, the air outside is slightly cooler. Firebeetles wink in the back orchard. Children catch them and tear off the beetles' glowing abdomens to wear on their hands and throats. Jewelry of a sort.

Cassie grows larger by the day. Her legs and feet are swollen. It's too hot to wrap them. Baz lent her a dress, a pink sack of a thing. It's too big – but not by much.

Damut made pants for her sons. Her self-appraisal was on target. She doesn't sew well. The legs are uneven, the crotches too low, and the pockets askew. I'm glad she didn't attempt to make a dress for herself. The blue one looks good on her and has to be more comfortable than wearing wool in this heat.

What else? The other day, I walked out to the cemetery with bread and jam for Calec Wessel. If he does have any teeth left, the jam should set them to rotting.

How could I forget! First Sec Jazuf liked my Blazing Pudding! He told Cyril it was 'enchanting.' Hickten Jazuf must be more of an idiot than I thought.

517, 7/9. Katre Haesyl is sixty-five years old today. He has been in my thoughts all day. Now that Tobb's asleep and Cassie has gone, memories crowd my mind.

If ever I loved a man, that man is Katre. Yet there were times I hated him. If ever a man deserved mercy, that man is Katre. Yet there are times I wish him dead.

Katre Haesyl. Lord of Evald. He fathered Sythene. Yet he showed me more affection than he did her. He called her, "Praechall's daughter," until Praechall died, then Sythene became, "Lord Lonntem." I don't remember a single instance when he spoke her first name. Perhaps he did when they were alone. Perhaps, when no one could see, he held her on his lap, kissed her sacred brow, and expressed the love of a father to a daughter. Perhaps.

Katre Haesyl. Lord of Slaves. He believed himself to be without power, thus it became true. When Praechall died giving birth to a son who soon joined her in death, Katre swore he would never partner again. Yet he allowed Vics to force him into a marriage with a Dray woman. When she and her Mule son were murdered, he displayed no emotion.

He wore tragedy like a cloak on a snowy night. His royal demeanor secured the love of his people. "Poor Katre," they would say. "He suffers so."

Katre Haesyl. Bearer of the Crescent. He is the last of his line, the last to bear the crimes of his ancestor. I remember my last conversation with him. We were in his sitting room. A portrait of Daith Haesyl hung on the wall. The chairs were arranged so when we sat, we half-faced each other, half-faced the painting. Katre wanted to discuss my involvement with the Kinship. I did not, and answered his probing with a minimum of facts. He became more and more blunt, unusual for him. When I continued to evade his questions, he removed his signet ring and placed it on the tea table between us. Then, as if I were now free to speak openly, he asked, "What sort of poisons do ye use to murder thy Vic friends?"

"They aren't my friends," I replied, "and I don't murder them. They're executed for crimes against the people of Evald."

"How can ye be sure of their guilt?" he asked.

'Dynnas be judge,' would've been the standard response, and I almost said it, but knew if I did, his next question would be, 'Do ye claim the wisdom of a god?'

As I pondered what to say, my gaze fell on his ring. A marvel, that ring. Dynnae crafters still produce wonders, but nothing like the Old Masters did. That ring is etched in my mind. Stones embedded on either side of the Haesyl Crescent represent the Double Triangle of Uttebedt. Ocherest stones. Blazing white on a royal hand. Black as night when worn by any other.

I sat there, absorbed by the reflection of his ring in the gloss of the table, and remembered being in that room as a child. Remembered crawling about on the floor while Katre and my mother chatted over tea. Remembered Katre giving me the ring to play with, as if the precious relic were a child's toy. Remembered sliding the ring onto my thumb, the stones winking black. I may have thought Katre was my father, but the ring knew he was not. The ring knew.

And so I lifted my gaze. "My lord, I know they're guilty. I see treason in their eyes. I see Utte blood on their hands. I know."

"Ye've had the Training, to be sure," Katre mumbled. He scooped up his ring and returned it to his finger. The stones blazed even brighter as though pleased by his touch.

When he stood, I did also, assuming he intended to dismiss me, but he drew me to the portrait and bade me to study the image of a man who had lived five centuries ago. Daith Haesyl, partner to Huhtha Lonntem and signer of the Cyntic Treaty. Daith Haesyl, who surrendered Evald to protect his eldest child, and murdered his youngest.

"Look ye close at his hands," Katre commanded. "Do ye see Utte blood upon them? Look ye close at his eyes. Do ye see treason within?" Then Katre turned to me. He had the same handsome features of his ancestor. He held out his hands, the same long-fingered hands of Daith, adorned with the same glowing ring. "What do ye see, Soehn Biehr?"

Katre Haesyl. Beloved Lord of Evald's Lost. Tonight, I think of you with honor. Tonight, I share your wish for death, a wish I couldn't grant you. Tonight, I remember.

517, 7/18. Returned from the meadow this evening. I counted eight bodies along the road when I went. Eleven on the way back. The Games bring more than coin to Tiarn.

517, 7/20. Something happened to Damut while I was gone. I detected a strange air about her yesterday, and she was unusually quiet, but she's such a moody woman, I didn't think much about it. Today I scanned her and picked up a sense of desperation, bridled by pride.

No one's talking. Cassie swore she hadn't noticed a difference. A lie. I offered her a hopence for the truth. She shook her head. "I don't know nothing."

All Tobb would say was, "Damut learnt her place."

Cyril shrugged when I asked if anything had happened. "I weren't here," he said. "Went into town, I did." Wasn't here for what? If someone beat Damut for sassing, there's no overt damage, no welts or bruises. But the stubborn resolve that toughened her has broken.

517, 7/25. Damut was raped while I was gone. Tonight after Tobb fell asleep, I got the truth from Cassie. I'd been pressuring her for days. She weakened when I offered three hopence, but agreed to speak only after I swore not to act on what she'd say, nor tell anyone who told me.

"Damut were bragging," she murmured as she stitched the coins into her hem. "Showing off her wedding bracelet and acting a proper lady. Said we was brothids, she did. And her, not wearing a bonnet, like a brothid herself, she was."

The women organized Damut's rape. They planned it during my free days. Waited until Cyril had gone into Tiarn, then set her up. They held her two boys and forced them to watch while the men 'taught Damut her place.'

Don't women bear enough misery here? Why must they be cruel to one of their own?

I asked Cassie if Tobb had been in on it. She patted his leg. "No, not my Tobb." But further probing revealed it wasn't virtue that held him in check. The other cooks didn't want to share a woman with a poxed man. Tobb was to be the last to have Damut. Cyril returned and put an end to the 'lesson' before Tobb had his chance.

I swore at Cassie. I damned her.

She sat on Tobb's bed, by Tobb's feet. He snored. She whispered. "What was I to do? I tolt them they shouldn't mess with a kor-man's girl. Tolt them you'd turn into a demon and spit fire. But they says you wasn't to know. And Grutin, he says he weren't feared of no demon and if you did find out, he'd tend to you. And to Damut, he says he'll kill her boys. And to me, he says ..." She put her arms around her bulging belly. "What was I to do, Kor-man?"

I wish I were a kor-man. Or a memsa. If I had a memsa's power, I'd char everyone here. A memsa would forgive them. Better to be a kor-man. But I'm neither.

This world would be a pleasant place if people didn't inhabit it.

517, 7/26. After evening meal I asked Damut to go walking. Her boys came with us. We strolled down Lower Main and past the yards, then broke off the road and aimed toward Perimeter.

Royal guards, in preparation for the Games, have been sparring in the lower paddocks. They were there tonight, their swords clanging in the warm air. Damut stepped closer to me as we passed them. Her arm brushed mine. Though I've been trained as a sensitive, I wasn't born with the ability. I don't often receive the cutting images naturals do, but when her arm touched mine, a bolt of terror shot through me – her terror. "I'm not going to harm you," I said. "I want to go where we can talk without being heard. That's all."

She nodded. Her younger son, Basal, moved between us and took my hand. Malison, her older boy, stayed by her right side. We stopped at the edge of Perimeter and stood as if waiting for a carriage. I put my back to the setting sun. With her boys present, I wasn't sure how to approach the subject of her rape. "Found out yesterday," I said, then asked if she had been injured. A stupid question.

She shook her head. For a moment, a spark of her former self burst through; anger flushed her cheeks. She waved up toward the kitchens and sunlight flashed on her brass marriage cuff, the innocent bangle which, in part, had caused her trouble. "Those bastards are worse than Uttes!" Then she fell weeping against me. Begged me to marry her and take her away. Promised to be a good wife to me.

I told her I couldn't replace her late husband, couldn't leave my position here. Basal, wailing, clung to my legs. I doubt he understood more than the fact his mother was distressed. Never have I been so uncomfortable. I tried to soothe Damut. Told her I had discussed the incident with Cyril and he thought it wouldn't be repeated. Told her to try to forget it. Worthless advice. From over her shoulder, I saw Malison glowering, and my thoughts turned from her to him. What sort of man will he become? Does hatred burn in his veins as once it did in mine? Was I looking upon a future assassin?

517, 8/11. I knifed Grutin today. My only regret: he'll recover.

The day began with an argument between Cyril and me. While cleaning out the storerooms yesterday, he found a cache of apples. This morning, he wanted me to render them into sauce. I thought we should cart them down to the yards. They were withered, a good half of them rotten. Fit for pigs. And with a fresh crop ripening, we'd soon be sick of apples. Old Wix agreed. Cyril wanted sauce. Angry at Wix for siding with me, he snatched Damut from him and ordered her, Cassie and Mira (a floater today) to do the peeling and coring. I didn't have to help them, but I was also annoyed with Wix (he had yielded too quickly) so I decided he could do without me for the entire day.

We carried the baskets outside. Cassie sat on a stool – she's so big she has trouble getting up and down. The rest of us sat on the ground. We had paring knives, blades no longer than our thumbs. Damut's sons sorted out apples too rotten to bother with and, for a while, it was pleasant. The morning was warm, but the kitchens shaded us, and a breeze kept us cool. Mira and Cassie began talking about child rearing, a subject women never tire of discussing. Cassie coaxed Damut into the conversation, either an attempt to rekindle their friendship or to please me. Who knows.

I blocked their voices and listened to wind in the leaves. The apple trees are so weighted with fruit gardeners propped up the limbs with poles. They reminded me of Cassie, those trees, heavy with new life. Their leaves seemed to rustle with gossip like the women around me.

As our shade shrank, the sun heated not only us, but the apples. The area smelled like a cider press, attracting a horde of wasps. We worked faster. Malison continued to help by gathering peels. Basal napped beside Damut, sweat sparkling on his young brow. I hoped we'd be done by mid-afternoon.

Then Tobb and Grutin came out. Both of them were free today and both were already drunk. As I expected, Grutin scoffed at me for doing women's chores. Tobb tried to divert him by teasing Cassie and boasting about how large his son would be. But Grutin wanted someone to torment. When I ignored him, he started on Damut. Tobb tried to hush him, so Grutin switched to Tobb, laughing at him for missing his turn with Damut and goading him to take her now.

What happened next isn't clear. Grutin reached for Damut. Malison charged him, fists raised. Grutin kicked the boy away. Mira screamed. I'm not sure when the knife left my hand. One moment I was holding it, the next it was gone. I can't recall throwing the damn thing, but I caught Grutin in the center of his blazon. Must have been then Mira screamed. After her voice faded, it was quiet. I remember hearing the leaves rustling. I don't know who was more surprised – Tobb, Malison, the women, Grutin ... or me.

Grutin stood gaping, a bit of blood beginning to dampen his tunic. Had I been using a proper knife, he would have been dead. And he knew it.

I got to my feet, plucked the knife from his chest, gave it to Malison, and told the boy to fetch a clean one. "Don't want to spoil the sauce," I said.

Later, Cyril reprimanded me. He doesn't like his cooks quarreling, especially over a woman. I told him it was an accident. And it was. Had I been thinking, I would've considered the blade's size and aimed for Grutin's throat.

517, 8/15. This morning Grutin complained about Basal being underfoot. Later, while carrying a kettle of hot gravy, he tripped, the gravy went flying and if Malison hadn't yanked his brother aside, Basal would have been scalded.

Damut is afraid Grutin plans to kill her boys. More than one child has died from a mishap in these kitchens and it would be difficult to prove intent to murder. She needs to leave. But to where? It's too late in the year for her to find a position in the city. She won't survive on the streets and I can't support her. She has family in Eastland and if I borrowed on future wages, I could hire a carriage to get her there, but she refuses to consider it. She won't return to Eastland without a husband. Damn her pride. I'm not about to marry her. I'm not responsible for her situation. So why do I feel guilty? She's an adult woman. She can solve her own problems.

517, 8/17. Some of the women complained about Malison sleeping in their room. He can't be more than eight, but Mira and a few others claim he's been ogling them while they dress. To keep peace, Cyril told him to move in with the boys. He'll be the youngest one in there.

517, 8/18. Malison was beaten last night. By the other boys, I assume. He won't tell me. Both of his eyes are blackened. His shoes are gone. Stolen? Undoubtedly, though none of the boys had the courage to wear them today. This afternoon I saw him slip a knife under his shirt. "A good way to get yourself killed," I told him, but didn't force him to give up the knife. He'd only steal another. He intends to sleep outside tonight.

Tomorrow is the first of my free days. I had planned to leave for the meadow today. After evening meal, I went down to the stables. Jenner said I could use the roan mare. I had her saddled and was leading her from the stall when I spied Malison in the doorway, awash in the red light of sunset. Soon as he caught my eye, he ran, but that one instant of seeing him was enough to prick my soul. I unsaddled the mare. Told Jenner I'd leave in the morning.

Malison isn't my responsibility. There is no sensible reason for me to care what happens to him. No one else seems to care. Yet the balance of Dohlaru eludes me. Which is the greater sin? To care too much? Or too little?

The moon should have risen by now. Had I gone to the meadow, I would be spending the night outside. Why not do the same here? Indeed, why go to the meadow at all this month? I can fast here as easily as there. True, I can't see the mountains from here, but do I really want to punish myself with the sight of home?

517, 8/19. Tobb is sitting on his bed, staring at me as if at any moment wings will sprout from my shoulders. It's been this way all day. The wide-eyed stares and sudden hushes when I enter a room remind me of when I was the Soehn Biehr. At least a dozen people have asked when I'll be leaving. "Moon's near full," they say. "Shouldn't you be visiting your wife?" They know I'm not married. But it's easier to say 'visit your wife' than 'become a demon.' They expect me to transform before their eyes, and it both fascinates and frightens them. To them, my fasting proves it will happen.

At noon, when I was loitering in the dining hall, Cyril came up beside me. "Can't you eat when ..." he started to ask, then waved a hand to finish the question without words.

"I'm not hungry for cooked food," I answered loud enough for others to hear. Why not play the kor-man?

I paused in writing to glance at Tobb.

"Didn't touch Damut, I didn't," he stated quickly. "Didn't smack her boys neither."

"Then you have nothing to worry on." In truth, no one has anything to worry about. Superstition is protecting Damut and her sons for the moment. But after the moon has grown full and begins to wane, and I haven't become more than I am ... What will protect them then?

"You spending the night out again?" Tobb asked.

I nodded. I'll go out as soon as I finish this entry.

Darkness brings a glamour to this place I hadn't noticed before last night. Perhaps the bright moon created the illusion. Shadows of the fruit trees stretched over the silvered ground. I found Malison curled up among the roots of an apple tree. He was awake when I went out. I didn't sit beside him, but near enough so he knew I was there, near enough for me to see moonlight shimmer on the blade of the knife he held. Near enough for me to watch the knife slip from his grasp when he fell asleep.

It's Malison, not I, who is being transformed. I sense a hardness growing in him, a crust that will seal his heart as mine was sealed long ago. He has distanced himself from his mother. He knows he can't protect her. Knows she can't protect him.

He was my shadow today in the same way I was his last night. Always near. Not close enough to speak. But wherever

I went, he was there, watching. I feel him now, standing in the orchard with his gaze fixed on the kitchens, waiting for me to come out. Even before he's dead, he's haunting me. And he will die. If he stays here, he'll die. If not in flesh, in spirit.

Last night, as the moon followed its path through the stars, I wondered if I should kill him. An easy death would be better than a life of pain. His soul is still pure. Would death be a kindness? I can think of no other way to save him. I don't have the connections I once had. Cyril is of no help. Nor is Jenner. "Let him go," they say.

Damut doesn't understand. She frets over Basal, yet Malison faces the greater danger. He's adrift. Within a week, he'll be on the city streets where he's sure to fall prey to slavers and list masters. With a life of abuse before him, wouldn't death be a blessing?

I pray for another solution. Perhaps I should address my prayers to Dynnas, but it's Sythene I dream of when the moon grows full. It's to her I send my pleas.

Sythene, just this once, hear me. God, child, memsa, or lord. I don't care which part of you listens to prayers cast upon the wind. Just this once, answer. Let me see another path for the boy. Not for my sake, but for his, guide my feet so I can lead him to salvation, guide my hands so they can deliver life instead of death.

517, 8/20. When I came in this morning, Cassie had a pot of tea ready for me. Fasting when no food's about is simple. I rarely feel hunger in the meadow. Fasting in the kitchens is more difficult. I was hungry and succumbed to a cup of tea.

The early women were the only ones up – except for Basal, with Damut. She gave him and Malison bran cakes to eat. Bending, she kissed Malison's cheek and started to embrace him. He pulled away and went outside again. Through the window, I saw him by the cold spit. Bruises lent his face a dark cast in the pale light. I had decided to kill him.

When I drained my cup, Damut came over to refill it. She told me she had noticed Malison tagging after me the day before. "Just like a father to him, you are," she said.

How does one respond to such a comment? I said nothing and, putting down my cup, went outside. Basal started to follow. He's torn between Malison and Damut. At some level, he, too, knows she can't protect him and he's beginning to look to his brother for security. I told him to return to his mother and he obeyed, reluctantly. She'll lose them both, I thought at the time. One way or another, Basal will leave her.

I walked past Malison, went up Lower Main to Main and across the road. I didn't need to look to know he was behind me. I entered Royal Wood, went a short way along a path and waited. It was cool and dim beneath the trees. When Malison entered the Wood, I continued eastward.

I wanted to place his body in hallowed ground. He was born a Mearan. The least I could do was send him to Loric. The distance between us closed until he was on my heels. He chose to come, I told myself, as if that lessened the crime I planned. He chose what I have to offer.

We were almost to the cemetery before he asked where we were going. I answered with another question. "Do you like living in the High Lord's kitchens?"

He, of course, replied, "No."

"Well, we're going to a better place."

When we reached the edge of the Wood, I pushed aside a branch to see the Temple of Loric and Calec's cottage. No smoke was coming from the chimney and I assumed the old man was yet abed. His pony was grazing in the field of graves. The sun hid behind a bank of clouds.

Malison moved beside me. "It's a graveyard."

"Are you afraid of ghosts?" I asked.

"My father's a ghost," he whispered.

I asked if he wanted to learn how to throw a knife. He said, "Yes," as I knew he would. He untucked his shirt, withdrew the knife he had stolen and gave it to me. It was a thick-bladed, single-edged knife, better suited for dicing celery than slitting a young throat. But it would serve my purpose. That I also knew. I'd spent all night projecting how the morning would unfold and, except for indulging in the tea, it had happened as I had imagined.

Damut kissed her son farewell. Malison followed me of his own free will. Without fear, he placed the instrument of his death into my hand. We were at the appointed place, at the appointed time. The stolen knife was warm from the heat of his body. I had only to use it. Yet I hesitated, and again prayed for Sythene to show me a different path.

"Aren't you going to show me?" Malison prompted, as if to echo my prayer.

I smiled at him. Such trust he had in me. If only there were a safe place to send him, I thought. A place where he could learn kindness instead of the brutality so common in this world. No gentle place came to mind. I put a hand on his shoulder to prevent him from bolting. As I lifted the knife, a partridge burst from the Wood. A bow thrummed. The partridge fell dead.

"Natals," Malison breathed and pressed against me, his fear as palpable as the knife in my grasp. No doubt Cyril had stuffed his head with warnings of natal hunting parties. The boy still didn't realize why I had led him to the cemetery. Nor did I for that matter.

The hunter wasn't a natal. It was Calec Wessel. When he bent to collect his prize, I called from where the boy and I were hidden, "Nice shot." Calec nearly jumped out of his skin. He hadn't known we were there.

I'm not sure why I spoke. Had I been silent, I could have waited for him to leave, killed the boy and gone, but since I had already given our presence away, I stepped out from the Wood. Calec laughed, "Just in time for breakfast," and the three of us tramped down to his cottage.

It was easy to resist his cooking. He boils everything. I watched him and Malison eat, sitting side-by side, and the idea began to form that this was where the boy should live.

After the meal, I asked Malison to clean the pot. He obeyed. There's a spring near the cottage. I sent him to fetch water, then had him sweep the floor while Calec and I stood outside chatting. When the task was completed, I asked if the temple needed swept.

"Could use it," Calec admitted, and Malison headed across the road with the broom. When the boy was out of earshot, Calec picked at a grease spot on his shirt, avoiding my gaze, as he scolded, "Not my business, but you shouldn't beat your son, not a good son like him. Now my girls, maybe I should have. But my father never beat me, so I didn't beat them girls neither."

Here was the gentle hand I'd been seeking. Why hadn't I thought of him before? "The boy isn't mine," I told him, "and I didn't beat him. Someone in the kitchens doesn't like him. Needs a new home, he does."

"You don't say," Calec mused.

I spent most of the day with the old man. We brought out chairs and sat under the quince, moving the chairs as the shade shifted. Whenever Malison finished a chore, I gave him another. Small chores, ones he could do without assistance. He didn't complain.

Calec, I knew, was impressed. Finally, he hinted, "Could use me a boy." He went inside and when he returned, offered me a lit pipe.

I don't usually smoke, but the pipe was a token. My taking it would open the door for Calec to take the boy from me. So I sat and smoked with him – he uses dixel cut with briar leaf. We passed the pipe back and forth as Malison brushed the pony. Across the road countless graves housed the dead. We three were alive to enjoy the day.

Calec tapped ash from the pipe, then fussed with the thing as if debating whether to reload it. "Could use me a boy," he restated. "How much would one like him cost?"

"In Tiarn? A good twenty daekahs." I paused long enough for the price to gel. "He's not mine to sell though. Has a mother, he does. And a younger brother."

"Does he now," Calec grumbled, setting the pipe down. "How much she asking?"

"Marriage," I said. "The price is marriage." I told him the little I knew of Damut. I didn't mention her rape. Few Mearans would wed a raped woman.

Calec wasn't opposed to marriage. Nor was he eager for it. "Girls don't take to the quiet life." But he agreed to meet Damut. And Malison agreed to stay in his cottage overnight. I promised to bring Damut in the morning.

I had no right to commit her – as she hotly informed me when I told her of the deal. Tomorrow I'll take her and Basal out to the cemetery. If she wants to come back here, I'll bring her back. But I hope she lets Malison stay.

Did Sythene answer my prayer? Did she guide me to the cemetery and place Calec in my path? I want to think so, but I doubt it. Even if, somehow, she knows the Kinship's report of my death was false, why would she care about me, or the boy? But I need something to believe in. And though I see her only in my mind, Sythene is all I have left.

517, 8/22. Ended my fast when I returned this evening. Cyril sat with me while I ate, asked where I'd been the past two days. Told him I'd been in the Wood. I expected him to ask about Damut. He didn't.

Tobb followed me into our room, shut the door and leaned against it. He, too, asked where I'd been. Told him the same. "In the Wood." Then he asked about Damut and her boys. "Cassie seen them leave with you," he said. "Where are they? Lost in the Wood?"

I had just taken out the journal. I turned to stare him in the eye. "I ate them."

He paled about two shades, made the sign against evil, then slid out the door. Fool.

Damut opted to stay with Calec though she made it abundantly clear she wouldn't share his bed until their union was legal. Today they went into Tiarn, filed the papers in the courthouse (Palace Courts don't handle such trivia) and mouthed the vows at the Grand Temple. Calec wanted me to go with them. I didn't want to be in the city during daylight. Nor did Damut want me along. I tended her boys while she and Calec became legally joined.

The boys and I tidied the cottage (there's only one room) and aired Calec's bedding. A stable attached to the rear of the cottage had a rick of straw outside the door and, stealing a bit of it, I wove a pallet for Basal to sleep on. Malison, with a little help, wove his own. After raiding Calec's stores, we baked a seedcake, traditional fare for a Mearan wedding. Eating the cake supposedly ensures a happy and fertile union. I had set it out to cool when Calec and Damut returned. Neither of them was in a mood to celebrate. She was wearing a black felt bonnet and a grim visage. Wouldn't speak to me at all. So be it.

517, 9/1. Though the lords have yet to arrive, everyone with the slightest royal connection is moving into the palace. Few, if any, bring their own cooks, and their rapacious appetites are straining the capacity of these kitchens. I don't finish work until evening meal. Tobb, roasting meats for the next day's breakfasts, eats by the spit. The scullery women work into the night. And Cyril ... He may lose the rest of his hair by year's end.

Almost overnight, the city swelled to triple its size. Swordsmen crowd the streets and fill the taverns. Many camp along the river, denuding the banks of vegetation and fouling the water. Stray dogs and cats have vanished. Floating bodies are a common sight. Welcome to Tiarn.

517, 9/3. Before we received our wages today, Cyril told us our free days have been reduced to one a month. He reminded us of the daekah bonus we'll be paid Gurn 4 and promised to let us take turns leaving early during the Games.

Later, he and I spoke privately. He told me I could have my usual days, but said if I took four, I wouldn't receive the daekah. My staying through the full moon last month has made him less wary of the kor-man. To enhance the proposal, he offered me first pick of a day each month and repeated his promise of letting us attend the Games.

Watching savages batter each other in the Prelims doesn't interest me, but the daekah ... Saving half my wages won't put the price of a horse within reach by spring, not one capable of mountain travel. I'll need gold. I could barter my necklace, but Sythene gave me this amulet. I'd like to be wearing it when I die. I still have holdings in Evald, properties hidden under various names, but I can't tap into them without going through the Kinship. Poverty locks me into a life of obedience.

I remember when I first came here. I wondered if I could make the people believe I was a Mearan cook. It was amusing in the beginning. The challenge of the ruse brought satisfaction. I've played other roles – merchant, scribe, tailor, horse breeder, minstrel ... Once I performed as a juggler in a troupe of acrobats. But those were short acts of illusion, lasting only long enough for me to accomplish my task. A day, a week, or a month at most. Never years.

I no longer pretend to be a cook. I am one. There is no challenge in maintaining the coarse tongue used in these kitchens. Writing Universal in this journal is more difficult than it would have been six years ago. Six years. I have been here six years. Pray Dynnas, have mercy on my soul. Let my exile end before I forget who I once was. Don't let me die as a Mearan.

517, 9/18. Cassie went into labor this morning. Her screams pierced the clatter of the kitchens. There was talk the child was too big for her, but by midday she had given birth. The child, to everyone's surprise and Tobb's disappointment, is a girl. Cassie named her daughter Untha, the name of the High Lord's current wife. Mira brought the girl into the dining hall and made a fuss of showing her about. Untha is the ugliest child I've ever seen – huge body and a small head. Tobb's progeny for certain.

517, 9/26. Today is my free day. Yesterday evening I walked out to the cemetery. It was dark when I got there, the cottage quiet. I roamed up through the cemetery, then settled down by Liana's grave. The widow's tears I'd planted last spring are blooming, stalks of white bells vague to the eye at night, but not to the nose. Their scent sweetened the air.

I've discovered something odd about myself. I enjoy being in the cemetery. I'm at ease among the dead. I had hoped to spy a ghost and left my mind open for a probe, but my senses detected nothing. Not even from Liana. As the moon rose, bright as a watchman's lantern, I thought of my partner and son. I wish I knew where their bodies were discarded. I'm certain they weren't given an Utte funeral. Were they left to rot in some alley? I avenged their deaths too quickly.

At dawn, Damut came out with a pail and walked to the spring. I ambled down to meet her. She must have just risen. Her hair was loose, her feet bare. The cream-colored dress she wore hid her shape. The garment appeared to be two pieces of cloth simply basted together, something a pauper would wear. She needs more practice sewing.

We didn't say much. She asked if Cyril knew she was now Reverend Wessel's wife. I told her he did, though people in the kitchens call Calec "the gravedigger," not "Reverend Wessel." She nodded, went inside and sent Malison out, probably to shoo me away.

The boy seemed pleased to see me. He showed me the felt shoes Calec made for him, then invited me to join them for breakfast. I refused his offer. Better all-around for me to leave.

517, 10/3. Went into Tiarn at nightfall. Beggars on every corner. Half my wages vanished into their filthy hands. The taverns were packed tight. I bought ale from a cart-vender and, as I drank the stinking brew, I listened to the streams of people passing by. Men and women from near and far, chattering in all sorts of tongues. I felt distant from them. Separate. I had no one to chatter to.

When I worked for the Kinship, there were times I traveled alone. People I've cared for have died or moved to where I couldn't follow. I've felt loss. I've grieved. In the meadow, I'm alone. But I never felt the loneliness I felt today. I miss the companions I used to know.

Once I was the son of a Vic Chairman, the son of a memsa to the Royal House of Evald. When I became an assassin, the person I'd been ceased to exist, just as the assassin ceased to be when I became a cook. It's as though I died, was reborn, died, and was reborn again – all within the span of a lifetime, all within reach of my memory. But not within reach of my touch.

Is the way I feel now a small measure of how Sythene feels? She can recall hundreds, if not thousands, of lifetimes. Does she hunger for familiar voices from long ago? Scan crowds hoping to spy the face of a loved one who has been dead centuries? Does she wake each day longing for a past age and cursing the stretch of her memory? If so, how does she bear the pain?

517, 10/19. Macon D'brae and his party arrived this evening. I happened to be in the front orchard when the riders appeared, their white-stag-on-green banners flapping over their heads. There was no carriage and since the lords weren't expected until next month, I assumed the riders were Verdi advance troops. A quick probe hinted otherwise; the emanations I detected had a protective quality that could only mean someone of import was among them. The probe also revealed a woman. I wouldn't have spotted her without the Training. She was dressed as a man.

The group halted near the palace steps. Half of them dismounted. One of Trivak's guards sped down to greet them while another went inside. Soon First Sec Jazuf came out, nervous hands toying with his gold chain.

Macon D'brae wasn't wearing a crown, but any fool could have picked him out. He's a broad-shouldered man, brown hair, bearded. Jazuf gave him a polite nod. With all the yapping and milling about no one noticed me. If I'd had a crossbow, I could have taken them both.

Another man also captured my attention. He was a good head taller than the others and could only be Ceither Tulley. Four years ago, his name was on everyone's lips. Three times Verdi Champion and each of those times, the Verdi team won the Finals. Seeing him, I understand why. He's the size of a Dynnae warrior. I'm sure he hasn't been quickened, but I wouldn't want to tap blades with him. The woman must be his. They stood together and when they followed D'brae up the steps, she held his arm.

I went down to pass the news to Cyril. I mentioned my surprise that D'brae hadn't arrived in a carriage.

"Northmen are savages," Cyril said. "Near as bad as Uttes, they are." Savage or no, at least D'brae can sit a horse properly. That's more than I can say of Fesha Trivak.

517, 10/30. Today was my free day. I didn't fast. There seemed no reason to deny myself food. Last night was the full moon. It rained. This morning I went to the stables. I didn't want to enter Tiarn in daylight and there was nowhere else to go. I'd rather have no free days than just one.

Jenner hired so many hands he didn't need my help. Despite the extra horses from the Verdi party to tend, men found time to loiter – and rehash the nasty gossip that's been spewed repeatedly since Lord D'brae arrived.

Calling Verdi people Stags or Greens, even cursing them, is to be expected. From a Mearan prospective, they are rivals. But the talk has gone beyond the petty slurs I recall hearing four years ago. True, I didn't dine at Cyril's table then, so maybe I heard less. Plus Grutin wasn't here during the last set of Games and he certainly heats the chatter. He claims he spent a year in Verdina, working in a silver mine. That in itself is a lie. Yet for the fools here, it adds credence to further fabrications, such as tales about

Verdi families eating their own children, Verdi women coupling with hounds and other beasts, and so forth.

I discount every word Grutin utters. It's more difficult, however, to tease fact from fiction in the gossip Cyril and Jenner relay. They've dredged up rumors about Macon D'brae from twenty years ago. They say he killed his father to gain his throne. And killed his first wife, mother of his heir, to marry a Dray woman who beguiled him. "Macon's witch," they call his present wife, and blame her for Verdina's luck in the Games. They claim she imbued magical strength into Ceither Tulley. They say he's half Dray, half Verdi and half horse. Three halves total more than a whole, but that fact doesn't deter them. "Tulley's more than a man," they counter, "Macon's witch, she seen to that." Then they mutter knowingly, "She's a Ciard."

I haven't studied Drayfed's royal families, but Ciard strikes a vague memory. Can't place where or when I've heard the name before. Doesn't matter. Nor does it matter if the old rumors are true. Macon wouldn't be the only lord who's worn a bloody crown. But the slander irks me. Maybe I'm just weary of hearing it. During evening meal yesterday I expressed doubts about the tale of how he ascended Verdina's throne. Jenner said I'd see proof if I spent a day in the stables, which is another reason I went today.

Jenner's proof is dubious. Each day, he says, two Stags saddle three horses (the third supposedly for Macon), leave and come back in less than an hour. Two lightly-armed Stags did enter the stables a little past noon today, saddled three horses, left and soon returned. I confess it was a bit mysterious. Jenner has ears throughout the palace and he was grinning like a stoat in a hen house, so I played along and asked if he knew where the Stags went every day.

"To visit the Stag natals," he said. "Only them natals don't let the Stag Lord in the compound. The Stag Na-Kom, he were

Macon's brother, mate, and if he was aching to see him, that door would swing wide. When it don't, can't mean nothing but that Na-Kom don't want Macon in."

I exposed my ignorance by musing aloud that surely Macon could order access to the Verdi Compound.

Jenner scoffed at the idea. "Them natals live and die for their na-kom. Macon's crown don't mean nothing to them. Nor High Lord Trivak's neither. They don't obey nobody but their na-kom, and nobody orders a na-kom about."

I hadn't realized natals were so autonomous. Even if true, however, and even if Jenner's assumption of a feud between Lord D'brae and Na-Kom D'brae is correct, it's hardly proof Macon killed their father. Feuds between brothers occur for a myriad of reasons. What may be of import is the degree of the Na-Kom's anger. Would he throw the Finals to spite his brother? A betting man might consider this possibility when placing a wager on the match. Which could explain why Jenner hasn't mentioned the feud to Cyril, or anyone else in the kitchens. Except me. And he made me promise to keep quiet about it.

Other than gossip, not much is new. Tobb spends more time with Grutin and less with Cassie. He complains her child keeps her busy. True enough. A scullery girl watches over Untha in the hallway while Cassie's working. The location is convenient for Cassie – I swear she dashes out to feed Untha thirty times a day – but it's too close for me. The child wails constantly. I don't want to bicker about it though. Cassie isn't to blame. I suppose I've become her spy now, albeit an unpaid one. She asked me to tattle if Tobb brings another woman into our room. So far he hasn't, and I hope he won't. I'll hate lying to her.

517, 11/2. My Blazing Pudding won me entry into the palace. I went up with the house staff to a warming kitchen on the fourth floor. I was not impressed. The stove only held six bowls at a time. I didn't have to serve the stuff, just prepare it, and the incident wouldn't be worth noting except for one fact – the kitchen had a southern window.

I sat on the sill while the puddings baked. I could see the Church of Eshra – and the flat roof of the Saeween. From above the Saeween looks like a black diamond painted on the ground – a perfect diamond, corners aligned with the cardinal points. It isn't a secret Dynnae crafters built the Saeween; anyone with the slightest knowledge of the Dynnae would know no other group could have built the damn place. What I didn't expect was the white line which runs between the east and west corners, dividing the shape in half. The Double Triangle of Uttebedt?

I sat on the windowsill, staring down at that unholy roof, so dazed I nearly burned the first batch of puddings. Why would the Dynnae put the royal mark of Uttebedt on the Saeween? A jest? I can only guess the temperaments of the Dyns who lived five centuries ago, but if they were anything like the Dyns I've known, humor was not their strength. Were they angry at being forced into slavery and marked their work with the royal seal to prove their loyalties? Or did they know they'd be slain when their work was completed, and marked the roof to hint of something more they had done?

The Saeween can't be solid since the Finals are held inside. Or so everyone is told. Are the Games a lie? Do the lords meet and decide among themselves who will win? Unlikely. If the Games were fixed, they wouldn't allow Verdina to win the purse three times in a row. The Saeween must be hollow with a combat arena inside. I'll accept that as fact. And I believe it's a reservoir of power. Does it have other functions? Dyns are masters at creating things that are more than what they appear to be.

Lying on my bed, it's amusing to ponder the possible secrets of the Saeween. But I'm not curious enough to want to pass through those dark walls and find the answers.

517, 11/10. Crey Maisouff, Lord of Somer, entered Tiarn today. He arrived by barge, then he and his people paraded into the city, across the bridge and through the park to the palace.

Tobb was working the spit. He heard the blare of trumpets and shouted through a window to the rest of us. Nearly everyone went up. I wanted to see if Maisouff really carries a staff made from a bull's member as Kara claimed.

Between blasts on their trumpets, criers announced the 'finest swordsmen in the world.' The swordsmen were on foot and wore orange tunics emblazoned with a black bull's head. A live bull bedecked in ribbons chased anyone who stepped near. His handlers, expertly diverting him, provided safety with a semblance of danger. Women in feathered costumes danced alluringly to entice watchers close again. Jugglers tossed up flaming torches. Tumblers leaped, rolled and walked on their hands. Boys wearing little or nothing stood on the backs of ponies and waved banners. On and on. Drummers preceded the royal carriage. I glimpsed Maisouff as he climbed the palace steps. He did carry a staff, but I couldn't tell what it was composed of.

"That's how a proper lord should enter Tiarn," Cyril told me later. "Not sneak in like those damned Northmen."

The Soms definitely put on a show. And Lord Maisouff apparently intends to enjoy his stay here. The impression I detected from D'brae was he would rather be elsewhere. Yet he came three weeks early. Why? To discuss business with the High Lord before the other lords arrived? Or to visit his na-kom brother? Mend a breach in their relationship? According to Jenner, the daily rides to the Verdi Compound have ceased and

D'brae never made it past the door. But at least he tried to see his brother. I can appreciate a man who sets priorities. The Games are more than feathered women and trumpets. There's a million daekah purse in the balance. I'd rank winning the Finals above a damn parade any day.

517, 11/12. Lord Banuri Sarum of Drayfed came at midday. Also by barge and carriage. I didn't go up, but Tobb yakked my ear off about it, so I might as well have. "They brought wizards! And a ram with blue horns!" As if I care.

Cassie didn't go up either. She's lost the weight she gained during the summer. Untha cries incessantly when she isn't nursing. The child seems to grow each time she feeds. It's as though Untha is sucking the life from Cassie.

517, 11/31. I chose today as my free day though the moon isn't full. Tobb thinks I'm a fool for not going to the arena to watch the Prelims. Maybe I am. I haven't gone outside all day. I purchased a bottle of wine from Cyril, but so far I've only uncorked it. Temptation.

My mouth is dry. My stomach wants filled with something, anything. Wine would suit it fine. But I won't give in to the desires of my body. Not yet.

This month has been a lue-mout. The moon is hungry. My flesh is hungry. My soul is hungry.

Sythene is twenty-four today. I haven't seen her for eighteen years. Seems like a lifetime. Eighteen years of hunger. Eighteen years of darkness.

My memory of her is like the candle in this room. A flicker of light to break the gloom. A small flame of hope, burning on a waxen heart. My desire to contact her is like the bottle of wine, uncorked and ready to be served. I must resist.

Sheever's Journal, Diary of a Poison Master

In my dreams she is yet a child. When I'm awake, I try to imagine her as she is now. Did she grow tall like her mother? Does her red-gold hair still curl about her face? Does she wear it long, bind it in braids, or crop it short? Has tryadett yellowed the whites of her eyes? Are the centers still the deep green color of jade, or have they lightened with age? Does she still hum to herself when she drifts into thought? Today, this moment, is she slim, or heavy with child? Has she already given birth to a daughter, heir to her crown? I would sell my soul to see her one last time, even from afar.

I envy the people near her. I envy Daemis Brandt, though I've never met him. Did she choose him as a partner to align herself with his foster father Dyn Luka Massu? Or did he win her heart? How did they celebrate this day? Did he share her company? Did they seclude themselves and sip warmed mead from golden cups before warming each other in bed? Whether or not politics forced their union, does he make her smile?

I remember the one occasion I dared to ask her for the honor of being in her service.

"How would ye serve me, Novice Mysuth?" she queried.

'How indeed?' I thought and let the matter drop. I would ask again, I decided, after I became a memsa. Then I would have a worthy talent to offer. And when those plans failed, I accepted the fact I would never serve her.

But now. Now I wish I could go to her. Wish I could kneel at her feet and ask again to be in her service. And if she posed the same question, I know how I'd answer. "Lord Lonntem, I will serve ye in any capacity ye desire."

I would shine her boots and consider myself lucky. I would groom her horses, mend her clothing, scrub her floors. Blessed day, I would cook for her. Kill for her. Would damn my soul for her. If only she would ask.

I can resist the wine no longer. Drunkenness offers sleep, and a chance to dream.

517, 12/18. A fever has infected everyone around me. An ailment called the Games. Stags aren't the only people debased these days. Soms have become "Bulls," or "damned Orange Backs." Drays are "Rams," or "Blue Demons." An onslaught of hostile gossip has defamed Lord Maisouff and Lord Sarum. Forgotten is the fanfare of their arrivals. Wags report foul deeds from their pasts and the treachery of their evil wives, just as with Lord D'brae.

The Games were supposedly created to end all wars. I'm amazed they haven't sparked one. The air stinks of venom. It's unsafe for a lone man to walk about. I've stayed put and can only imagine what Tiarn must be like. Brawls in the streets? Rampant murder? Undoubtedly, if these kitchens are a taste of the prevailing mood.

Red and black are the only colors we're allowed to wear. If Cyril ordered us to dye our skins, I'd be the only person reluctant to comply. Everyone here is insane. State pride has stolen their wits. When troopers come up to cart off their food, they're greeted with cheers and encouraged to take extra helpings. No one remembers that less than a year ago some of those men had extra helpings of Vraden. "Our Victorious Hawks," people boast, though nothing's been won yet and much has been lost in stupid wagers.

Tobb, after betting and losing his own coin, robbed Cassie of the coins stitched into her skirts. Is she angry? "Tobb'll wed me when he wins a tidy sum," she sings.

Cassie will die an unmarried woman. As for Tobb, he and Grutin have become best mates. Both of them sneak out before their work is done and go to the arena. Tobb staggers into our room late, reeling drunk and blathering. I would complain if there were someone to complain to. More often than not, Cyril is gone as well.

517, 12/30. The Preliminary Games ended today. Everyone wanted to attend the closing ceremonies and see the natals ride in to meet the State Champions. Cyril said the senior cooks could go. For three coppers, I let Grutin go in my place. Cyril was pleased with the deal. He put me in charge and went to the arena with Filson, Padder, Wix (Old and Young), and just about every other cook who's been here more than a year.

Since the palace was nearly deserted, it was an easy day despite being short-handed. I took the liberty of tapping a keg this afternoon and offered free ale to everyone, women and all. Cassie fed Untha a brew. The child stopped her usual fussing and actually slept quietly.

Rebic was on the floor of the dining room, passed out, when Cyril and Filson returned with Jenner. I was ready for a scolding, but Cyril's spirits were high. He rolled Rebic under a table, then ordered another keg tapped. Within moments, Tobb appeared, cup in hand. I swear he can smell free ale from a league away. After downing a brew, he picked up Cassie and swung her around. They haven't been getting along of late. It was good to hear her laugh.

Soon the dining hall was full – cooks, stable hands lured up by Jenner, and even a few troopers who stopped by – all of them jabbering about the State Champions, rating the natal teams and laying odds on who will win the Finals.

The Verdi natals are the oldest of the four legions. The Soms are next oldest, then the Mearans. The Drays are the youngest. Youth or experience, which weighs more? Is choosing the middle ground the safest wager? Then there's witchcraft to consider. Is Macon's wife, a Dray witch by all accounts, more powerful than the wizards in Lord Sarum's employ? Will their spells clash and bounce harm back against the Stags and Rams, leaving the field open for the Hawks and Bulls? Or will Loric protect the Hawks from all dark forces, and magic won't be a factor? Or maybe the Eshra priests, who are supposed to be neutral, will ensure a fair battle. Such nonsense I listened to.

A man named Cron, one of Trivak's guards, earned the title of Mearan Champion. Ceither Tulley is again Verdi Champion. I didn't catch the names of the men who won for Drayfed and Somer. Doesn't matter. Verdina is the state to beat. Cyril is certain we'll break the Stags' winning streak. I'm not as sure.

The Drays are young, but this isn't their first time in the Games. The Verdi team is the oldest, but their na-kom is Macon's younger brother and Macon didn't look much older than I am. There is their possible feud. But I doubt Na-Kom D'brae would throw the match and endanger his men (not to mention lose the purse) merely to irk his brother. Eliminate age, magic and the feud. If one assumes the natal teams are evenly matched, then the skill of the champion is what tips the balance and only a fool would wager against a man the size of Ceither Tulley.

Tobb is one of those fools. He wagered his daekah bonus – which he has yet to receive – that Meara will win. With whom did he place the wager? With a royal guard.

"Don't you think," I asked him, "that if a man who knows Cron is betting against him, maybe you should, too?"

Tobb laughed and shook his empty head. "Three to one odds, mate. I'll have me four daekahs when our Hawks win." And he'll have none if the Hawks lose. I tried to explain this to him, but he snarled, "You don't know nothing! You didn't go to the arena, not once, you didn't!" He had me there. Taking my lack of knowledge into account, I'm glad I was sober enough not to wager at all.

517, 12/32. Finals night. It's illegal to be outside after dark.

Storm clouds rolled in this morning, shrouding the sun as if to shorten the day even more. We served evening meal early. After eating, I went out for a breath of air. The sky was black overhead. Light rimmed the western horizon. The filtered sun looked like a moon as it slipped through the span of thinner clouds and sank from view. The sight reminded me of Sythene, hidden behind the veil of Uttebedt. Few non-Uttes know she exists. Dyns and memsen created a web of lies to shield her from Unbelievers. They keep her safe, but unseen by the world.

As I stood there, I wondered what sort of person I would be if I had never met her. If I'd never seen the sun, I wouldn't miss its golden warmth. One can't miss the unknown. A crack of thunder ended my musing.

Cyril called out for me to unfasten the shutters. I helped him close them, but before going in, I glanced westward once more. The horizon had reddened. Black and red, the colors of the sky matched my tunic. It seemed to be an omen that the Hawks would win the Finals.

As soon as I stepped over the threshold, the clouds released a torrent of rain. Cyril locked the doors. He gathered us into the dining hall, counted heads to make certain we were all present, then brought in a cask of wine. "Victory wine," he called it, "aged in a special cask."

Indeed. I remember the wine he served four years ago. It was laced with sportha. This time it was heavily dosed with ophren, a cheaper means to the same end – proof First Sec Jazuf has his eye on costs.

Cyril had every man, woman and child drink a toast. The men drank two cups, as did Baz, her mounds of fat earning her a man's portion. I managed to secure a third before Cyril realized I'd had my share. I yawned along with everyone else and plodded to my room, as did they to theirs. Tobb collapsed, fully clothed, onto his bed. I waited awhile, then lit a candle and began to write.

Is everyone in the palace drugged tonight? If so, why? And who ordered it done? The Eshra priests? They may not want any witnesses when they open the Saeween. The natals? They may not want anyone near when they bring their na-koms to the Finals. But the na-koms entered the Prelim arena with thousands of people watching. Did the lords order the drugging? I've heard rumors they enter the Saeween without escorts. A good assassin could pick them off as they walked from the palace. Now that's an intriguing thought.

If all four lords were slain in a single night, what would happen? Firstborn sons would be crowned as quickly as possible. There'd be confusion, but war would be unlikely. However, if Fesha Trivak were spared while the other three lords were slain, it would appear as though he had planned it, and sons of the dead lords might proclaim war against Meara.

Would the Church restore order? Who controls the lowlands? Are the priests more than judges and advisors, more than an unholy common thread connecting the States? Are they the true power behind the separate thrones? If so, assassination of the lords would accomplish nothing. Is this what Sythene meant by the illusion of government? Does the Eshra Church, not Vic armies, prevent her from reclaiming Evald?

518, 1/1. I was first to rise. The storm had passed and when I opened the shutters, the world looked wet and new, as if the night had given birth. A fresh day. A fresh year.

Cyril was up next. I heard him shouting to wake the others and dumped a jar of bidda leaves into hot water. Slowly, the kitchens came to life. The bidda didn't go to waste. Everyone except Cassie complained of a pounding head. A long sleep must have been what she needed.

Cyril told me to make apple tarts. He rarely spends time in the oven rooms, but this morning he hung around my workbench, sipping tea, while I rolled dough. A runner came to inform us we didn't need to prepare food for the Stags. D'brae and his people had left. Grutin whooped. He had wagered against them and D'brae's departure seemed to indicate Verdina had lost.

Cyril muttered, "Them Northmen always leave early."

Soon another runner came to cancel Trivak's Gurn 4 banquet, a strong hint the Hawks may have lost also. Cyril sent a boy up to Main Road to watch for the banners, then poured more tea – he'd had at least five cups – and stood behind me, so close I heard him slurping.

The boy returned, out of breath from running. Cyril snapped, "What color?"

"Green and white," the boy panted, and everyone in the room cursed. The Stags had won for a fourth time.

Cyril told Grutin to finish my tarts, then drew me into his room. He wanted me to check his tallies of the year's expenses. I thought his timing was odd, but didn't argue.

He sat on his bed as I added the sums. Now that he has mastered writing, he keeps good records. Unfortunately, they proved he spent well over what Jazuf had allotted. (Staying within the constraints would have been impossible.) Cyril believes Jazuf intends to replace him with a more educated man, someone from outside the kitchens. "It were the reason for the ledger all along." He thinks he should act before Jazuf does, step down as head cook before he's fired, and promote a man who will allow him to remain here.

"Filson, he'd do me fair, like I do Old Wix. But Filson, he can't read nor write, nor Padder neither, nor nobody but you and if Jazuf knowed you could work a pen ..."

I understand his worries, but I don't want to be head cook and I told him so. He sat still a moment, looking like a hound that had been kicked too often, then he broke into a dissertation about his life. I had heard most of it before.

"Earned me two coppers a month," he said, "and spent them coppers each month until Sal were made head cook. Sal, he makes me his right hand, he does, and doubles my pay, but tells me to save coin. 'Put bits aside,' says he, 'you never know when your betters might cast you out.' Sal, he beat me blue, but he gived fine advice as well."

Curiosity forced me to ask what had become of Sal. Cyril tugged on an ear. "Were an accident. We was unloading a wagon of syrup, we was, when two barrels come loose and toppled. Crushed poor Sal, them barrels did."

If a turd had dropped from the ceiling, it would have smelled less than his tale.

"Were an accident," he repeated, then coughed as if to clear the lie from his throat. "But I does what Sal tolt me and all them years I keeped stashing coins." As he rambled on, I 'keeped' wondering where he'd stashed these coins, and would he notice if a few were missing? The idea of petty theft vanished when he confessed he had wagered the whole lot on a Hawk victory.

Fear of dismissal caused his insane wager. He's too old to be hired elsewhere. He had hoped he would win enough to live out his days in comfort. "On the streets, I'll be. Begging. After all them years of work." Then he wept. Not a wetness in the eyes. Great sobs. The sobs of a man enduring torture. Snot hanging from his nose, he asked again if I'd be head cook.

"I don't want the post," I said and walked out.

His problems are of his own making. Like Tobb, Grutin and countless others, Cyril placed wagers with royal guards. Fools. If they don't pay in coin, they'll pay in flesh.

518, 1/2. The kitchens have become a way station for gossip. Tongues did more work today than hands. Crey Maisouff departed at noon. This much is no doubt true. But it was said that before he boarded his riverboat, he slaughtered his pet bull, ate its heart raw, and mounted its head on the prow of his barge. There were variations of the tale: the Som Lord had the decks of his barge washed in the bull's blood; he let the beast gore two women before the slaughtering; he ate not only its heart but also its liver.

A list of those injured or slain in the Finals has supposedly been posted on the front door of the Church. I haven't gone to look. A crier supposedly announced the same information yesterday evening. I didn't hear him. The majority of wags said Cron and the Som and Dray Champions were listed as slain. Yet five people said Cron was seen last night in a tavern, hoisting a brew and toasting Na-Kom Trivak. These people didn't see him personally. They'd heard he had been seen.

Besides a champion, there are seven natals, plus a na-kom, on each team. That's true. Gossips say all the natals were injured or slain, yet none of the four na-koms was harmed. No one thinks that's odd. It's commonly believed na-koms are immortal. More likely, they don't partake in the actual fighting. No sense in spilling royal blood.

According to the house staff, Fesha Trivak is seething over the Hawk loss and is searching for someone to punish. He wouldn't dare direct his anger toward his na-kom brother; Na-Kom Trivak has a legion of swordsmen at his disposal. Thus, so the rumors go, First Sec Jazuf is the target. The High Lord supposedly had told him to draft a bill that would ban prior champions, namely Ceither Tulley, from the Games. The Church refused to approve Jazuf's bill and when the Stags won the Finals, Trivak ordered Jazuf flogged. I don't believe it. The house staff also said Trivak is leaving tomorrow with the Drays. Said Trivak and Lord Sarum are conspiring to have Ceither Tulley assassinated. That I believe.

Gossip is like thread wound over a spindle of truth, changing its shape.

By all accounts, the Verdi natals left Tiarn after the Finals, clearing the way for a new Verdi legion to arrive. (I didn't know this was their last time in the Games nor, apparently, did anyone else. But it may explain why Macon tried to see his brother. The feud may have been a dispute over where in Verdina the Na-Kom and his men would retire.) Take this spindle of truth (if they truly left their compound), add a few strands of gossip, and we get: the Verdi natals flew over the city, dropping gold coins as they went; they rode out, tossing coins to all they passed; Briss summoned them to a secret land where they will live as gods and since they won't need coin, they slit their money sacks and let coins dribble out for the less fortunate to find.

Two common threads emerge from these tales. The Verdi natals left. And Verdi gold is scattered throughout the city, waiting for any poor fool to claim. Do I intend to waste my time looking for these coins? Not hardly.

Jenner had the most interesting gossip concerning Finals Night. He said a pounding woke him and when he opened the stable doors, there stood Macon D'brae and Ceither Tulley, fresh from the Saeween. D'brae helped Tulley inside, ordered Jenner to watch him, then left.

"Were dark," Jenner said. "Couldn't see nothing. Tulley, he stands there, quiet-like, while I fire a lantern. When the light strikes him, I near lost my breath from fright. Were like a dead man, he were. Next to naked and slick with gore. His cheek were cut clean through to his teeth, blood oozing from mouth and jaw both. But it were his eyes that set my skin to crawling. Wild, they was, and staring at nothing. When I asks if he were wanting a stool to sit, he turned them eyes on me and my knees starts to quaking. Then he walks out. Not a word he says. Just plain walks out. I tolt him to stop. Tolt him D'brae wants him to wait, but he keeped going and I weren't about to chase him."

Lord D'brae returned with a full troop of Stags. When Jenner reported Tulley had gone, D'brae struck him with either a metal rod or a sheathed sword. (Jenner lifted his shirt to show his bruised chest, so he was hit with something, but the weapon varies from telling to telling.)

"Smacked me right good," he said. "Then D'brae hisself and a dozen Stags, they goes out searching for Tulley, while them other Stags starts slapping saddles on their mounts. The whole lot of them yapping in that tongue of theirs. Yap like hounds, Verdi do." Each time he told his tale, Jenner paused at this point to make barking sounds.

"Were near dawn when D'brae gets back," he continued. "Tulley, he were a raving madman. Five Stags was holding on to him and that girl they bringed was cooing like a dovey-bird trying to calm him. Then D'brae, he grabs Tulley by the ears and shouts square in his face. All of a sudden, Tulley, he's gentle as a child. Lets them others clean and dress him. Lets a healer stitch him proper. Don't make a whimper and don't say a word. Then they all mounts up and by first light, they was gone, every damn one of them."

How much of Jenner's tale is true? I didn't catch any overt lies, but I'm sure he exaggerated. One thing is certain – Ceither Tulley survived the Finals and if he isn't murdered in the next four years, D'brae will probably enter him in the Games again. I wonder how much D'brae pays him.

Rumors aside, Cyril paid off his wager, then spent the day drinking. He charged us an extra hopence for each pitcher of ale. He's desperate for coin. The last I saw him (after the keg ran dry), he was by the spit, retching.

Tobb suffered a mild beating from two guards. They wanted to remind him of the daekah he owes. Grutin avoided similar treatment by hiding in the women's privy.

With most of the cooks destitute from lost wagers, I felt wealthy this evening, too wealthy to worry about saving coin. I bought Tobb a pitcher to cheer him after his beating. And I bought two for Jenner. I wanted to hear his tale again. His barking imitation of Verdi makes me laugh.

518, 1/3. Not all of the recent gossip has been false. Trivak left with Lord Sarum this morning. Prissen went with them. Who knows what will be discussed as they float downriver. Plotting murder is as good a topic as any.

There is a sheet of parchment nailed to the main doors of the Church. I didn't go over to read it. I'll accept the rumor that it's a list of those slain in the Finals.

First Sec Jazuf was executed. Guards hung his nude body from a pole by the palace steps. A sign around his neck said, 'TRAITOR'. His back bore evidence of a flogging. He had been disemboweled. An untidy end for a first secretary. Mearans have a penchant for slitting bellies. Quite a few of their laws have disemboweling as a penalty. But the guards could have clothed Jazuf before hanging him for all to see. Like my father, Mearans have no respect for death.

Jazuf's fate pleased Cyril. He may be allowed to stay on as head cook, or so Undersec Olinad told him.

Tobb and Grutin are scheming to slip out of the city as soon as they're paid tomorrow. With two daekahs between them, Grutin has convinced Tobb that they'll fare well on the road. He promised to show Tobb the world. Cassie is determined to go with them. She won't listen to reason. "Tobb's mine, he is, and I'll follow after him." I don't think Tobb wants her along, but Grutin isn't opposed to the idea. That's what worries me.

518, 1/4. There was little to celebrate today. At noon, we shut down the ovens, as always on Gurn 4. The paymaster arrived late. Undersec Olinad came with him, wearing a false smile and Jazuf's gold chain. We were not given our promised bonus. The deal had been with Jazuf, the Undersec explained. None of us spoke out to complain. Our pay was minus the two-copper raise Jazuf gave us last year.

Tobb gathered his few belongings. He couldn't stay now even if he wanted to. I followed Cassie into the women's quarters, the first time I had been in there. The room is foul smelling and overcrowded. I can't blame her for wanting something better, but I pleaded with her to stay. "Think of your daughter," I told her.

"I am," she said.

When sure she wouldn't be swayed, I gave her the coin I've been saving, 22 coppers. She considered it a fortune and started to refuse it. Stupid woman. "Bundle it with the child," I said, then made her swear she wouldn't tell Tobb. She kissed me. Her mouth tasted bitter.

Tobb and Grutin were waiting for her in the hall. They both had capes and boots. Cassie had a shawl Baz gave her and shoes too big for her feet. Untha wailed in her arms, wanting fed, as they slipped out the north door.

Mira was unhappy to see Grutin go, but wise enough not to go with him. She motioned to the closing door and muttered a prediction, "Cassie'll end up sold, she will."

Cyril drove us into the dining hall. "It's a new year!" he declared, as if we didn't know.

Tomorrow is the full moon and the first of my free days. I had planned to leave for the meadow today, but the sky threatened rain, and with food, ale, and warmth about, I was easily persuaded to delay going. The temperature dropped toward evening. Wagers were placed on whether or not it would snow. I bet a hopence it would.

At dusk, three guards came looking for Tobb and Grutin. Cyril told them the two had left last night. Most of us were still in the dining hall and no one countered the lie. The guards smacked Cyril and demanded payment of the debt. Cyril gave them a cask of wine, but they wanted someone to work off the debt. Cyril offered them Izzy the half-wit.

Baz clasped her daughter tight, nearly smothering poor Izzy between her huge breasts, and begged the guards for mercy. This amused them. They tormented Baz, pinching her, lifting her skirts, slapping her behind. All the while Izzy struggled to get loose. No doubt she needed air. When she managed a good breath, she squalled that she wanted to play. The girl, though probably in her late teens, has the mind of a three-year-old and, if given the chance, I think she would've gone willingly with the guards.

They, however, rejected her as being too skinny. In her place they claimed a girl named Anar, the eldest child of a woman who died five years ago. I remember her mother because she was the first to die here after I'd been hired.

Anar is about fifteen. A pretty child. She has two younger sisters that she raised in her mother's stead. She and Rebic have been bedmates for the past year. Rebic didn't try to stop the guards from taking her, didn't beg for mercy as Baz had done. Nor did anyone else. No one faults the guards for the theft of a child. Izzy or Anar, it hardly mattered. "It were their due," was the common opinion. "The debt were paid." Indeed.

Vraden died last Gurn 4. Now Anar is gone. Twice in a row, the guards have celebrated a new year by preying on us. Us! Why am I writing us? I'm not one of these people!

I should have gone to the meadow. Greed kept me here. Greed for the daekah I didn't receive. I should NOT have given Cassie my savings. She'll give it to Tobb and he'll drink it away. This room is quiet without his snoring. I stare at the name carved over his bed and wonder where he and Cassie are spending the night. Damn them and Grutin as well. They may be cold tonight, but they're free.

518, 1/5. The early women played Loric this morning, relighting the ovens, reheating yesterday's spice cake. When I got up, the aroma of clove ended my plans to fast. A wet snow was falling outside. I carried tea and cake into the dining hall. Since the kitchens were more or less closed today, none of the other cooks were up. I had the hall to myself.

As I ate, the snow turned into a mixture of hail and sleet. I thought of why I shouldn't go to the meadow. The road would be crowded with people leaving Tiarn. Travelers might be camped in the meadow. There would be no chance of spying the moon in such stormy weather. When the sky cleared this afternoon, I told myself that with Tobb gone, our room is now mine. Why not take advantage of the privacy and pray here? The truth is going to the meadow required more effort than I could summon.

I've lost the will to fast, lost the desire to pray. I didn't want to be cold and hungry. I chose comfort over renewal of my soul. I'm not pleased with my choice. When I finish this entry, I intend to don my cape and go up to the front orchard to watch the moon rise.

518, 1/6. It's almost dawn. Cyril locked the doors. I had to climb in through a window. I was freezing. I stoked an oven and heated water for tea. The early women were awake by then, so I brought the whole pot in here. I want to get my thoughts on paper, but my mind is buzzing. I may have solved a piece of the riddle the memsa in Eastland told me.

"Heed ye well," she said, "when the Victors don a new face. Tis a sign the end of thy toil in exile draws nigh." I assumed Victors meant Vics and a new face meant a new Vic Chairman. I assumed it went with her prophecy that I'd see my death written in ink and my life would be spared by a man who would rule my home. I assumed she meant a future Vic Chairman would spare my life. Were my assumptions wrong? Do the two predictions have nothing in common?

The idea first came to me when I went up to the front orchard. Tattered clouds scudded over the stars. Royal Wood shielded the eastern horizon. The wind cut through my clothes like broken glass as I waited for the moon to rise.

I walked toward the palace. Security is lax when the weather's foul. Storm lanterns glared from watch posts, but the guards had gone inside. I was alone except for Jazuf, swinging from his pole. Crows had pecked his flesh and the bones of his face shone in the darkness. He had a new face, I thought, then the memsa's words flooded my mind. Could Jazuf be the Victor she foresaw? As a Mearan, he was by law a Vic. But a Victor? It was too cold to stand there beside his mistreated body and debate the matter with myself.

I didn't want to return to the kitchens for fear I wouldn't come out again. I walked out to the road, then to escape the wind, turned east onto Natal Way. The oaks along the road leading to the Verdi Compound are ancient and their thick limbs interlock overhead. Walking beneath them, even in winter, imbues the sensation of being in a tunnel.

Natal Way splits behind the Verdi Compound and circles around it. I emerged from the shelter of trees and stood at the Y in the road. The moon had risen, pearly white, edging the clouds near it with silver lace. Beautiful – except the Verdi Compound, looming ahead of me, ruined the view.

All four compounds are the same, colossal towers of mortared stone without a single window to break the monotony. Each has two entrances: a door for foot traffic and an archway for horses, wagons and such. Staring at the back of the Verdi Compound, I wondered why anyone would want to live in so depressing a structure. I've seen prisons that looked more inviting. If I were the Verdi Na-Kom, I thought, the first thing I'd do with my winnings would be to hire an architect and construct better living quarters.

Then the notion struck me. What if Victors had nothing to do with politics? The Games. Who were the Victors? The Stags. And the Verdi legion had left to make room for a new legion. The Victors would soon have new faces!

It isn't wise to linger near a natal compound but, stupid from excitement, I went around to inspect its front. A padlock sealed the door. Iron gates blocked the archway. I peered through the bars. Moonlight lit an inner courtyard of packed dirt. I noticed other archways cut into the interior walls, but detected nothing alive in there.

When does the new Verdi legion arrive? I don't know. My fever of hope is cooling. I'm so eager for a sign my exile is finished. Yet I have no coin to buy passage home and no proof the Verdi departure is the sign I hope it is. Am I grasping at air?

518, 1/7. I asked Cyril when the new Verdi legion would arrive. "Between now and four years from now," he said, which I already knew. "Depends on the young na-kom's birthdate. They comes when the na-kom were seventeen."

I have no idea when Macon D'brae's second son will turn seventeen. Nor does Cyril, but lack of knowledge didn't keep him from rattling on. "Then it depends on how long it takes them to get here and that depends on the season. In winter them Northmen could gets held up by snow. In spring floods could block their way." He went through each season, then cursed the fact he'd wagered his savings on the Games. "Should've waited," he declared. "Them Stags'll lose next time for certain. No team wins first time in. Not never."

My hope died with his comment. If Victors don new faces concerns the Games, it might mean when a non-Verdi team wins. The next chance for a Verdi defeat won't occur for another four years. I can't survive here that long.

518, 1/8. I spent my last free day in the stables and made two ugly discoveries. The first is Jenner didn't try to wean Prissen's stallion from panix salts. He just continued giving him the drug. Now that Prissen is out of the city, Undersec Olinad ordered Jenner to have the horse butchered. I also learned that Anar is being kept in the barracks. The guards are charging for her services. Unless one of them has a license as a list master, they're breaking at least three city ordinances. I mentioned this to Jenner.

"Who's going to tell on them?" he laughed, then winked. "They're only asking a hopence for her, mate."

These people sicken me.

518, 1/9. I was in a storeroom and overheard Baz and Cyril in the hall. She had discovered Anar's fate and was upset that it could've been Izzy. Cyril assured her that when he offered Izzy to the guards his intention was she'd launder their clothes. Baz believed the lie, but the truth fluttered in his voice. Cyril doesn't like Izzy, never has, and had hoped the guards would kill her.

Something else I detected: whether brother and sister, past lovers, or both, the bond between Baz and Cyril is even deeper than their outward actions imply. They trust each other – more than they should.

518, 1/32. Three weeks of rain. Rats, washed from their usual haunts, scamper through the kitchens.

Filson complained that a leak above his bed dripped onto his feet all night. He envies the woodwork Tobb constructed and wants to bump me from this room so he can have it. Cyril refused to allow him, and I know Filson won't move in with me. No one wants to share a room with the 'Kor-man.'

I confess I've enhanced my demonic status with brutish sounds at night – growls, snarls, and whatnot. No one comes in here, not even during the day, but other than privacy, Filson has nothing to envy. Along the east wall, Tobb's woodwork – including the niche he built for this journal – is wet. I built a niche in the north wall, by my bed, but I doubt it will stay dry. I can't store the journal under my mattress. It, like everything else, smells of mildew.

I snatch moments of sleep, then wake in a sweat and lie in darkness. The nights are long. I listen to the rats prowl beyond my door and imagine this room is a grave.

518, 2/3. Went into Tiarn. The city has shrunk in population. Half the streets were flooded. Beggars sat atop mounds of litter to avoid the lakes of stinking water. Most of the shops were closed. I roused a smith and had him craft a box for this journal. Tin was all I could afford. I had him fashion it with space to hold a pen and a bottle of ink. The box offers some protection, but moisture rules the air. My blankets are damp. My clothes are damp. Everything is damp.

I wake from dreams and weep. I must forget the past. I never loved a woman. Never had a partner. Never had a son. Never watched them die. Never can forget.

518, 2/6. Rain, rain, rain. This afternoon I napped in the dining hall until Jenner woke me before evening meal. Ever since his encounter with Macon D'brae, he considers himself an expert on Verdina, and he decided his latest knowledge was of more import than my sleep.

The new Verdi Legion has arrived – if his gossip is correct. He got the information from royal guards who got it from the troops assigned to escort the natals to their compound. He said they said the natals numbered in the millions. Not hardly. To illiterate Mearans anything over a hundred is a million. If I remember correctly, the Seto Pact limits a natal legion to five thousand.

Jenner also said Na-Kom D'brae appeared to be sickly. The guards told him D'brae had difficulty sitting his horse and needed help to dismount.

"So does Fesha Trivak," I argued, "but no one would describe him as sickly."

What compelled me to defend the Na-Kom? In part because I was in the mood to quibble. But also, as Jenner related his third-hand tale, I visualized the young D'brae entering Tiarn, soaking wet from the steady downpour. Once through the gates, he and his men can't pick up and go if displeased with their new home. By law, they're doomed to live within the walled park and city until a new legion comes to replace them. In essence they were exiled from Verdina and imprisoned here – or so I imagined while listening to Jenner.

I doubt, however, Na-Kom D'brae considers himself an exiled prisoner. If he continues his uncle's winning streak, when he does return to Verdina, he'll do so as a hero. I won't waste pity on him or any other natal. More important to me, was he what the memsa meant by 'Victors don a new face'? Did his arrival set her prophecy into motion? His entering exile a sign mine will soon end?

My free days begin tomorrow. Rain or no, I'm determined to go to the meadow if only to prove I enjoy more liberty than the natals. I can leave Tiarn when I choose. Maybe this time, I'll choose not to return.

518, 2/10. Returned this afternoon. Wet and starving. The meadow was a sea of mud and rotting grass. In places, the river and the road were one and the same. Twice I had to swim. Almost lost the horse Jenner lent me. Too tired to think. Hope I'm too tired to dream.

518, 2/15. The rain stopped this morning, but the sky hasn't cleared. Not a single patch of blue.

Cyril caught me napping in the dining hall. "Your moon-howling didn't help, eh?" he said, then gave me a vial of ophren. "Sleep in your room," he ordered.

I don't want to induce a trance. Don't want to use skills learned in the past. That life is over. It never happened. I'm a cook. Nothing more. A tired cook.

518, 2/16. Anar was dumped in Valley Green. The bee tender was checking his hives for water damage and found her body. There'll be no inquiry. No arrests. No punishment.

I didn't go to the cemetery. Cyril, Rebic, Anar's sisters, and most of the women went. When they returned, they were laughing about Damut and Calec. Damut's with child and Calec claims he's the father. The women are sure the child was conceived during Damut's rape. They bickered over the child's true father.

"Were Grutin who done her," Mira swore. "My man had her three times, he did." Her pride over the fact 'her man' assaulted another woman is beyond my comprehension.

Old Wix was among the group listening. He rarely takes part in idle chatter. I assumed poor hearing prevented him from keeping up. But he must have washed out his ears. Just as the tittering was waning, he shouted, "Loric knows it weren't Calec who done her. Calec were limp twenty years back." And laughter over Damut's fate began anew.

No one mentioned Anar, though Rebic promised he would tend her sisters. Tend them in his bed, no doubt. A pity I didn't die instead of Anar. I've lived longer than I should have.

Today I am forty-one years old.

518, 3/7. I've wet my pen and don't know what to write. Should I fill these pages with nonsense? Or save them until I have something worth recording? Is anything that happens here of import? Why do I bother? What will I do with the journal when it's completed? Send it to my mother? Let her know what happened to her son? I don't want her to know. And if I have contact with her again, I want it to be face to face so I can hear her response when I ask why she betrayed me.

Perhaps I should post this journal to Lord Haesyl. Or to my grandmother. Is she still alive? If she read what I've written what would she think of me? Thylla, I'm sorry I didn't become the man you hoped I would be.

518, 3/15. A soggy stay at the meadow earned me a single reward – on the second day the sky cleared briefly and gave me a glimpse of the mountains. Snow on the peaks glistened in a stray beam of sunlight. Will I ever travel those peaks again? Smell crisp mountain air? Drink from a cold stream? Hear the wind howl through the passes? Thoughts of home shatter my heart.

One thing is clear. The arrival of the Verdi natals was not the sign I hoped it would be.

518, 3/27. Cyril invited a list master here. He acted surprised when the man arrived, but it was a ruse. The man declared himself an innkeeper seeking young employees. Silken clothes, silken tongue. Two women and a boy were with him, all three plump and well-dressed, and eager to boast how much they earned 'tending beds at the inn.'

Every girl in the scullery begged to be hired. Several boys, more aggressive, demanded to be chosen. Both of Anar's sisters, five other girls and two boys were put on the man's list. Cyril accepted the role as father and signed their names. No force was used, no laws broken. The purse Cyril earned on the deal must have been fat enough to banish his worries. He lowered the cost of ale to last year's price. Everyone was pleased.

518, 4/3. I walked past the Verdi Compound. A dozen natals were raking dead grass and leaves from the compound's perimeter. They paused in their work to gawk at me. They are so young! Scarcely more than boys. Yet all were armed, swords on their hips, knives in their boots, merely to rake leaves.

I quickened my pace. Young or no, they emoted danger. I agree, however, with Cyril. The Stags are sure to lose the next set of Games. I must learn patience.

518, 5/32. Four cooks Cyril hired last year left. He doesn't intend to replace them. With Trivak still gone, there isn't much work. Is the High Lord delaying his return to snub Verdina? I assume he usually welcomes a new legion. Is his absence intended as a slap to the D'brae family?

518, 6/8. There are rumors of plague in the southwest. An embargo has been imposed on livestock from the area and the city of Driden is under quarantine. Or so the gossips say.

High Lord Trivak and Prissen have returned.

518, 7/20. Hot weather has reduced everyone's appetite. I finished work early, then strolled through the Wood to the cemetery. The Wessel family was resting in the shade under the quince. Both Malison and Basal have grown taller. Calec has grown fatter. He proudly displayed Damut's third son and proclaimed himself the father. "A miracle," he said, which is why he named the child Loren, after Loric. He went on about the surge of life that has returned to his organs. "I'm the sire, I am," he said countless times.

I saw no reason to argue the matter. He grinned when I told him the child looked like him, and the child does in a way – neither of them have teeth.

Malison took me by the hand, and he and Basal led me to the garden they had planted beyond the spring. Row by row, Malison announced their crops – beans, coriants, shallots, squash – as if I couldn't see. "And we'll plant more next year!" he exclaimed when we came to the end of the patch.

Damut had walked to the spring. She was wearing her blue dress. A breeze stirred the skirt about her bare legs. She called us over, then sent the boys in search of the ripest melon. Two marriage cuffs clasped her left wrist. Her felt bonnet spoiled her hair. "When you brought me here," she said, not looking at me, "I hated you. Treated me like a slave, you did. But Calec's a good man, he is. A good father to my boys. And I don't hate you no more."

I stayed through the evening, feasting on melon and sharing a pipe with Calec. Damut asked me to visit during my free days this month. I promised I would.

On the trek back, a half moon lighted Perimeter Road. Locusts sang in the Wood. I'm pleased Damut's hate for me has faded, pleased the darkness which had been in Malison is gone, but I don't know if I'll visit them again soon. Their happiness makes my life seem more barren.

518, 7/31. Got back from the meadow today. The weather was ideal, but I couldn't concentrate on prayers, couldn't separate mind from body. Each night when the moon rose, I thought of Sythene. In the old tongue her name means promise and, each night, my promise to visit Damut and Calec pestered me. If I break my word, how can I expect Sythene to keep hers?

So I left the meadow this morning and instead of riding straight to the stables, I stopped by the cemetery. The Wessels were outside under the quince. None of them recognized me at first, then Malison came running to greet me. On the surface, all seemed well. Basal and Loren were asleep in the grass. Damut and Calec both smiled and stated their joy I'd come. Yet unease shaded them as surely as the quince. I had interrupted an argument.

Malison immediately wanted to ride the horse. Damut objected and, I admit, the beast was high-spirited, unsafe for him to sit alone. (Jenner often lends me whichever horse most needs a firm hand.) But with Damut's permission, I hoisted the boy up into the saddle with me. We rode across the lane and up into the common graveyard, out of earshot, then I asked him why his mother was upset.

Like most children, Malison was glad to tell his side. "She said you'd not come and I said you would!"

I doubted so small a thing as my visit had caused the amount of disruption I sensed. With a little probing, I got more. Calec wants him to become a reverend and, upon Calec's death, take over the position of Temple Keeper. Malison wants to be a cook. To be anything else, he feels, would be a betrayal of his father's memory.

"You're a cook," he stated, tilting his head back to look at me. That look told the tale. For some reason, he's bonded with me instead of with Calec. It explained the cloud over Damut and Calec's pleasant greeting. They had hoped I'd disappoint the boy by not coming. And here I was riding him about on a horse neither I, nor Calec, could afford to buy. So what to do?

I reminded Malison of his father's death, then asked him if Calec, living so far from royal protection, ever worried about being slain by robbers? The boy said, "No."

"He doesn't even worry about natals?" I motioned up toward the trees. The Dray Compound can't be seen from the cemetery, but I assumed the boy knew of its proximity.

Malison shook his head. "We've seen natals now and again and Calec tolt me not to go near them, but he don't worry on them. They'd not harm a reverend."

"That's right," I agreed, and he fell silent. He's bright enough to figure it out.

518, 8/5. Runners sped through the kitchens this morning, warning us not to stray onto Main Road. The Verdi Na-Kom was scheduled for an audience with the High Lord.

The warning prompted a dash up to the front orchards. Spying a na-kom brings good luck. Touching one brings bad. The belief has a simple foundation. People who see a na-kom up close and live to tell of it consider themselves lucky. No one touches a na-kom and walks away. Bad luck indeed.

Good luck or bad, the front orchards are hotter than an oven during the day, and I wasn't about to roast. In the empty kitchens, I continued rolling pie crust. By the time I shoved my pies in to bake, the women and children had returned. Soon the cooks, too, gave up their watch. At midday, Jenner rushed in, face scarlet from sunburn, and convinced Cyril, Filson and few others to go up again.

The die was cast in late afternoon. We, the unlucky, had to listen to every detail (over and over) throughout the evening. By all accounts, the Verdi natals were young, disciplined, and very well armed. By most accounts, Na-Kom D'brae was drunk. More likely the viewers were woozy from sunstroke. Some said his hair shone like gold. Others swore his hair was as black as a crow's wing.

518, 8/6. Just one comment: the house staff strengthened the idea that the Verdi Na-Kom is a sot. Rumor has it the young D'brae came drunk to his audience and spewed wine on High Lord Trivak. That would have been worth waiting to see!

518, 8/18. More gossip from the house staff. They say Prissen became betrothed while in Dartsport. Marriage is several years away, but he brought the girl and her parents here with him, and the girl has taken ill. The gossips say Prissen dallied with her and she's with child. The girl, Wacha Leyourd, is eleven. She and Prissen are cousins.

518, 9/3. Returned from the meadow last night. I did a little praying and a lot of thinking. Got back late. Was too tired to stay awake and write. Having time today to gel my thoughts hasn't helped. My mind is in confusion.

When I arrived at the meadow, I set my horse out to graze as usual, bathed in the river, and began to recite the usual prayer. "Lo, I be a sinner ..." I could not finish it. Why, I wondered, do I stay in Trivak's kitchens? Because a memsa I met by chance told me to? Why do I believe her? "Heed ye well," she said, "when the Victors don a new face. Tis a sign the end of thy toil in exile draws nigh." Have the Victors donned new faces? Maybe, maybe not, but none of her other predictions have happened.

"Darkness," she said, "shall mark thy brow, and a circle of glass shall bless thy chest." What does this mean? Is it sheer nonsense? "Ye shall taste what ye have given by thy craft and Pheto's door shall stand ajar." Does this mean I will be poisoned? There are a few poisons I'm not immune to, but they aren't common. I have only partial immunity to mesinale. A large enough dose would cause my death. But the Snakes don't offer mesinale for sale and if they discovered my whereabouts, they would want me alive, not dead. And it hasn't happened.

"Ye shall hold fire upon thy palm." Hasn't happened.

"Ye shall witness thy death in ink, yet thy life shall be spared by a man who shall rule thy home." Hasn't happened and isn't likely to happen while I'm living here.

I stood on the riverbank, drying my hair over a fire, and mulled each prediction. Then a horrid thought occurred. What if the memsa I encountered had been sent by my mother? I'm sure Ry'aenne knew I was working for the Kinship. I'm sure she wanted me to stop. It would be like her to use religion to get me to comply. Few memsen would disobey her orders. Can a memsa lie? It may be rare for one to, but not impossible. It is impossible for me to determine the veracity of a prophecy. Something that has yet to occur is, by nature, neither true nor false.

I put the wages I received today on the crate I use as a table. Coppers in one stack, hopence in another. Should I give half to Mearan beggars? Does the act of charity truly lighten my soul? Even the beggars think I'm a fool.

Living here is torture. I hate the people around me. Why don't I leave? And go where? To Evald? I'd be arrested the moment the Vics discovered me. If I got inside the Keep without being seen ... It wouldn't be fair to place Lord Haesyl in such an awkward position and I couldn't live as he does, never stepping beyond his domain.

I could leave here, find an agreeable woman and settle down somewhere. And be like Calec? Not hardly. I could work for the Kinship again. Snakes pay better than Trivak. I could go where I please, buy what I please, without a thought of expense. With the Snakes, I'd get news of home, maybe even of Sythene. That's what I miss most. News. Yet it would come at a price. There's only one skill the Snakes would pay me for. I'd rather not murder again.

I have been here seven years. Should I stay? Was the memsa true or false? Faith is believing without needing proof. Cassie had faith in Tobb. That's why she left with him. At what point does faith become insanity?

518, 9/10. Wacha Leyourd, betrothed of Prissen Trivak, died. She was not with child. She died of fever. Gossip of her is spoken in whispers. No one wants to say it, but everyone fears she died of plague. The Leyourds, a noble family, hail from Driden and, though they've lived in Dartsport the past year, their connection to a plague city is enough to spark panic if not controlled.

Wacha's social standing should earn her a spot in the exclusive Grand Temple Cemetery, but that's smack in the middle of the wealthiest section of Tiarn. House staff say the owners of homes there have kicked up a fuss. They say there's talk of burying her in one of the cemeteries outside the city walls. An alternative plan is to quietly tuck her in Park Cemetery, a respectable place at a tolerable distance from people of import.

Wherever the High Lord decides to plant the girl, if he has any sense, he'll make a show of it. Anything less will confirm the rumors of plague, and he'll have an empty city.

518, 9/12. A fine day for a funeral.

The highborn, resplendent in gala costumes, assembled on the palace steps, awaiting the High Lord. The lowborn, clad in our usual, gathered in the front orchard, weeping and wailing, earning the hopence we each were paid. The young corpse, oblivious to us all, lay beneath a shroud of flowers, her wheeled bier poised before a line of carriages.

A reverend from the Grand Temple had been hired to officiate. Wearing a gown the color of egg yolk, he stood on the bier's prow, a torch in hand to guide the unfortunate Wacha into the realm of the dead. Calec, in yellow and red, perched like an old rooster on the bier's stern and waved his smoking ball of incense to deter Wacha should her spirit stray. His pride shone as brightly as his dress, for beside him stood Malison, clad in a gown of yellow and white, a young disciple of Loric.

The wailing increased when Fesha Trivak emerged from the palace. A scarlet apple, he wobbled down the steps, Prissen, just as round though not as tall, a radish in his wake. Behind them, Trivak's third wife, Untha, descended, stunning in gossamer silk. Then the Leyourds, parents of Wacha, came arm in arm into the sunlight. With their hopes of snuggling closer to the royal house as dead as their child, they were, perhaps, the only ones truly weeping.

When the procession to Park Cemetery began, we raced down to prepare the funeral banquet. Laughter bubbled from every mouth as we chopped, mixed, kneaded, and sweated over the ovens. Disposing of the dead incites joy in the living.

Yet beneath the gaiety flowed an undercurrent of fear. Did Wacha die of plague?

518, 9/25. Mira coupled with Cyril yesterday. She ended the night in Filson's bed. I didn't spy on her. She bragged about her achievement all day. She must believe her conquest will elevate her status. Why else sleep with two old men?

518, 9/28. A Court Medico inspected the kitchens. Cyril lined us up and the medico breezed past, a rapid assessment of our health. He advised us to eat more salt and ordered Cyril to report any of us who fall ill. "So they can receive care," he promised though only a fool would've believed him. "No burials," he warned, "until I've seen the bodies." Cyril babbled an oath to comply.

518, 9/31. What began as a quiet evening exploded in a ruckus. Cyril and I were in the dining hall discussing the allotment of apples the gardeners had left us. The day had been grey and drizzly. Most everyone was abed. Cyril bribed me with a pitcher of ale into staying up.

Baz sauntered in. (Despite her size, she's amazingly light-footed.) With Izzy asleep, she was in good humor and wanted ale, but didn't want to pay for it. She pawed Cyril with her fleshy, red hands, whining and teasing until he surrendered. Hefting the full pitcher, she chugged down the brew, her gullet rippling. Pitcher drained, she ambled out and left us in peace, sated – or so I thought. Within moments shouts erupted, then a scream so shrill I thought my head would split. Cyril and I sped into the main hall, as did many others, awakened from sleep.

The scream had come from Mira. Baz, thirsting for more than ale, had paid Filson a visit and, catching Mira in his bed, seized her by the hair and dragged her from his room. Filson, mouth agape, stood naked from the waist down, his manhood, the only portion of his body lacking fur, pointing like a pale finger at the brawling women. It withered when his audience burst into laughter.

Deflation of the prize didn't dampen the conflict. Mira clawed and kicked, shrieking the whole while, until Baz sat on her. Personally, I was grateful for an end to the racket, but Cyril, who rarely gets involved in disputes among the women, coaxed

Baz off (with the promise of more brew) before she crushed the life from Mira.

Nulan, Mira's son, helped his mother up, then raced after Baz and struck her in the back with his fists. Cyril spun around and threatened to toss the boy out of the kitchens. Nulan sulked to his mother. Filson retired for the night, alone. And the evening again became quiet.

518, 10/2. War has erupted between Mira and Baz. No armies will invade, nor nations crumble. A petty war. What's at stake? Not Filson. He's merely a tool. Baz, due either to her age or her link to Cyril, is the unofficial matron of these kitchens. Mira covets that position. Her attempt at a coup (bedding Cyril) failed. Half the women here could claim the same. She lost a major battle when Baz snatched her from Filson's bed. Today she unleashed her latest weapon – gossip.

"Baz," Mira said to anyone who'd listen, "is laundry staff and should sleep down in Fieldtown with the rest of them washer girls. She don't belong in these kitchens! Them other wash-girls, they eats and sleeps down there. They got kettles and stoves and food and beds. Baz don't need to come up here except to takes and brings our washing!"

To me, Baz has always been an assault to the eyes and, when possible, I avoid any room she's in. But she accepts my soiled clothes without harassment, returns them cleaner though often more fragrant, and (as long as she doesn't choose my bed) I don't care where she sleeps.

Will gossip win the war? Not hardly. Baz is too well liked by the people here, her ties with Cyril too strong.

War aside, I plan to leave after work tomorrow. Jenner promised me use of the roan. Hope the weather clears.

518, 10/6. A chilly stay at the meadow. Constant mist gradually soaked me. Was ravenous the whole time. I got to the stables early this afternoon. Usually I curry whichever horse I've been lent, especially when it's the roan, but I was so hungry, I relinquished her to one of the stable hands, and hurried up to the kitchens.

I wanted something hot and went into the soup kitchen. Filson was there as I expected, but to my surprise, Nulan, Mira's son, was assisting him. I ladled myself a bowl of their beef barley, then strolled over to where Pinark was tending a kettle of bean and onion.

Filson followed me, wanting my opinion of Nulan's soup. I told him it was fine, which it was, though it could have used a dash of jorum to enhance the flavor. I then asked when and why he had accepted Nulan as an apprentice.

"T'other day," was the when. The why was more elusive. "Always did have an eye on him for teaching," is what Filson said, a lie if I ever heard one.

"Nulan's fourteen and more," Pinark joined in. "If he don't learn the trade, Cyril will toss him out. He'd be daft for it, too. Nulan, he'll make a good cook, he will."

Obviously, the war had progressed. When predicting the outcome, I hadn't weighed Nulan's part in it. In my defense, I'll say he's a child one tries to forget. Big-boned like his mother, he became a bully even before he moved from the women's quarters to the boys' room. If smacked, he would do chores on occasion, but after his father left, Nulan endured Cyril's hand, ignored all threats and did nothing. No work that is. Loafing about, pinching brew and fighting, he encourages other children into poor behavior. The only thing more surprising than Filson teaching the boy is Nulan agreeing to be taught.

As I ate the soup, Filson and Pinark went on and on about 'wonderful' Nulan. Their glowing comments ruined my appetite.

I came in here to change clothes. I had just skinned off my wet shirt when someone rapped on my door. It was Mira. No one's been in this room except me since Tobb ran off. I let her in, but left the door ajar.

She gave me a cap sewn from scraps. "To keep you warm when you're out riding."

I tossed the cap onto Tobb's bed. She sat beside it, thinking, I assume, his bed was mine. "Awhile back," she said, "Cassie tolt me you was aching for a girl."

I told her Cassie was wrong. She pouted a moment, then went to the door, but once there, she turned to fire a last arrow. "I'll wash them clothes for you, Kor-man."

I told her Baz would wash them. She said, "They'll stink like that old sow. I'll wash them proper. Can do it right in the scullery and them clothes'll smell fresh."

I told her the stink kept fleas off me. She scowled, slid out and slammed my door.

I sat with Rebic during evening meal. He was wearing a new rag cap. Indeed, everyone at our table sported something new. A patchwork muffler, brass buttons stitched as decorations to a sleeve, a small blue jar that could fit into a pocket and hold whatnots. Bits of trash crafted into things of use. All given by Mira. Throughout the meal, I heard only praise for her and Nulan, her 'hard-working' son.

To test the depth of Mira's influence, I mentioned Baz, saying I had given her an armload of muddy clothes to wash.

"Old sow," Rebic said loud enough for all in the room to hear, "ought to get out and live in Fieldtown where she belongs. Her and her dimwit girl stink up this place."

A few whispers followed his remark, but when no one, not even Cyril, defended Baz, Rebic blared, "It were Baz who killed my Anar! Them guards, they'd have took Izzy, but Baz tolt them, 'No! Take Anar!' Were Baz who killed her!"

To blame Baz for Anar's death was absolute insanity. During Rebic's outburst I focused on Mira, sitting between Filson and Nulan. I have no doubt that she twisted the truth and fed it to Rebic until he believed it. He's become her instrument, and her pleasure in watching him perform was evident. I underestimated her. With gifts, gossip and perhaps a little bed warming she's tipped the balance in her favor. She, too, should leave these kitchens. Her talents are wasted here. She belongs in government service.

518, 10/9. High Lord Trivak and Prissen 'secretly' left the city.

518, 10/14. Glorious weather drew me outside after work. Blue sky, warm sun. There's a hickory grove a safe distance behind the Som Compound and, determined to put the day to good use, I decided to gather nuts for the Wessel family.

Royal Wood was brilliant, trees like gaudy noblemen, their leafy gowns in hues of wine, crimson and yellow, set afire by sunlight. Leaves already fallen rustled underfoot and seemed to glow along the paths, luring me on, while flat-topped rocks enticed me to sit and linger.

The hickory grove was a place of enchantment. Sunny leaves diffused a golden light. Squirrels dashed overhead. The air seemed to vibrate life. Boar and dwarf deer had trampled the underbrush so I could roam at will and, though many nuts had yet to fall, more than enough were at hand. I hummed as I filled the sack I'd brought.

Then I became aware of the smell. Dirt, dry leaves. Not unpleasant. Merely the scents of autumn that I smell each year. Yet today the smell flung my mind back in time.

It had been a day like today, the weather teasing the world with a last burst of warmth before winter. I was twelve. My father had coerced me into attending a party at the Howyls. For some reason I can't recall, I didn't want to be around Leister Howyl, so I stayed by Juboe, listening to him chitchat with other guests. Bored witless most of the evening, I perked during a conversation between him and Tyman Wincle, a member of the Vic Council. They were discussing the Children of Liberty, an elusive group of Uttes and half-breeds who supposedly met at taverns (tagged Liberty Pubs) to plot the overthrow of the Vic government. A man believed to be a leader in the group had been arrested that day by the Vic Police.

Tyman nudged Juboe and said, "The damned Utte should face the Blacksmith." I knew Tyman meant my father should interrogate the man, for it wasn't the first time I'd heard Juboe referred to as the Blacksmith, but on this occasion I was stupid enough to ask how he had earned the title. When my question incited laughter, I assumed the answer must be humorous.

Juboe slapped me on the shoulder and said, "You're old enough," which led me to believe the answer must contain an erotic quality, intriguing me more. But instead of an answer to me, he spoke to Tyman, "Your house?" Tyman nodded, then walked over to Cinnar, a young warrant officer, who soon afterward left.

Juboe made a final round of the party, thanking each Howyl, trading quips with this person and that, bestowing compliments on every woman present. By the time he finished, I'd forgotten my question. We linked up with Tyman as we donned our capes. A carriage awaited.

The house we went to wasn't Tyman's home, but owning several properties was common among Juboe's friends, and I thought nothing of it. Cinnar greeted us, a sign that more than a late bout of drinking would occur. "All's set," he said, then escorted us down steps to a room at the rear of the house, a room he had prepared for Juboe's use.

A pot of mulled cider on the hearth hob scented the air with rich spices. On the mantel, twin lamps burned, their porcelain bellies ashine. Baskets of feynuts lined one wall, bounty from the season. At the room's center, a table held tools of a smith's trade: hammer and anvil, chisel, tongs ... And strapped to a chair, a naked man sat, head bowed as if he were contemplating the size of his manhood.

Tyman opened the back door, for the room was stifling. Dry leaves and smells of autumn gusted in. The naked man lifted his head. His eyes, like mine, were grey. Juboe the Chairman, a hand on my shoulder, asked him his name and the names of others in the Children of Liberty.

The man replied in Utte. Juboe the Father pinched my shoulder until I translated. "I know nothing." Then Juboe the Blacksmith began his work. Shattering bones, crushing fingers and toes, searing flesh with rods of hot iron – the smith enjoyed his occupation.

The man refused to give his name, refused to name others and, though he understood Universal, refused to speak it. I repeated his words for the Blacksmith. "I have no name. There are no Children of Liberty. No Liberty Pubs. I know no one."

The man had been arrested, charged with sedition, tried and convicted in a single day. In Evald, justice can be swift. Yet his sentence of death was a lengthy process.

Each time the man swooned, Tyman filled our cups, Juboe cracked hard-shelled feynuts between his palms, and we drank the warmed cider and ate the tender nutmeats – while Cinnar revived the object of the night's labor.

Why didn't I run from the house? I did rush outside once to retch in the yard. And I did pray the screams would arouse neighbors. But it must have been a neighborhood of the deaf. And I couldn't leave. Here was a man stronger than my father. I had to witness his victory.

Why didn't I beg Juboe to quit? I did. "Stop," I said when the man, his teeth hammered out, could scarcely speak. "Father, stop. I can't bear the way he's looking at me." To remedy my complaint, Juboe gouged out the offending eyes.

When the man died, still nameless, his secrets died with him. He inspired such awe in me that years later I visited taverns in the Utte quarter, searching for the Liberty Pubs.

Uttes can be as foolish as Vics. My ability to speak the tongue bought acceptance. The pubs did exist, I found, as did a group called the Children of Liberty. Their goal, rather than revolution, was to teach Uttes to read. The pubs supplied space for classrooms. Would the truth have saved the nameless man? Not hardly. Though legal, educating poor Uttes would have flamed Vic suspicions. They would've presumed the schools were a front for more devious schemes, true or not. How does one prove a negative? The moment that man had been arrested, he was dead. And anyone he had named would have shared his fate.

These memories crowded my head as I carried the sack of hickory nuts to the cemetery. When I got there, Calec and his family were abed. I left the nuts on their stoop.

While walking back, I imagined Juboe's ghost striding beside me, and I had to laugh. When the day came for me to face the Blacksmith, I lacked the strength of the nameless man. I lost the battle and would've betrayed everyone I knew. But Juboe didn't have the sense to ask.

518, 11/7. Unable to remain neutral in Mira's war, I sat with Baz and Izzy at evening meal. Cyril joined us. Extra chairs were taken to other tables. Izzy drooled as she ate, and Baz ... I wasn't hungry anyway. None of us had much to say.

Afterward, Mira waylaid me by the privies, a fitting spot for her to deliver her gossip. She began pleasantly enough, "Seen Damut of late?" I told her I hadn't. "Were a shame," she said, "how Cyril threw Damut out and her, with nowheres to go, has to bed old Calec."

I told her Damut chose to live with Calec. "They're man and wife," I added just to prick her, but my weapons were dull compared to hers.

"Do Calec know she were raped?" she asked, and I felt my blood thicken. I lied and said I told him about her rape before the wedding. "Did you now," she mumbled, then asked, "You know Cyril paid me to set her up for it?" When I didn't respond, she smiled like a swordsman when an opponent drops his guard, tasting the kill before the fatal blow. "Cyril, he were tired of her mouthing and tolt me to lesson her. Tolt me he'd turn his back so as nobody would know his part. Gived me a hopence for it, he did."

I didn't need to question Cyril. I knew her words were true. And clearly the purpose of her confession was for me to withdraw support from Cyril and thus Baz, but did she think I'd join with her? She was as guilty as he. And why bother? With everyone else on her side, why worry about me?

I must admit she baffles me. What is her goal? To demote Baz and succeed her as matron? It's accomplished. Whether or not Baz eats and sleeps here, she's lost the esteem she once held. Does Mira want to ensure a place for Nulan? It's accomplished. If the boy tries even a little, he'll eventually secure a position as a cook.

Thinking back on Damut's stay here, Mira used the same tactics on her as she did with Baz. Convincing others to dislike her and, with Grutin's help, inciting fear so those few opposed to the rape would be too afraid to stop it. I haven't yet sensed the element of fear, but I haven't really scanned for it either. Maybe with Grutin gone she decided to use gifts instead. Buying loyalty can be as effective as fear when one's rival is poorer than oneself.

Much of the recent gossip has been directed at Cyril, with again the intended result of mustering dislike. Has Mira lifted her aim? If Cyril were removed as head cook, what would she gain? As a woman, she'd never be allowed to take his place. So why attack him? For spite? If so, Cyril had best watch his back.

Something else. With Damut, Mira waited until I was gone to set her up. Tomorrow my free days begin. I had planned to leave at first light, and still do. Should I warn Cyril? I think not. He can handle himself. Besides, he helped create what Mira has become.

518, 11/11. A cold, but greatly needed, stay in the meadow. Being away helped clear my thoughts. But I stayed too long. I rode the horse into a lather getting back and barely made it into the city before the gates closed. The portal guards delayed me further. They were questioning everyone entering the city. Meara isn't Evald. It isn't necessary to carry identity papers and travel permits aren't mandatory, though if this plague scare continues, it may become so.

I lied to the guards, told them I was a special courier for the High Lord and had dropped off a package in Brithe. Why the lie? Both the horse and the saddle carry the Hawk brand, and no guard in his right mind would believe one of Trivak's cooks had gone out riding. The interrogation was hardly brutal. One guard mentioned that High Lord Trivak had left Tiarn last month and asked who had sent me. But Trivak's departure was supposed to be secret and when I asked where he had gotten the information, there were no more questions. In fact, the guards treated me to a dipper of spiced wine.

Jenner had waited up for me. "Thought you weren't to make it," he said. While I tended the horse, he burned my ears with the latest developments in Mira's war. The gist is Nulan assaulted Izzy, probably broke her arm, and would have killed her if the laundry foreman hadn't intervened. Jenner said Cyril paid Nulan to do it. It's impossible to gauge the truth of secondhand news, but Cyril's dislike of Izzy isn't a secret, and Jenner believed he'd paid the boy. I didn't defend Cyril, for I had decided not to become involved in the war. Something I've learned: if one does not react to gossip, the informer hushes more quickly.

When Jenner hushed, I trudged up to the kitchens. Cyril was alone in the dining hall. He, too, had been waiting for me, and delivered the same line, "Thought you weren't to make it." He had tea and bread ready for me and, though the tea was cold, I sat to drink it.

Cyril sat across from me. "Hear about Izzy?"

I told him what Jenner told me, including the bit about him paying Nulan. He didn't deny it and perhaps felt I wouldn't have believed him. "Mira's gone too far," was all he said and with that, I knew the allegation was false.

He remained silent while I ate, but when I stood, he asked, "You ever kill somebody?"

I sat down again. "Were an accident," I said and let him fill in the rest.

"I knowed you had." His head bobbed. "Knowed it were why you comed here. Weren't it always the way? A body dies and they blames the cook." He stretched his coarse hands toward me. "Sheever, I needs me an accident now."

As Soehn Biehr I received countless bids for my service. Some wanted the target to know who had ordered his death,

167

but more often the bid was presented with a request similar to Cyril's. "Soehn, it must appear to be natural." Yet never in my life as a Poison Master was I approached in quite the same manner as this evening. No formalities. No mention, delicate or otherwise, of payment. Merely an open-handed plea for another's death. Had I not just returned from the meadow, I may have agreed to do it. Instead, I cautioned him of the risk. If Mira died, accident or no, he would have to report her death to the medico and even if her head were bashed in, the medico might panic and order all of us slaughtered. I suggested he simply discharge Mira and send Nulan packing as well.

"I can't," he grumbled. He didn't elucidate, but a tender heart isn't preventing him from being rid of Mira. She must have something on him. I was too tired to pursue the matter and left him with his troubles.

I thought I could sleep easily. Obviously, I can't. Damn Mira. And Cyril, Baz, Nulan. Damn them all, and everyone else in these kitchens. What annoys me most is none of these people have the slightest concept of true power. They squabble over nothing and hurt each other in the process. What does it matter where Baz sleeps? Or who is head cook? No one here is of import. If we all died tonight, the world would happily go on without us.

I realize that to the people here, these kitchens are the world. Perhaps they wield what insignificant power they possess because it is so insignificant. If not used, it may appear to be the nothing it truly is. But why not use it for good instead of inflicting harm? Why involve innocents such as Izzy in a game she surely can't comprehend?

In the meadow, I devoted considerable thought to Sythene. She's someone who knows the sting of true power. I wondered how she'd handle the situation. But imagining her involved in Mira's war was, and is, impossible. This place and its people are so petty. Compared to Sythene and her world, we're a puddle of tadpoles.

518, 11/12. Baz didn't cart our soiled clothes to the laundry today. She plunked herself onto a bench in the main hall. Izzy, right arm heavily wrapped, huddled against her mother, whimpering. To anyone passing by, Baz shouted, "Look what Nulan done! Needs punished, he do!"

From my workbench I could glance into the hall. A few women stopped to chat with Baz. None of the men did. There is a measure of fear involved. No one wants to take on Mira.

I didn't need the skills of a sensitive to know Izzy was in pain. I scanned her anyway. Physical aspects are the easiest to detect. The girl's arm is broken below the elbow. If it isn't set, she'll lose use of her arm.

I never made a study of the healing arts, but I've seen more cracked bones than I care to remember, and I've set quite a few. When I worked as a defense advocate, most of my clients resided in my father's prisons. Setting and splinting bones became as routine as filing papers.

I didn't offer to splint Izzy's. By afternoon when I was tending my ovens, I had put her out of mind. Until I heard a wailing in the hall. Nulan was there, not doing anything overt, just tormenting Izzy with his presence. I stepped out and hinted, "Shouldn't you be helping Filson?" He sneered at me before going back into the soup kitchen.

My path of neutrality, so clear in the meadow, is beginning to haze.

518, 11/13. I tended Izzy's arm. Over protests from Baz, I summoned Cyril into the act. "Can't do it with the girl awake," I insisted, and Baz relented though she believes the lie about

Cyril paying Nulan. She's lost some of her trust. Cyril supplied the ophren. He forced a healthy dose down the girl, more than necessary. She slept through the day and is still asleep as far as I know. If Baz can keep her from fussing with the splint, the arm should heal. Mira wasn't pleased. "Kor-man," she warned when she caught me alone, "stay out of it. I'll take you down with Cyril, I will." Stupid woman. I can't go down much further than I already am.

518, 11/16. I'm restless. Not because of the weather. It's cold and clear. Not due to Mira's war, nor worry of plague. Those are mere distractions. A sensation, or rather a lack of one, is affecting my mood. This is difficult to express. I don't totally understand it myself. It concerns Sythene and how she affected me. How does one describe a feeling? Imagine being frozen, then having a steaming blanket draped over one's shoulders. Not exactly comfort. Sharp. Biting. Not exactly pain. It awakens the spirit. That isn't accurate.

An example: during the time she visited me in secret, often I would doze while waiting for her. When I woke in the night, I didn't need to check each room in the suite to see if she were there. I could sense her. And after she went to Uttebedt to be crowned, I could still sense her existence. Like the glow on a far horizon at the approach of dawn. When deep in prayer, even here I've sensed her steamy blanket about my shoulders and felt a reassurance, a knowing, as one knows the sun will rise.

That feeling is gone. Has been for a while. How long? I'm not sure. When does a lover know love has fled? Long after the spark has chilled. Passion cools without notice until the day one becomes aware of its absence.

When last in the meadow, I foolishly wrestled with the mundane hassles caused by Mira's war and was unable to imagine Sythene involved in such matters. I realize now I was unable to imagine Sythene at all. Not imagine. She's yet in my memory. I was unable to sense her. Thinking back, I haven't felt 'the knowing' for months. Not this season. Not the past summer. Since spring? Since the Verdi natals came? Since Gurn 4 when I chose the physical comfort of these kitchens instead of the spiritual comfort of the meadow? Was it gone before then? Since the Games ended the year? Or before? And what does it mean?

The obvious deduction is Sythene no longer exists in this world. I refuse to believe that. The problem must lie with me. I have lost the capacity of profound prayer. Yet I wish I could verify that she is alive. In the lowlands the only people privy to such information would be Kin. But even if I went to the Snake House, and even if the Snakes recognized and greeted me, would they tell me anything? If a past assassin appeared from nowhere, would I supply him with information about Sythene? Not hardly.

I must believe she is alive and well. I do believe the skills I once had are deteriorating. She is alive. I want to believe it. Yet the unknowing makes me restless.

518, 11/17. At evening meal Cyril announced he has decided to teach Nulan how to read and write. Then he took the spare keys to the storage rooms from Filson and bestowed them on Nulan. It's an unofficial way of stating he has chosen the boy to be the next head cook. This must be what Mira has been after all along. The war, I assume, is over. With her as the victor. Whatever she has on Cyril must be damning. Nulan is the worst possible choice as a successor.

It's cold. I stole the blanket from Tobb's bed.

518, 11/18. Colder today than yesterday. Nulan spent the day with Cyril. Mira strutted about, bragging. Baz may have lost the war, but the weather restored her to favor. When she came up from the laundry, she had more clothing than she'd taken down. Most of the children now have socks, albeit over-large, and a few got heavy tunics that need a little stitching to repair holes.

Mira demanded the best of the tunics for Nulan. "He's to be Head Cook!" she declared. "Can't have him taking sick!" By her haughty demeanor, one would think her son were heir to a crown. And he acts the part, wearing the spare keys around his neck as if they were gold, bossing the other boys, smacking the women. Soon he'll be bossing and smacking the cooks.

Izzy is doing well enough. The incident changed her. She doesn't try to slip from Baz's sight, and hides behind her when Nulan is near. Baz should be happy.

518, 11/19. We've shuttered all the windows. People coming up to eat don't remove their capes in the dining hall. The oven rooms are drafty but tolerable. And also dark. I stepped outside this afternoon to prove to myself it was indeed day not night. Hoarfrost whitened the ground. Wind scoured my face as I squinted at the sun. Light without warmth.

Can't shake my depression. Unable to pray with conviction.

518, 11/21. Nulan unlocked the stores and stole a keg. By midmorning every man in the soup kitchen was drunk. Cyril yanked me from the spare kitchen, and he and I did soups. It was the first I've seen him cook. He knows his way around a kettle, but he criticized everything the women did. I contemplated shoving a turnip in his mouth.

The house staff get top pick of the day's goods. Kwint, chief of staff, goes around with Cyril and selects what he considers worthy. Usually meats and pastries are chosen, then whatever else will fit is jammed onto their carts. Soups are virtually ignored which works fine. The troopers collect their portions and the remainder is ours.

Today, however, Kwint found Cyril sweating over a pot of pork and lentil. "You're cooking!" His staff swarmed in behind him like flies chasing a turd barrow. "Is Filson ill?"

"Drunk," Cyril blabbed. "Me and Sheever here done the work of five men today."

Kwint's face reminded me of a ham butt, his eyes two cloves punched into the fat. A fur ruff supported his chins. "Why," he drolled, "you deserve a reward." The manner of our reward became evident when he tasted Cyril's lentils. "Wonderful! On a cold day, hot soup is perfect!" He went from kettle to kettle, sniffing, slurping, and selecting half of them to be carried out.

Cyril's ears flamed red as blisters. I knew he was counting kettles, subtracting the number the troopers would take and wondering if we'd have any for ourselves. But what could he say? He left with Kwint to go around to the other stations. Soon afterward the troopers came and cleaned us out except for a pot of onion broth we'd intended for gravy.

The women grumped. "A full day's work and nothing to show." No one would go hungry. There's always plenty of bread and cheese and a bite of meat besides. Maybe after being griped at all day they needed to gripe themselves. But I'd heard enough. I headed for my own station to see if my twist rolls had been finished.

Cyril and Kwint were gossiping in the hall. Cyril beckoned me, then clamped a hand onto my shoulder as my father used to do when he knew I wanted to slip away. Death was the topic. Apparently, a runner had been unable to work. I missed the reason why. Two of his friends covered for him. They were found out. All three were tossed from the bridge and drowned in the river. "It weren't plague?" Cyril asked, voice wavering.

173

"No," Kwint stated, "but the medico's orders were clear. Every illness must be reported." His lips shone with grease from something he had tasted. His clove eyes gleamed as well. The anxiety his tale had wrought in Cyril pleased him. "Filson's drunk, you say?"

Cyril nodded, his fingers drilling into my shoulder. "Drunk." The pressure didn't ease until Kwint led the parade of rattling carts away. Then Cyril asked me if I could swim. I said I could, which is true. Thinking of the river, I added, "Not well," which is also true.

"I can't swim a stroke," he muttered. His hand slid to my elbow and he steered me down to the women's quarters. He grabbed a hall lamp before going in.

The room appeared to be unoccupied. In a far corner, a candle burned atop a crate. He went toward it. I followed, tramping on bedding. Women don't enjoy the luxury of cots.

A clay idol of Loric stood on the crate amid an array of buttons and beads, the candle like a fiery staff beside him. It was the closest portrayal of an altar I'd seen in the kitchens. A girl slept before the altar, shivering despite the blankets covering her. Even an idiot could deduce she was ill with fever, but a quick scan confirmed my appraisal. Between her and the rest of the room, a line of salt had been poured – a demon barrier. Similar salty shields have been poured in front of my door on occasion.

Cyril stopped short of the salt. His lamp lit the girl's face. Her name is Onji. She works in the scullery. Most of the girls here bloom into womanhood scrubbing pots. Her mother, Helsa, works in the spare kitchen. Indeed, she was assigned to my bench after Cassie left. This link, I assumed, was why Cyril had led me in there.

Half-awake, Onji whined about being cold. Mounds of bedding lay near at hand. Cyril didn't pick any up to spread over her. Nor did I. We stayed safely on our side of the salt and when he said, "Let's go," I eagerly obeyed.

In the hall, he offered me a sip of wine. I trailed him to his room. He closed his door, shutting out any warmth we might have received from the meat kitchen across the way. I sat on the stool, leaving him the chair. Glass clinked as he hauled a cache from under his bed – five bottles and a jug. "You being a korman," he said as he jerked out a cork, "you probably seen lots die of plague."

"A few," I lied, holding my cup ready. The reason for the lie is simple. Cyril believes, as do most Mearans, that plague is caused by demon minions of Krich, god of the Netherworld. He also believes I'm a part-time demon and if my dubious status was the reason I was at that moment in his room, cup in hand, I saw no reason to rupture his delusion.

"Well?" he demanded. He angled the bottle above my cup, not pouring. "Do Onji have plague or no?" Clearly, I would not receive wine without the proper answer.

Truth is I've never seen a body with plague. Vics gossiped about it in Evald, especially when visitors came from the lowlands with tales of whole cities dying in a sixtnight. But they blamed demons as well, claiming the fiends jumped from person to person, entering through the nose or mouth. Remembering such nonsense provided no tools to assess the current situation.

I stared at the bottle, the ruby fluid poised on its glass lip, and recalled an incident with Luka Massu. During the time I worked with him, or rather, he worked on me, his potions often left me weak and I'd lie in a side room until I recovered. On one occasion, he and another Dyn discussed an outbreak of plague in Uttebedt. With calm precision, as if plotting a military campaign, they debated ways to contain it. She wanted everyone in the region immunized. He vetoed the idea due to expense. I remembered him saying a victim had to display specific symptoms before their relatives merited immunity – intense fever, spotted skin, and swellings along the throat, groin and under the arms.

All this flashed through my mind in an instant. Fever did possess Onji, but her face was unblemished. "No," I answered Cyril with confidence, "she don't have no plague." Wine gushed into my cup. After it was full, I suggested he fetch the medico – just to be safe.

He mumbled something I failed to catch and filled his own cup. For a while we drank without conversation. When we drained one bottle, he cracked a second and when it was gone, he unplugged a third. Neither of us mentioned a desire to attend evening meal. If drunkenness is the goal, an empty stomach is far superior to a fed one.

As a young man I could get giddy from a single glass of mead. Half a bottle and I'd be in a stupor. Now, I can still become intoxicated, but the sweet oblivion so easily reached in my youth is next to impossible to attain. I have Luka to thank for that, I suppose.

Tonight I couldn't drink fast enough to stop a worm of guilt from chewing my brain. Why had I ignored Onji's pleas? It would have taken only a moment to spread another blanket over her. I wondered if I should press Cyril to fetch the medico. Would he know how to help her? Not likely. I wouldn't trust a Mearan to tend a scratch. Besides, I reasoned, the medico would probably order her thrown off the bridge and maybe us with her.

I rummaged my mind for courses of action. Dyn healers sometimes applied heat to sweat out a fever, and other times they iced a person to counter the body's heat. How did they determine which would promote health? I have no idea. Luka taught me to kill, not cure.

Toward the end of the third bottle, I wondered if Onji truly did have plague. Would it sweep through the kitchens with the speed implied in the tales? By morning would we all be ill? If not plague, what was causing her fever? Had she nicked herself on a rusty pot? Why hadn't I checked her for an injury? I reminded myself that Wacha Leyourd, Prissen's bride-to-be, had died of fever. She was about the same age as Onji, but I could think of no other connection.

Cyril coughed, preparing to speak, and I hoped for a silly diversion, but his mind had spun along a similar path. "If Onji was to die," he presumed, "would you bury her proper?"

"No," I admitted. "I'd bury her in the Wood."

Cyril belched as he stretched for a fresh bottle. "Loric damn the Wood. Feeding her to hogs would be easier."

The chill of the room seeped through my clothing. He was not extrapolating. "Other children have died?" I asked.

He spat out the cork and topped our cups. "Seen Mira's daughter of late?"

Indeed I had not. Nor had I noticed one less child among the horde. "She died of fever?"

He nodded. "Mira, she don't say her girl were sick. She bringed me the girl dead."

We guzzled the fourth bottle as he disgorged the unpleasant truth. He and Mira hacked up the corpse and dumped the pieces in with the food scraps that are carted down to the stockyards. According to him, and it sounded true, the idea was hers. Afterward, she blamed him, and threatened to go to the medico and reveal his deception.

"I tolt her," he said, face flushed from the wine, "I'd say she were the one who done it. But she tolt me nobody'd believe a mother done it. I tolt her if the medico sniffed plague, he'd kill us all. She don't care."

Mira's threat may have been a bluff, but Cyril bought her silence by promoting Nulan. Confession out, he moved onto his bed. I opened the fifth bottle, and then the jug. Cyril, slurring like an old sot, prattled on about Nulan and demons until his speech shrank into gibberish. He achieved oblivion. Damn him.

I staggered out for a breath of air. Clouds blotted the stars. A light snow had begun to fall. Mearan snow. It won't amount to much. Shivering with cold, I couldn't escape thinking of Onji shivering while her body burned from within. Some poisons produce that effect. Could Mira have poisoned the girl? And poisoned her own daughter as well to benefit her son? Such deeds aren't beyond her madness. But she had no access to Wacha Leyourd.

A good sensitive could probe Onji and discover answers. But whether or not she has plague, the girl is far more dangerous alive than dead. A good assassin would lessen the risk and hurry her demise.

Standing out in the darkness, I clasped my necklace and lifted my gaze. I thought of Evald, white with winter. Of Sythene, more brilliant than the sun rising above an icy peak. Snowflakes patted my face like the cool fingertips of a woman hoping to rouse a dozy lover. How I wish all this were a dream. I didn't pray for guidance. One can fail only so many times before the courage to try is lost.

O Winter, send thy cold caress
To freeze my heart with tenderness.

518, 11/22. I'm drunk. Worse – or better – than yesterday. I should snuff the candle and try to sleep. But I can't snuff my thoughts.

This morning I overslept and woke with a headache from last night's indulgence. When I finally got up, the other early cooks and women were huddled by the ovens, gulping tea. Craving privacy more than warmth, I told Helsa to serve me in the dining hall.

Sheever's Journal, Diary of a Poison Master

The sun had yet to rise, but I spread the shutters on a window, curious about the weather, and stood transfixed – a downpour of snowflakes glistened in the lamplight. How I've missed the shy enchantment of an honest snowfall, the breathless excitement that hushes the world.

Excitement. My father felt most alive when delivering pain. When he became the Blacksmith, elation loosened his stance, passion strengthened his voice. The first snow of winter would bring a similar change in me. By spring, I'd curse it, but the first snow would ignite a zeal for life. It would be as if I could feel the pulse of the whole world.

I remember a year when I was with Ayros at the Falcon and a group of Snakes came to make a bid. The first snow of the season began the day they arrived. Tarok was with them. He wasn't a Master yet, but he acted as spokesman for the group and plied me with mead while he sweetened their offer. I couldn't concentrate and went out on the porch.

Tarok followed me, meadskin in hand. "Soehn Biehr." He was always insufferably polite to me. "Soehn Biehr, the man deserves to die. Surely ye agree to that much." Ever the diplomat. Little wonder he became a Master.

I walked to the edge of the porch and leaned against the rail. The snow swirled down, thick and fast, blurring my view with dizzy movement. Excitement flooded my senses. Tarok was a tick on my ear. With gold, he tempted me to commit murder when I felt I could reach out and catch life on my palms. Damnation, I'm rambling.

This morning I gloried in the sight of the snow, feeling more alive than I have in years. Then Helsa brought my tea. She's a small, quiet woman, as bland as Calec Wessel's cooking. Easy to work beside. Unlike Cassie or Damut, Helsa is easy to ignore. Yet she succeeded where Tarok had failed, for her sobs wrenched me from the window.

"Please, Kor-man," she begged, "chase the demon from my Onji like you done with Izzy." Fool. I said I could do nothing and turned again to the window. But the snow's spell had broken. I agreed to look at her daughter.

The late women were in various stages of dress when we entered their room. Dimness protected their modesty; candles here and there threw patches of light. Helsa hustled me through the crowd, announcing, "The Kor-man were going to chase the demon from my girl!"

Several candles lighted the corner – the crate was encrusted with wax – and amid the flames, the idol of Loric gazed stupidly at all who approached. More trinkets had been added to the pile of offerings. Do these women truly believe a god can be bribed with buttons and beads?

As we neared the salt line, Helsa covered her nose and mouth. Protecting herself from a jumping demon? Perhaps. But the stench of soiled bedding induced me to do the same.

Onji lay as she had yesterday, feet toward the crate. Her fever had plainly worsened. She was no longer conscious. I envied her that, for my head was splitting.

A hopence glinted on the girl's brow. I had seen this custom before. The coin attracts the demon causing the sickness. To cure the victim, the coin is tossed out a window – swiftly, lest the tosser succumb to the demon's powers. The women's room has no windows.

Women gathered behind me, blocking any chance of a rapid exit. I stepped over the salt line and turned as if to address them. Expectation adorned their flat faces. They wanted magic from me. So I plucked the hopence from Onji and slipped it into my pocket. One hopence richer, I would have left then, if Helsa hadn't spoken.

"Kor-man," she breathed, "will my girl get well now?"

Her heartbreak bit my soul. I wanted to say, 'Yes, the demon is in my pocket. Your Onji will now be well.' I could not utter the lie. Instead, I knelt and, drawing back blankets, I exposed the naked chest of her daughter. Onji is a child, thirteen at most, and thin, her ribs more prominent than her breasts. Her body summoned no lewd desires in me. Even so, I was less than comfortable as I groped her while Helsa and the others looked on. I found nothing – no swellings to indicate plague, no festered cuts to explain her fever. A scan revealed only what my hands and eyes told me. Discovering the fever's cause would require a deep probe, a procedure I hadn't done for a decade or more.

Fear delayed me. I've known sensitives who were witty until they probed too often, too deeply, or the wrong person – such as a Court Sensitive who can scour a mind and leave one with the intellect of a squash. Neither Onji nor any woman present had the ability to scour me. Nor did I fear probing too deeply and getting entangled in the girl's mind. Luckily for me, the risk of entanglement increases in proportion to one's talent. The risk I feared was failure. Or was it success I feared? Either way, it made me pause.

"Helsa," Mira snipped, "he's spoilt your girl!" Her remark goaded me into proceeding.

Adept sensitives can probe from a distance. Today I did it as a beginner would. I placed a hand on the girl's brow and a hand on her bare chest. To enhance my meager skill, I slid into a trance – and the room vanished. Only Onji remained, hot as a griddle beneath my palms.

The trick to probes is imagery. I imagined her as a bathing tub, the sort I had at home where I could lie back and enjoy a good soaking. She didn't resist, a poor sign, as I climbed in. Variations of heat disclosed what I sought – an injury, a puncture in her young womb.

A shriek jolted me. Sweat ran from my face as I broke contact with Onji. I longed to be buried in snow. A hand touched my shoulder. Still open from the probe, I looked up and for an instant saw Helsa as her daughter would – the homely creature was my mother. Then I recoiled from the grief spewing into me – Helsa's grief. I knocked her hand from my shoulder and staggered to my feet. My headache crashed back with a fury. Mira didn't help ease it.

"The Kor-man," she shrilled, and her hostility gored me, "he were the one who tainted Onji! With demons, he tainted her! Like he done my daughter!"

I stumbled toward her, then pitched onto my knees. Hating the weakness, I struggled to close the breach in my mind. The crush of women impaled me with their suspicions.

Baz bellowed, "It were you, Mira! You let them demons in! Snatching my hammer! Seen you practicing on your daughter. Tolt you she were too young. Tolt you she needed a rinse. You'd not listen! With Onji you done the same. Tolt you not to smooth the road without no rinse. Tolt you she'd not live to pleasure your boy. I tolt you!" Her words make more sense now than when I heard them.

Mira's denial failed to pacify Baz who thundered, "I want my hammer!"

A woman shouted, "Give it up, Mira! Baz, she done us all and knows how it's done proper!" Demure Helsa became a zealot, yelling, "Take it from her!" And Mira went down beneath a swarm of squealing women.

Baz emerged and swung the trophy high. The implement looked nothing like a hammer, more like an ornately carved cow's horn, leather cord fastened to the blunt end. Eyes wild with triumph, she focused on me. "You!" she boomed, swaggering toward me. "You seen what no man ought!" Baz is an imposing figure, especially when one is, as I was, kneeling on the floor. Add to her massive bulk a mob of panting women and I can only say the sight could wither any man. I envisioned her ramming her hammer into my chest. Yet I could not move.

Helsa sprang to my aid. "Sheever's not no man! He's a korman! He's taken the demon hisself to save my girl! You bust him, Baz, and that demon will get us all!"

Ignorant savage. Yet her inane babbling provided me with a weapon. I stood, almost recovered from the probe. Baz knew the balance had tipped. Clutching her hammer, she retreated into the mass of women as if they could protect her. I asked how the hammer was used. The women were aghast. Baz didn't want to tell, but I withdrew the coin from my pocket and offered it, demon and all. Here's what I learned:

When Mearan girls mature enough to desire a man, they undergo a ritual called 'Og Inet Unc Bisce-furn' which translates roughly to mean 'breaking the rock to smooth the road.' It is not a rock that is broken. Baz, as matron, had performed the ritual on most of the women here. The hammer confirmed her station. When she lost her position, Mira acquired the hammer and its responsibilities.

Baz assured me the ritual is harmless if done properly. She said the rinse Mira didn't know how to brew promotes fertility, then she turned on Mira and declared, "You killed your own daughter! And Onji as well!"

Mira retained enough spite to mutter, "Least I didn't tell no man nothing he oughtn't know."

To deny her any leverage, I went to the makeshift altar and swore to Loric I would never reveal the secrets of the Og Inet. A worthless oath, but it sated the women.

I would've liked to have learned more about the rinse which I suspect reduces the risk of infection. I didn't, however, want to push my luck. I told Baz to rinse Onji, then I left the room, taking four of the women with me.

Perhaps due to my probe, or perhaps because I craved an excuse to go out in the snow, I was determined to ice the girl. I commandeered a roasting pan from the meat kitchen, and the women and I carried it outside. Snow cascaded down, diffusing the sunlight and working its magic on me. I laughed as we filled the pan. The women doubted my sanity, but none would defy a man with a demon in his pocket.

When we lugged the pan back inside, I peeked into Cyril's room. Nulan was at the desk, alone and snoring, paper and pen before him. I instructed the women on how I wanted Onji chilled and sent them off to do it, then I hurried to my station, for I was late.

Cyril had begun my work. "The girl dead?" he asked.

My excitement melted like the snow on my shoulders. "Not yet." I donned an apron. "How's Nulan doing with his writing?"

Cyril grunted. "It'd be easier to teach a chicken to talk." Neither of us smiled. "Don't matter," he mumbled. "Don't nothing matter no more."

The day passed quickly enough. Kwint came snooping, but spying Filson satisfied him. After the house staff had gone, I pinched a dab of sugar cone and went to check Onji. She lay in the roasting pan as if in an icy coffin.

Baz considers the Og Inet Ritual harmless, and I understand it has been done for centuries, but in my opinion, it's unholy, unnecessary, and unsafe. Did Wacha Leyourd die from a botched Og Inet? I'd wager on it.

I shoved the sugar into Onji's mouth, an Utte custom, to sweeten the taste of death, then added a copper to the paltry offerings to Loric. She won't be blessed with a burial, but who knows, maybe gods can be bribed.

If not for the weather, I wouldn't have regained my humor. Mearans are so unaccustomed to snow they become alarmed when it's deeper than their boot soles. By late afternoon, it was to their calves. I watched from a window as troopers, unable to move their wagons, walked up to fetch their rations. They stepped ever so cautiously and when they slipped, as they invariably did, they'd jerk and twist, arms flapping like plucked geese, then squawk as they fell. On their descent, they trudged single file, melting a path with their kettles.

Jenner had a different approach. He raced up, slipping and sliding, wolfed his food and fled, "Before it's deeper!"

When the women began cleaning the dining hall, Cyril invited me to his room for another bout of drinking. He sank into his chair and sighed, "It's the end of the world."

"Cyril," I said, "it's snowed here before."

"Not this much," he argued as he filled our cups. "Never this much. The end's come."

I ceased trying to dissuade him when he vowed to drink all the wine in storage so it wouldn't go to waste.

Now, I wonder. The weather is odd. And though my skills have waned, they aren't gone. My success with the probe is proof of that. So why can't I sense, even faintly, Sythene's distant existence? Has she departed this world? If so, the world may decide to die from sorrow.

518, 11/23. Up late again. After eating enough bidda to numb my head, I asked Helsa if Onji was still being iced in the roasting pan. She said yes. A lie. Not that it matters.

Baz camped outside the spare kitchen. She isn't a subtle spy, but I doubt she intended to be subtle. Izzy was unable to sit still beside her mother. Splinted arm bound across her waist, she danced and twirled and chanted nonsense. Baz should have named her Fidget.

I don't mind being under observation. Couldn't stop it if I did. Baz isn't alone. Every woman here is watching me, waiting for me to reveal their petty secrets. Hoping I will? Mira certainly does. She'd destroy me in a heartbeat – if she knew how. She wants Cyril more than me though. He underestimates her. Fool. He leaves himself open. Today he didn't rise until past noon. He ate bidda, drank tea and returned to bed.

No wine tonight. I'm sober. Too sober to record my deeper thoughts. My room seems colder than last night. Sythene's birth date is a week away.

518, 11/24. The boys neglected to fill the coal bins last evening. When the early women, intending to do the chore themselves, couldn't open the north door, they ran screeching through the hall, waking anyone with ears. Several meat cooks threw their weight against the door to no avail. Cyril, stinking drunk, was incapable of thought. Filson assumed control. He ushered Cyril back to bed, then asked for volunteers to go out and see what was wrong with the door. What was wrong, of course, was snow.

I nudged Rebic. He's young and strong enough to pull me from a drift if need be. Plus he was standing beside me. "We'll go," I said for both of us. Armed with shovels, we scrambled out a window. Wind blasted us as we dropped into waist-deep snow. It was impossible to tell if it was still snowing or if the flakes whirling about and stinging our eyes were being driven aloft by the gale. We dug the door free and cleared a path to the coal shed before racing in to thaw ourselves. Neither of us had gloves.

The stockyards failed to make their morning delivery. Filson again asked for volunteers, but no one offered to lug up fresh meat. He unlocked Cyril's cache of smoked fish and salt pork.

When the house staff came, Filson complained to Kwint about the stockmen. "Thump their heads," he claimed he said, and Kwint – according to Filson – promised to do just that. "A bit of snow weren't no excuse for slacking!" This was meant, I'm sure, as a jab at Cyril.

The troopers came through the palace to fetch their portions. Jenner didn't show at all. Filson wasn't worried. "He'll eat with the stockmen like he used to. Weren't till him and Cyril got tight that he eats up here."

I heard all this at evening meal, wind howling outside, Filson blowing in. He'd enjoyed his day of ruling these kitchens and wanted us to know how well he had done. To secure an audience, he tapped a keg and doled out free ale. Not free. We had to listen to him boast.

Mira, who had been somewhat invisible the past day or so, cut in with an attack on Cyril. "He scolds my boy for nipping brew and look at hisself this morning. Staggering, he was! He ought to stop being Head Cook, he ought."

Baz jumped to Cyril's defense. "All them years he works, not never taking free days like we done. Deserves a day now and again, he do." Every woman except Mira voiced agreement, and Filson's bragging gusts abated. The balance of power has settled into its old position.

Pinark stitched the hole in the conversation with a simple observation, "Some weather, eh?" This produced a mesh of comments that supported forecasts of doom. Never has it been so cold. Never so much snow, never so dark. The world is freezing over. The sun will never shine again. This is the last year of the world. And so on.

Rebic, musing aloud, wondered if Loric was at that very moment spying on them, deciding who would enter his Garden and who would not. His eyes rounded as though the idea never occurred to him until he heard himself say it. And he did not gape alone. Jaws fell open with such a rush of gasps one would have thought the room teemed with hooked fish. Women jerked their children to bed as if loitering in the dining hall were a sin. Men, less willing to admit they feared for their souls, slunk away gradually. Soon I had the keg to myself – for a moment.

Baz returned. "A last sip," she said as she filled a pitcher. I've yet to see her drink ale from a cup. She slurped the froth, then sat on a bench across the table from me. It's been more than a week since she's done laundry and her usually red-rimmed eyes are a clear blue. Lesions on her face and hands have healed into shiny patches. Even so, she is not something one would care to gaze upon. "Been minding you, Kor-man." She tipped her head as if to eye me from a fresh angle. A tuft of hair poked through a hole in her bonnet. She leaned forward to get closer, her great breasts swelling and spreading on the table like rising dough. "You've not tolt nobody."

"Tolt?" I questioned though I knew damn well she was talking about the Og Inet. "Tolt nobody about what?"

She chuckled, "Sharp one, you is," and wiped her mouth as if to infer the matter closed. But she went on. "Mira needs punished. And her son Nulan. They needs punished!"

"Not by me," I stated.

Her bosom expanded with a breath before she nodded. "By vote then," she said. I have no idea what she meant. "Weren't your place no how." She stood to guzzle her brew and sauntered out. Finally, I was alone.

All day Sythene flitted though my mind like a butterfly along a rose hedge, too elusive to catch amid thorny distractions. If I were alone, I presumed, she would land. But when Baz left, Juboe intruded. "You're wasting favors on nobodies," he admonished. It was a lecture he often crammed into my ears. Yet as I heard his voice in my head, I imagined him sitting where Baz had been. My father wasn't a large man. Baz could make two of him. He was taller than I am though, and more muscular. Solid. Like a damned rock.

As his image formed in front of me, he escaped the confines of memory and blurred with reality. "If you're determined to waste time in these kitchens," he chided, "why not punish Mira and Nulan? Do it right." A little drunk and more than a little startled, I knocked over my chair getting to my feet. He laughed, "Where's your cry for justice now? Do it, son."

I left his ghost, went out and brought in coal, a chore the boys had again neglected. It's miserable outside, cold as death. How could snow elicit joy one day and misery the next?

"It isn't the snow," says Juboe's ghost. He tracked me in here, appearing from nowhere like a foul odor. He wants to stir my anger, but I've retreated behind a shield of Dohlaru and feel nothing. Still, he's difficult to ignore.

Either I'm drunk or mad, for I visualize him lounging on Tobb's bed, legs crossed at the ankles, his boots shiny – razor boots, metal edges in the soles. He had his polished each morning. I see him clad in black with red piping on his collar and cuffs. Mearan colors. His mother was of Mearan descent. Who knows what his father was. Bastard.

Juboe was a handsome man, broad forehead, square jaw. He had, as they say, 'strong features.' A scar cleaved his lower lip and curved under his chin. He had a plethora of stories to explain the scar. Lies. I pried the truth from him one night. We had gone through the day side by side, maintaining the illusion that I, on parole, was again the obedient son. When evening stole the sky's light, I watched as he shook from the hunger. "Father," I said, "tell me about your scar." He cursed me, swore he'd have me hanged. But when pain bowed his head, he confessed. The truth? Back when he was a Nobody, a Somebody wearing razor boots kicked him in the face. I nearly pitied him that night, nearly set him free. Lie. There was no mercy in me.

His ghost smiles, shameless. He's sure my recounting his downfall will trigger memories of my own. Truly, I must have achieved Dohlaru, for it seems we were equally cruel. My partner and son? Casualties in a private war. The ghost wants me to write of her. I haven't spoken her name since she died. Tonight I could. My room stinks of ale, not dampness and rot. Screams won't haunt me tonight. Dohlaru ices my heart. Juboe doesn't believe me. I'll pen her name for my eyes – and his – to see. Clariz. Proof enough?

"Not snow," he says. I'm confused. He sits up. "Change sparks your blood. Not snow."

I'm not insane. I know the form on Tobb's bed is a projection of my mind. But real or no, this ghost knows me better than I do. It is change. The first snow of winter, the first blossom of spring. In Evald, I craved a change in the political weather. Desired it so badly, I killed Vics trying to achieve it. This isn't what I want to record.

"You could've been Vic Chairman," he taunts. "Could've changed Evald without damning your precious soul."

Not true. One doesn't change a mountain by scaling it. From the crest, one is awarded a change of view, but only an idiot would believe the mountain had vanished. Becoming Vic Chairman would have damned my soul as surely as murder did.

"How do you know?" Juboe prods. "You didn't try it."

I don't want to argue with him. Why is Sythene silent in my mind? Why can't I summon her memory to battle his?

"She and I were cut from the same cloth," he claims. There's some truth in that. She was born on his birthday so, naturally, their charts show similar traits.

Many cultures place significance on one's date of birth. Uttes trace it down to the moment a child enters this world. Sythene and Juboe were born in Lassamout, Moon of the Wolf, signifying strength of character. On the thirty-first day. Three and one added equal four, implying endurance. The thirty-first is the seventh day of the month's fourth week. Seven signifying a tilt toward the spiritual. The fourth week indicating strength of purpose.

Both she and Juboe were strong. I can't dispute that. Where their birth charts differed was the hour. Memsen assign a symbol to each hour of a day. Juboe was born at eight in the morning, the sign for which is a square within a square. This indicates a desire to control and maintain established order. Juboe lived up to his chart.

Sythene was born 37 degrees past midnight. Thirty-seven reduces to ten, a number of completion and high achievement. But a dagger-shaped symbol, the satalith, rules the midnight hour. It is not considered the best time to enter the world. Indeed, it's the worst. The satalith represents upheaval. Destruction of the old to make way for the new. The moment of her birth, when the clock-watcher called out the official time, I may have been the only one present who was pleased. Praechall's daughter was destined to end Vic rule. I was sure of it.

My mother – when I presented my conclusion – neither agreed with nor disputed my opinion. "Birth charts can be tricky," she said in the flat tone she used to obscure the truth from a person trained to detect lies. Yet enough emotion leaked through to reveal she saw more in Sythene's chart than I did, and whatever she saw frightened her. When I pressed her on it, she snipped, "If ye wish enlightenment, my son, study lore!"

My study habits annoyed her. At the time of Sythene's birth, I was a sixth level novice, the phase when a novice devotes himself to study, meditation and prayer. I clerked in the Vic law offices, continued my secular education with both Utte and Vic tutors, maintained a social life, and employed two hundred or so people, half of them brothids.

Loehl Ohmswreith understood my need for activity. As memsen go, he was exceptionally flexible, tutoring me at all hours of the night. Ry'aenne was stiff as ticky-tack. Each of her letters ended with a reminder to study. And when she returned to Evald, she'd snare me after morning prayers and question me on where I had been the night before. My answer didn't matter. She'd issue the same advice. "Busy feet carry simple minds. If ye wish to overcome thy chart, my son, ye must focus thy passions." Though I harbor bitterness for Ry'aenne, she was adept at her craft. My birth chart is full of twos: second month, second week, two degrees into the second hour. The cross is the symbol for two and implies indecision, a scattering of forces. I'm certainly scattered tonight.

My grandmother gave me more practical advice about my inborn nature. Thylla often dined with Katre Haesyl – before Praechall came. After Praechall came, Katre was occupied, so whenever possible I'd dine with Thylla. I assumed she missed his company, and I enjoyed hers. The arrangement began the day Praechall arrived. Talk about change. Praechall brought more change than a snowstorm.

Before her arrival, I enjoyed complete freedom to roam the Keep. I didn't enter occupied suites, of course, but most of them stood empty. If I wanted to stroll the throne room, or even sit the throne, no one cared. Katre never used it. And when I entered his presence, a simple bow was enough. He did enforce protocol on Vic secretaries, having them walk backward when leaving and so forth, and his manner was eternally regal, but compared to Praechall ...

The day she came, I left the Keep after morning prayers and when I returned, Dynnae guards barred me from entering. My name wasn't on the roster of those employed in the Keep.

"Thy list be in error," I lied, "I work for Undersec Demasoot." Two of them ushered me inside. Every corridor bustled with people, none of whom I knew. The guards led me directly to Thylla's suite. Luckily, a servant let me in.

Thylla's face gained a few extra wrinkles that day. Change didn't excite her. "Me'acca," she sighed, "ye shall dine with me this eve?" She was a tiny woman, but until that instant, I never thought of her as frail and, though I had other plans, I didn't have the heart to refuse her.

We dined old-style, sitting on floor pillows. Her low-table was glossy black, top decorated with a runic calendar. She sat by Wyemout, Moon of Flowers, red roses painted before her. I sat by my birth month, Ve-ausmout, Moon of Hidden Passions. Between my elbows, a man and a woman, faces veiled and the rest of them bare, engaged in lovemaking. I covered the engrossed couple with my forearms, then had to uncover them while a servant washed and dried my hands.

"Thy mother arrived with Lord Lonntem," Thylla stated as bowls of this and that were placed on the table. "She regrets she cannot escape her duties to see ye this eve."

I hadn't seen Ry'aenne in years, but she was the last thing on my mind, for I was again shielding the table with my arms. We had yet to receive plates. I was fifteen? Sixteen? Young enough to be embarrassed viewing the lovers in Thylla's presence. Old enough to be aroused.

"Thy mother," she continued, "was displeased to learn ye've become a list master. The scriptures forbid the selling of another's flesh for gain or pleasure."

"I sell nay one, grandmam." A flush burned my cheeks. "I merely buy papers. Thus brothids may keep the coin they earn. Tis nay sin to barter one's own flesh."

"Ye tread a thin path, Me'acca." Servants stood ready with plates, awaiting her nod, a signal I prayed she would give. "Thy mother frets that ye may forsake thy studies to cavort with these brothids whose papers ye own."

"Cavort?" I choked as if the word were a peach pit. "Nay, grandmam, I shan't forsake my studies."

"Study, yea, ye must study the scriptures. But study also what lies afore ye." She motioned to the lovers hidden by my sleeves. "Ye were born beneath Ve-ausmout, Me'acca. If ye should cavort, forget not thy veil."

She nodded to the servants. A plate swiftly cloaked the amorous pair, and I was relieved to discuss another couple – Praechall and Katre. Years before, the two had partnered by proxy, their union ordained by prophecy, and the date of their contractual agreement selected by memsen. The birth of their first child, also ordained, was to occur at the turn of the century. This was the autumn of 492.

"Do the memsen not worry," I asked, "that a child may be conceived during her visit?"

Thylla replied with what may have been the best advice ever given me. "One does not question a Lord of Uttebedt."

I first saw Praechall from a balcony so jammed with people, if we had all inhaled at once, someone would have fallen over the rail. Rich, poor, half-breed or pure, all lumped together due to our place of birth – Evald. Being a memsa failed to win Loehl an exception. He was squashed beside me. Below us a sea of heads lapped at the dais steps – natives of Uttebedt, sending up a riotous clamor.

I lie in bed, drunk on cheap Mearan ale. How can I express my emotional condition that day? Naive awe? The double throne I knew well, large but not grand, armrest between the two seats. A tapestry behind it portrayed the Double Triangle of Uttebedt amid the winged crown and sword of the Lonntem Line. Emblems of power. This was new. This was what impelled us in the galleries to elbow and poke one another, straining to see, then stilling, awed by the sight.

Juboe's ghost hoots, not impressed. The Vics knew Katre's partner was a citizen of Uttebedt. Juboe himself signed the papers granting Katre permission to bring her 'with her own escort' into Evald. But the Vics didn't know she was a Lonntem. Even if they had, the import would have sailed past them. Fools. Five centuries of living among Uttes, yet they had no grasp of Utte culture. Yes, they knew the Lonntem family ruled Uttebedt, but pathetic Vic chroniclers depicted Lonntems as men. The idea of female bloodlines was too novel for their thick heads. Thus the Vics had no concept of the significance of Praechall holding Court in Evald. Since Huhtha's death in the war, no Lonntem had sat Evald's throne. All of us in the galleries believed we would witness history being made.

"But you didn't," Juboe nags. Damn him. We believed. Lust packed the galleries that day. A lust for freedom more potent than any lover's kiss.

Silence struck like a broadax when Dynnae warriors marched from behind the tapestry. Their footfalls pounded as they descended the dais stairs. They fanned out on the bottom step, then stood at attention, a lethal screen between the crowd and the throne. Memsen and Dyns filed simultaneously onto the stage. The Dyns, Salla Tree blazons on their chests, arced to the left. Memsen arced to the right, looking like shadows in their dark fahsatas. Both groups circled the edge of the dais, then turned to face the throne rather than the crowd.

We in the galleries thought Praechall would be next. We shoved and squirmed to get closer to the rail, all of us ready to explode with our desire to espy the woman we hoped would free us from Vic rule. When another person clad in a fahsata emerged, someone near me hissed, "Be it she?" A fahsata, with its hood raised, totally conceals the wearer's identity, deflecting even the scan of a sensitive. What clued me to the fact we were not yet viewing history was the person walking toward the throne carried an enormous ledger. The person pronounced Court in session. Later I discovered he was Ybbard Maer, Praechall's First Sec.

Maer recited an agenda, then accepted comments from the crowd, pointing to a person or calling a name and granting permission to speak. His gaze never rose to the galleries. Most of the business concerned problems with the move in location: grumblings about housing, questions such as was it safe to leave the Keep without an escort, and so forth.

Evald had once been the capital of Uttebedt. Yet they spoke as if it were a foreign state. I should have realized then that to them Vics WERE foreigners and Evald's Uttes were worse than Vics. Our ancestors had surrendered the city. But I was blind to the subtleties of Court. It was all so new, so confusing, so wonderfully civilized.

The session went on for hours. We roasted in the galleries. I was about to sacrifice my place for a breath of air, when everyone below suddenly dropped to their knees.

Praechall bewitched me at first sight. Tall, slender, hair the shade of autumn wheat – these are mere physical traits. The majesty she projected stunned my senses. Straight-backed, she strode to the throne, the famed winged crown atop her brow. Ziamford Massu, Luka's grandfather, trailed her. (I write his name knowing more now than then.) A withered giant, he would have escaped my notice except in his arms he cradled the Lonntem Sword.

The crown and sword were mythic objects, seen by me in paintings or stitched on cloth as with the tapestry. There they were. Real. With Praechall, Lord of the Uttebedts. I could not budge my gaze as she settled onto the throne. Ziamford offered her the sword and when she seized that golden hilt, I expected fire to shoot from the crystalline blade as the legends asserted. It emitted no flame.

Ziamford joined the other Dyns and knelt. Praechall rested the sword across her lap. "First Sec." Her voice resounded like the clang of steel. "Ye may rise."

Maer was the only one permitted to rise. The session continued with everyone else, including old Ziamford, on their knees. Praechall added a comment here and there, but there was no inspiring speech about ending Vic domination, no acknowledgement of the fact that she was the first Lonntem since the War to sit a throne in Evald. She didn't stay long. As she strolled from the dais, she snapped names and several memsen scrambled up to hurry after her. I recall being surprised that one of those summoned was my mother. Katre never appeared that day. Nor did he ever appear and fill the seat beside his partner.

Though my itch for an immediate overthrow of the Vics went unscratched, awe of Praechall inspired me to attend sessions of Court. Mobs in the galleries thinned, affording me more comfort, and gradually I realized why there had been no historic speech. When Praechall came to Evald, the borders of Uttebedt stretched to encompass her. She may as well have remained in her own city of Karamorn. Politically nothing had changed. Even so, my hope that she would free us didn't die. I was, as I said, naive.

During the winter of 492, Evald received far more snow than is outside these kitchen walls now. We were accustomed to snow. Sleighs replaced carriages and the city went on as usual – ruled by Vics. When Utte nationals left the Keep, they were issued Salla Tree brooches to wear. Vics assumed anyone sporting the emblem was a Dyn and though they noticed a high number of

Dyns roaming about, they were so wary of the Dynnae, no one dared issue a complaint. For a while, Vics asked me, "What's going on? Why all the Dyns?"

"Oh," I'd say casually, "it's because of Katre's partner." That's what we called her when speaking to Vics. They'd nod as if they understood and go on their way.

Chairman Juboe questioned me more thoroughly. He suspected Ry'aenne was in the Keep. He never asked directly though, and I didn't supply the information.

Thinking back, it was a good year. I was blissfully busy. I trained servants to handle my clerking duties. They'd bring me the forms each night and, unless something odd developed, I merely added my signature. Other servants brought whatever written assignments my Vic tutors gave me. I'd study scripture with Loehl until dawn, go to morning prayers, rush into the city and do anything needing personal attention, then race back to meet Loehl in the gallery. He often brought food. Eating during Court was rash perhaps, but to the people below, we didn't exist.

After Court my Utte tutors claimed me – philosophy, mathematics and such – until evening prayers. Memsen always gathered after the service and I, as did other novices, volunteered to serve them tea. This pleased my mother. These people, her peers, were the core of the Order. "Listen and learn," she told me. I did. Memsen may be the most holy people alive, but they gossip like shopkeepers.

Following late tea, I'd eat and discuss politics with Thylla. If the desire arose, as often it did after dining on her table, I'd visit a house I owned near the Keep, 'cavort' until midnight and return to meet Loehl who never scolded me for smelling of perfume. Sometime in there, I slept.

Early that spring a rumor began. Praechall, the Dyns claimed, was with child. I heard it while serving late tea. The memsen didn't believe it. None of them had envisioned a child born before the predicted date.

I was still wearing my white novitiate gown when Thylla and I sat to dine. The painted lovers between my elbows no longer embarrassed me. We had dried our hands when Katre walked in. She and I stood and bowed. He nodded to me, then spoke to her. "May I join ye, Undersec Demasoot?"

The simple interaction seemed odd after months of watching Praechall. As a servant positioned a pillow for Katre, Thylla jested, "Thy partner set ye free tonight, eh?"

Katre sat, stone-faced. "Lord Lonntem be done with me," he said, and I knew the rumor was true.

Weeks passed and even the most doubting memsen admitted the unthinkable had happened. They pushed themselves to new limits, but none could envision the child. The cloying odor of tryadett permeated their gathering room. Memsen, dozy from the drug or locked in trances, ignored my offers of tea. Loehl's easy nature turned suspicious. "The others be blocking me," he snarled, and our nightly scripture readings became chances for him to augur without distraction. I warmed his mead, prepared his tryadett, and when he cried out, I clutched his body while his mind swam in the void. He saw nothing. "Tis as if," he confided, "a blade had ripped a hole in time."

The memsen, exhausted, reasoned the child must be dead, but Dyns cited physical evidence to the contrary and calculated it would be born during the twelfth month of the year. All of us prayed the child would be male, for no heir to Uttebedt's crown should be born under the Beggar's Moon.

One summer day I was in the gallery, looking down at Praechall as First Sec Maer prattled about something. Suddenly woozy, I bent over the rail. The heads below seemed to rush toward me. Then a blinding vision jolted me. Loehl pulled me

199

back. "Wolves," I blurted, "I saw wolves." And before the day ended the Memsa Tribunal had cornered me.

It's one thing to serve tea to memsen, another to be the object of their attention. Especially Tribunal members, Dohlaru judges all. Mercy was a stranger to their hearts as they stared at me and mumbled to themselves. Since I lacked the ability to repeat the vision, they decided to 'help' me. When my mother offered me tryadett, I knew the process would be unpleasant. She assured me the chance of addiction was minimal. "The cure be within the vial, my son." But I refused the drug, afraid I would be one of the lost souls who, though cured of the need, couldn't resist the desire.

Maer was chosen to do the forcing. I sat on the floor. He knelt behind me, hands on my nape. "Shut thy eyes," he instructed. Moments passed. I stifled a yawn. His hands crept up my neck, my face, fingers warm against my eyelids. As I relaxed, I wondered what he'd do if I fell asleep. My head bobbed when I lost the support of his hands. "Look!" he commanded, then rammed hot pokers into my eyes. Images flared in my mind: Juboe standing on a dirt floor, feathered pen in one hand, horsewhip in the other. And me, lunging, clawing out his heart.

The ghost jeers, "A false vision, boy."

He's yet with me, keeping vigil from Tobb's bed. I didn't kill him and, in that respect, he's correct, but at the time my vision horrified me. When Maer yanked out the mental pokers and asked what I'd seen, I lied, "Naught. I saw naught." So he thrust them in again. Fresh images arose. I walked the streets of Evald. Corpses lay in the gutters. A woman shouted from a window, "Have ye seen my son?" A boy ran toward me, then fell and died at my feet.

I woke up in my suite, my mother bathing my forehead with a cool cloth. "Do ye recall anything of import?"

"Nay," I breathed. "Naught of import."

"Don't fret on it." Her hand like silk brushed across my brow. "Tis the child. The child blocks us."

Juboe's ghost just stood up. "You shouldn't have told her about those visions."

I didn't tell Ry'aenne, or anyone else. Oh. My mistake. I told Sythene. We were discussing my birth chart. She didn't read it the way my mother – or any other memsa – had. Indeed, she envied the twos in my chart. The cross, to her, symbolized choices.

"Ye must understand," I remember her saying, "I learned the craft long ago. Time has changed many things. What I divine for ye, Me'acca, be a series of choices. Be wary. Each new path shall grip ye fast. Once ye tread upon it, ye shan't be able to turn and go back." She was right, of course. Anyway, it was then I recounted my visions. She couldn't explain them.

"She knew what they meant," the ghost alleges.

He's by my bed now. I wish he wouldn't come so close. His presence sickens me. That can't be. He isn't real. "Stop trying to bring her back," he warns.

He's correct about my intention. I hope to activate my memory of Sythene by recording events prior to her birth so she can be born anew in my mind.

He's put a foot on my cot. I see the sinister gleam of his metal-edged boot sole. Real? If I believe that, I've lost my mind. "Son," he says. "Sythene was the one who had you exiled. All because of those damn visions."

That's absurd. Juboe laughs. Not even he can believe such a lie. He steps back to Tobb's bed and sits, elbows on knees. Why can't I make him disappear? His eyes shine, tryadett eyes, the whites yellow from the drug. "You didn't give me the chance to fight it," he charges. True. The drug I fed him lacked the cure. He was addicted from the first sip. What a joke. Everyone thought

I was his puppet when in truth he was mine. The ghost isn't amused. What does he want? Pity? He'll get none here.

"The lake house," he breathes, a weapon to pierce me.

Memories rush back. Shadows accrue greater menace. Cedar and granite outside, oak and marble within. As a boy I called it home. When Ry'aenne ditched him, Juboe ordered the house boarded up. I wish he had burnt it down.

I sensed danger when he offered me the house. I was at the notary registering my son's birth. Juboe came in, as if by chance, and insisted he certify the document. "Can't risk any errors," he said, face so benign, then he smiled. "Am I ever going to meet this family of yours?"

I saw the shadow of his mask and donned a mask of my own. "We'll get together soon."

"Tell me when," he pressed. "I'll open the lake house. Make the occasion special. If Clariz fancies the place, it's yours. A late wedding present. Just pick a date."

"Soon," I repeated. It would've been never. But I wrote to Ry'aenne, seeking advice on how I could forge a truce between Juboe and me. Her initial response cautioned me to avoid him. Soon, however, she sent a second missive that urged me to accept his invitation. "Go, my son, without delay. I foresee a fresh start for ye and thy father."

I assumed, as she knew I would, that a 'fresh start' would be for the better. Damn her. What prompted her treachery? Did she hate him more than she cared for me?

I set the date with Juboe, and the terms – no guards, no servants. Clariz worried more than I. She feared he wouldn't approve of her. He was at the house when we arrived. I introduced them and served as interpreter. He kissed her cheek and cooed over his grandson, three months old. His genuine delight lulled me.

He led us on a tour. Despite the efforts of soap and polish, every room stank of decay. I blamed the odor for my unease. If a plot was afoot, I reasoned, a sane man would have sprung the trap the moment we had entered. Here was Juboe, my son in his arms, guiding Clariz around that grand old house, pausing to relay tidbits from my childhood. He fit the part of a happy grandfather. The afternoon light was fading when he ushered us into a meeting room. My son was fussing. Juboe handed him to Clariz, then steered her to a chair by the windows. "Tell her how I'd catch you here reading at midnight."

She smiled when I translated his words. Sitting in the chair, she unfastened the front of her gown to feed our son. Juboe left us briefly. He returned with a decanter of wine and crystal goblets. The bounce in his step should have warned me. But I wanted peace between us. I trusted Ry'aenne. I ignored the faint whiff of deception.

Clariz rarely drank mead and never wine. Juboe winked at me, "More for us, eh?"

I remember fog creeping over the lake, remember Juboe refilling my cup, the flash of alarm when I noted he had yet to sip his own. "She's beautiful," he said, diverting me.

I swayed, dizzy, as I turned to see Clariz, our son at her breast. Beyond her two lawmen waited in the doorway. My goblet crashed to the floor. Then I slid into darkness.

The ghost sits half in shadow. "Clariz was a nobody," he says. "You never loved her."

Is that true? My mother arranged the union. "You need a partner," she said. Clariz, an orphan, had been raised within the Order. "She's perfect for you."

Perfect, but not for me. She was too innocent. Too obedient. Too accustomed to serving memsen. The day we met, I tried to scare her away by suggesting we test our compatibility in bed.

She was too polite to object. When I learned she was with child, I could hardly refuse the contract. Did I love her? We had too little time together. Working as a defense advocate ate my days, and my nights – Luka Massu stole those.

"You should never have mixed with him," Juboe mutters. Ha. Juboe's the one who taught me to court the somebodies of this world, and few carry more import than Luka. It's no coincidence that the capital of Uttebedt rests on Massu land. The family trails only Lonntems in political power – and that may be illusion. Every Dynnae warrior assigned to guard a royal house is trained at Brakten-Nore, the seat of the Massu estate. If the Dynnae is the right arm of Uttebedt, the Massu family is its fist.

My ties with the Dynnae were fragile at best. So I was surprised when Luka attended the Rite of Union between Clariz and me. His presence caused a stir. People who caught Luka's eye either enjoyed remarkably good fortune, or were found dead.

After the ceremony, he presented gifts: a cradle for her, and for me, a ruby brooch shaped like a Mearan hawk. The brooch was a slap to my lineage. I thanked him anyway. His interest in us inspired the notion that my requests to enter Uttebedt hadn't been in vain. Clariz was, after all, native-born, and I was now bound to her. Luka had come, I prayed, to determine if the security restrictions against me could be waived. I endured his insult. And when he invited us to dine with him, I accepted.

I expected a formal evening and advised Clariz to dress accordingly. We weighted ourselves in glitter. His suite was on the royal floor of the Keep. We hardly needed an escort, yet a guard came to fetch us. She led us into a chamber where a low-table bespoke plans for an intimate gathering. Glass doors offered a view of a snowy terrace.

Luka entered from another room. He had reddish hair and the physical grace of every quickened person. A thick moustache angled sharply past the corners of his mouth to frame his chin. It made his mouth appear wider than it was, especially when he smiled. He did not smile at us. He was clad in a plain tunic and leggings, his only jewelry a ring bearing his family's crest. He must have thought us clods.

On sable rugs and ermine pillows we sat around the table, evenly spaced, stiff as pegs around a prayer wheel. A harpist began a mellow tune as servers dished out food. I hoped the evening would progress better than it started. A fool's wish. Conversation was terse. Yet he invited us back. We dined with him nearly every night that winter.

During meals, he doted on Clariz. He had an uncanny smile; her shyness melted under its glow. He soon had her so at ease that after she'd eaten, she'd stretch out 'to rest,' and he'd switch to Universal, a tongue neither she nor his servants understood. He spoke it like a Vic. Privacy attained through language, we'd drink and talk until she woke or, more often, dawn.

Most of the chatter was a masquerade. In the midst of a debate on civil law, he'd ask, "Why do you serve the Vic courts?" It would seem an innocuous query. My clients were paupers. I rarely won an acquittal. Why shouldn't he ask why? But the subtle change in his tone added weight to the question. Luka set a mood of privacy and comfort, conditions conducive – especially with the mead – to free expression. None-the-less, the talks were an inquest.

Oh, he was clever. We'd be discussing the advanced age of Katre's First Sec and which memsa might replace her, and he'd ask in an off-hand way why I hadn't become a memsa. I'd explain that very few novices actually earn a brand.

"True," he'd agree, "but most fail in the process. You reached the ninth level. You've taken all the vows required by the Order, passed all the obstacles except Final Testing. No novice stops at that phase without a reason. Did the memsen bar you from Final Testing?"

"No," I'd say, "I decided against it."

"Why?" he'd ask, and I'd sweat for an answer that would satisfy him without destroying my chances for the waiver.

He had a keen interest in religion. His knowledge of scripture so impressed me, one night I dared to ask if he had studied awhile as a novice in the Order.

"Me? A novice?" He laughed. "My father would've disowned me." Then he peered into his chalice as if to divine his future. "I believe in the wisdom of Dynnas. I'll raise my children in the faith. But solving the problems of this world will require more than prayers."

World problems became a recurrent theme of our talks. He expressed a desire for his children to inherit a stable world and though he praised Sythene, he worried the memsen were steering her in the wrong direction. This was hardly treasonous. Memsen and Dyns have argued for centuries. Besides, the expectant edge in his voice told me it was all part of the inquest. Sprinkled throughout, he solicited opinions about war with the Vics. Would I feel obligated to side with my father's people? Break my vows to take part?

My stance on the matter had tempered over the years. I could honestly say any war should be sanctioned by the Memsa Tribunal in accordance with Uttebedt's laws. Such a sanction would rescind everyone's vows. And so on.

By year's end, he granted me permission to address him by his given name. My hopes for a security waiver soared. And when he began his unholy work on me, I swallowed the foul liquids he bade me drink. I accepted his claim they would make me immune. I presumed he meant to protect me from disease. His insistence on secrecy didn't alarm me. Dyns thrive on secrets.

Proving trust was another step in earning the waiver. Or so I assumed.

I discovered the truth by accident. It was early spring, the weather pleasantly warm. I had been retching on and off the whole day, ill from a potion he'd fed me that morning. Clariz and I joined him for dinner. He fussed over me as he usually did her, coaxing broth down me, then bidding me to lie on the fur rug. I dozed during the meal. When I woke, they were gone, the suite quiet. Still unwell, I went onto the terrace. A gibbous moon dripped light on the courtyard below. Shoveled snow formed walls along the paths, yet the air smelled of crisha blooms. I had lingered awhile – long enough to feel the night's chill – when I heard voices inside. Luka was speaking with Etolie, one of Katre's guards. I was the topic. Etolie asked how long my transformation would take. Luka responded, "I cannot rush him, or he shan't survive."

"Perhaps he shouldn't," Etolie cautioned. "Creating a soehn biehr from the Chairman's son be a dangerous sport. We can never again allow him near Lord Lonntem."

It was like a kick to the head. I should have stayed put but, dumbstruck, I went in. If surprised, Luka didn't show it. "Soehn Biehr," he addressed me, as though I were already an assassin, then he spoke Universal, emulating our private talks. "The Memsa Tribunal will never sanction war. For our children's sake, we must protect the world's future through other means."

Etolie jutted in, "Killing justly brings honor!"

"Be still," Luka ordered, knowing this insane credo wouldn't overcome my repulsion. "You must be wondering, Me'acca, why you were chosen. Why not Etolie instead? He'd be willing, even eager. Why pick you?"

Why I'd been chosen was irrelevant. I was wondering how to refuse and remain alive.

Luka threw his wide smile at me, then walked after it, closing the distance between us. "You're perfect. Trained for government service, a profession of cunning and deceit. A ninth level novice. No one will suspect you."

I backed out onto the terrace. He pursued me. "You want to say it wasn't fair to begin without your consent. But, Me'acca, you would have refused. You want to refuse now. Want to remind me of your oath of non-violence. Want to say you're not capable of murder."

The stone railing struck my spine. He moved alongside me. "Memsen can afford ideals, my friend. The rest of us must choose between being hunters – or prey."

He talked about Evald, the disgrace of five centuries of Vic control. I thought about his deception. He said if we did nothing, we'd pass that shame to our children. I thought of what a fool I'd been. "We must assume the burden," he asserted, then asked, "Could you kill to protect Clariz?" I imagined her a hostage and me a slave to his whims. I nearly choked on my anger. Etolie loomed in the doorway, weapons aglint. I walked toward him with the slim hope he might let me by. Luka's voice snared me. "Consider your potential, Me'acca. Surely some of your father's blood flows in you."

As I swung around to face him, a blaze of obscenities burst from my mouth. I cursed him and every member of his family – or as many as I managed to name before his fist silenced me. My head cracked against the terrace floor. In a heartbeat, a blade pricked my throat.

"Dyn Massu!" Etolie shouted, "not here!"

Luka shoved the knife into a sheath hidden under his sleeve. Pain shot through my side when he booted my ribs. "Take this Mule," he gritted, "from my sight!"

Etolie snatched me up and hustled me down to my suite. I fretted through the night. At dawn, I went to see Katre.

Etolie was on duty. He led me into Katre's dressing chamber – and stayed. Katre greeted me with a wan smile, then dismissed his attendants. Etolie remained. Securing privacy with language wasn't an option; he spoke Universal better than Katre. The situation exposed a mere fragment of Luka's power, but it was enough to daunt me. I bowed to Katre. "Forgive me. I should not have come so early."

Katre deciphered my anxiety. "Tisn't so early as ye may imagine, Me'acca. Dyn Massu has already left for home this morn. Did ye two argue yestereve?"

"Nay," I alleged. I knelt to help him into his day slippers. "My lord, I've been ill of late, and if my health should worsen ..." I looked up at him, praying he could read on my face the truth behind my words. "Clariz has nay family. Will ye grant her thy protection?"

Katre glanced at Etolie before stating, "I shall do what I can for her."

I could ask no more of him. For months, I thought each day would be my last. Etolie seemed to be everywhere, watching. But after my son was born, my winter with Luka Massu sank into the depths of memory – until the lake house.

It just occurred to me that perhaps I misjudged my mother. I'm certain she foresaw danger in my encounter with Juboe, but is it possible the outcome was mutable? If so, when did I err and set things reeling into disaster? When I drank the wine? Even in the cellar was there something I could have done or said to alter our fate?

I woke bound to a post, hard wood against my back. Lanterns lit the dirt floor, the walls buttered with mold, and the lawmen sitting on barrels and sharing a jug – Tanner and Horst, two young toadies with ambitions. A strap around my throat cinched tighter when I tried to free my hands.

Juboe strolled from a pocket of shadow. A coiled whip hung from his belt. "Don't fight me, son." He loosened the neck strap enough to let me take a breath.

"Where are they?" I exhaled.

He feigned ignorance. "Where are who?" Behind me, my son whimpered. Juboe chuckled, "You mean the Uttes? They're here." He tugged on my ear. "Stupid Fool, you forgot what you are." He cited the Racial Purity Act, the section forbidding Mules to breed. "If you'd told me you wanted children, I could've fixed it. I'm not your enemy. But you broke the law. I have to set things right."

He produced documents: an annulment of partnership, a denial of paternity. I agreed to sign them if he'd release Clariz and the boy. "These first. And use your real name." He untied the rope binding my wrists, put a pen in my hand. I signed. He retied my wrists. The strap again squeezed my throat. "Swear this Utte and her bastard mean nothing to you?"

I swore. He signaled his men. Tanner carried my son into the light. Horst brought Clariz. Her gown was torn, her face bruised. "Me'acca." Her voice sounded hollow. "Forgive me."

Juboe pulled her to his side. "She entertained us while we waited for you to come around. Do you care?" He was testing my oath. I told him, "No, I don't care."

"I understand why you wanted her." He stared at me as his stinking hands groped her. "Care if I take her again?"

"Father, we had a deal."

"I'll keep it if you do."

I couldn't look at her. "Take her again if you want."

He released her. If she had fled that house, maybe I'd be with her tonight. But she ran to me instead. Her lips brushed mine before Juboe jerked her away. She fought him. An error. He wrestled her down. Our son began to wail. "Shut him up!" Juboe yelled. The boy squalled louder. Clariz scratched and bit. Her strength amazed me. Yet she had no chance of winning.

Juboe ordered Horst to hammer pegs in the dirt. He sprawled atop her while Horst tied her down. She shrilled my name when he entered her. He cursed her, called her Ry'aenne, then collapsed. I thought the worst was over. But when he stood, he trembled with rage.

He snatched my bawling son from Tanner and dangled him in front of me. "Do you care what happens to this bastard?" Was there a correct answer? I said, "No." And my father strangled my son. He flung the body against a wall.

I lacked time to grieve. He pointed at Clariz lying uncovered in the dirt. "Do you care what happens to her?"

"Yes," I said and begged for her life. That, too, was a wrong answer. He uncoiled his whip. And all was lost. Screams splattered the walls. Tanner bolted upstairs. I fled as well. A door opened in my mind and I ran in, hiding like a child in a cupboard. The screams died. The whip cracked on. "You'd best learn from this," Juboe warned, but by then I was beyond his reach. Horst cut me from the post. I didn't recognize the thing pegged out in the dirt, couldn't identify it as a woman. Did I love Clariz? I didn't even know her.

Juboe walked me upstairs, told me he'd revise the laws so I could marry a Vic woman. "One of the Howyl girls, eh? Would you like that?" I didn't respond. He shook me as if to jostle out an answer. Silence. He accused me of being obstinate and sent me to state prison.

A day, a year, or an instant passed before the cell gate groaned open and Ebe Metreek swished in, dogged by Gregor, one of his pets. Ebe was Primary State Advocate and as bound to Juboe as a kite's tail, yet he emoted surprise at finding me there and blathered about parole. Gregor squatted beside me.

211

His lamp tossed light over his boyish features. "Sir, he's in shock."

Ebe crouched down and, with a moist hand, stroked my neck. "Fetch the Chairman. This has gone too far."

Juboe came as if to rescue me, his fingers like talons ripping me from the floor, clamping my shoulder as we walked from that filthy place. He took me back to the lake house.

Servants had arrived in my absence. They bathed and dressed me, rubbed salve on my neck and propped me up in a chair. "Grief has shattered his mind," one said. "He cannot even hear us." Not true. I was acutely aware of my surroundings. I heard, saw, smelled everything. Debris clogged the chimney flue and traces of smoke improved the stench of the room. The men policing me quarreled over a wager. They pried my jaws apart to see who had won. "Ha!" the winner crowed, "told you the Smith left his tongue."

Insanity. My body was clay to be molded. My mind, clay to be written on. I existed in another space. Outside, rain disturbed the lake. I created a new one, water smooth as glass, serene. Outside, the wind wailed like my dead son. Yet I felt no sorrow. No hate. Nothing.

If I could have eliminated reality, I believe I'd still be in that space, with a lake flat as a mirror, reflecting nothing. But my mind continued to record everything around me and when a servant whispered Clariz's name, emotion tainted my sanctuary. My lake churned. Then Luka surfaced like a bloated corpse. His fist smashed my face. I fell, as I had on the terrace, hitting my head. He yanked me up, struck. I fell. He yanked me up. Over and over, the scene repeated. My eyes exploded in their sockets. Teeth and blood dammed my throat. My head split like a rotten melon. All this without my body leaving the chair. How can I be sure? Each evening Juboe asked my wardens if I had moved or spoken. "No," they always replied, "he's been quiet all day." Juboe would curse, then bend over me and say, "I know you hear me. Stop this nonsense." He'd wait a moment, then bark, "Put him to bed!"

Every evening the same. When Juboe arrived, Luka would drop me in the chair. As I was carried to bed, I'd feel his boot slam into my side. He'd batter me through the night, boot me again in the morning, batter me the next day, and so on. Illusions. I craved pain and created Luka to deliver it. Why him? Why not? His fists were as good as any. He never tired of hitting me. I never tired of the pain. I'm not sure how long my insanity lasted.

"Six days," Juboe's ghost says with confidence.

How could this phantasm know more than I? Yet the number hardly matters. The day it ended, a storm brewed outside. Wind slapped waves on the lake. Juboe came up behind my chair and wrapped his hands around my skull as if to crush it. Luka's fist bashed my face. I didn't fall, didn't hit my head. Luka vanished. I was stuck in reality.

"Son," my father said, "I won't let you starve yourself to death. Dine with me tonight." He twisted my head so I'd see Tanner and Horst beside him. "Or they'll cram food down you!"

I joined him. He sat at one end of the table, I at the other. Lamps bridged the chasm between us. "Your brothids have been sold. Your other properties soon will be. From now on, you'll live here. We'll be a family again, son."

"Books," I said, ending my silence. "I have books in the Keep. May I fetch them?"

Juboe collected books with a passion. I knew he couldn't resist the lure of more. I swore if I entered the Keep, I would come out again. I had no plan for revenge. No pride either. I begged to go that night. He assigned Tanner and Horst to escort me, officers of the law. They shackled my legs. The carriage driver was a half-breed I'd known since I was a child. Instead of going to the Keep's main entrance, he drove us to the south court. His deception failed to alert the lawmen. They hauled me out into a pelting rain. The gates stood open, untended, another hint that more than my hastily planned escape was afoot. Horst noted the oddity, but failed to heed its message. I balked at the gates. He shoved me forward.

Vapor lamps spat puddles of light in the courtyard. The shackles forced me into a mincing gait. We passed the peach grove without seeing a soul. Then Etolie, like an uprooted tree, stepped onto the walkway. For an instant, I thought Luka had finally sent him to slay me.

Tanner held a knife to my back. "Tell him we're your escort."

Etolie didn't need me to translate. He let us by.

It could be argued my downfall occurred that night, in that wet courtyard. I was nearly to the arched entry when the lawmen cried out. Etolie had seized them from behind. I could've gone on and entered the Keep. But he shouted, "For honor!" And I grabbed Tanner's knife.

The bastards refused to die simply. They kicked me as I hacked and stabbed. Even their blood fought me, spurting hot at my face as if to blind me. I gained no honor from that butchery. Madness. Etolie finally let the bodies slump to the ground. I dropped the knife on top on them.

"Well done!" Luka praised – the real Luka. I saw him sheltered in the archway. "Soehn Biehr," he summoned, and I hobbled toward damnation. There was no turning back.

"Luka's hound," the ghost mocks.

Not true. Luka didn't own me. I picked my targets. He placed one ban on me: Juboe wasn't to die by my hand. Fine. I didn't want my father dead. How could I be certain his soul would suffer? Addicting him to tryadett served my purpose and couldn't have been easier.

I returned to the house with two books of verse and a chalice. Juboe asked about his men. I confessed I'd killed them. He clapped my shoulder. "Finally you're a man!"

I gave him the chalice and posed a toast. So cold my heart as he raised his cup. With no pain to ease, the drug produces euphoria. Juboe howled with laughter when I told him what I'd done. "You think you can get away with this?"

In truth I thought I'd be hanged. But the drug was already in him. Only death would free him from the hunger for more. For that alone, I was willing to hang.

His Vic friends noticed the yellow streaks in his eyes, but some of them had streaked eyes, too. It was a symbol of status, proof they had the wealth to hire a Dyn healer to assist them through an illness. None of them were addicts. The Dyns always supplied the cure – after payment for their services had been rendered.

As Juboe's strength waned, Vics would pat my shoulder and say, "He's so lucky to have you as a son." Or predict, "He'll get well," and pump my arm until I agreed. Vics adored the Chairman. Their affection for him lapped onto me. "Tend your own health, too," they'd fret, for I truly did not look well. I was downing Luka's potions at a risky pace. My hair greyed rapidly, and some days my skin developed rashes or blanched into a lifeless pallor.

Why didn't Juboe expose me? He had ample chances. Pride may have held his tongue at first. After the drug had eaten his mind, no one would have believed him.

Luka was correct. I made the perfect assassin. The Vics – incredible fools – sought my help in finding 'this damned Soehn Biehr!' I warned each target, signed notes slipped into a pocket or left on a desk, giving the option of resigning from office. Each man showed me his note, each asked my advice. "Resign," I told them. How simple could it be? Life or death. They chose. I took no innocents.

The ghost is gone. Crept back into my mind? He's different than the Luka I created. That illusion was limited. This one seems to possess a will of its own.

Voices in the hall. Is it morning? Damnation. I had intended to write of Sythene, not Juboe. He's laughing in my head, "The night she was born, you worked for me." Lie! We traded favors, that's all! And we wouldn't have if Bibaloe Howyl had been jailed as he should've been!

Who am I arguing with? Myself? Insane fool. I've written through the night and accomplished what? Sythene is mute, less real than Juboe's ghost.

518, 11/25. Exhausted. Need sleep. So why did I wet a pen? To record the exciting events of my day? The stockyards delivered fresh meat. Onji is well enough to drink broth. Helsa kissed my cheek in gratitude. That's it.

How my life has changed.

518, 11/26. Jenner came up for evening meal. He was bent on religious chatter more than food. He's gotten it into his head that Krich is breaking Loric's seal on the Netherworld. "The dead will rise," he warned. "An army of ghosts and demons will slaughter us all. The seal's cracked, Mates. Already Krich were casting plague demons right and left!"

As far as I know there hasn't been a single case of plague either in the palace or the city. Jenner, however, offered solid proof of demonic activity – snow. "Ghosts and demons, mates. Loric can't stop them, can't melt the snow. If we want protection, we got to give Krich his due."

After he had badgered us into agreeing we should pray to Krich, he left our table to accost another group. He won few steadfast converts. Nearly everyone quickly recanted – in whispers, so he wouldn't overhear and return.

"What do you think?" Cyril asked me.

I shrugged. I don't much care which god these savages pray to. I have enough trouble tending my own faith.

Jenner's wild talk sounds ludicrous, but what if he's correct? Juboe lurks on the fringes of my mind. Is he my own creation? A manifestation of my guilt? Or is his ghost real? I can't believe his soul entered Loric's Garden. Has he escaped from the Mearan Netherworld? Or did Eshra, not Krich, claim his soul? Juboe did turn to the Church before his death. He had little choice, thanks to me. But I had little choice as well. Luka yanked me out of circulation.

"You're taking too many risks," he ranted. "Don't you realize the Vics asked the Church to sniff you out?"

I knew. So what? I didn't intend to survive.

Luka let me go – disguised – to view the body that was supposed to be mine. The corpse was decomposed, but it wore my ring. The Vics were sure I was yet another victim of the Soehn Biehr. I could have continued. Being dead was an ideal cover. Yet Luka kept me a virtual prisoner until the Snakes could smuggle me out of Evald. Why?

We last spoke the night before I left. An odd meeting. I'd never seen Luka so ill at ease. "You'll be safe in the lowlands," he said. "The Kinship will furnish everything you need." For an instant whatever conflict raged inside him surfaced on his face. "Me'acca, I ..." Then a smile washed the evidence away. "Don't get yourself killed before we send for you. We're not finished, Soehn Biehr."

When he said it, he believed he would send for me at some later date. As did I. To hone my skills, I hired myself out to the Snakes. And waited years for a day that never came. Maybe I should've stayed. Waited a bit longer. And ignored the memsa at the way station? No. I had come to a juncture in my life and she clearly was a signpost. The Soehn Biehr had to die.

The corpse I left fooled the Snakes. I planted more than a ring. All my poisons, my weapons, even my clothes. I had to char the body – as any thief might after finding a Kinship dagger on the man he'd just killed. Blur the identity of the victim. Take the item of greatest value – an amulet that could be melted down and sold. Hide the rest in brush. A robbery scene, placed on a trail used by Snakes and, with wet leaves smoldering, sure to be found.

When Luka heard of my death, was he relieved? Or sorry he had hurried me out of Evald? I could've accomplished so much more. Could have died, as Etolie would say, with honor. What was I being saved for? This? Again I'm waiting for a day that may never come. Only now, if that day should arrive, I'll be useless to Luka or anyone else.

Juboe murmurs in my head, "Go now. Pick up and go."

Ghost? Demon? Hallucination? Whatever he is, he tells me what I want to hear. I don't want to listen. Don't want to believe him. He's a liar. Yet what he says sounds true. Why can't I force him to go away? I miss the sweet hum of Sythene's voice in my mind. It's as though he's replaced her, snuffed out her light with a cold breath. He draws me deeper into darkness.

I understand Jenner turning to Krich. If one god fails to answer prayers, why not invoke another? But will Krich change the weather? Or will Jenner be the one who changes? I should have argued with him, should have told Cyril to continue praying to Loric. No good will come of courting Krich's favor. Evil begets evil. We must resist.

518, 11/27. Sunshine brought cheer this morning. No one could stay out and bask. A freezing wind stripped the sun of heat and the glare was blinding. We contented ourselves with beams of light blazing through cracks in the shutters.

Jenner appeared during the afternoon, blinking and bumping into things. Faulty vision didn't suppress his glee. "Look what one night of prayer done!" he declared. "One night! And already Krich, he gave us the sun!"

His absurdity went unchallenged. Last night I may have considered opposing him, but sleep honed my wits. Never compromise a vital alliance. Juboe taught me that, and it's sound advice. The snow will melt. People will return to their senses. I can't afford a war with Jenner. Who else will lend me a horse on my free days?

518, 11/28. This morning Mira clutched a cloth bundle while a group of women, Baz in the lead, marched her up and down the hall, shouting "Guelfik!" which means – literally – "sour milk."

The purpose of the bizarre parade eluded me but as the day progressed, I noticed none of the women spoke to Mira, nor did the men except to issue orders. At evening meal, she sat alone in the far corner, near the window where a broken shutter lets in the worst draft. I assume she's been ousted from the women's quarters and the bundle is her belongings. I also assume being shunned is her voted punishment.

Jenner came up late – the scullery girls were clearing tables – but he wasn't after food. He wanted us to go to a meeting in the stockyards. The only one he snared was Nulan. The boy must realize he has no future here. Maybe he hopes Jenner will hire him on in the stables.

Mira may have guessed this and fears losing him. "Nulan!" she barked as he headed for the door. "Don't go out in that cold! You'll catch your death!" He didn't even glance her way.

Cyril, bursting with joy, invited Filson and me to share a bottle in his room. I declined. The one thing more tiresome than hearing Cyril whine is hearing him gloat.

518, 11/29. I fasted today. Helsa, who seems to have made it her duty to tend to me both on and off the job, worried that I was ill. I'm not. I simply needed to clear my head. Can't say fasting helped. Now I'm hungry and can't sleep.

Juboe has been a constant presence. He's trying to blunt the sharp memories with gentle ones. Beguiling me. He wants me to admit he was a good father.

It's true he sometimes read to me when as a child I had trouble sleeping. If I wandered down and interrupted a meeting, he'd draw me onto his lap rather than send me to bed. I can recall dozing, ear to his chest, soothed by his voice. I loved him then. Wanted to please him.

Ry'aenne also held me on her lap during official meetings. Also read to me. I preferred his choice of books, fanciful tales aimed to intrigue a young mind. But I loved her then as well. Wanted to please her, too. Pleasing both of them was impossible.

My parents were such opposites – yet so alike. Juboe existed in the real world, in real time. What was happening at the moment was of import. This isn't to say he forgave debts or failed to plan his next move. He forgot nothing. Each step had a purpose. But everything hinged on his satisfaction at that moment. Ry'aenne also forgot nothing. Each of her steps also had a purpose. But for her the moment was transitory. She existed in the future. I remember the first fast I shared with her. How old was I? Three or four maybe. We sat with Juboe as usual for evening meal. Servants arranged platters of food and I thought I'd swoon from the sight. "The boy's too young to fast," Juboe complained. "He'll never grow if he doesn't eat."

Ry'aenne retorted, "His soul shall grow, husband."

"Look at him!" Juboe waved at me. "He's hungry! Aren't you, boy? Tell your mother you want to eat!" Immediate gratification or eventual salvation, how does a child choose? On that occasion my mother won.

I remember her taking me up on the Rim, teaching me to ride. She boosted me onto the saddle, then swung up behind. My feet didn't reach the stirrups. We left the Keep's high stable and rode the steep trail that coiled up the cliffs. "Ye've naught to fear," she murmured, as if I could possibly be afraid with her arms about me. When we gained the narrow but relatively flat Rim, she gave me the reins and I steered the horse toward the crest of Mount Ahsett. Never one to waste an idle moment, she tested me as we rode, "What does Evald mean in the old tongue?"

"Chalice," I responded, then looked at the city below. Enclosed by cliffs, it did resemble an empty cup, the lake a blue-green drop of residue. If I shut my eyes, I can summon the image. I liked the city best when seen from the Rim. Far above the misery below. In spring, snowmelt cascades down the stone, a thousand waterfalls, as if to fill the cup. But it never does. The chalice is flawed. A southern crack allows the lake to drain into the Olamett Valley.

The State of Evald controls ten leagues of the Olamett River, from Lake Falls to the paper mills at Border Falls. Vics call the valley the Farms, a joke of sorts. The Farms are labor camps. Prisoners cut timber, raise cattle, grain and so forth. Several times a year, Ry'aenne would visit the camps and offer religious guidance to the legally enslaved. She took me along when I was young. She tested me as we rode then, too, having me recite this or that, or speaking in one language and I'd translate into another.

We'd go from camp to camp, spending nights in visitors' cottages, cross Mill Bridge and come back on the other side of the river. Though we carried identity papers, the Vic guards never asked to see them. They knew she was Juboe's wife and when we'd arrive, they'd halt the day's work and she'd cry out, "Come ye who desire the blessings of Dynnas!"

I'd squeeze her hand as prisoners shuffled to us, leg irons jangling like mail. I thought they were the most heinous criminals in Evald. The opposite was true (debt was the most common offense) but my child eyes saw the men as fiends. When Ry'aenne told me Juboe had committed them to chains, my opinion of him swelled to heroic proportions. I realize now she meant to portray him as callous. Yet was she less so? She didn't buy the men's freedom. Their physical welfare didn't interest her. Her business lay in souls. To any convict who asked, she performed the Rite of Grace, accepting his sins as hers. Not once did she refuse. Why, years later, did she refuse me? I had not yet become an assassin. My sins were petty. Did I not grovel enough for her? Didn't weep at her feet and beg for redemption?

Damn her. I hated going to the Farms and she knew it, yet insisted I go. The least she could have done was allow me to enjoy the ride. Was she hoping to smother the Vic half of me with incessant recitals of worthless knowledge? I know she resented Juboe's influence on my upbringing. "Thy father tempts ye to sin," she'd rail, and maybe she was correct, but we differed on our definition of sin.

The Howyls' barge, for example. Every summer the Howyls entertained a select group on their barge. While servants rowed the damn thing around the lake, the Howyls and their friends drank until they spewed over the side. It was the premier social event of the season.

When my parents lived together, the barge was a point of contention. My mother forbade me to board it. Lake Bahdala is sacred to Uttes, a physical representation of the spiritual realm of

Sheever's Journal, Diary of a Poison Master

Bahdala. One could drink from the lake, and to have one's ashes cast upon it was the ultimate final blessing. But to "frolic" on it, as Ry'aenne would say, was close to blasphemy. To Juboe, not going to a Howyl function WAS blasphemy. He never missed an outing on the barge.

I'll concede this: the barge was not a proper place for a child, especially an Utte one. Besides the temptation to overindulge in drink, there were always brothids aboard. Sin was rampant. But Ry'aenne extended the ban to all social activities near or on the lake.

Evald doesn't experience the staggering humidity of a Mearan summer, but after the snow on the arms of Mount Ahsett has melted, the cliffs surrounding the city magnify the sun's rays. On hot days, Vic boys go down to the piers and swim. Leister often invited me along and I'd create some excuse rather than confess I wasn't allowed.

Juboe took my side on the matter. "The boy should learn to swim," he'd argue.

Ry'aenne refused to budge. I recall one spring. I was eight or nine. We were on a Farm trip. Snow still whitened the road, but already I was dreading a summer of excuses and, between spouting bits of catechism, I pestered her about learning to swim. Where in the scriptures, I harped, was swimming deemed a sin?

In response, she led me off the road and up over Smuggler's Pass to a small tarn. A solid layer of ice didn't deter her. She scratched off her right glove and extended her hand over the frozen water. Pulses of light burst from her palm, melting a hole in the ice. "If ye cannot control thy desire," she grated, ire thinly masked, "then swim!"

My first year aboard the Howyls' barge occurred the same year Ry'aenne left Evald. Before leaving, she confided the reason she had pushed me to study – while I was in her womb, she had a vision of me serving as Katre's First Sec. She was so confident her vision was accurate she installed me, a ten-year-old, into the suite traditionally occupied by the Utte First Sec, bumping the memsa holding the post into another suite, one further from the record room. The effrontery of her action appalls me now. I suppose it proved Ry'aenne's power within the Order. At the time, I thought nothing of supplanting the First Sec from her living quarters. I fully intended to earn my brand and pursue the path my mother envisioned. So the following summer when Juboe wanted me to go rowing with the Howyls, I balked.

"Your mother isn't here to stop you," he goaded and since she was supposed to be dead, I could hardly argue that she'd find out about my indiscretion. And she did find out. Within a sixtnight she admonished me in a letter. A waste of ink. The affair was punishment enough.

From the moment we cast off from the docks, I felt ill. The oars were barely wet when Leister and a slew of his cousins herded the brothids into cabins below the top deck. Juboe prevented me from joining them. "You're too young." But Leister wasn't much older, and I could have handled a premature dalliance far better than the amusement the men had planned – fishing.

Living in these kitchens has accustomed me to the smell of cooked fish. And I've known Uttebedt natives who ate fish. My partner loved steamed trout, and Luka occasionally provided it, always with the comment, "Imported." To avoid insulting him, I nibbled the stuff at his table. But I've downed poisons more eagerly than those fishy morsels.

I once asked Sythene if fish in Lake Bahdala ferry souls between this world and the next. She said it wasn't true. But at the time of my barge excursion she hadn't been born, and I believed, as did most Uttes, that eating fish from the lake was akin to eating human flesh. When the men, Juboe included, began yanking up the gasping creatures, I was horrified. Worse, a brazier stood ready so the fish could be grilled and eaten immediately.

"Father," I whispered, "I can't do this."

He nodded, understanding, yet wanted me to appear Vic even if I wasn't. "Don't bait your hook," he advised.

As morning aged into afternoon, I drank wine to curb my hunger, a mistake to be sure. Leister and the other boys decided to swim while the oarsmen rested. They'd dive into the lake, swim to a rope tied to the prow, clamber up and dive in again. I watched, besotted, from the rail. It didn't seem difficult. Bibaloe Howyl came up beside me. Bibaloe was Leister's uncle. He also sat the Vic Council. Sober, he had a mean streak. Drunk, he was nothing but mean. "Why aren't you swimming?" he demanded. "Afraid the water will sizzle your Utte blood?"

Some of the boys overheard and gathered around as he dared me to jump, prove I was a Vic. I had no idea where Juboe was. Leister pushed through the dripping crowd and offered to go in with me. I shucked my clothes. Hand in hand, we perched on the rail. "Ready?" he grinned. As we plummeted down, I heard Juboe roar, "He can't swim!"

The water was unbelievably cold. I sank like a stone. Leister pulled me up and towed me to the rope. Something brushed my leg, probably his foot, but I imagined a disembodied spirit trying to drag me into the depths. Faster than a rat I scrambled, yelping, up the rope.

Bibaloe laughed at my fright. I didn't quite catch his derisive remark. But Juboe did. In a blink, Bibaloe flew over the side. Politically, it wasn't a wise move. Bibaloe never again cast his vote in Juboe's favor.

Instead of a scolding, I reaped lessons from the incident. We walked to the lake at night. And with the moon as our sole witness, Juboe taught me to swim. I remember his strong hands holding me afloat. I trusted him with my life. He was a good father then. And I a good son.

518, 11/30. Fasting today was easier than yesterday. I tidied my station during evening meal, then went into the dining hall afterward. I've yet to pry Juboe from my thoughts and was reluctant to enter the silence of my room. I hoped someone would be in the mood to chat, but there's little new to say. Mira unrolled her bedding in the corner that's become her quarters and everyone else turned in early – except a few boys who gathered around Nulan, listening to him preach.

I sensed danger there. The boy spits drivel more adamantly than Jenner. "Dispatch Nulan," Juboe advised in my head, "before he's out of hand." I got up and left.

I don't doubt Juboe's assessment of the situation. If the weather doesn't break, Nulan will likely cause some sort of trouble. But I'm not about to kill the boy. It isn't as Juboe claims. I don't fear getting caught. With planning, it could be done with next to no risk. But I refuse to entertain the idea. I've had my fill of killing.

518, 11/31. I've been numb to hunger. Helsa is sure I'm ill. Soon as I hung up my apron, I bathed. Cyril thinks I'm crazed. Maybe I am. I have nothing clean to wear. My hair's wet. I nicked my chin shaving. I'm cold. And I stink anyway. I don't know what I'd hoped to accomplish. It seemed I should do something to acknowledge Sythene's birth date.

I was honored to witness her entry into this world. Everyone of import was there. Praechall sat the birthing chair as if it were a throne. Not once did she cry out in pain. Dyn Ducia Iamun served as Chief Medico. Ybbard Maer was scheduled to deliver

First Blessings. Memsen chanted prayers. The rest of us waited in breathless anticipation. The enormity of the event clenched my mind.

I can't do it this way. This is like the worthless trivia a first sec would file. Such and such happened. So and so was there. All went well. Glossing the truth. True, everyone of import was there, but that implies I was of import. I was among the few Nobodies present. My vision of wolves got me in. The other Nobodies had also reported dreams about wolves. If Sythene had been born under the Beggar's Moon, we would've been barred from the room.

True, Praechall's birthing chair looked like a throne, but she didn't sit it until the last moment. True, she never cried out in pain, but she cursed like tavern keeper. Pacing back and forth with poor Dyn Iamun chasing after her, begging her to stop drinking so much mead. She ordered all of us to leave and when no one obeyed, she hurled threats and declared her child would not be born that night.

True, First Sec Maer was scheduled to bless the child, but he never did recite the passage. True, memsen chanted prayers, but they were praying for their own souls, for they were about to be party to sacrilege. The rest of us waiting in breathless anticipation? It was a madhouse. The only time we became breathless was when Sythene nearly died. The enormity of the event clenching my mind? Nonsense. Juboe ruled my thoughts that night, as he's trying to do now.

Mere hours before Sythene entered this world, I bargained away a man's life and committed petty treason. I don't want to write of these things. Nor of the truth surrounding her birth. It has never been recorded. I've read Maer's official account. Though longer than my initial version, it's similar. The breathless and mind clenching are direct steals from his. I don't blame him for glossing the truth. Every person there swore an oath not to reveal what had been done to Praechall's child. If we had not sworn, we would not have left the room alive.

I'm not sure I want to break that oath. Yet if I write of that day, I should do it honestly, or not at all. Maybe not at all is best. I lied from the start. I haven't been numb to hunger. I'm starving. And so cold it's difficult to hold the pen steady. This won't work. Sythene may not be gone from this world, but she's gone from me and nothing I write here will bring her back.

518, 11/32. Nulan transferred to the stockyards. Mira begged her son to stay, begged Cyril to forbid it. She may as well have been begging stones to sprout ears.

Juboe has been silent all day. My head seems oddly light – and empty.

518, 12/1. A fresh storm brought more snow. To no one's surprise, our monthly shipment from the city failed to arrive. Lucky for us Cyril habitually overstocks.

518, 12/2. Cyril went into the palace to meet with the chief steward. While he was gone, private cooks came down and raided our supplies. Kwint oversaw the foray. The theft was launched at our busiest time, so they might have escaped quietly if Filson hadn't caught wind of it. Shouting curses, he ran down the hall as if his pants were afire and the rest of us spilled out to see what was going on.

Kwint attempted to calm the situation. There's no love lost, however, between base cooks and privates. Kwint, a true coward, shrank back as Filson blasted him with foul language. Two privates dropped their plunder and fled through the connecting door. It seemed the others might follow. But soon Cyril arrived – with the steward.

The steward has the appearance of a man who's never savored a meal. So many layers of wool hung from his gaunt frame he looked like a cloak pole. His no-nonsense air brought silence though, and when he demanded to know the cause of the uproar, it was Filson who shied.

"A small misunderstanding," Kwint offered graciously.

The steward pointed a glare at him, then told us (as, I assume, he'd already told Cyril) that troopers had been sent to hurry our supplies, but until everyone was again fully stocked, the private cooks could take what they needed from our stores. Indeed, as he spoke, they carted off sacks of flour, our best cheeses, and who knows what else. We're to begin rationing tomorrow.

The steward said members of his staff would "supervise" us and warned that anyone caught pilfering would be flogged.

518, 12/3. Rationing got off to a sour start. Six pettymen have been assigned to spy on us. They showed up early and scolded us for eating brancake with our morning tea.

The new rules are simple. Cooks are allowed to sample what they're fixing, but women are not, and children have been banned from the oven rooms completely. This means no snatching a roll from the cooling racks, no begging a dipper of soup at noon. We're to have one meal each evening. Tonight we dined on baked onions and pickle bread.

Getting paid failed to sweeten the day. Cyril took three coppers from my wages for the wine I drank last month. He stole more from Filson, nearly his whole pay, charging him for wine plus the keg of ale the rest of us drank. Filson's purple with rage. He pledged to stop buying ale and bullied the rest of us to do the same. A boycott won't last. Ale is one of the few items we have in abundance.

518, 12/8. End of the week and no shipment. Nor word from the troops sent to fetch it. The steward's spies are still with us. They tell us what to cook, dole out how much we'll need, then nose about, jotting down figures in their hand ledgers. They leave each evening, but none of us is fool enough to break into the stores and cook more than we've been allotted.

Other than a general feeling of discontent, however, we've adapted to the situation. The women have become gifted thieves. While one distracts whichever spy is present, another pinches a tart or roll and hides it in her skirts. Mira isn't included in their sly sport. She's paying dearly for her war with Baz. The women set out our evening meal and Mira's table is always skipped. She'd have nothing to eat at all if not for Onji.

The girl has been well enough to work since rationing began and when she cleans up, she scrapes the meager leavings onto a plate and gives them to Mira – often with a chunk of bread from her own pocket. I don't know why she decided to feed the woman who almost killed her, but no other female could risk it without being shunned herself.

518, 12/10. Jenner came up this evening to peddle his religion. He said crowds have been gathering to worship Krich. I assume he's had better luck winning converts elsewhere. Services are every other night, on odd days, Krich's days, which left him free tonight to help himself to our platter of turnips. Cyril and I have become his prime targets. He thinks that as a kor-man I have special access to Krich and if he wins Cyril over, he'll be able to snare us all. "Just go to one service," he challenged. Cyril is rightfully cautious. Services are held in the slaughterhouse.

518, 12/11. My free days begin tomorrow. Cyril won't let me work through. He says the pettymen have our schedules and any change might spark suspicion. We're not busy enough to claim I'm needed. "Catch up on your sleep," he advised.

518, 12/12. This morning I stood in line while the pettymen gave assignments, hoping they'd forget I was off. They didn't. Indeed, they banned me from going to my own station. I waited by the doorway while Helsa brought me a pot of hot water. We've run out of tea. "Tell Baz," she whispered, "I can't sneak her nothing. They was watching too close."

I found Baz sulking in the dining hall. She accepted Helsa's news with a simple nod, shook her head at my offer to share the hot water, then wobbled onto her feet and sighed, "Might as well go back to bed."

I moved to a table near the wall where heat from the ovens on the other side warmed the bricks. Sipping water, I struggled against thoughts of food. I had planned to go for a stroll. With all the shutters closed this place is like a rabbit warren. A walk up to Main would be refreshing – or so I believed last night. I roused my ambition shortly after daybreak, with a slight alteration. Rather than go as far as the road, I'd simply exit the west door, go around the kitchens and enter from the north. Even this modest plan dissolved. Snow had piled outside the door. I shouldered it open, then stood there squinting. The light was unbearable. And what was there to see? Snow. I dragged the door shut and returned to my seat.

About noon, Cyril tried to entice me into buying ale. "Good way to pass a day." I passed on his suggestion. I don't want to be the first to break Filson's boycott. Cyril mentioned he had a jug of wine in his room, but when I didn't bite on that either, he yawned and stated his intention to nap.

During the afternoon a group of women hauled in a sack of rags and gossiped as they patched tattered clothing. A gaggle of children played a brief game of tag. But mostly it was quiet. My heels on the table and my back against the bricks, my mind was moldering when the west door scraped ajar and Nulan squeezed inside.

The boy's face was bruised. From a beating? He tracked snow on the floor as he limped through the room and into the hallway. Had he come to see his mother? To beg Cyril to rehire him? It was something new to think on.

At evening meal I had the misfortune to sit between Cyril and Filson. They've been sparring since payday, but their past friendship had softened the blows – until tonight. The onion soup had been ladled out when Filson smirked, "We could all be rich, mates." His method to attain wealth was to pray to Krich – and give a donation. Fool. What little he had left of his pay is now jingling in Nulan's pocket. "Every coin gived will come back tenfold," he claimed, then leaned around me to aim at Cyril, "I'll fetch back what you stolt from me!"

"I took what was owed!" Cyril roared, stinging my ear. And the battle was on. Cyril ridiculed Filson for letting Nulan swindle him. Filson accused Cyril of preventing any of us from going to the yards. Cyril called Filson a liar. Filson declared he would attend tomorrow's service and called Cyril a coward for being afraid to go.

I swear Filson's head is hollow. First Mira filled him with bile and now her son has done the same, for they were Nulan's words being spat from his mouth. Cyril had few options. He stated he'd go to tomorrow's service. Later he asked me to go as well. I told him I'd sleep on it.

518, 12/13. Boredom enticed me to join Cyril and Filson's trek to the yards. Rebic and three meat cooks came along – Padder, Woset, Tlan. Courage in numbers.

We left after evening meal. Filson insisted on using Lower Main which troopers had cleared days ago. "So we won't get no snow in our shoes." The western sky was rosy, pale stars beginning to shine. The road, hard-packed ice, was slick as wet marble. I clambered atop the snow. It was crusty enough to provide good footing and I easily plunge-stepped down the grade. No one else followed my lead. They linked arms, thinking they could stabilize each other. Each slip of a boot slammed all six of them onto their asses.

Two hundred or so men had gathered in a holding pen outside the slaughterhouse, milling about as docile as cows, their needs met by stockmen. A bonfire in the pen's center provided light. Near the troughs, food in the form of greasy pork lay in heaps on a table fashioned from an old door. Ale, too, was for the taking, wooden bowls on hand for those who had neglected to bring cups.

We had barely wet our lips when Jenner latched onto us. He introduced us to Col who runs the yards. Col's a heavy-set brute, bald, with a shaggy beard. Cyril, Filson and the meat cooks already knew him, though not by his new title of "Uchidon" which translates roughly to mean "Blasphemer." Col thanked Filson for his donation. "You'll get your wish, mate. You bringing fresh sinners binds it tight."

Recruitment was part of the arcane deal – which explained Jenner's persistent attempts to snare us. And losing to Filson irked him. He clasped my arm in a last bid for credit. "Uchidon, here's the one I told you about."

"The kor-man?" Col eyed me as if I were a rival. "Hear you're a demon when the moon's full. It's full tonight, Kor-man. Where're your wings?"

"Don't believe all you hear," I said, which vexed Jenner more. "Besides, the moon hasn't risen yet."

Col muttered something about unholy retribution, then left us to greet a pair of latecomers.

For a while it was merely a social gathering, albeit an odd one due to the mix of people who didn't mix at all but stayed with their own. Most were working class and the few who weren't disguised themselves as such. Glints of silver from tipped flasks betrayed their higher station. Col, chatting with each group, was a needle and thread, stitching patches into a whole. Nulan, too, served this purpose. He wore an old gown over his clothes and carried a 'staff' – it was simply a tree branch, but everyone knew he represented Loric. A tattered Loric. A Loric bereft of luck. As the boy-god made his rounds, jeers erupted. Several troopers cuffed him. One booted his backside. Their actions left little doubt as to how the evening would turn. Yet the sky was clear and the fire warm. I could have stayed until the barrels were dry – or until moonrise when I had planned to slip away.

The preaching began when Col shouted, "The gods are at war!" He circled the area between the men and the fire. "Krich and Loric locked in battle!" He snatched Nulan from the crowd and pretended to be wrestling with the boy. "Who will win, mates?" Any fool could see the match before us was no contest. But men cried out the obvious answer, "Krich! Krich!"

Col seized the boy's staff and rapped him with it. Nulan, whimpering for mercy, dropped onto his knees. Col raised the staff, victorious, and threatened to strike the boy again. "Run, you bastard god! Run!" It was all rehearsed, but when Nulan jumped up and ran, the pummeling he received from the crowd must have hurt.

Col tossed the staff into the fire. The world will be turned upside down, he predicted. The dead will rise and slay the living. The righteous will be punished and sinners rewarded. The poor will be rich, the rich poor. All this is to happen at year's end, when Krich will break down the gates of the Netherworld and the battle will rage in this world. Only those obedient to Krich will be saved. To prove obedience, Col instructed us to bring others to honor Krich. He closed this portion of the service by inciting the crowd to chant, "Damn Loric, Krich rules!"

Then stockmen herded us inside. The slaughterhouse is brick with a slate floor. Easy to wash. We dodged carcasses that hung from hooks in the ceiling as we followed Col toward the killing trough. Troopers scrambled to get in close. We cooks settled for the rear. I found a bucket and, standing atop it, could see well enough over Tlan's shoulder. Lanterns lit an idol crafted from wicker and dung. Immense in size and smell, the idol was mostly human in form though its face had a snout. Its member jutted upward to attest its potency.

Col donned a mask made from a cow's skull. Holding a cleaver, he asked for offerings. "Every coin will return tenfold," he promised. He didn't say when. Yet there were fools aplenty. Coins rained at his feet. Twice he asked for more, waving the cleaver as if to use it on the stingy. Too little, he claimed, would bring Krich's wrath upon us. When threats failed to generate added profit, he turned and bowed to the idol. "Accept these meager gifts," he said, then delivered a prayer in which he begged Krich to forgive those of us who had yet to believe, and to protect those who did. "Who now wishes to receive Krich's blessings?"

Nulan crawled from behind the idol. Still in the role of Loric, he gripped a squawking chicken by its feet. I didn't catch his words, but the symbolism was clear.

Col hacked off the bird's head. "See, mates," he stated, "even gods will bow before Krich." As if the boy's performance were proof. "The low and the mighty will bow. And will be saved!" He smeared chicken blood on Nulan's forehead, then shook the dripping bird at the crowd. He scoffed at those who avoided being splattered. The blood, he said, would protect them from demons and the hungry dead.

While he anointed the faithful, someone produced a medibox of laetris and passed it around. The cooks didn't know what it was and abstained. As did I. Jenner, though, snorted a healthy portion. Most of the other men also indulged and the pitch of the assembly heightened.

A pig was pushed out from behind the idol. Cloth around its neck fluttered like a cape. A crown of sorts had been tied atop its head. "The High Lord!" a stockman yelled, to be certain we'd comprehend the parody, "It's Fesha Trivak!" The pig charged into the crowd. Carcasses thumped the unwary as men, laughing and cursing, jostled each other while chasing the pig. Stockmen finally caught the thing and forced it back to Col.

"Do you," Col addressed the pig, "accept Krich as your god? No?" he answered for the animal, then asked the gathering, "What'll we do with him, Mates?"

A response, first issued by a stockman, was picked up by others and shouted, "Kill him!"

Col turned to the idol. "O Mighty Krich," he intoned, "take this gift. And bless those who worship you." He slit the pig's throat. Capturing its blood in a tin basin, he ordered, "Come! Drink the power of Krich!" And men lined up to gulp his evil sacrament.

Cyril huffed out. I shrugged at Jenner as if to imply I'd rather stay, then escaped as well.

The moon had risen, and the stark beauty of the night contained more sorcery than Col's nonsense. I started up toward the orchard. Drifted snow had smoothed the terraces into a rippled slope. Apple trees poked through the crust, black on silver. How long has it been since I've walked in moonlit snow? Perfect snow. Soft enough that I could kick in toe holds.

Firm enough to hold my weight. Highland snow. I could have imagined myself close to home – if Cyril, behind me, hadn't been raving in Mearan.

He blamed Col for "twisting things so nobody can tell right from wrong," and blamed others for being too stupid to see the outcome. "Col, he was always trying to be bigger than he was, but messing with Krich is too big. If he don't stop, them gates will open all right and demons will fly out after us. We'll end up kor-men like you, Sheever."

I doubt he needs to worry on that level. I detected no resident force in the idol. The danger I saw lay in Col's power to manipulate. And his reckless stretch beyond religion into politics. He may have dubbed himself Blasphemer, but the High Lord's judges might pin another label on him – Traitor.

Cyril was still ranting when we reached the kitchens. We entered through the dining hall. Mira was curled up in her corner and pretended to be asleep, but I'm certain she was awake, listening, as Cyril said he intended to pray for Loric to send an omen to "set things straight." He wanted me to do the same. An omen, though, can be interpreted too many ways. Instead, I'll pray that the wealthier observers in tonight's crowd weren't spies planted by the State Advocate.

518, 12/14. Filson slept through morning assignments. I worked in his place, though to call it work is nearly a lie. The women chopped the vegetables and pettymen decided how much of what went into which pot. I stirred and, on occasion, tasted. Soup bones allocated to us were picked clean. I couldn't help but think of the mass of pork given away last night. Does the steward know what's happening in the yards? Or are we the only ones being watched?

518, 12/15. The ale boycott is over. Filson ended it. Damn his luck. And my stupidity.

I idled the morning away in the dining hall, in peace. Rebic, also free today, got up about noon. By then, aromas from the day's work glutted the air. He babbled incessantly about food. I suggested a dice game, thinking it would distract him, which it did. And for a while it was harmless; our cautious wagers slid back and forth between us. Even when others joined in, I won more than lost. Then Filson finished work and I lent him a hopence so he could have a throw. Arrogant benevolence. When will I realize I don't have the resources I once enjoyed?

Filson won. And won and won. Soon he called for Cyril to tap a keg. I should've stopped then and spent what remained of my coin on drink. But before each roll, Filson invoked Krich to bring him luck and I wanted to prove him and his notions false. Against all odds though, he continued to win. Every damn roll! When I pulled out of the game, no one else dared wager. Needless to say, after evening meal, there was a rush to the yards.

518, 12/16. Filson is poor again. As are the fools who hurried to forge a covenant with Krich. Today they tried to drum up a dice game with those of us who hadn't gone to the yards, but they had no coins of their own to wager. I spent the last of my pay on brew and drank it in front of Filson.

518, 12/23. Not much new to record. No shipment yet. Flour won't last another week.

The rift between Cyril and Filson has widened. A new one has split Old and Young Wix. Father and son are on opposite sides of the religious war. A pity. The bread cooks were the tightest group in these kitchens. Old Wix always identified himself with them, which may be why he never developed a close bond with the cooks in the spare kitchen. He ate with the bread cooks, spent his free time with them, and they treated him with respect. But Young Wix went to the yards and convinced the cooks under him to convert as well. Now they snub Old Wix.

Cyril welcomed him at our table, but it's difficult to converse with him, especially if the topic is not one that should be shouted for all to hear. The man can read lips, but his gaze is rarely on us during meals. He watches his son and former mates.

518, 12/27. Cyril's omen arrived in the guise of Malison. He came through the north door, leading Calec's pony right into the hallway. The boy's face had been painted white, a dab of saffron on his forehead. He has entered baimyot. I can't think of a concise translation. For disciples of Loric, baimyot is a sacred time – and silent. The boy was totally mute. Nor would he meet another's gaze, but made a point of looking elsewhere, and when too many faces surrounded him, he shut his eyes rather than be accidentally tainted.

To say his appearance caused a stir would be an understatement. The pettymen were agog. One raced off to fetch the steward while another ordered food and drink for the boy. Idiot. A disciple in baimyot can't accept anything unblessed by a reverend. Malison didn't refuse with a head shake. He didn't acknowledge our existence.

Cyril quickly used the situation to his advantage. "It's a sign! A sign from Loric Hisself! He sent the boy to show us He were stronger than Krich!" Maybe he would have won over the yard-goers, maybe not. But when the north door opened again and a brace of troopers announced our supplies had arrived, we swarmed out to unload the wagons, and even Filson praised Loric.

The steward officially ended rationing. We cooked with a frenzy. No one went hungry tonight. Except Malison. He wandered off during the mania, leaving Calec's pony in the hall. An initial search turned up nothing, then I found him in here, asleep on Tobb's bed. He's still there, still sleeping. I covered him with a blanket. He can, when he wakes, choose to ignore it.

Jenner heard the news through the troopers and came up to share our feast. The topic around every table was Malison. Cyril insisted Loric sent the boy in answer to his prayers. Jenner asserted Calec sent him because they were running low on food. The road to the cemetery hasn't been cleared, according to the supply chief, so their wagons couldn't get through. Calec's monthly provisions were left with us. Did Malison just happen to arrive on the same day?

Padder suggested we load up Calec's pony in the morning and see whether or not the boy leaves with the goods.

Jenner countered, "He'll get hisself robbed." He waved down protests. "Not by no Mearan. But what if he runs into a band of hungry natals? Foreign natals, who don't pay no never mind to what he were. Verdi natals were a bloodthirsty lot, mates. I knowed. I seen Ceither Tulley …" He started a rendition of his tale about Tulley, Macon D'brae and the rest showing up in his stables after the Games. I broke into his story and volunteered to escort Malison to the cemetery.

Cyril cautioned, "You'll get yourself killed." His concern for me is secondary. He doesn't want Malison to go. Though he'd never admit it, I'd wager he'd lock the boy up, if given the choice, and keep him like an amulet. The magic he's hoping for has already happened though. Tonight Old Wix dined next to his son. Baz chatted with Mira, then invited her to sit with the other women. It's as if the boy were a balm, healing old wounds. And though today is a 'Krich day,' not a soul mentioned going to the yards.

Indeed, when (in response to Cyril's warning) I said I'd scare away natal attackers by turning into a demon, more than one hand discreetly made the sign against evil. Loric has regained his hallowed image.

I had to argue with Jenner to get use of a mount. I reminded him of his promise to lend me a horse whenever I wanted. He finally consented to my taking the roan. And Cyril had to admit I'm owed a free day for when I replaced Filson. So it's settled. If Malison decides to go, that is. He may have other plans – or rather, whatever force sent him here might, for something is moving him. The boy nearly glows with power.

He's jarred my memory as well. I know now when last I felt Sythene's distant vitality. It was the night I kept watch over Malison in the back orchard, the night I prayed for guidance, the night before I led him to Calec. Is it her hand I sense on the boy, her power guiding him? A better sensitive could tell, but I can't. I also can't let him escape my grasp. I don't mean that the way it seems. I'm not like Cyril. I don't want to lock the boy up. I want to set him loose and follow him. If he is a link to Sythene, I can't let the opportunity slip by. Hungry natals on the prowl or no, if he leaves tomorrow, I'm going with him.

518, 12/28. This morning when I woke, I sensed Malison in my room. He was not as he was last night. Confusion is what I read from him. I snuffed my disappointment, got up and cracked the door to let in light. He was huddled on Tobb's bed. He flicked me a glance, then averted his gaze in keeping with his baimyot status.

"Wait here," I said. He isn't supposed to hear anyone except a reverend and he didn't respond, but he stayed put when I went into the hall. Though well before dawn, nearly everyone was up, eager to see what Malison would do. I was in no mood to answer questions.

The pony, his belly full of turnips the children fed him, had spent the night in the hall – and left a mess. Padder had stacked

Calec's supplies nearby, but had no idea how to load them on the animal. There was more than the pony could carry anyway. I asked if someone would fetch the roan from Jenner. Cyril himself went down to the stables.

As I packed up the goods, Padder wanted me to include a beef roast left over from yesterday. Old Wix offered two loaves of spice bread. Baz and the women brought out blankets and a patchwork dress for Damut. Everyone wanted to add a little something. By the time I had finished, there was space on the roan for only one rider.

"You still going with him?" Cyril asked.

To be honest, I hadn't decided. There seemed little to gain. Jenner was correct about the boy being an attractive target. I wouldn't be much protection. But I couldn't send him off alone and expect to sleep well. I nodded to Cyril, then went back to my room and shut the door behind me. I don't need light to find my way around. I explained the situation to Malison, told him what I wanted him to do and, as I spoke, I went to the nook, removed my journal and stuffed it under my tunic. The tin box would deflect an arrow shot at my chest. I was thinking of myself, not the boy, and maybe that's why I hadn't brought in a candle. Acts of cowardice are more easily performed in the dark. I donned my cape, which hid the bulge of the journal, before opening the door. Malison obeyed my instructions perfectly. We were out of the kitchens by daybreak.

He rode the mare. I led Calec's pony. The roads were clear as far as the bridge. We continued on Perimeter. The broken snow from the boy's trek out made the going more difficult, for the holes had frozen rock hard. We were headed into the sun and the glare blinded me. I tripped constantly and worried the mare might also and crack a leg. We were near the turn onto Cemetery Lane when I spied a man struggling toward us. It was Calec, out looking for Malison. He said they had been praying in the temple yesterday when Malison simply stood up and walked out. The belief that Loric had 'favored' the boy satisfied Calec.

When we reached the temple, he pulled Malison from the mare and pushed him inside. The two of them have been living in there to prevent the boy from being tainted by his mother. The moment we were alone, Calec stated, as if an order, "You'll stay. Damut needs company."

I wasn't sure what he was implying, but I didn't like the sound of it. I muttered an excuse about Cyril expecting me back by evening, said I was scheduled to work tomorrow.

"You'll stay, Sheever. It's the Will of Loric."

And so I'm here in his cottage. Damut's asleep in the bed with Basal, Loren in a crib alongside. I chose a place by the hearth. The stone floor makes a hard bed, but I'm comfortable – physically. It's my mind that lacks ease. A melancholy air clings to Damut. Little wonder. Calec won't speak to her. "Tell your mother," he said to Basal, "Sheever's to stay." We were standing on the cottage stoop. Calec won't cross the threshold. Nor take food from her hand. She passes the kettle to Basal to pass on to him.

Calec has tried to appease her. He earned a tidy reward for his role in the funeral of Wacha Leyourd. Or maybe the sum was a bribe for letting a possible plague victim be buried in his cemetery. Whatever the reason he was paid, he used it to buy Damut an iron stove. Clearly, he isn't snubbing her due to anger. It's his religion. Yet his actions must hurt her the same.

Like a docile Mearan wife, she accepted my invasion of her home, her head bowed, as if her black bonnet were made of lead. She wears the shapeless cream-colored dress atop the brown wool dress she brought with her from Eastland. The combination is for warmth, but it seemed to express her fate, her present life smothering the woman she had been.

The stove embodies the remnants of her pride. When I entered the cottage, she stood in front of the thing, as if to shield it from sight.

"I hope you don't expect me to cook," I said.

A glimmer of a smile eased the tension in her mouth. "I'll do the cooking. If you'll help bring in wood." Help, indeed. The woodpile is a block of ice. She's been using a grub ax to break loose enough to heat both the cottage and the temple. The chore was so difficult for her that she had skimped on her portion, keeping just enough for the stove. The cottage was chilly. I brought in more tonight and lit a fire in the hearth. It's snug in here now, and pleasant lying before the fire, writing in this journal. Too pleasant. A part of me cautions I should leave.

Yet there's work to be done. After the sun had softened the snow, I climbed up onto the roof and, with the ax and a shovel, cleared off as much as I could. The thatching had handled the weight so far, but if more snow falls, the roof may fall too. I also improved the path between the cottage and the temple, and smoothed another to the stable.

There are four stalls in there, but only one is usable. The others are packed high with generations of Wessel clutter. Rusty wheels, a carriage seat, and such. There's no shortage of feed though, and the pony seemed pleased to share his stall with the mare. And pleased with the attention. Damut has fed the animal, but he hasn't been curried nor his bedding changed for who knows how long. I raked the old, but didn't take the time to lay down fresh; the rick is buried under a hill of ice.

There are chores here. I won't be idle. And my journal isn't a problem. I didn't try to hide it from Damut. I pulled the box from under my tunic and told her it contained my recipes. "Don't want them messed with."

"Mali kept his writ down," she said, referring to her first husband. She told me to put the box on the mantel, then instructed Basal to keep out of it.

I suppose I'll stay another day or so to help her. I'm lying. That isn't why I decided to stay. Nor is it because Calec ordered me to. I'd like to solve the mystery of what possessed Malison and why he went to the kitchens.

The idea he came for food would be plausible if I had found the family starving. But they weren't. Damut welcomed the supplies, especially the butter and Padder's roast. Calec hasn't been hunting so meat is scarce. But produce from their garden fills a corner of the cottage, root crops and apples. Herbs and braided onions hang from rafters. The Wessels haven't gone hungry. What possessed the boy, and why? I don't know. But if it happens again, I hope to be near.

518, 12/30. It's late and I'm tired. It was difficult waiting for Damut to fall asleep. This one-room cottage seems large enough to the eye, but offers little privacy. Though she was abed and hidden by shadows, I could hear her sobbing.

She and I have clashed. It began yesterday. I had used the grub ax to uncover the rick and wanted to teach Basal how to tend the pony. I thought it would relieve her of one of the burdens placed on her. When I took him into the stables, he ran screaming back to Damut.

She defended him, "He's too young."

Yet the boy must be nearly six and when I was that age ... Basal is not me. He's afraid of the pony, and the mare terrifies him. Someone has to learn though. Letting the beast stand in his own waste until spring is not an option. "You want his hooves to rot?" I scolded.

"No," she mumbled, then told Basal to watch over Loren, plunged her hands into the big square pockets she'd stitched to the front of her dress, and followed me outside.

Lack of easy access to water is a problem. Snow is the only source. I told her earlier that I'd need a fair amount and she had melted enough to fill two pails. I could have used more. Lack of space added to my frustration. Damn Calec and his whole family for saving every bit of trash they ever owned. I had to lead the animals outside and I worried the mare might stray. There wasn't a damn thing to tether her to. If I lose her, Jenner will have my head.

Damut stood shivering from cold while I cleaned the stall. After I had laid down fresh straw and brought the mare and pony in, she began poking about in the Wessel trash. "If we got rid of this," she mused, picking up a harness that fell apart in her hands, "I could get a cow."

The woman was dreaming if she thought I was going to clear out that mess. "You can't even tend a damn pony," I said – too harshly, I admit – "let alone a cow."

She turned away so I wouldn't see her weep. Damnation.

Today was worse. She fixed porridge again. I've never cared for the stuff. Unlike yesterday, I declined the bowl she filled for me, said tea and the bread I smelled baking would be breakfast enough. Her eyes welled with tears. Loren was fussing. The boy is amazingly good-natured and rarely cries, or so I thought. His crib has wheels and each day Damut rolls it near the stove where the air is warmer, and where he can see her moving about. This morning seeing her spurred his agitation. He clutched the bars of his prison and pulled himself onto his feet as he bawled for attention. She asked me to hold him while she checked the bread. I told her I'd rather not. She burst into sobs.

I felt like a turd. But Loren ... He's older than my son ever was, but only by a few months, and has wisps of curly dark hair as my son once had. I couldn't.

I spent most of the day outside, knocking loose the wood and restacking it, so she'll have less trouble after I'm gone. The woman is exhausted.

Calec came over this evening to fetch a pot of stew. I escorted him back to the temple. "Damut has more to do than she's able," I said, and suggested I spread word – when I returned to the kitchens – that he wanted to hire a boy. I hoped to find out how much he'd be willing to pay. If it was more than Cyril pays the boys to shuttle coal, I was certain I could entice one out here.

Calec refused to discuss it. "Don't need no kitchen boy. Loric sent you, Sheever."

We had crossed the road and were at the temple by then, and I asked him how Malison was doing with his studies, how long before he'd be finished, or at least be out of baimyot.

"Smart boy, he is," Calec crowed. But the answer, when I finally squeezed it out of him, was another year or two, maybe longer, before Malison can reenter the world.

"Reverend Wessel." I called him by his title to imply what I was about to say had nothing to do with friendship. "I work in Trivak's kitchens. Not here. I have to go back. Soon. If you care for your wife, hire a boy to help her."

He opened the temple door. I glimpsed Malison, aglow with candlelight, kneeling by the altar. "Loric bless you, Sheever," Calec said before going in and shutting me out.

A coal of anger burned in me when I went into the cottage. Damut had used the last of the butter to make pastry dough for pocket-pies. They were meant to impress me. She stuffed them with cheese. I told her they were as good or better than any I'd tasted, which was true.

Could she simply accept the compliment? "If I had me a cow," she began, "I'd have butter on hand and could bake enough to sell and earn a coin or two."

Could I simply let her dream? "You have enough to do," I grumbled. "Who'll milk the cow? Who'll churn the butter? And what fool would come way out here for a damned pocket-pie? This is a cemetery, woman! The dead don't eat!"

Damut didn't eat tonight either. She went to bed, sobbing. I tidied up after Basal. The boy didn't like me before. He must detest me now. I detest myself.

When Loren started squalling, I went outside so Damut could nurse him in peace. I sat on the stoop until I thought I'd freeze. The lamp had been snuffed when I came in again. And Damut, feigning sleep, sniffled in the dark. I don't belong here.

518, 12/31. I apologized to Damut this morning. Told her I was testy because Cyril had expected me to return days ago.

"Don't want to risk losing your spot," she said with a shade of sarcasm, then asked about the kitchens. I told her nothing had changed. Maybe I should have mentioned Mira's troubles. Might have cheered her. But I'm not much of a gossip. I extolled her quince jelly instead, as I lathered it onto my third slice of her bread. Praise softened her. She poured more tea into my cup. "You going today?"

"I'll finish restacking the wood."

She correctly assumed I meant 'yes,' and asked me to stay longer. "Just till year's end. Go back Gurn First."

The way she phrased it reminded me of Col, the Blasphemer, and his predictions for year's end. I didn't repeat his forecast of doom to her, merely replied, "I'll think on it," but it was Col I thought about today.

The wood's restacked. I carried a week's worth to the temple. Tended the mare and pony. Spent more time outside than I should have. It's cold as a judge out there. My fingertips show early signs of frostbite. But I needed time alone. At dusk Damut called me in. I could smell squash baking, spiced with cinnamon and clove, could read the question of my staying in her eyes. She had a kettle of soup and hot bread for Calec and Malison. I picked up the kettle and, mumbling that I'd save him the trip, went out again.

Snow crunched underfoot as I walked to the temple. The blush of sunset had purpled. It would be a fine night for a ride. If I had winter clothing. Breathing warmth onto my hands, I quickened my pace as I returned to the cottage. "I'll stay," I told Damut, "till Gurn First."

I don't believe the world will end tomorrow night. I couldn't be that lucky. But if Col is correct and the dead will rise, what better place to be than a cemetery?

518, 12/32. A change in the weather. The day started cold as ever. A vicious wind woke me before dawn, banging at the shutters, howling over the flue. The noise woke Damut and her boys as well. She seemed frightened, but went about her morning chores so calmly, Basal was asleep again by daybreak. She sat at the table to nurse Loren. I finished my tea and stated I'd bring in wood. There was plenty already; I'd brought in extra yesterday, and filled every spare pot with snow, so there was plenty of water. But a full pot of snow shrinks to a mere third of water. I altered my statement, consolidated the water and went out with a pail.

I didn't get far. About two paces. With ice underfoot and that damn wind, I slammed onto my back and couldn't stand up again. I crawled back inside, strained to close the door and bolted it shut. "Windy?" Damut quipped.

"A bit," I laughed and returned to my seat, though I angled the chair to diminish my view of her. I've seen countless women nurse their children. I don't know why seeing her do it bothers me. She doesn't look like – like my partner. And the more I've seen Loren, the less he reminds me of my son. Still, it makes me uneasy.

The wind raged the whole day. There was little for me to do. Certainly not cooking. She tested me on it. She's run out of meat again and was looking through her stores, musing aloud, as if seeking advice about what to fix. I asked her if she had any cloth to spare. She turned around to gape at me, her face pretty with surprise. "Cloth? What for?"

I told her I'd like to make a pair of gloves. The idea amused her. She supplied a swath of wool felt, shoe quality, and her sewing kit. "Want me to make them?"

"I'll do it," I said. "You cook."

Sewing is not a craft I enjoy, but I can ply a needle. I learned the trade to get close to a clever bastard who had reneged on a deal with the Kinship. He knew he had erred and took elaborate precautions to evade retribution. His weakness lay in a fancy for high fashion. Fool.

Damut was impressed enough by my gloves to ask me to make her a pair, which I did, and mittens for Basal. Gave me something to do so I wouldn't intrude while she cooked, which may have been an error. She served a cheese and carrot concoction that was ... interesting.

I don't know why I'm rambling on about all this. None of it is of import. It seems I'm trying to focus on the beginning of the day to avoid thinking about its end. I'm half afraid to record what happened. Maybe I fear that once on the page, the incident will be over, finished, and I want to savor it, like warmed mead on a dry tongue. Or worse, maybe I fear that while finding the proper words to describe it, I'll realize nothing happened. The incident was sheer imagination. Ah, that's the pith of my fear. How much of reality is truly real and how much do our own minds create to satisfy our needs? But I know I'll eventually record it, so why delay?

As I've written, the day was windy and I stayed inside. Calec didn't show at dusk. It was hailing then. The pellets sounded like nails hitting the shutters. Damut reasoned aloud that he probably hadn't wanted to go out. She might have been hinting I should tote their food over. I was feeling guilty about not feeding the horses, but if I went out to do it, I was certain she'd openly ask me tote Calec's food, and I envisioned myself blown off my feet and wearing her carrots and cheese. I said nothing. "They probably yet have a bit of yesterday's soup," she added, again as if to herself. When I didn't comment, she let the matter drop, though she left the pot where the contents would stay warm.

It was past dark when the wind and hail stopped. The sudden quiet was more unnerving than the noise. Damut rushed Basal into bed. I donned my cloak and lit a lantern.

"Where you going?" she shrilled when she noticed me.

The high pitch of her voice jarred me and maybe it was her fright I sensed, but it became my own. Gloves on my hands made the moment seem even stranger as I gathered the pot of carrots. "For Calec and Malison."

She nodded, but, clearly, did not want me to leave her. She kept by my elbow as I walked to the door. When I opened it, I nearly bumped into a sheet of ice. I struck the ice with my fist, twice, before it shattered. The world outside was glass. I lifted the lantern and my gaze landed on the old quince. Trunk buried, its upper limbs sprawled atop the snow, dark yet glistening, like a fallen beast, wet with sweat, twisted in agony.

"Don't go out," Damut whispered.

"I won't be gone long," I assured her. I skated to the temple, pounded on the door and yelled for Calec. He finally cracked the door.

"What is it?" he hissed, visibly shaken, then snatched the pot.
"What's wrong?" I asked.
"Nothing," he lied, and the door thumped shut.

I slid to the stable. The pony tamely greeted me, but the mare was jumpy, snorting and stomping in the limited space. I fed them and damned myself for not bringing water. The little remaining from yesterday had frozen. I left the lantern there and started back to the cottage.

The moon had risen, thin as an eyelash. Not a single cloud marred the blaze of stars, which made me wonder where the hail had come from. I had reached the corner of the cottage when I heard – or imagined I heard – my name. Not Sheever. Me'acca. The voice was muffled and seemed to have come from across the road, in the common graveyard, or beyond, up in the trees. Col's prophecy about the hungry dead poisoned my courage. Hair on my nape stiffened as I stood listening. Silence lasted an eternity. Then a low moaning began, again from the west, seemingly from the trees at the upper border of the cemetery. Again I thought I heard my name, mixed in with the moaning. "Me'acca."

A sudden gale struck with such force it knocked me hard onto my seat – knocked my wits as well, for it took me an instant to realize the wind was hot. Not warm like a south breeze. Hot. Searing. Like a blast from a smelting oven. Ice, rapidly thawing, began cracking and popping around me. My instincts screamed for me to get up and run.

Before I could move, the temple door burst open and Malison strode out, hands raised as if to catch the wind. I couldn't see his face. Candlelight behind him provided little more than a silhouette. Calec lurched through the doorway and tried to stop the boy from going further by seizing him from behind, but yelped and let go.

Water from melting snow flooded the shoveled paths. Malison splashed a few steps toward the road, toward me, then halted and stretched upward. With the wind flapping his gown, I half expected him to leap up and fly.

Lightning streaked overhead, hundreds of flashes. The quick changes between light and dark dazzled my eyes to near blindness, yet I believe I saw the boy's hands afire with power, sparks snapping around his fingers. I closed my eyes and scanned him. And almost swooned. The force within him was immense, and at its core – pain. His, no doubt.

I broke the scan and shouted, "Stop!" A useless act. But no more so than Calec's. He wailed prayers, begging Loric to not harm the boy. His ranting may have fooled my ears, but I swear ... No, not swear. I thought I heard Malison cry, "Tyat!" Danger – in the old tongue.

A clap of thunder ended it all. The lightning vanished and the air cooled. Malison collapsed. Calec snatched him up and carried him into the temple. He refused to let me touch the boy, or even look him over.

I collected the lantern from the stable, then stood outside awhile. When memsen wield power, they leave a 'scent' of sorts. To a good sensitive, a memsa's scent is as clear as a signature. The scent I detected tonight was unlike any I've known.

Damut was crouched by the hearth when I entered the cottage. "My boy all right?" she asked, rising to meet me.

"Fine," I answered.

"What happened?" she breathed.

"A change in the weather," I said as casually as possible, but my voice failed to calm her. She wanted me to sleep in the bed tonight. There was space beside Basal, enough for us both, so I laid down with her, held her until she slept, then left her with her son.

How much of what I heard and saw tonight actually occurred? How much was colored by fright and imagination? I don't know. Nor can I decipher what, if anything, it means.

519, 1/1. This morning, and the new year, dawned cool, but not as cold as it has been, nor as hot as last night. Damut, keeping the deal we'd forged, didn't ask me to stay longer. She's too sly for that. She asked me to help her uncover the spring before I left, reasoning – correctly – that it would thaw faster if exposed to sunlight. The trick lay in finding the damn thing.

We went out at midmorning, leaving Basal to tend Loren. The snow was too soft to support us. On each step my foot would punch through and I'd sink up to my crotch. Damut, trailing me, had worse trouble than I. After fifty paces or so, I stopped to wait for her.

She halted as well. The skirts of her dresses were bunched up and sopping. "Can't you shovel me a path?"

"I can't shovel the whole world. Show me where the spring is, and I'll shovel a path from it to the cottage."

"I don't know where it is exactly." Hands against the snow for balance, she pulled one leg from a hole and swung it forward into the next. I caught a peek of her sagging stocking, her bare thigh, red with cold. I suppose I should have pitied her. But she expects too much of me. At least she had gloves.

When we neared the area, I let her stay put and direct me to where she thought the spring was. The first site, I'm sure, she knew was wrong. She just wanted a cleared spot to stand in. I dug down until I hit dirt, then she moved in. Sweat ran off me by the time I had dug the fourth hole. I stripped down to my shirt. By noon, I had uncovered six wrong guesses. I was working on the seventh when Calec came out and sat in the sun on temple's stoop, smoking his pipe.

I called to him, "How's Malison?"

He called in return, "Sleeping," which worried me.

I kept digging. As I – again – struck dirt, Damut uttered a warning, "Riders."

There were twenty, riding double file, the two in front breaking the way for others. A good third of them carried quivers and bows. One had a slain stag draped over his saddle. They were headed toward the temple – slowly, for the snow crested as high as their mounts' bellies. Writing of them took longer than it did to assess the danger. The sight of their bright blue tunics and white ram-and-star blazons set me in motion. But snow hindered me as well, and I knew they'd reach the temple before I would.

Calec rose onto his feet. I prayed he'd go inside. Instead, he waved his arms, as if to shoo off a swarm of hornets, and shouted, "Go away, you damned natals!"

Archers in the group veered out of the tight formation and cocked their bows.

"Don't shoot him!" I cried. In a blink, the archers aimed at me. I was thirty paces away, maybe less. Near enough for their aim to prove true. I froze in place and held up my empty hands. "We're not armed," I said, then, for some reason, repeated the statement in Universal.

The Drays purred to each other before one spoke to me, also in Universal, "You the Holy Man?"

"Why do you want to know?" I asked, which prompted another discussion. My chest remained a target as I continued toward Calec. I hoped the archers would cast a warning shot before firing one to hit. They let me scramble onto the stoop beside Calec, then addressed me again. The conversation that followed was tedious, tense and confusing. All they wanted was a prayer sent for Na-Kom Sarum. But the Dray who spoke

Universal wasn't fluent in the tongue. I couldn't always understand him. Nor would he just come out and ask for a prayer. He wanted to know about the temple, about Loric, and if a reverend was the same as a holy man. Each word we spoke had to be translated for his mates, just as I had to repeat everything for Calec.

When he finally asked for the prayer and I passed on the request, Calec flatly refused. "I'll not pray for some savage! Them Drays want to win the next Games, is all. I'll pray for Na-Kom Trivak, I will. You tell them so!"

I smiled at the natals, at the archers who had not once diverted their aim from my chest, and said, "The Reverend will be happy to pray for Na-Kom Sarum's good health."

They left the stag and a fat wineskin as payment, which made Calec doubt I had 'told them proper.' I swore to Loric I had, and suggested they had hoped the gifts would change his mind. "Fools," he called them, and I agreed. We sat together on the stoop. I assumed his knees felt as weak as mine, though now I think perhaps not. His faith is strong enough he probably believed Loric would protect him. I, however, needed to sit, as the natals rode off.

Damut brought over my tunic and cape. (I hadn't realized how cold I was until I took them from her grasp.) She voiced her pleasure with the stag. "We've meat again!"

"We're not to eat it," Calec blurted, then caught his slip and nudged me. "Tell her, Sheever. It were tainted. This too." He poked the wineskin with a wool-covered toe. "Tainted. Tell her. And tell her she weren't to be coming over here neither. Her place weren't here."

I didn't need to tell Damut. She walked back to the cottage. I lingered. I wanted to find out if Malison had been damaged last night, but getting information from Calec was more difficult than chatting with the Drays. He told me nothing until I said I planned to leave today.

"The boy's hands were sore," he offered, "frostbit. If he had gloves like yours ... Where'd you get them gloves?"

I told him I had made them. He asked me to stay long enough to make Malison a pair. I pulled off the gloves. "Give the boy these. Better yet, bring him out to try them on, so I can see if they fit."

Calec took the gloves inside, shut the door, and a few moments later came out again – alone. "It would mean a lot to the boy if you'd stay through Gurn Four."

"Did he just tell you that?"

"Mean a lot," Calec repeated, then gave me a razor. "Need a shave, you do. Look like a stinking savage."

I breathed a curse – after he went in – then dragged the stag behind the stable, skinned and dressed it. Nosing through the Wessel trash, I found a crate and used it to pack the meat in snow. I left it in the stable, then brought the wineskin into the house and set it on the table.

Damut didn't comment on the wine, nor anything else. We dined in silence. Basal toted food to the temple and returned with dirty pots. I offered to clean them. "No," Damut said through tight lips, "it weren't your place."

I sat by the hearth while she nursed Loren. When he fell asleep, she put Basal to bed. Then swooped down on me. "You're staying." A statement, not a question.

"If it isn't too much trouble."

Her mouth twitched. She was spoiling for a fight. "Where'd you learn that foreign talk?"

I told her Universal wasn't foreign. "Mearans speak it every day in Tiarn."

"Not no cooks, they don't. Where'd you learn it?"

"My father taught me. A scribe, he was."

"Scribe? I heard he were a smithy."

Obviously, she had listened to the gossips in Trivak's kitchens, but I'd spouted so many lies over the years, I had no idea what she knew, or thought she knew. I told her my father had been a smith until a horse kicked him and broke his arm. "Needed a new trade, he did."

"Is that so." She hauled a stool over, plunked herself onto it and stared at me. "You wasn't born in Eastland, was you? You ever even been there?"

The belief that liars always avert their gaze is a myth. I met her stare dead on. "I was born in Eastland. I haven't been there in years though. No doubt the city's changed by now."

"Eastland don't change much. Know that shop on Baker's Street? The one with the yellow slipper tacked over the door? That slipper's been there forty years or more."

I blocked a laugh. "Your memory is better than mine. I remember that slipper as red."

She blinked, looked away, then stood. "You've been there. That don't prove nothing."

Her probing continued while she scrubbed the pots and tonight's dishes. I did well with landmarks, and explained my ignorance of people she named by saying we'd simply had a different circle of friends – which certainly was true.

"You don't recall my husband Mali? You must have heard of him. Every cook in Eastland heard of Mali Baker."

It would have been easy to say I had at least heard of him, but smelling a trap, I shook my head. "Sorry. I must have left Eastland before he became famous."

"Mali were older than you, Sheever. He were famous before you was born."

I suppose that was the trap. My falling into it seemed to satisfy her. She hushed until she wiped the table. "Them Dray natals," she said as she sopped up melted snow that had dripped off the wineskin, "why do you think they stopped by today when they never did before?"

Good question. Maybe the odd weather had unnerved them as it had everyone else. Drays pray to so many gods, it must be easy for them to adopt another, even a foreign one. I thought this was as good an answer as any, and I gave it to Damut. Clever woman. She had set another trap. "How come you know so much about Drays?"

Common knowledge in Evald is not common here. "I don't know nothing special. Just heard the same gossip as you."

"I never heard gossip about them having a slew of gods." She rinsed her cloth, squeezed out water, then dried her hands on her dress. "Don't you trust me, Sheever?"

Instead of an answer, I told her about the venison in the stable. "If you don't want to eat it, I'll toss it. But I thought it would be good for our Gurn Four dinner."

"You're staying?" Her smile, which bloomed when I nodded, withered when I repeated what Calec told me. "You're staying for Malison," she stated, then huffed, "We'll eat the stag. Tainted or no. Don't matter to me. I'm tainted as is." Shortly thereafter, she went to bed.

Is she jealous of my interest in her son? It's I who should be jealous – of Malison. He's caught the eye of someone with power. Yet it's pity I feel. People with power don't care if they harm those of us who lack it. The boy is nothing more than a lute being played. But by whom?

It would be comforting to believe a memsa, especially Sythene, knows I'm here. And it's possible the memsa by the way station told another of her ilk where she had sent me. But it's unlikely. She didn't know my name and didn't ask. I was simply another sinner to her, gone from her mind the moment I left her presence. Memsen don't care.

So why would one expend so much energy last night just to warn me? Is that truly what happened? If so, what was I being warned about? The surprise visit of the Dray natals? There was danger there, but surely not enough to warrant such a deluge of power. Memsen don't waste power. Overuse can suck the life from them. Last night doesn't make sense.

It's arrogant of me to assume the display was the work of a memsa, or meant for me. I should learn from the Drays. If I believe Dynnas exists, how can I say other gods don't? And if Calec believes Loric is favoring Malison, who am I to say he's wrong? My hearing 'danger' in the old tongue isn't difficult to explain. I didn't hear it. I thought it. And hearing my name whispered on the wind? Imagination.

I glanced at the wineskin. I'm too tired to be tempted. I still need to shave. My clothes are stained with stag's blood. I am, as Calec said, a stinking savage. But I'm too tired to care.

519, 1/2. The snow has been turning directly into vapor. Fog as thick as Damut's porridge hid the quince from view when I went out this morning. I used my own devices to locate the spring and found it on the first try. A stiff kick broke the ice seal. Fresh water gushed out.

I dug the path I had promised Damut, then led the horses out and gave the stall a good scrubbing. (The mare did stray, but I had more wits today. I tethered her to Calec's pony. They didn't roam far.) I carried wood and did any other sweaty chore I could think of. All the while Damut was heating water – lots of it.

A chunk of ice filled the rain barrel, but the chunk was loose and floating. With effort, I emptied the barrel, and it was into there Damut was pouring the hot water. When I had finished the chores, the barrel was full and steaming. I shucked my clothes and climbed in. Such bliss.

Damut was intrigued. "What if somebody was to come by? Them Dray natals maybe. What if they was to come back?"

"They won't," I stated. It was evening by then and the fog had gotten thicker during the day. "Or if they do, so what? What're they going to see?" I sank under the water, then bobbed up again. "You should try this, woman."

"Me!" She feigned shock, but the idea had occurred to her. She simply lacked the courage to act on it. "I can't do nothing like that. Not," her voice dropped to a whisper, "naked. I haven't been naked since I were born."

She picked up my clothes, saying she'd wash them, and took them inside, but soon came out again, offering a quilt to cover my nakedness until my clothes dried. She left the quilt on a snowbank, went in and came out, this time to offer a mirror the size of her palm. "So you won't cut yourself with the razor."

The mirror was glass. There was no place to set it. I asked her to hold it for me. She hesitated, as if afraid to get too close to a naked man, or to the barrel itself. "Don't you trust me?" I asked in the same tone she had used when asking me the question last night.

"No," she admitted, then edged closer, eyes pinched shut, mirror stretched out like a shield against evil. My reflection, so much clearer than in the brass mirror in the men's privy, shocked me. I've aged. I stared at the crisp image though the sight stole my joy.

"What's wrong?" she prompted.

"Nothing." I lathered my beard, then commented on the mirror being glass and jested, "Sure you're from Eastland?"

"Sure, I'm sure." Her eyes slitted open. "Mali bought me the mirror. From the Snakes." She spoke so earnestly, as if I truly doubted her origin, that I laughed, regaining my humor – then Calec stepped out of the fog. He had trekked over to collect his food and wasn't pleased with what he found. "Tell my wife," he scolded, "that she weren't supposed to have that foreign mirror no more. You tell her that her lie were found out."

She fled into the house. I made excuses for her. "You told me to shave, Reverend. I needed the mirror to see."

He grunted. "Never heard of a man who got naked just to clean off his beard." He took the razor from me, tipped my head and shaved my jaw. "Damut, she gets lonely out here. Don't blame her. And you out here, young as you are. Don't blame you neither. Loric forgives."

I hissed when he nicked me. "Let me do it."

"Be still!" He pushed my head back, and I held my breath as the razor scraped under my chin. "Don't blame her nor you. Don't want it shoved in my face is all."

My face was raw when he finished with it. I suppose I should be thankful he didn't slit my throat. I told him nothing was going on between Damut and me.

"Hush!" he commanded when Basal brought out food. He calmed to say, "Just set it down, boy," and waited for him to go inside, then railed at me, "I don't want her boys spying nothing!"

After Calec left, I stayed in the barrel. I wished the fog would clear so I could see the stars, wished Damut would bring out a lantern so I could see my way to the door. The air turned frosty and the water chilled. I groped for the quilt, stubbed my toe finding the door. Food waited on the table for me. My clothes, still wet, hung from a cord stretched between hooks in the rafters. Damut and her sons were asleep. I should leave this place.

519, 1/3. Damut woke in a sour mood. She banged around the cottage, making more noise than necessary, chucking wood into her stove, slapping pots onto its top. She flung hot bread onto my plate, slopped porridge into bowls for her and Basal, then scowled at the wineskin still on the table where I'd put it days ago. "You ever going to drink that?"

"Only if you drink it with me."

She shook a spoon at me. "I'm a reverend's wife, Sheever, case you forgot."

I glanced at Basal, wondering if he remained loyal to his mother or served as a spy for Calec. I decided to err on the side of caution and would have said nothing, but Damut refused to let the matter rest. "Foreign wine," she grumped, "probably no good anyhow."

"Drays make the best wine in the world," I stated.

"That something you learned in Eastland? Were it your smithy father who learned you? Or your father the scribe?"

"My tongue learned me. Pity yours didn't learn to be quiet." That shushed her, but she began to weep, quietly, as though if she didn't sob aloud, I wouldn't notice her tears, wouldn't scold her again. I got up from my seat.

Fog cloaked me as I went to the stable. I fed the pony and saddled the mare. She was eager to stretch her legs. Beyond the paths though, the snow was deep and the going rough. When I tried to force her up the trail the natals had broken, she balked, so I let her stop and just sat her. I wasn't angry with Damut. Merely tired of the way Calec treats her. Tired of her pathetic attempts to grip a shred of dignity. Tired of it all. And guilty as well, for I'm the one who brought her here. I'm to blame. When will I learn to stop toying with other people's lives?

I turned the mare and rode back to the stable. Damut was there, stag haunch in her grasp, soiling her gloves. "Thought you'd gone," she murmured, then started an apology.

I cut her off, "Don't. There's no need." I led the mare into the pony's stall. Damut hung around me, as if to watch, while I stripped off the saddle.

"My boy Malison could use a bit of meat. If Calec thought you'd caught us a deer ..." She had already devised a ruse, but needed me as an accomplice. I suppose it's a sin to lie to a reverend. In my view, however, he's to blame for her duplicity. And one more sin added to my soul hardly matters. After I agreed to abet her, she cooed, "If that Dray wine's good as you say, I'd not mind a taste of it."

I doubted she wanted even a drop. Duplicity has become a mode of survival for her. I considered suggesting we dump the wine, but couldn't compel my mouth to utter the words, so I forged a deal with her. "I'll match you cup for cup."

We returned to the cottage together. Basal was playing with Loren, trying to teach his young brother to speak new words. His patience is endless. Loren's babble is indecipherable to me, though Basal and Damut seem to understand it. The boys entertained each other while she and I prepared tomorrow's feast. I'm certain she thought I'd take charge. I did nothing unless assigned a task. Having no butter or cream limited what could be made, and frustrated her. But the aroma of roasting venison lightened her mood. Plus she enjoyed bossing me.

I carried a pot of stew to the temple and told Calec I'd borrowed his bow and shot a deer.

"Thought I heard you out riding this morning," he said, tipping the lid. Steam blurred his toothless grin. "Now weren't this better than that tainted meat them Drays tried to pass off on us?" Does the belief that something is pure make it so?

I learned nothing of Malison. Calec was even more reticent about the boy than he's been, if that's possible. He made me swear I'd be here tomorrow and, after I did, he shut the door.

Soon as I got back, Damut told me to fetch water. I hesitated (we didn't need it) and her mantle of control slipped. "It might be foggy in the morning," she expounded.

"It's foggy now and getting dark." But I picked up two buckets and went to the spring.

She met me on the stoop when I returned. "Sheever, I want me a bath tonight."

I made several trips to the spring. After we'd eaten and her boys were abed, she created excuses for changing her mind such as a bath would be too much trouble, or it was too cold. She was afraid of the dark, afraid of getting caught, afraid to have me out there with her, afraid to be out there alone. I let her fret – and continued heating water and filling the barrel. When it was ready, we crafted rules. I'd stand guard with my back to her, the lantern behind me, and there would be no conversation and no peeking. I confess I broke my word on that part. I wanted to see if she had cheated by wearing an underdress. Her marriage bracelets were all she had on.

She didn't stay in the water as long as I had last night. But afterward, as she raced behind me for the door, she laughed like a thief who'd just stolen a crown.

I waited until she summoned me in. She had donned the patchwork dress, but her feet were bare, her hair a wet mat soaking her shoulders. "Don't want you catching cold," she said in a rush, still excited over what she'd done. She fairly floated to the table where she'd already poured two cups of wine. She gulped hers down, then coughed, "Good."

The wine was excellent, a dash of woodruff perfecting its flavor. "Don't drink this one so fast," I cautioned as I poured her another. "There's nothing to prove." We carried our cups to the hearth and sat on the floor. She had a comb and started tugging at tangles in her hair. It hurt my eyes to watch. I took the comb.

There's something intimate about teasing snarls from a woman's hair. And for me, erotic. When I first became a list master, I'd stop by after clients had gone, as did most listmen.

Unlike them, I didn't go to collect payments. The brothids would be fresh from their baths, warm and scented, clad in loosely bound robes. I combed their hair to relish the smell of them, and catch glimpses of what clients had paid for. The fetish amused my brothids, but when I was older, busier, and more versed in ways of sharing pleasure, a few of them would – on occasion – still ask me to comb their hair. And if I had the time, I happily obliged.

Damut wore no perfume. The dress offered no glimpses. Her hair is long and thick. Not glorious. Yet begging to be pampered. She was skittish when I took the comb, as if I planned to stab her with it. When I separated a lock of hair, her back tensed. I eased tangles from the end, moved up a little, then a little more, seducing the lock until the comb ran smoothly along its length. Her spine melted. Her hands lay limp in her lap.

"Sheever," she purred, "you ever miss Eastland?"

"Sometimes," I lied, choosing the next lock to seduce.

She sighed. "I miss it every day."

We spoke in whispers so we wouldn't wake Basal and Loren. She did most of the talking, about her parents, her two brothers and her husband, Mali. Her life had been nothing like mine. She was a baker's daughter, her marriage to Mali part of a deal to get her younger brother a spot at the Double-Ox Inn. Yet I was struck by the fact that, like me, she longed for her past, for her home. "Mali were famous," she praised.

Perhaps. But the man was a fool. I remember before the Games, when Cyril went into Tiarn looking for cooks to hire. News of his search spread as far as Eastland, but became twisted by gossips. Mali believed he'd be paid a daekah each month to bake for the High Lord. Greed lured him from the safety of the D.O. Greed claimed his life.

I shouldn't be so harsh. The man wanted more coin to support his family, to buy Damut more trinkets like the mirror. He took a risk and lost. The only difference between him and me is I risked more – and when I lost, others paid the cost. His wife is alive to mourn him. Which of us is the better man?

Wanting more seems to be a flaw common to humankind. We are never satisfied with what we have. If I were suddenly transported back to Evald and had everything I once had, would I be satisfied? I wasn't when I had it all before. Will there ever be a day when I look around me and no matter how much or how little I have, it will be enough? Acceptance. Is that what I was exiled to learn? The lesson may be impossible for me to master.

Damut hasn't learned it. In the kitchens, she had food and warmth. She wanted safety and a new husband. She has both now, but they're no longer enough. Tonight she again spoke of getting a cow. I had finished with her hair and we were sipping wine, when she voiced her desire for fresh cream. "If I had me a cow. And some chickens maybe ..."

She stretched out on her side and propped up her head with a hand. Her left arm nested in the dip of her waist. "If I'd a way to get my pies to the markets ..." Dreams shimmered in her eyes. Her hair flowed over her breasts into a pool, and firelight gave it the illusion of luster.

While she babbled about pastries, I imagined unhooking the miss-matched buttons on her dress. In Evald it would be a capital offense for a Mule like me to couple with a Vic woman. Tonight, the illegality of the act spurred my fantasy. She would remind me that she was Calec's wife. And then, her morals supple with wine, a sweet surrender. I imagined her nude in the flickering light. Imagined the taste of her. The warmth of her body molded against mine.

She disrupted my musing, lifting her gaze from the fire to ask, "What're you thinking?"

I smiled. She was never in danger of being spoiled by my touch. Though my mind burned with desire, my corpse of a body did not. "I was thinking you should teach Basal to cook. Then when he's older ..." I shrugged. "Who knows?"

She sat up, aroused by fresh dreams. "He could get himself a spot at a bakery in Tiarn! If I only had ..."

Tonight was a night for fantasies.

519, 1/4. I've become complacent. Dangerously so. I believed I could always pass as Mearan. Understandable. I've spoken Mearan for so long now that, at times, I catch myself thinking in that damn language. Speaking the tongue, perfecting the common accent is not enough. In the kitchens, it's easy to blend. Flaws go unnoticed in twilight. Staying with the Wessels is akin to being seen under a noon sun.

It would be easy to sleep. I'm tired. The cottage is quiet, Damut and her sons abed. Peaceful. The hearth fire is warm, comforting after a cold day. Rushes of alarm that flooded me earlier have all subsided. Exhaustion fills the void. Sleep would come quickly. Yet if I value my life, I must examine the issue now, before more errors are made.

Note: I cannot rely on my knowledge of Mearan culture, knowledge gleaned from Mearan Vics in Evald and from my experiences in Trivak's kitchens. In Evald, Mearans have been cut off from their motherland. Their customs have been warped from centuries of rubbing against other cultures. And the people in Trivak's kitchens may not reflect typical Mearan behavior as I once thought.

Example: my father always celebrated a new year on the First, as did all Vics I knew. There was nothing religious about it. People from all faiths gathered together. Men got drunk, women complained, and children stuffed themselves with sweets. It seemed more or less the same in Trivak's kitchens. True, it was on a different day, and they put out their fires at noon – something no one in

Sheever's Journal, Diary of a Poison Master

Evald would do in winter. But I assumed the way they celebrated Gurn Four, everyone gorging themselves from noon on, was how all lowland Mearans did. Not so at Reverend Wessel's house.

My problem extends beyond this, however. I must appear friendly. Yet I cannot actually care. Caring breeds errors. Though I didn't come to Tiarn to spy, if I'm caught, no one would believe otherwise.

Today bears evidence of my sloppy actions. The day began awkwardly. Damut overslept. When Loren began to whimper, I rolled his crib to the hearth before he could wake her. Candied carrots kept him content. Basal was less easy to satisfy. "I'm hungry," he whined, but refused to touch any food prepared yesterday. He threatened to create a ruckus when I told him I shouldn't use Damut's stove. Imbecile. I should have let him wake her. Instead, I fried him skillet cakes over the hearth fire. It's an old recipe, and a simple one, taught to me by a Snake back when I was learning how to manage without servants.

I didn't think twice when Basal grumbled that he hadn't had them before. I smeared them with quince jelly, rolled them so they could be held, and smiled when, after his first bite, he too seemed content. It's wrong to write I didn't think twice. I didn't think at all. Skillet cakes are not a Mearan dish.

My error became evident when Damut woke. She had slept in her dress and got up in a rush, hair loose and wild about her face. Maybe being the last up unsettled her. Maybe she was anxious about the day's feast, for nearly everything needed a bit of heating. Who knows. But she focused on the skillet cakes. She had seen them before – no doubt being munched by Snakes. She didn't say this, nor did she utter a single question about them.

"You don't want these," she told Basal and took the cakes from him. "I'll fix you porridge." Her back seemed stiff enough to break as she bent to open the stove door.

I went to the stable, grabbed a pail, and headed for the spring. The fog, which has persisted for days, had thinned slightly. I saw Calec, like a ghost in the mist, as he left the temple and punched through the soft snow to join me. "Fetching water, eh," he stated.

I thought it a good time to repeat my opinion that Damut was overworked and he should hire someone to help her. Another error. I should stay out of their affairs.

He nodded, as if agreeing, but he had his own agenda. "Been praying. Now I see Loric's plan." Determined to relay his insight, he held me hostage by the spring while he prattled on. I set down the pail and snugged my cape, hoping the damp air would chill him before it did me.

The pith of his epic spun on the betrayal of his first wife and their daughters. The Wessel family, saving not only generations of trash but also coin, had accumulated what he considered a fortune, which he inherited. And though his family had lost favor with the Crown, the wealth proved Loric remained pleased with centuries of devotion. Then 'his girls' ran off, taking the fortune with them. The fact Loric allowed this tragedy to occur disillusioned Calec. He slacked off on his holy duties, doing the bare minimum, and fell into a slovenly style of living.

"A lapse of faith," he said and nudged my shoulder as if to rouse me, for I had pulled up the hood of my cape and was watching snow soak his felt shoes. "A lapse. Then Loric sends you, His servant, to lead me back to Him. I didn't see His mark on you that night when you come knocking, asking for a cooking pot. Near ready to poison yourself, you were."

I looked up at him then, remembering the mushroom dinner he'd spoiled, which added to the moment's irritation. I assumed the purpose of the conversation was to convince me to stay permanently. "I'm not Loric's servant, Reverend. I'm a cook in the High Lord's kitchens."

"Yes, go on," he urged, "confess. Loric forgives."

I know Mearans can buy absolution. It was a facet of their faith my father never utilized. "Not worth the cost," he'd say and, considering the number of Juboe's crimes, he was probably correct. The price of unburdening his soul would have been enormous. I never heard of anyone being absolved without payment. Nothing in Evald is free.

Calec, however, didn't seem to want coin. Indeed, his expression bewildered me the most, neither pious nor greedy, yet with a glint of anticipation, as if he already knew my sins. I told him I had nothing to confess. "It's Gurn Four," he prompted, as if a reminder of the date would loosen my tongue. "Loric's Day."

I shrugged, completely baffled, though I soon wished I had confessed to something, for he continued talking about his "lapse" and how he would not make the same error with Damut as he had with his first wife, to whom he had bestowed numerous gifts and liberties. He believes women are weak by nature, easily gulled into sinful desires and vulnerable to the lure of foreign amusements. I envisioned him retracting Damut's stove, which I'm sure was crafted in Verdina.

"Balance," I recommended, using Sythene's favorite hedge, "it's all about balance. A girl needs some fancies, or she'll wander off for certain."

"Could be right," he mused, rubbing his jaw.

I spied my chance and wandered off myself, citing chores as an excuse. I spent extra time grooming the mare so she'll pass the inspection Jenner's bound to give her. I also wanted to concoct a lie for Damut. She's brighter than most and not likely to swallow a prickly falsehood. Wrong. Even as I record the day's events, I'm exposing my flaws. Damut is no less a fool than anyone else. The truth is I've become too fond of her. I didn't want to feed her a lie.

Despite the extra time in the stable, it was well before noon when I returned to the cottage. I froze in the doorway. Calec was inside, standing between two chairs positioned in front of the hearth. His presence was enough to elicit surprise. Odder still, he seemed to be engaged in direct conversation with Damut. But what stunned me was the fact he held my journal, open in his grasp. Idiot. How could I have left such damning evidence lying about?

He flicked a page as he glanced up and saw me. "What sort of writing is this, Sheever?"

The fire behind him had died down, but I half-hoped he'd toss my journal onto the hot coals. "It's in code," I lied. "Don't want nobody stealing my recipes."

"Mali done his the same," Damut said. She was by the bed, twisting her hair into a bun.

I don't know why she opted to defend me. But the edge in her voice hinted that I had interrupted an argument.

Calec closed the book. With a finger, he traced the gold crescent on its cover and I held my breath, wondering if he recognized the symbol, then he returned the journal to its box and put it back on the mantel. "The dress you bought my wife were too tight."

"Baz sent the dress," I clarified, trying to calm my unease and make sense of the situation. More was happening than I could readily perceive. "It were her daughter's."

Note: I cannot afford to continue relying on the ignorance of others.

Damut slipped her cream-colored dress over her new one, donned her bonnet, and moved to the stove, the dutiful wife. Calec extracted Loren from the crib and sat with him in one of the chairs. Basal knelt on the floor by Calec's feet. It was all so strange. Everyone seemed to know his place. Calec motioned for me sit in the other chair. "Long ago," he said as soon as I complied, "men ruled the days. And demons ruled the nights." With that as a prelude, he recounted a religious fable, something about an ill-fated pact that led to mass starvation.

In retrospect, I should have paid attention. The story may have relayed the spiritual foundation of Gurn Four. I can't blame Calec. Like most purveyors of religion, he can weave a good tale. Basal stretched up from the floor, competing with Loren for Calec's lap, and listened with mouth agape, as if hoping the words would fall onto his own tongue. And Damut, loading the table, often paused to hear various parts. But my mind ran along a different path.

The errors I made today, if made when I was Soehn Biehr, would have been fatal. I could not relax. What if Damut had shared her suspicions with Calec? What if he had only pretended to not read Universal? Or if he had recognized the symbol of Evald's Royal House? I could only guess how long he'd been in the cottage. Perhaps he'd gone there directly after we'd spoken at the spring. Perhaps Damut had steered him to the journal. Perhaps her defense of me had merely been a ruse. And most critical to my worry, Malison was not present, nor had anyone mentioned him. A logical assumption was he had been sent to fetch troopers.

I remained seated, even though I expected the door to burst in at any moment, but I could not listen to Calec.

"A miracle!" he exclaimed, clapping his hands and jarring me into reality. "From thin air foods of all kinds appeared. And Loric says, 'Let the feast begin!'"

The end of his tale led to the meal. Calec brought Loren with him to the table and both of them gummed the soft meat Damut had boiled especially for her husband. Concern numbed my appetite. Damut and Calec chatted amicably about mundane issues, problems caused by the weather and such.

It was all too normal for my imagination to accept. Wouldn't I, too, be pleasant to hold a naive target at ease while I readied the blade? Rapport or manners mean little. I thought of Tarok who had marked his own brother-by-law for death. Of Ayros, the most affable and deadly innkeeper in Meara. How could I believe the Wessels were mere innocents?

Calec uttering my name snared my attention. He was talking to Basal, scolding him mildly for not helping his mother more. "You don't want Sheever sending some kitchen boy here to take your place, do you?"

"No," Basal mumbled, his mouth smeared with honey glaze from raisin clusters. "But horses don't like me."

"I'll tend the pony," Damut said.

"No, I will," Calec stated. "You have enough to do." He wagged a finger at Basal. "Loric watches. So be good in the coming year. Never forget who brings us the miracle feast. When we forget, we let night into our hearts."

As if on cue, Damut stood. She doused the stove and hearth fires, sending up hissing clouds of steam, then moved around the room snuffing lights until only a single lamp on the table remained burning. Calec pinched it out. "In the dark of night," he intoned, "demons roam free."

"Loric save us!" Basal shouted – piercingly – again and again. He was never truly frightened. Damut opened the door and, when light from outside seeped in with the mist, he was grinning. The whole family, it seemed, was acting in a play. I alone didn't know my role.

The cottage cooled rapidly. While Damut washed up Basal, Calec asked me what I expected in the new year. I said I hadn't given it much thought, the worst possible answer, but I had yet to grasp the tradition of Gurn Four.

Damut, under the auspices of tidying the table, fluttered around us like a moth, as Calec salted me with questions about my family. I quickly gathered he wanted to know if I had been raised properly, believing in Loric. I told him my parents hadn't been strict.

"That explains the whole apple." He deviated into politics, cursing the Eshra Church and the High Lord for the deterioration of morals in today's families. "Them Trivaks don't give no example for good Mearan folk to follow."

His faintly seditious words relieved me. This was not a man bound to the State. Worry of imminent arrest vanished and – finally – I understood. On Gurn Four, Mearans confess their sins and promise to do better in the new year. He asked if I had ever had a lapse in faith.

"Many times," I replied, wondering how he'd rank acts of murder.

He tapped my chest. "Must be dark in there."

I nodded and told him I'd lost my faith completely.

He smiled, satisfied. "You wait. Tonight'll be special. Loric Hisself is coming. You'll find your faith." He didn't stay much longer. Taking a platter Damut had prepared for Malison, he directed us to pray for Loric to 'chase them demons' from our hearts.

After he'd gone, I went out and sat on the stoop. It was brighter there and no less cold than inside. Toward sunset Damut, wrapped in a blanket, joined me. "Both boys are asleep," she said, as if I should care. We sat quietly, neither of us comfortable with the other, as the fog blushed and gloom settled in. When it was too dark to see, she tried to cross the gap separating us. "Calec says I can keep my mirror. Did you tell him to?"

"No," I said, though my advice at the spring may have swayed him. "He wants you to be happy here."

"Here," she grunted, "is my punishment. I'll never escape this graveyard. I can never fix the sin."

Once more today I was baffled. And if pricking my curiosity was a ploy to engage me in conversation, it worked. I did uncover the answer. Her sin was she had left her dead husband, unburied, on the road. Living among graves, seeing them daily as a reminder is, according to Calec, her penance. If she stays until she dies, Loric will forgive her 'lapse.' Her other option is to find and bury Mali's bones – an impossible task.

In my opinion, Calec is using guilt to keep her here, an abuse of his religious power. Not that memsen have never abused power to gain personal ends. My exile may be proof of such abuse, especially if my mother was involved in it.

"If I were Mali," I offered, "I would've wanted you to snatch up the boys and run. You did right. A body can rot above ground as easy as under it." Even this was an error. To a Mearan, the soul of an unburied corpse is damned.

As if to remind me of the culture, she probed, "You'd choose to spend eternity in the Netherworld?"

"To keep my wife and children safe? In a heartbeat."

"Mali," she sniffled, "he'd not feel the same. He always said he'd be Loric's top baker after he died."

"Then he was a fool." Using the topic to correct this morning's blunder, I heaped blame on the dead and questioned Mali's decision to journey without an escort. "Snake caravans travel to and fro often enough. They don't charge much for tag-alongs. And nobody robs the Snakes."

"You ever done it?" she breathed. "Ride with Snakes?"

"Where'd you think I learned to fry skillet cakes?"

A nervous laugh exposed her relief. "You did have me wondering on that." She scooted closer to me. "We was going to ride with Snakes, had it all set, but Mali weren't sure of them. And when border troopers said they was on their way here and would take us for no charge ..." Her voice trailed off and I strained to see her in the dark.

"You had a troop escort and were still attacked?"

She leaned against me and I put an arm around her, as she expected. "Them troopers was the ones who done it."

I can't afford to feel compassion for this woman.

The same is true for Calec. He returned with Malison, before midnight most likely, but late enough. They came waving torches and chanting warnings to any demons who might be slinking about. Malison, playing the role of Loric, performed a quaint ceremony before he lit the kindling Damut had placed in the hearth. I can't recall his words. I was too busy scanning him. His hands are tender (he wore my gloves) but not badly damaged. Of more import, there was no presence surging in him. He was merely a boy, a bit worried about forgetting the proper words.

Damut virtually blazed with pride. Not so Calec. His disappointment stank like rancid butter. He wanted a show, lightning and power, as it had been the other night. He wanted to be able to say, "There's proof Loric exists."

I was still in a scanning mode when my gaze landed on Basal. Roused from sleep, the boy was awestruck by his brother's portrayal of a god. Maybe religion is more suited to children. I wish I could believe as I once did.

I blunted my purpose by rambling on. The evidence, though, is on every page. I've lost my perspective. I cannot forget my oath. Ever. Each member of the Wessel family is a citizen of Meara. According to law, each of them is a Vic. Likeable or not, they are my sworn enemies.

519, 1/5. I'm here again. In the kitchens. Arrived before noon. I caught Jenner chatting with two of his stable hands, the three of them huddled together like plotting thieves.

He rushed over to me. "We thought you was dead!" He ordered his men to tend the mare without giving her so much as a glance. "Talk to Cyril yet?"

I told him I had not. "Something I should know?"

"No, nothing." Jenner will never be a good liar. I could've pried the truth from him, but was tired from staying up late last night. I guessed Cyril had hired another cook to replace me and fumed as I trudged up to the kitchens.

The dining hall was a shambles, as always on Gurn Five. A few women were tidying up from yesterday's revelry. I went straight to Cyril's room, didn't bother to knock. One of the scullery girls was in bed with him. I shook him, cursing, "Damn you, wake up."

He blinked, rubbed his face, then greeted me as Jenner had, "We thought you was dead."

I was in no mood to dance around the matter. "Did you hire someone to fill my spot?"

"Loric's Fire. Where would I get me another cook with all this snow about?"

"Fine," I said, my temper cooling. "Then I'm to bed." Coming in here was like falling into a hole. I stowed my journal, then dropped onto my cot. Dreamed of Juboe. We were in the lake house, but it wasn't the usual dream. He was at a desk, pen in hand, a stack of warrants before him. "If you don't want these signed," he said, "just tell me."

"And the price?" I asked.

He smiled, that damn confident smile which cut his face whenever he knew he'd trapped me. "A favor is all." I woke with a start, my heart pounding, and for an instant, I smelled the corrupt stench of him, here in the dark with me. I scrambled out into the hall.

Most of the cooks and a handful of women were lolling about in the dining room, nearly all looking the worse for wear. Seeing them seemed strange. No, that isn't correct. Recognizing them seemed strange. I felt out of place, as though I'd been away years instead of a week. I wondered how I could know these people. They were all gaping stupidly as if wondering the same about me. Cyril handed me last month's pay. I gave him a copper back and uttered, "Ale."

"A copper's worth?" he questioned.

"Fetch it," I ordered.

Cyril laughed, "You must've gone dry."

I drank Baz-style, standing, gulping straight from the pitcher, not caring the room was silent, everyone watching. Finished, I had Cyril fill it again. As I started to guzzle the second pitcher, Old Wix squeaked, "Sheever." White hair, watery eyes, he reminded me of a Vic Councilman I'd murdered. "Is all well with Calec and Damut?"

"Calec's fine. Damut and her boys are fine." The resistance suddenly snapped – like a tight sock, once over the heel, rolls smooth – and I donned the proper role. "Stuffed me with religion, Calec did. Spent the whole of yesterday praying. Not a drop of nothing worth drinking."

Old Wix cackled. "Missed all the excitement, you did."

"Hush." His son poked him with an elbow. "We was tolt to say nothing to nobody."

"Sheever's not nobody," Cyril argued, "he's one of us." Dam loosened, the flood followed. My ears were the only fresh ones and every voice wanted to fill them. Filson gave the best accounting which, simmered down, is this: Nulan is dead and Col has been arrested.

The death occurred at year's end. Col and Nulan were performing a show similar to the one I saw, a mock battle between Krich and Loric. According to Filson: "Nobody was doing no harm when a fierce storm comes out of nowheres and we starts to panic cause we knowed Krich, he'd broke down them Gates, and somebody shouts we should kill Loric so ..." Somebody did. Col was arrested the next morning, on the First, though no one saw him deliver the fatal blow. By afternoon, Eshra priests were snooping about.

I wanted that part clarified. "They were here, in the kitchens? Asking what, exactly?"

All agreed the priests had been here, four of them, interrogating each fool who'd been to the yards – ever, even on nights other than the murder night. All agreed they had been taken one by one into Cyril's room and questioned in private. And all said they'd been told to keep quiet. But not a soul could recall a single question asked. Mind probes? I'd wager on it. If I'd been here, I would've been taken in there as well. Could I have blocked a probe? Not stinking likely.

Tonight's chatter prompted me to muse on what I witnessed on year's eve, the warning I thought I heard. Is there a connection? I still believe the power unleashed was focused on the temple. But it was immense. The storm seen here may have been a backwash.

Alternatives. Was there a second focal point? Rebic's version of the events credited Col for the storm. Impossible. I may not be able to wield power, but I can spot those with the skill, and Col is not among them. A second focal point, however, placed near the Church might have been used to cover the main thrust directed at the temple. Makes sense. No priests came snooping out there. And it is the power's source they're interested in, not Nulan's death, though people here don't realize it. Idiots. The murder of a nobleman might spark an investigation, but unless he was close to the High Lord, Eshra priests wouldn't get involved.

Proof of point: at least ten Vic officials died by my hand before the Church became interested in the Soehn Biehr. And it was the possible threat to the State itself, not to an individual, which brought the priests in. They don't rule over internal affairs. The only exception that comes to mind would be if a crime involved natals. The Church does have jurisdiction over them and, from what I've heard, usually lets them off with a fine, regardless of the weight of an infraction.

A trial for a yardman's killer would be kicked down to common court. Priests wouldn't waste their time on it, not on Nulan's behalf anyway. The aroma of power drew them. Taking that as a given, what occurred on year's eve still doesn't make sense. Why expend so much energy, let alone twice? Pray Dynnas, did a memsa die that night?

Now there's a phrase I haven't spoken in a while. Pray Dynnas. It used to drip off my tongue like sweat off a mill slave. I've drifted further from my faith than I can imagine. But not so far that I wouldn't mourn the loss of any memsa and it is possible one or more had to burn their total life force to create the effects I saw. I pray not.

Again the question, why? What if the main volley was aimed here, directly at the Church, a prelude to war, and Col was arrested on the chance he might have served as a conduit? As Malison did. Was the temple event truly meant to warn me? I want to believe memsen know I'm here. But who would sacrifice so much for so little gain? My mother? No. Ry'aenne gave me up for dead long ago.

One thing is certain: no memsa would perform such a deed without Sythene's order. Yet she has conventional powers at her fingertips. If she knew I was here and wanted me out, she could pass word through the Kinship. The Snakes would fetch me one way or another. She'd use them before placing a memsa at risk. If she's yet alive. Why can't I sense her in this world? Is she gone, felled by an assassin? Impossible, I think, but she wouldn't be the first lord to meet that end. I could rest more easily if I didn't know how simple it is to kill. Questions. I can't solve them with the information I have and I'm not likely to gain more. The world is changing and I'm stuck in this hole. No one knows I'm here. Accept it. Tomorrow I go back to work.

519, 1/7. Gossips among the house staff are confident Col is being held by the Eshra priests. Before sunset, I went out on the road and inspected the Church – from a distance. I saw no damage, thus learned nothing. And it was stupid. I warned myself of this sort of insanity at Calec's. What's wrong with me? Do I want to be arrested? Do I need to be?

That made me pause. I'm recalling the memsa's predictions. The part about seeing my death in ink and being saved by a man who'll rule my home. I assumed she meant I'd see my death warrant, maybe even would be shown the damn thing by this man, whoever he is. I assumed I'd be given the chance to escape. Never did I consider she meant I'd be arrested, yet that makes more sense. Arrested here, tried and convicted, then sent home for execution. Is that what will happen? I must think this through before I do anything rash.

Would I be sent home? Maybe. If officials here knew I was a citizen of Evald, they'd delay the execution until Evald's Chairman was notified, and wait for a possible transfer appeal. Considering the speed at which most officials file paperwork, I might sit rotting in a Mearan jail for six months or more. I could endure that.

If Leister Howyl is still alive, he's still Vic Chairman. Would he sign an appeal? Maybe.

I'd have a better margin of safety if I didn't use my own name. When I was a clerk, I created records for several non-persons, an easy way to hide ownership of odd bits of property. I could use one of those identities. But the name would mean nothing to Leister. He wouldn't bother with a transfer. I'd have to use my name to gain his attention. But I'm legally dead. He might request confirmation of identity, a physical description, maybe pose questions only I could answer. Would he use diplomatic channels for this? Or go through the Church? I don't know who Evald's current ambassador to Meara is. But that post has always been held by a Howyl. Leister might opt to turn the matter over to a member of his own family. Everything would depend on who knows what about me.

Sources I once had informed me the Church concluded I was the Soehn Biehr, despite the deaths that occurred after my feigned demise. Was Leister told? Or does he still think I was one of the victims? Doesn't matter. Leister's tongue was always loose as a brothid's garters. If he receives a notification on me, everyone in Evald will know. The Eshra priests will step in. No question about it. I'll disappear into the Church just as Col has. For how long?

The Eshra Church was founded, supposedly, with the lofty goal of world peace. World domination is nearer the truth. The Seto Pact gave the Church authority to settle suits among the Four States, or between them and Evald. Sounds harmless. Yet, in effect, the Pact raised the Church above all laws. If I become a ward of Eshra, no legal document – not even a pardon – can force my release. Being arrested is not a way to get home. And if it happens? If that's what was foreseen? Then by logical progression the man who saves me, the man who will rule Evald, would have to be an Eshra priest. If that's the future, I pray I die before it comes to pass.

519, 1/10. Juboe entered my dreams again and, surprisingly, Cassie. She was walking barefoot down a road, her red hair swinging past her waist. I called to her, "Where's Tobb?" She didn't turn. Then I noticed Juboe beside me. "Did you care for her?" he asked.

I don't know why Cassie was knocking about in my mind, but the dream prompted me to brave the cold and walk into the city. Most of the streets are passable, snow pounded into slop by countless feet. There were no beggars I recognized. Nothing like a hard winter to sweep out the chaff. New faces begged for sympathy – and coins.

519, 1/15. I was scheduled to be free today through the 18th. But Cyril insists I make up the week spent at Calec's. No matter. The weather's yet cold. Riding to the meadow would be more trouble than it's worth.

Curious fact: by all accounts, the Eshra priests took Nulan's body and no one has seen it since. Why would they want it? What purpose would a corpse serve? No idea.

Another curiosity: Mira has become a martyr of sorts. Well, maybe that isn't so curious. She did lose both of her children. But no one recalls her hand manipulating events. If she hadn't grabbed power from Baz, her daughter would be alive. If she hadn't coerced Cyril, her son might be also. At least some blame should rest on her brow. None has. Pity is her latest tool and she's honed it to a fine edge. She spends each night in Filson's bed – no complaints from Baz. Filson gained a cloak of innocence on the deal. His part in luring others to the yards has been forgotten. He's now the man who will give Mira another child.

So where did they shovel the blame? On Jenner's head. Cyril banned him from the kitchens. It's possible he acted on his own, without a shove from Mira; the ban occurred while I was gone, so I can't be certain the cause wasn't simply a feud between Cyril and Jenner. But the result is the same. Their friendship is severed.

519, 1/17. Went up to the road and stood shivering to watch the full moon creep above Royal Wood. How many poets have penned testaments to the moon's beauty? How many lovers have whispered lies while bathed in its light?

By day humps of unmelted snow are spotted black from soot and yellow from urine. Tonight, beneath the moon, those same humps shimmered like silver. Illusion. That's what the moon creates, a veil to hide the truth. With or without it, the night is just as long.

519, 1/30. I've been avoiding the circles of gossip. I don't want to be involved with these people. I work. I talk when necessary. I live inside my mind.

519, 2/3. Wages day. Went into the city after work. Met a one-eyed beggar from Drayfed. He knew only a few words of Mearan. We conversed in Universal. I empathized with him being so far from home and gave him two coppers. He swore he wasn't a beggar, said he'd earn the coppers by reading my fortune 'in the bones.' At least I think he said bones – his accent may have fooled my ears. "Another day," I told him, and he palmed the coins as fast as all the other beggars I bumped into this evening.

519, 2/16. Argued with Cyril this afternoon. Over nothing. I was simply in poor humor and wanted someone else to be as well.

It's been a month and a half since year's eve, and nothing more has happened. If my presence here were known, I would have been contacted by someone in the Kinship, given instructions, told to leave or sit tight. Some word would have come. I can only conclude the event at the temple was not meant for me. Sheer luck that I witnessed it.

I chose to come here. No one forced me. I chose to tidy my trail so I wouldn't be found, not even by friends. Even so, I feel ... abandoned. As when my mother left me in Juboe's care. Surely she realized his influence, unchecked by hers, would damage my soul. I was just a boy of ten. Harmless. Why didn't she take me with her?

Abandoned. As when Sythene left Evald for Uttebedt. I know she had to be crowned there, where her people lived, not where Mules like me resided. But she had the power to bend the laws. She could have taken me with her, if she wanted. Clearly, she was not so inclined.

I remember when she presented me with the amulet I'm wearing, its etched gold now hidden beneath filthy cloth. I remember how I knelt before her so she could put it on me.

"Keep this near," she said, her sweet breath caressing my face as she lowered the chain over my head. "Always, Me'acca, near thy heart." She pressed a warm palm against my chest. "May it serve as a reminder of this moment, for the time shall come when ye doubt my affection." Sythene, that time is now.

Today I am forty-two years old.

519, 2/21. Dreamed of Juboe again. He was in the south courtyard of Haesyl's Keep, walking a path toward the lily pond, leaving red footprints in his wake. I can't recall much more of the dream, but it unlocked a cache of memories. All day I've thought of that pond. Circular in shape, the low wall around it was of a brownish substance that at times felt like stone and other times felt ... odd, more akin to flesh. I didn't often sit on its wall.

In winter, the pond was always free of snow and the chest-deep water never froze. Each spring water lilies stretched up from their submerged pots and spread leaves across the surface. In summer, the musky perfume of their blooms saturated the whole courtyard. The scent of passion, my grandmother called it, and cautioned me to avoid the place on sultry nights. "Ye have enough passion in ye now!"

The most interesting feature of the pond was the statue of a woman at its center. Knees bent, head bowed, she seemed to be rising onto her feet, one hand down, the other raised as if she were catching her balance. Water sprayed out from the back of each shoulder, and when the wind was calm, the fans of water appeared to be wings.

Common knowledge held that the statue was a depiction of the birth of Arumethea Lonntem, the first Lonntem to wear the crown of a united Uttebedt. According to legend, she was born from a tear that fell from the left eye of Dynnas onto the bloody ruin of a battlefield. Indeed, many in the Keep referred to the pond as the Eye of God, or simply the Eye.

I don't believe the legend. But I do think Arumethea existed. I believe she managed to unite the warring clans. Unfortunately, the peace she forged didn't last. The vast history of Uttebedt is rife with civil wars. Every time a new peace was stitched together, a Lonntem plied the needle. Perhaps Arumethea's legend helped in that regard.

Today, while mixing muffin batter, I thought of the men I crudely murdered in the south court. Had it not been raining, I would have heard Arumethea's wings spraying the lilies. Had it not been dark, I could have seen her, rising from the Eye. Would the sight have stayed my hand?

This morning's dream linking Juboe with the pond didn't shock me. In real life, he met Sythene there. It happened after Praechall's death. A funeral pyre was being built on the lake's shore and Sythene was to light the flame, which meant she'd be leaving the protective domain of the Keep. I suppose the Dyns worried Vics might interfere. At least that was the official reason for the encounter, though agents could have ironed out any difficulties. There was no actual need for Juboe and Sythene to meet face to face.

I remember he summoned me to his suite in the State House beforehand to discuss the matter. He had wanted me to go along as an interpreter and I'd eagerly accepted, but Dyns rejected the idea. "They want one of their own," Juboe told me. He was clad in a purple dress tunic, the four-spoked wheel, symbol of the Vic government, stitched in gold on his collar and cuffs. Standing in front of a mirror while an aide combed his hair, he grumbled, "A royal." He knocked the aide's hand away in a glint of anger. "Named Luka Massu. Know him?"

"No," I said, which was true at the time, but I'd heard of Luka's reputation. I honestly believed my father would be assassinated that day. And I didn't warn him.

He asked me to stay and wait so we could dine together afterward. "I hardly ever see you anymore." I recall feeling ashamed I'd betrayed him. Though I couldn't have been too upset. I broke into his wine cabinet and got pleasantly drunk while he was gone.

He did return, shedding his cloak as he strode in, snapping orders for his aide to bring us food. He snatched the cup from my hand and downed the wine yet in there.

His appearance surprised me. I don't mean the fact he was alive, though that may have influenced my reaction. His hair was disheveled, his face dabbed with sweat – and the day had been frosty. "Didn't you take a carriage?"

"Of course I did." He headed toward the bedroom, then paused, turned to me and said, "Uttes sure are a gruesome lot."

We dined on a table that would have served nicely as a desk, in a room that may have once been a clerk's office, window so small it hardly seemed worth looking through. A good son would have insisted Juboe move into a proper house. A good son would've nagged him into seeking a life beyond his official duties.

"You thought Sythene was gruesome?" I probed after we'd been seated.

"No, not her." He had washed up and wore an ecru shirt tucked neatly into his pants. "They wouldn't let me inside the Keep so we met outside. By a pond. Know the place?"

I nodded. "So?"

He frowned at me, as if thinking: Stupid Fool, must I explain everything? "The girl's mother is fresh dead."

"Her brother as well. He died last night."

"That just makes it worse."

I didn't understand his reasoning, nor did I wish to aggravate his temper, so I asked his opinion of Sythene.

"She's short," he said.

"She's a week shy of being three."

"A child," he agreed, though it seemed he said it to convince himself she was not an adult. Sythene had that effect on people. "They'd dressed her, head to toe, in red. That's the color of mourning for Uttes, isn't it?"

"Yes," I confirmed, not adding red was also the color of battle. "What did you discuss?"

"She asked to enter the city for the funeral. I told her she could. Then she hopped down and went inside." Getting information from him was like pulling ticks from a hound.

"She hopped down?"

"From the wall of that damned pond. She's short. And I wasn't about to kneel. So she stood on the wall, I sat on it and we were more or less level." He motioned for the aide to refill his wine cup. "Could've used you, son. That fellow Luka wasn't straight with me, I'm sure of it. Maybe not straight with her either. She'd jabber away and all he'd say was, 'You may sit, Chairman.' I pity the girl. She's too young to know who to trust."

I must have lapsed into silence, or maybe my face showed my disappointment, for he softened his tone. "I can't lie to you, son, she's a bit strange. How many young girls would ask if I'd ever hunted wolves?"

I choked. At that moment, at the age of nineteen, I finally realized Juboe was the stupid one. He had learned nothing from my mother, his wife. Why? He'd expected her to adapt to his culture and made no effort to study hers. Stupid. The proof was there, for Juboe hadn't weighed Sythene's question with the fact her dead brother was born under the wolf's moon, as was she. Regaining my composure, I asked, "How did you respond?"

He shrugged. "Told her I hadn't. She advised me not to start. Said hunting wolves was a dangerous sport. Strange, eh? Think her translator was fooling with me?"

Odd how well I remember our conversation, but not what we ate. Would that be different now that I'm a cook? I distinctly recall watching him chew, staring at the scar on his lip, wondering if I was pleased he had, by accident, answered the lethal question properly. Then I looked down at my plate. What was there? I have no idea. But I was gazing at it when I asked, "What was so gruesome?"

"The statue in the pond!" He threw down his fork. "The girl's mother was just murdered, and they haul her out in the cold to a statue of a slain woman, stabbed in the back, falling into her own blood! If you don't find that gruesome, then you've more Utte in you than I thought!"

I didn't bother to explain the legend of Arumethea. Any hope for a civil evening had fled. I did counter one point. "Praechall wasn't slain. She died in childbirth."

"Believe that," he grunted, "and you're a fool."

Sheever's Journal, Diary of a Poison Master

I spent the night in a brothid house. The next morning I entered the Keep through the south court. Someone had put red dye in the pond, and I understood how Juboe misread the statue's intent. Water spraying from Arumethea's back could have symbolized blood gushing from wounds. And maybe to some it did. There were others who believed as Juboe. Rumors Praechall had been poisoned were widespread. But sharper minds than mine checked into the matter and no evidence was found. So why am I dwelling on all this now? Am I trying to fool myself by remembering days when my life had worth? Those days are gone.

The moon is full tonight. I had planned to go out and watch it rise, but I've decided not to. No more illusions.

519, 2/30. The rains have come. They're late this year.

519, 3/3. Wet weather has forced me to be more social. To delay coming in here each night, I linger in the dining hall, staying up with whomever is off the next day.

This evening was more interesting than most. Being paid lightened the gloom. Rebic and Filson were hot for a dice game. I won more than lost. Have nothing to show for it though. Spent my winnings on ale in a vain attempt to be drunk enough to enjoy the conversation.

I'm sick of hearing fools repeat the tale of Nulan's death, each swearing they never believed Col could raise Krich from the Netherworld. Why, then, did they go down to the yards last year? Jenner forced them to go is how they tell it. Did mind probes erase the fact Filson challenged Cyril to go? I wish my memory was as poor as theirs.

The nightmares are worse than ever. Juboe is potent. Though I haven't again seen his ghost, the fear I will torments me when I'm awake. When I sleep, he rules. My partner's screams echo in the dark. I can do nothing to help her. Only months ago I defied the ghost and wrote her name in this journal. I could not do so tonight.

519, 3/4. I went out after work despite a downpour. Had to get away. Was soaked through by the time I reached the bridge. The river's high. I watched debris bob past until dark, then crossed over into the city. Streets were nearly deserted, the taverns packed full. I turned into an alley behind the markets, the beggars' domain. Rain failed to dilute the smell. Rotting food and human waste, the stench was overpowering. I didn't get far when a man yelled, "Slaver!" and the place erupted, every man racing away, leaving their meager goods in the discarded crates that serve as homes.

I was too tired to chase after the fools. I could have pledged to return tomorrow, but I no longer trust my oaths and if I held onto the monthly allotment, I might lose it in a dice game. So I went from crate to crate, placing a coin on each soggy nest of rags. How do people live like this? Why am I not elated that I have more than they? Isn't that why acts of charity are performed? The giver is supposed to feel smug about being better off. For me, it's simply a chore. I'll rest no more easily tonight because of it. Indeed, I've reached the point where I'll need to induce a trance if I want to function tomorrow. I've already selected the scene. Lake Bahdala. I'll make the water smooth as a mirror. Juboe can't touch me there.

519, 3/23. My first free day this year. Helsa's been rapping on my door each morning. The sound draws me from my nightly trance. Today she delayed waking me until past dawn. I'm sure she acted on Cyril's orders, for he was waiting in the dining hall, pot of tea and nut rolls as bait. "Sit and have a bite," he lured me, "before you're off traveling."

I told him I wasn't going this month. We've had less rain of late, but the west road parallels the river and is bound to be flooded. I don't want to lose the option of going to the meadow in future, however, so I'd planned to spend the day ingratiating myself with Jenner. "Thought I'd lend a hand in the stables," I said to Cyril.

"They'll not need you," he predicted. "With the High Lord gone none of us is busy." His assessment, though accurate, skirted the reason he'd risen to intercept me. He and Jenner have yet to patch their feud. "You'll find nothing but trouble in the stables."

"I am free today," I reminded him.

"Go," he grumbled. "Nobody listens to me. Go and see if I weren't right."

The back orchards were shady and cool as I walked down the terraces. The roof of the stables, in sunshine, steamed. I found Jenner in the lower paddock, exercising a bay stallion – or trying to. As I approached, he was hitting sod. He got up and brushed off his pants, then limped over. "Thought you'd quit going to Brithe."

"Not had a chance." I explained how I had to make up the week spent at the cemetery.

"Can't blame Cyril. You was gone them days." Jenner leaned against the railing, as if already weary from a day's work. "If he catches you down here ..." The pain of lost friendship blistered his voice.

"Cyril knows I'm here." I watched the bay prancing along the far rail, head high, a magnificent creature, much more valuable than the horses Jenner usually lends me. "Want me to give him a good run for you?"

"The stallion? Can't let you take him to Brithe."

"Not to Brithe. Just a good run." We haggled over details. He wanted me to stay in the paddock, then sanctioned the back portion of Perimeter as safe, then loosened the restrictions even more. But he made me swear I wouldn't leave Royal Park.

Tension from the stallion spread to me the moment I sat him. He'd been cramped in a stall too long. I trotted him to Perimeter, then eased him into a canter and held him in the gait until we rounded the bend. The back road stretched due east, red mud baking in the morning sun. I relaxed control. The stallion shot forward. And the sheer exhilaration of speed canceled all thought.

I reined him down to a canter again to take the turn onto Cemetery Lane. I don't know why I went that way. Habit, I suppose, but I regretted the decision immediately. I didn't want to visit the Wessels. Damut was out in the muddy waste of her garden, hunched over from the weight of a rock she'd pried up. I saw her heave the thing aside and look up. A bolt of guilt pierced my back as I rode past.

When the lane rejoined Perimeter, I turned left. I've gone to the park's eastern point only once, to find out what was there, which is absolutely nothing. I went there today because I was toying with the notion of looping back to the cemetery and helping Damut.

I had slowed the stallion to a walk to give my guilt more time to either fester or ease, when a man on a black horse charged up from behind me and streaked past. An instant later a pack of horsemen swarmed by, laughing and yelping like hounds on the chase – and pelting me with clumps of mud. The stallion sprang to match the pace. He reared when I reined him in hard, and I barely kept my seat, but I stopped him cold. The other riders stopped as well, near the next curve, and turned their steaming horses around as if waiting for me to catch up.

I'm not sure how long we stayed there, eyeing each other. I admit I was dazed. And something more. Memsen speak of life choices as paths. A person may hit a fork and whichever choice he makes will alter his life. Or he may be at a crossroad and has the option of changing course or going straight ahead. I've made plenty of choices in my life, not all of them wise, but I always saw the options and could guess the outcome. Even becoming Soehn Biehr was a choice I made. I can lie, blame anger or Juboe, or even insanity. But when I held that knife in my grasp and decided to use it, I knew the path I'd chosen.

There is another type of life-changing encounter. "Bumping fate," memsen call it. With their vision, they can use this type to their advantage, shifting themselves or others onto an entirely different path with entirely different choices. It's for this ability memsen earn the respect and, at times, fear they deserve.

Today I was bumping fate. I could feel it. The potential existed to change the path of my life and nullify everything the memsa had predicted for me. But I couldn't see the choices, couldn't guess where they led. So I sat the stallion as if paralyzed while five of the horsemen pulled from the larger group and rode toward me.

They were all five filthy with mud, and all young – the oldest maybe twenty, the youngest not more than thirteen. From the little of their language I'd heard, I knew they were Verdi. If it were a Game Year, I might have fooled myself into thinking they were the sons of a small town in Verdina who had come to Tiarn together, safer that way. But it isn't a Game Year. And these men didn't appear vulnerable. All five carried knives in boot-sheaths. Their sleek saddles had all been adapted to house swords, and splattered hilts protruded past the knees of four of the five men. The fifth and least armed man – a boy really – halted his horse in front of mine. The other four circled behind and beside me. I visually searched the boy's clothing for a blazon, in vain, though I didn't need to see the stag-and-star. These men were Verdi natals.

The boy's gaze flitted from the man on my left to land on me. "You work for the High Lord?" he asked in perfect Mearan.

I nodded and wondered if I were staring at Na-Kom D'brae. A foolish idea, quickly discarded. The boy was too young. Nor would natals be likely to place their Na-Kom in such an exposed position. The idea, however, prompted me to scan the group waiting by the curve. D'brae might have been among them. Or not. Every one of them exuded a protective quality.

The boy, as if needing instructions, glanced again at the man beside me, causing me to do the same. He had dark curly hair and bright blue eyes. D'brae? I think not, but he was someone of rank. The man wore, like a cheap trinket, a gold daekah as an earring. He yapped something in Verdi, then the boy asked, "You on an errand?"

I couldn't decide which Mearan dialect to adopt – low, middle, high? I felt fate bumping me. Would not speaking at all be best? I shook my head to avoid an error.

"Good." The boy grinned. "Want to race?"

"Race?" I echoed without thinking.

"Aye, we've a fast mare. Want to race your stallion?"

I again shook my head. The boy frowned, then twisted around to shout behind him. A sixth man rode from the group, as if the five surrounding me weren't convincing enough.

Swordsmen – good ones – have a confidence that makes them appear to swagger even if they're sitting still. Men like Grutin try to copy that air of assurance. This man had the real thing. "What's the problem?" He spoke Mearan with a crisp Verdi accent. "We want to race, is all." With a cool gaze, he sized me up, his eyes the green shade of bottle glass. I heard the heavy clink of gold as he tore a money pouch from his belt. "Name your price, Hawk."

I chose to be viewed as lower class. "Can't. Too rich for my blood. If my stallion was to lose …"

"Briss Almighty!" He jerked the reins to steer his mount past the boy's. The horse he rode, still snorting steam, came muzzle to muzzle with the stallion. "I'm not talking of a wager, Hawk. Just a race." He shook four daekahs onto his palm. "Four if you win." A smile blunted the danger written on his face. "Five if you lose."

I was a breath away from saying yes. A mere heartbeat away – perhaps – from bumping my life onto a new path. Then a seventh man barked, and fingers closed over the gold. The offer had been withdrawn. I shifted my attention to the newest arrival. Na-Kom D'brae? There were hints. He rode a black mare with a white blaze which could've been the one to first speed past me. A silver brooch clasped the neck of his cape. A simple circle and cross brooch, except the massive emerald at its center was worth more than the other man's gold. The hood of his cape was up as if to conceal his identity. True, the sky had clouded over and a fine mist cooled the air, yet there was more to it than a possible chill. He deliberately kept his head bowed while he approached and, once near, he turned his mare to put his back to me.

The reaction of the other natals almost convinced me. They emoted more tension than the stallion had earlier that morning. Only the boy seemed at ease, confident his older mates would fell me if I misbehaved. But the hooded man could not have been D'brae. If he were, why would the forty or so other riders have remained by the curve?

"Damn you," he cursed the green-eyed man. "Must you encourage him?" His Universal was perfect, a mere tinge of an accent. Why this language for the scolding? Perhaps fewer of the natals listening could understand it. I wished the 'him' being encouraged was me, but knew better. The hooded man didn't give a whit about me. "That mare is nearly wild," he continued in the same tone, not irate, but not pleased either, "and he's been drinking since dawn."

"He's always on edge after a night in Tiarn."

"I know, I know." He started to push back his hood, then, checking himself, tugged it lower. "We'll tell him the Hawk's stallion is lame."

"He'll not want to hear that. Why not let them race? The mare's bound to win. So where's the harm?"

I'm recording a portion of their conversation not merely because I was privy to it – it struck me as odd. The hooded man clearly outranked the other, yet allowed him to state his opinion. And they both deftly avoided saying any name. While they argued about whether or not to lie to a man who undoubtedly outranked them both, I scanned the group more carefully, searching for D'brae. I felt stupid doing this, like a Mearan cook, and recalled last year when D'brae paid the High Lord a visit and the kitchens emptied, everyone rushing up to the road with hopes of earning good luck by spying a na-kom. Maybe that's what I was searching for, good luck. Picking out a drunken man didn't work. A full third of the riders fit that category. I gave up the search when the hooded man raised his voice, "Got that straight, Natal?"

The boy, who must have been daydreaming, snapped alert. "Aye, sir, lame, sir! I've got it straight, sir!"

I hadn't missed much, and any fool could have guessed the outcome, but the green-eyed man made a last attempt to promote a race. "What if he wants to go around again, and spots the Hawk riding a horse that's not lame."

"Good point," the hooded man agreed, and I worried they'd maim the stallion to cover their lie. "Give us a lead," he continued, changing languages to speak in Mearan, "then get the Hawk back in Trivak's stables. I want him off this road. If we come around again and spot him, I want his head on a post. Clear?"

"Aye, sir." His green eyes focused on me and relayed a surety that he'd obey the order. "You clear on that, Hawk?"

I nodded. The hooded man barked in Verdi, then he, the boy and three others rode back to the group, leaving just two to detain me. The delay was shorter than I anticipated. Apparently the lie was quickly swallowed. With a whoop, the pack sped off around the curve, and the chance of bumping my fate departed as well.

"Racing is one thing," the green-eyed natal said to me in Mearan. He dropped a daekah into his coin sack. "Escorting a damned Hawk is another." Two more daekahs clinked into the sack. "If you're smart, you'll ride straight home." He flipped the last daekah to me, an act so unexpected the coin thumped my chest and nearly fell before I pinned it against my thigh. "For your trouble," he said, then yapped to his mate, and both of them tore off after the others.

They had rounded the curve before I spread my fingers to ogle my prize. I could hardly trust my eyes. I pushed the coin into my pocket and kicked the stallion into a gallop. Needless to say, I did not stop by the cemetery.

Jenner was still by the paddock. He ran down to meet me, yelling, "Did you see them Stag natals!" He held the stallion's bridle while I dismounted. "They went screaming by just moments ago. You must have seen them!"

"Some riders passed me." I tried to sound casual, a difficult feat, for the daekah seemed to be burning a hole in my pocket, as we walked the stallion up to the stables. "You sure they were Verdi natals?"

"Sure, I'm sure. I know all about them Stag savages. Met Macon D'brae hisself, I did."

Jenner hung around, yakking about the D'brae family, while I rubbed down the stallion. Pity I can't verify his gossip. But he did know that the Na-Kom owns a black mare, claimed she was a gift from his father, Lord D'brae. "Troopers say she's fast as lightning."

"Any of them ever race against her?" I asked.

The question startled him, though after a moment, he murmured, "Missed your jesting, I have." Then he echoed my words, "Ever race against her," and faked a hearty laugh. "With a na-kom in the saddle, who'd dare win?" Indeed.

I bathed the stallion's left foreleg with feverflax, made a poultice of witchweed and bidda, and wrapped the leg. It won't harm him, though he'll favor the leg a day or two. I'd hoped to do this without a witness, but Jenner rarely argues with my advice on horses. "Getting a sprain, is he?" was his comment, and I responded, "It's safer this way."

It was noon by then and pouring outside. He invited me to eat with him. I accepted before realizing the meal was smoked fish. "We get it from the troopers," he said. I disavowed my hunger and sated my belly with ale.

We spent the afternoon sitting at the mouth of the stables, watching the rain, drinking and talking. He spoke of Col and the events surrounding year's end. He swore he didn't see who killed Nulan. The priests did question him, and he recalls nothing about the interrogation.

Toward evening, he suggested we dine with the troopers. "They're not a bad lot," he asserted, but I'd had my fill of armed men, and refused. "Fieldtown then?" he asked.

Fieldtown isn't really a town, just a cluster of shacks that serve as homes for common laborers – stockmen, laundry staff, field hands, and such. Jenner pointed out who lived where, not that I cared. We were soaked through when we entered an oblong structure on the verge of collapse. The place was packed with squalling children and noisy, stinking adults. Smoke burned my eyes as Jenner grabbed my arm and pulled me to a table with two empty seats. The reason they were vacant was soon apparent. The roof above them leaked.

I would not have stayed if Jenner hadn't been working so hard to please me, fetching food – garlic and fennel soup, and biscuits – and trying to entertain me, though he had to shout for me to hear him. The others at our table were women. Jenner knew them and introduced me. They were milkmaids, which made me think of Damut wanting a cow. He flirted with a maid across from us, a black-toothed creature he called 'Sugar.' She flirted with me. I felt ill.

Happily, the maids had finished before we came, and soon left. Stockmen took their places. Jenner knew all of them as well. I recognized a few, but didn't attempt a conversation. I learned what I wanted to know by scanning them. They had all endured extensive probes. The mental damage was evident. There was no life behind their eyes.

"They weren't the same after Col were taken," Jenner confided when we left the place.

The rain had stopped, and the moist night air cleansed my mood. I stated my intention of going up Lower Main to the kitchens, explaining it was easier than the terraces to navigate in the dark. An excuse to part with him. He thanked me for spending the day with him, blathered on about how much he'd missed me, though we both knew it was Cyril's company he missed, not mine. He asked me to visit him tomorrow. I promised I would.

I entered the kitchens through the north door and tried to sneak past the dining hall, but Cyril snared me. He wanted an accounting of my day. I told him I was too tired.

"Too drunk is what you are," he chided.

"That too," I agreed and came in here and shut my door.

Obviously, I was neither too drunk nor too tired to give an account of the day. The daekah helped considerably. Each time I glance at it excitement springs anew.

Many coins bear symbols that indicate their origin. The markings don't change a coin's value. All must meet the standards set by the Church, and thus are interchangeable. The Four States and Evald are bound to the standards by the Seto Pact. Convenience binds Uttebedt. Though diplomatic ties are nonexistent, trade knots east and west.

Snakes will never receive the respect awarded Dyns, but the Serpent Kinship is, to a large degree, a branch of the Dynnae. Branch is too high. Root is a better analogy. Snakes peddle Uttebedt goods throughout the world, and Dyns skim the profits. Even if the buyers and sellers are foes, sharing a similar monetary system is handy, but not required – with one exception, the tribute paid by Evald's Lord.

The Cyntic Treaty states the size and weight of each daekah to be rendered to 'guests of the House of Eshra,' as it quaintly named the winning armies. The number of daekahs is also stated – one million, far too great a sum for Katre to lose each year. I don't know how his ancestors managed to make the payments, especially immediately after the war. Uttebedt must have been in chaos. Apparently, the tribute was paid, for 'Eshra's guests' squabbled over it, which created a need to amend the treaty with the Seto Pact, set up the Games, and so on. The Pact divided the tribute. A quarter went to support the Vic government, another quarter to the winner of the Games. The Eshra Church swallowed the other half.

I'm rambling. The point is the tribute Katre pays each year is raised in Uttebedt and minted especially for that purpose. He serves merely as a funnel. Tribute coins always have one side marked with a five-armed star. The other side bears the rune of an elemental force – air, water, fire, or stone. When daekahs were as common as hopence in my pockets, I never cared which rune they bore, or even if they were tribute coins. A daekah with a hawk stamped on its face was worth the same.

The daekah I received today is a tribute coin. Not surprising. No doubt the young Na-Kom's uncle won it in the Games. It's marked with the rune for fire. I've spent thousands marked the same. Is this one worth more?

"Ye shall hold fire upon thy palm," the memsa said. Applying flaming coals to hands or other body parts is a routine torture. I assumed her prediction meant I would endure such treatment. Now I look at the daekah resting on my left palm and wonder. Is this what she foresaw?

I want to keep the coin near me. Want to feel its weight in my pocket. Far safer to store it with the journal though. Maybe the coin is one of the predicted signs, maybe not. But its monetary value alone is significant. I don't want to lose the damn thing.

519, 3/24. Helsa roused me at the usual time. I donned the tunic and pants I'd worn yesterday, went out in the hall, then questioned my eagerness to start the day. So I lit a candle, came back in and stretched out again.

I was thinking of home when I dozed into a dream in which I was flying over the city. Lake Bahdala sparkled like a jewel in a stone setting. I spied the lake house and fell like a rock. The body I landed in was me as a nine-year-old. I was in my room, at my writing desk, and could hear Taneh behind me, tidying my clutter. Taneh had been hired as my wet nurse, though I don't recall her as such. My parents kept her as a handservant. She was deeply religious, which won my mother's approval, and demure enough for Juboe to accept.

"Look ye hither," she said in the dream, and I turned to see the shirt she held, my shirt, sleeve stained. "Must I warn ye each day to take care, child? Dynnas gives us ink and silk, but they were not made to be mixed." Her voice contained no anger. Taneh loved me unequivocally. A shame I didn't value her devotion. She was a nobody.

Baz shouting in the hall pulled me awake, though she may have also caused the dream, for she was calling for laundry. Still caught in the dream's web, I went out. She stomped over, frowning. "You been rolling in mud? Take them clothes off before you grind the dirt in."

As if I were yet a boy obliging a request by Taneh, I stripped off my tunic, and had unbuckled my belt, when Baz giggled, "You going to get naked right here?"

I laughed, "Fuzzy from sleep, I am," which was true enough. I headed for my room, but she pushed her mass in front of me and plugged the doorway.

"Sleepwalking, eh?" She was in a mood to tease and could not let the opportunity pass. "Dreaming of a girl, was you? So quick to shed them clothes." She poked my ribs. "You've not enough meat on you to feed a cat." Her rough fingers reached for my necklace, and I clamped a hand over the disk to keep her from it. This provided more fodder for her to chew and spit out. "Oooo," she wailed, mocking offense, "don't want me touching that. Who made them fancy braids? The girl you was dreaming of?"

Izzy came rollicking down the hall, no doubt wanting to take part in her mother's fun, but her arrival ended my ordeal. Baz stepped aside. "Go in. I'll wait."

The sudden abatement baffled me until I found her in the dining hall. She had brought me tea. "Didn't know if you'd be eating," she said, speaking as gently as Taneh would have, "what with the moon near full." I reasoned she had decided tormenting a kor-man held potential risk. Then Izzy bounded in from outside, scooped up an overflowing laundry basket which had been sitting by the door, and carried it out. The splint I'd put on her arm was gone, and might have been gone for weeks. I hadn't paid much attention to the girl. Baz had though. "Arm mended like new," she said as she took my muddy pants. "I won't again forget what you done."

The incident unsettled me. I shivered as I sat at a table. I had layered on two shirts, but both are old and thin, and even together provide less warmth than my tunic. The hot tea I gulped seemed to freeze in my stomach. I thought of the daekah and the clothing I could buy with it. Then tried to not think of the daekah. Possessing it has not changed my fate. A thousand pieces of gold would not change the path before me. Just as the finest wool wouldn't have warmed me this morning. My chill came from within.

I went to a window, hoping the view would distract me. Gardeners moved about in the orchard. My eyes watched them trim dead wood from the budding apple trees, while my mind delved my memory for everything I knew about fate lines. Some are fixed, firm as an iron rod. Others tenuous as a hair. Every creature has them. Invisible to all but those with the sight. Undecipherable to all but those with the skill to see where they lead. Even a tenuous line can become – with proper grooming – as solid as a paved road.

The scene before me endorsed my thoughts. The apple trees were like people, their branches lines of fate, with the gardeners, like memsen, pruning out faulty paths. One man, rather than climb to saw out a limb, threw a rope over it and tugged it down, breaking a healthy branch as well. Seeing this made me think of Praechall and the week prior to her death, when gossips leaked that she was ill. Living in the Keep that week was akin to treading a dagger's edge. Yet I never expected her to die. With so many Dyn healers at her bedside, how could she? There were rumors they had discussed cutting the boy from her womb with the intent to save her. But none dared to wield the blade.

One night, I'm not sure which one exactly, Sythene came down to my suite, distraught. I held her in my arms. She sobbed, "I cannot loosen the knot." I didn't understand what she meant – until today. Sythene saw her brother's fate lines tangled with Praechall's. Knotted so tightly that when Praechall died, her lines tugged his. The knot couldn't be broken. A lethal bump of fate.

I was born with the potential to become a first sec. My mother saw the line, pushed me along it, yet must have known it was tenuous. "Focus on thy studies," she so often implored. Why didn't I listen? That line is gone. A dead branch can't bear fruit. Maybe all my lines are gone – except the one that will lead me into the Eshra Church. I toyed with this conjecture months ago, then forced it from my mind, hoping I was wrong. Pray Dynnas, let me be wrong. But yesterday's potential bump seems to confirm it. And this morning, as I allowed these thoughts to seep back into my mind, a sense of doom overpowered me. I didn't hear Cyril come up behind me, didn't feel his hands on my shoulders until he turned me around to face him.

"What's with you, Sheever? You're shaking like a leaf." He released me then, and hurried back a pace, as if he, too, saw my fate. "You changing into a demon?"

I hugged myself and rubbed my arms, trying to warm my soulless body. "Caught a chill, I have."

"No wonder, stealing in drunk and sopping wet like you done. Warned you, I did, about going out in the rain."

"You were right," I said, which elated him.

He draped an arm around me and towed me from the window. "Why can't you just laze on off days like everybody else?"

I had neither the will nor the strength to oppose him as he led me to my room. He hesitated in the doorway long enough for me to pull away. I sank onto my bed. He came in and covered me, left, then returned with two loaves of bread, fresh from an oven. He placed the loaves on my chest, "To keep your lungs clear," and went out again.

I felt like a fool lying on my bed with bread on my chest. The aroma soothed me though. My tremors had stilled when Cyril carried in a steaming pot of clove wine. I sat up as he dipped us each a cup. "Why are you doing this?"

He shrugged. "Why shouldn't I?"

"I don't have plague," I assured him. "You don't need to worry about the medico."

"I weren't worried of that," he insisted, a half-truth. Lifting the candle, he pretended to inspect the woodwork on the walls. "Tobb did all this, eh." His action was a pretense because he wanted to close the door without stating a desire for privacy. He nudged it shut, then pointed to the name above the other bed. "This as well?"

"I drew the letters. Tobb carved them."

He sat on Tobb's bed. "I shouldn't have made you work off them days you was at Calec's. What with you learning me to write. And all you done this past winter. Tending Izzy and Helsa's girl Onji, and not spreading gossip about Mira's girl, you know, what we done with her." He was holding the candle in his lap and light flowing up under his chin caused odd patterns of shadow on his face. "What I'm saying is, I won't again forget what you've done."

The same words Baz had used earlier sounded more ominous coming from his mouth. He will betray me. Not betray. He won't turn me in. But when the time comes, he'll stand aside and let the priests take me. The strange shadows seemed to blur and his face reminded me of a moldy squash. I emptied my cup then, lying down again, shut my eyes.

"Tired, eh. Too tired for advice, I suppose."

"What do you want, Cyril?"

"What I don't want is trouble." He rustled about. I heard him slurp wine. "While you was gone yesterday, Mira were telling everybody that Jenner killed her boy."

"A lie. Jenner didn't kill Nulan."

"It don't matter. She'll stir things up. I don't want them priests in my kitchens again."

I opened my eyes to see him standing by the door, cup in hand. "What does she want?"

"Filson named as the next head cook, that's what. And soon as I name him, there's no telling what she'll do." Apparently, even a head cook needs to worry about being assassinated, for that's what troubled him. Mira is truly wasted here. She maneuvered her way past Baz into Filson's bed. Now only Cyril blocks her ambition.

"You're letting her set the rules," I said.

"Can't do nothing else!"

"Sure you can. Look at your options."

"Don't have no stinking options!"

"Sure you do." I swung my feet out of bed, refilled my cup, then offered him the dipper. He needed something to calm him. "You hold the reins, Cyril."

He sat down again on Tobb's bed, and we drank the wine and ate the bread, while we unraveled the matter. It would've been easier to simply tell him what to do. He'd learn nothing that way though. Besides, I enjoyed the distraction. I wish my problems were as plain as his.

The knowledge that my soul is damned is nothing new. But I always felt there was a chance I could alter it. That is, after all, why I came here, to earn the Rite of Grace and be cleansed. My hope for the Rite may have dimmed on occasion, but if it had vanished altogether, I wouldn't have remained here. This morning, however, for a brief while, I felt no hope, none, and the weight of certain damnation staggered me. I am a coward, for it is damnation, not the Rite of Grace, I deserve. Yet I pray I can earn the Rite.

Outwitting Eshra priests will be more difficult than outwitting Mira. I have neither the tools nor the knowledge to devise a complete plan tonight. But I can begin. The questions are the same for me as they were for Cyril – what are the facts and what are the options?

Fact. The memsa told me I would see my death written in ink. It's possible this means I'll be arrested and a death warrant will be penned and shown to me.

Fact. The memsa told me I would be saved by a man who will rule my home. I concluded months ago that the man she foresaw must be an Eshra priest. Why would he save me? I'll have something he wants and he'll offer a pardon in exchange. This should make me feel better. But it's likely he'll want what everyone else wanted from the Soehn Biehr. Would I kill for the Church? Maybe. Depends on the target.

Fact. Yesterday I felt a bump of fate. It occurred while in the presence of Verdi natals. I sense Na-Kom D'brae is the source of the bump, but it could have come from any of them. The hooded man perhaps.

Fact. Natals are born for the Games. They are wards of Eshra. Their fate lines must lead to the Church. I felt the bump because my line is headed in the same direction.

Option one. Initiate another bump. Possible result – I'm thrown onto a path that leads away from the Church. And away from the Rite of Grace? Alternative result – my fate line becomes entangled with theirs, which would mean no deal with a priest, no escape from damnation.

Option two. Avoid the Verdi natals. That shouldn't be difficult. Yesterday was a fluke.

Possible errors. I could be totally wrong, start to finish. Why didn't I feel a bump when I spoke with the Dray natals? Fact. The Drays have taken part in the Games. Their fate lines are already attached to the Church. The Verdi natals haven't been in the Games yet, not these Verdi natals. Their lines are yet in motion.

"Heed ye well," the memsa said, "when the Victors don a new face. Tis a sign the end of thy exile draws nigh." Will the end come after the next Games? Or is my arrest imminent? I met Col only once, but memory of me no doubt rests in his mind. Have the priests plucked it out?

Odd how after all these years of wishing for my exile to end, I now pray it hasn't. I wished my life away. Such a coward I am. More so than Cyril. I forgot to talk to him about Jenner. We need to remove him from Mira's armory. A truce between him and Cyril won't be enough to restore his reputation. But it can be done. I didn't spend years studying diplomacy without learning a thing or two. A common foe would work. But a common goal would be better. Mira won't know how to counter a positive aim.

These are petty matters. A diversion to ease my panic. I realize the noose may already be around my neck and my chance of escaping damnation is next to nothing. But false hope, I've decided, is better than none at all. Even a caged beast must hope for escape. How else could it go on living?

519, 3/25. Cyril made an announcement during evening meal. "There's been talk about who'll be the next head cook," he began. "I want to put the gossip to rest."

I could record the whole speech. I helped him compose the damn thing. And he recited it well, listing the duties of the post, stressing the importance of keeping the account ledger. He even paused, as I'd told him to, and took a drink, heightening anticipation, before naming the three men who would be taught how to read and write. Padder, Wix and Filson are the three. The meat cooks were happy. The bread cooks were happy. The soup cooks were happy. They all had a chance for one of their own to move up. Old Wix was happy for his son, and the other cooks in the spare kitchen looked to see my expression. Happy.

"That weren't fair," Mira snipped, "learning them all. Which of the three gets to be head cook after you?"

"The one who learns best," Cyril countered. "Now it might take a year or two to give all three a fair chance. But there's no hurry, were there, mates?" He waited long enough for comments about the wisdom of his decision to be murmured, then brought out the tricky issue.

The common goal I'd chosen was digging Damut's garden. I'd spent most of the day smoothing the deal, but didn't know if Cyril could sell it. The first protest came from Mira, "Why should we walk way out there and gets dirty, for what?" Filson sided with her, and others grumbled about wasting a free day, or claimed they were scheduled to work.

Cyril let them vent, then motioned for quiet. "First off, we weren't that busy here. We can get by without the kitchens staffed full. Those of you free who help us, will get another day free. Those of you set to work can choose a day out in the air, or over a hot oven." He cleared his throat on cue. "Second off, we won't need to walk. Jenner'll take us out there in a wagon."

"He killed my boy!" Mira spat.

Cyril voided her lie with a firm statement, "That weren't true and we all knowed it." We had rehearsed this, too. Mira's outburst had been easy to predict.

The moon is full tonight and maybe its power of illusion filtered into these kitchens, for Cyril sounded like an orator. "Many of you went to the yards last year. Some of you prayed to Krich. Prayed for demon spawn to run loose in the world. I won't name no names. I weren't like that. You know who's who." His gaze traveled from table to table, delivering shame.

"Mates, what was done by some hurts all. And all of us should make it right. Maybe you don't know Calec were a reverend, but he were. And you seen his boy come here in the dead of winter. Starving, we was, till that boy come, and our supplies come right after. It were a sign, and we need to pay Loric back. He gived us food. Now we need to help Damut plant food for Calec and them boys." Cyril deviated from the script only at the end. He mistook a moment of silence for failure, and added his own words to fill the gap, "So that's what this's to do."

What he didn't know was I had written parts for members of his audience, and they spoke their lines at the perfect time. Baz, Helsa, Rebic, Wix and Old Wix – I even had Padder set to stand up and declare, "I'll go!" Young Onji had the best part. She rose, thin as a wafer, and sang out, "We'll be tending Loric's very own Garden!" Using her was divine inspiration.

The dining hall became a hive, more people wanting to go than stay. Even those opting out couldn't help being touched by excitement. This caper might actually succeed. One problem. Damut doesn't know we're coming. She may not appreciate an army of fools wrecking havoc in her garden.

519, 3/26. A nearly perfect day. Considering we had to hitch up a second wagon and still couldn't fit everyone in, we got off to an early start. I rode ahead – not on the bay stallion. I rode the bony back of a plow horse that couldn't manage a gait faster than a trot.

Damut was out hoeing the field. She wept when I told her what was up, then dashed into the cottage to wash and change clothes. She came out, wearing her blue dress, as the mob rolled into view. "What will I feed them?"

"We've brought food," I assured her. Indeed, we brought everything we could possibly need. Jenner had mustered most of his own men, plus fieldmen, a tiller to work the plow, and two expert gardeners to tell us what to do. We had picks and spades and slings to tote any boulders we unearthed. He even pinched the pail of fresh cream I requested – in case Damut's humor needed to be soothed. "Told Sugar this were for you," he said to me with a wink.

Padder used rocks already on hand to build a spit, and roasted a calf. The women swept and scrubbed the cottage. Baz laundered anything not being worn, and rigged cords in the blooming arms of the quince so the clothes would dry in the sweet air and sunshine. Old Wix and Calec sat by the spring and smoked their pipes. Basal relinquished Loren into Onji's eager care, then ran across the lane with the other children. Laughter rang through the graveyard.

By late afternoon, we had doubled the size of Damut's plot. I spied a gardener chatting with her. I had paused to stretch, and watched him aim her gaze to various spots. He'd brought spare seeds and I assumed he was telling her what should be planted where. She nodded each time his pointing finger moved and, as her gaze swept over me, a smile made her face radiant.

When Padder yelled, "Meat's done!" we gathered on the green between the cottage and the spring. Women had set out the bread, pies and puddings we'd brought. Calec delivered a prayer and blessed us all, then Cyril tapped a keg and a festive air eased the ache of hard labor. The only thing the day lacked was music – and Malison. I saw him briefly in the temple's doorway, and imagined his thoughts to be similar to those which burned my mind as a boy when sunshine competed with dry books of law. He'll survive.

The unity won today didn't break when we returned to the kitchens. Though Mira tried her sour best, our gaiety spread like plague. Those who hadn't gone complained of missing the fun and wanted us to plan another outing. I don't think we could manage it again.

519, 4/1. There are rumors the High Lord will soon return. The house staff fanned the news to us this afternoon. Jenner confirmed it when he came up for evening meal. He'd heard it from troopers. Another bit of gossip, which he hadn't heard, was unveiled after we'd finished eating.

"Got this from Kwint," Cyril said, voice dropping to a whisper, and everyone at the table leaned toward him. According to Kwint the High Lord's wife – who has been here all winter – is with child. Cyril passed this hearsay with a smile and the cooks around him laughed. Yet, if true, Lady Untha's life may be in peril and whoever fathered her child is as good as dead. Jenner, I noted, lost his grin while the others roared. Maybe he's worried that one of his trooper friends is the guilty party.

How will this group react when I'm arrested? Laugh? Or will they be stricken mute, fearing for their own necks? Cyril could be charged with harboring a fugitive. Is that why he'll cooperate? To save himself? Why shouldn't he? My crimes are my own. None of the people here should pay for them. But will they? Law and justice don't always go hand in glove. Anyone who calls me a friend could be punished, innocent or not. Anyone I care for could be used against me. Friendship is a luxury I cannot afford. I know this, have known it from the beginning, yet the past week – Stop. I must not search for reasons to like these people.

I cannot like them. Use them, yes. Make them like me. Yes, so I can manipulate them more easily. They are tools. Nothing more. I must practice Dohlaru more often. Emotion is a weakness.

519, 4/3. After being paid today, the cooks were issued new uniforms. The event was taken as proof of Loric's pleasure with the garden we helped dig. Cyril, to push this further, gave all who had worked on the project the rest of the day off. With new clothes, a month's wages in hand, and half a day free, most of the cooks decided to walk into Tiarn.

I declined their invitation to go along. I've nourished the habit of not walking into Tiarn until dark and was reluctant to change. Even if it had been past sunset, I would've refused. The chance of being recognized is slim, but if it happens, I would prefer to be alone, not in the company of fools. They refused to accept my decision. Huge Padder hoisted me up onto his shoulder, as if I were a side of beef, and threatened to tote me into the city.

"Cyril," I called as Padder carried me toward the north door, "you go. Let me keep an eye on things here," which is what happened. They may have gone down to the stables and lured Jenner along. He didn't show for evening meal.

I ate with Old Wix who also opted to stay. "Were too far for my legs," he shouted in my ear. He planned to wait up for his son and the others to return. I retired early, thinking I'd write, which I have, but there's little else to record. No facts anyway. And I'm not in the mood to plunge into speculations. The tunic I received fits better than the last one.

519, 4/12. The High Lord arrived today. Runners spread the word. Cyril sent us up to the front orchards, told us to cheer. Trivak made a show of it, banners and trumpets, and a parade of guests he brought with him. He must have forgotten that he slipped out of Tiarn last autumn, supposedly in secret. Since he's back, I assume the plague scare is over.

519, 4/26. This should be brief. I intend to go to the meadow tonight. I'm nervous about going. Do the priests know I'm here? If so, they might toy with me, let me think I'm safe until it suits their fancy to pick me up. But they wouldn't allow me to leave the city. This will be a test of sorts. If I get past the guards at the gates, I can be confident my ruse is still secure. And if they detain me? Should I take the daekah? Would a single gold piece be a large enough bribe to sway guards into disobeying a Church order? Not hardly. I'll leave it here.

519, 4/30. Got back this evening. Made it through the gates with time to spare. No problems from the guards, today or when I left. It's reasonable to believe the priests know nothing.

Both Jenner and Cyril remarked on how relaxed I looked. "Done you good to get away," Cyril said, and I nodded, my mouth too full for a verbal response. This was my first extended fast since I can't recall when, and I was starving. Not much happened while I was gone. It's been busy. Trivak's guests have strong appetites. But I don't want to write about this place.

The meadow was a carpet, violets and blue fieldstars woven through shades of green. Larks sweetened the days with song. Frogs croaked tunes at night. Sensual delights. I am relaxed. And missing home. From the meadow, the Purnath Mountains seem so close, looming up over the trees. An illusion. Crossover Pass is days away. Days? Who am I fooling? For me, Evald is years away – if I'm lucky.

This trip was not wholly devoted to the physical. I had a revelation last night. I had bathed in the river at sunset, a cold shock to my body. Afterward, rather than don dirty clothes, I wrapped myself in a blanket to regain lost warmth. When the moon rose over the trees, I suddenly yearned for its light to touch every part of me including, and maybe especially, the soles of my feet.

I shed the blanket, stretched out on the grass and, as the moon slowly passed overhead, I felt the break between soul and body. There's a technique for this. Every high-level novice learns it. Breaking improves the chance of a clear vision. But I hadn't initiated the break. It just happened. It was also different. Before – always – my body felt heavy and my soul light. This time my body seemed to float while my soul sank into the sod. The nausea later was similar though. I retched up the river water I'd swallowed.

I wouldn't call this a vision, more a reminder of the weight of my soul. And of my fate. As I dressed, my mind ran through the memsa's prophecy again and I reached the same conclusion – an Eshra priest will offer me a pardon in exchange for my services. Somewhere in this journal I wrote that I might kill for the Church to escape damnation. Last night I speculated a possible target. If this priest is to rule my home as Vic Chairman, he'll need to dispose of the man holding that post. Leister Howyl? It would be unpleasant, since he was once a friend, but I could kill him. The moment I thought this, I glanced at the moon and saw my error. I can't kill Leister, or anyone else the Church may select. I can't make a deal.

My exile is a test of endurance. My arrest will lead to a greater test. If I want the Rite of Grace, I must prove I've changed during these years. No deals with the Church. I'm sure of that now. What I'm not sure of is me. How much torture can I withstand?

519, 5/15. A dark moon tonight. This month is a lue-mout. The moon is dark and hungry. My soul is dark and hungry.

A man was found dead on Main Road this morning. A runner sped through to inform us the man had fallen prey to thieves, hinting that perhaps the robbers had been Snakes. Cyril told us to be more careful, warned us for the thousandth time to stay out of Royal Wood.

The house staff brought more enlightening news. Fesha Trivak is divorcing his third wife. Lady Untha is expected to leave the palace tomorrow. Her destination is unknown, though gossips say her family has spurned her.

I went up to the road. No risk to me. Other gawkers were there, as was the body, nude except for a cloak of flies. The man had been castrated and partially gutted. Lethal wounds, for certain, but a slow death, I'd wager. He may have remained conscious until loss of blood caused him to swoon. Bruises darkened his wrists, ankles and the sides of his mouth. Bound and gagged? Most likely. His killers must have waited until he was too weak to cry out for aid, then removed the evidence, or thought they had. No thief would be so patient. And no Snake so careless. If a body is chosen to be a warning, Snakes leave the evidence in plain view. If not a warning, there wouldn't be a trace. This was done by amateurs.

Jenner supplied the last bit of what wasn't really a puzzle. The dead man, he said, was a minstrel hired last year to amuse Lady Untha during the long winter nights. Apparently, he performed his duty too well. Will she be forced to go past her dead lover when she departs? Undoubtedly. I wish her luck.

519, 6/2. Returned from another trip to the meadow. No problems. No new revelations. The river was warmer.

519, 6/23. Col has been released. Most of the early cooks had finished for the day and we were drinking ale in the dining hall when Jenner came up with the news. Filson, who last winter had given a fair sum to Krich, was hot to confront Col and demand repayment. He stirred up the other fools who had lost coin. "Said we'd be repaid tenfold, he did. Mates, let's go tell him we wants a piece of his wages till we're paid full."

I felt safe going with a group. Filson led the way, charging down Lower Main, Rebic jogging beside him, eight others at their backs. I lagged behind with Jenner.

"How much did you lose?" he asked.

"Nothing," I said.

"Well," he grunted, "you was smart."

Filson shouted at a stockman by the holding pens, "Where's Col?" The man motioned to the slaughterhouse and the mob swarmed inside.

Jenner hailed the man, then whispered to me, "Gim were brought in to run the yards. Tight as a virgin, he is." Despite his appraisal, he smiled as Gim strode to meet us.

Rebic peeked out of the slaughterhouse and waved me over. "They near starved Col to death," he said as I joined him inside. The place stank of offal though no carcasses hung from the ceiling. Filson and the others were across the room, close to where the idol of Krich once stood. I didn't see Col until I walked over and Wix stepped aside. Beard gone and thin as a bone, Col was squatting on his haunches like a beast. Spittle dripped from his chin.

"He's pretending he don't hear me," Filson complained, then yelled, "Listen up, Uchidon! You owes us, you do!"

Col didn't blink. I scanned him, then touched his brow to deepen the probe. There was nothing there. Nothing. They'd scoured him clean. Is this my future? I jerked back my hand and hurried outside. Jenner was yakking with Gim. I cut in and asked to borrow the bay stallion.

"Where you going in such a rush?"

"Nowhere. Just feel like riding." I swore I wouldn't leave the park and when he relented, I ran to the stables. Was I hoping to bump into the Verdi natals? Yes. And I would've challenged them to race. But I didn't see them.

I rode the stallion into a lather before I calmed enough to regain my senses. The past can't be altered. My chance for a bump of fate came and went. I chose to stay on my path. A second chance won't come. I should be able to accept my fate. Once I become like Col, I won't care. But I'm not yet like him. I can't stop my thoughts. Will the priests, when they're done with me, set me loose in Evald? Is that how I'll get home? Will I know I'm there?

"Ye shall be offered the Rite of Grace," the memsa said. I remember when she uttered that prophecy how I focused on the word 'offered' and felt smug that I wouldn't need to ask for the rite. It would be offered. Damn her. She must have known I wouldn't be able to ask. Will a memsa spy me drooling on Evald's streets and cleanse my soul out of pity? Damn them all.

Options. Leave this place now. Get out of Tiarn and never return. Result. Unknown.

Question. Is the soul worth more than the body? The soul is eternal and therefore worth more than the flesh. Why doesn't the catechism comfort me?

Question. Does Col still have a soul? His body is alive therefore a soul must inhabit it. The mind is merely a bridge between body and soul. If a bridge is swept away, the two banks of the river continue to exist. The concept of being reborn doesn't frighten me. Memory is shed before a soul returns to this world. My memory was shed before I was born into this life. I don't miss whatever knowledge I had in past lives. This will be the same. After the priests finish with me, I won't miss what I can't recall. There is no reason to dread the future. Yet surely there must be another option, something I've overlooked.

519, 7/6. Ended a miserable stay at the meadow. Hot. Was eaten alive by bugs. Unable to concentrate. I'm tired and hungry and covered with bites. Cyril paid me when I returned. I asked him to fill me a pitcher while I came in here to pull off my boots. Thought I'd write a bit, let my feet air, before donning shoes. Lie. I wanted to make sure the daekah was safe. It is. Nothing else of import to say.

519, 7/30. Must be near midnight. I'm sweating, and this room is cooler than outside. It's likely a mistake to record today's events. Putting them on paper will award them more import than they're worth. But it's too hot to sleep.

After work, Jenner and several cooks decided to go into Tiarn. They wanted me to go along. I declined. Instead, I chatted with Cyril awhile, resisting the urge to drink. I'd spent most of this month's wages on his brew and hated the idea of surrendering the rest to him. The urge grew, however, as the evening sun heated the dining hall. I had to leave. I walked to the bridge. No cooling breeze wafted up from the sluggish water. I kept walking and entered the city before sundown.

The markets seemed as busy as during a Game Year. Merchants had arranged their wares outside their shops, competing with cart vendors and squeezing the crowds into a jostling river. Being short did not enhance the ordeal. My view was restricted, but I felt exposed, especially when riders fording the throng passed by. My tunic had been too hot to wear, let alone a cape. I tried to convince myself the old shirt and pants I wore were disguise enough – no one who knew me in the past would expect me to be dressed so shabbily – but my unease didn't wane.

Propelled by the flow, I turned onto Fruit Street and got caught in an eddy. Peaches and early melons must have recently been barged in from Drayfed. Every vendor was hawking them, and their ripe aroma masked the stink of human sweat. But the smell had also drawn bees. Persons buying did so quickly then reentered the flood on Martway. I pushed through and continued on Fruit. Midway down the street the river dried to a stream.

A boy yelling, "One hopence, one hopence," attracted me. Actually, the kegs in the wagon on which he stood attracted me – specifically, the ram's head brands on them. I assumed they contained Dray wine. "One hopence" were the only Mearan words the boy knew. A chain attached to a ring on the wagon's sideboard looped down to a brass cuff on his ankle. A man, the boy's owner I presumed, lay beneath the wagon, snoring. I paid the boy and he filled a clay cup, not with wine, with peach brandy, too sweet for my liking and green, which accounted for the price. Yet I was thirsty and the stuff potent, so I bought another. This I sipped, in no hurry to rejoin the madness. Leaning against a wagon wheel, idly waving off bees, I began to relax, as daylight dimmed and stranger after stranger drifted by. Then a man stepped from the current and, pointing at me, exclaimed in Universal, "I know you!"

He had shaggy yellow hair and a grin wide as the High Lord's ass. A leather patch covered one eye; the other was brown. His Dray accent surfaced when he spoke again, "Don't recall me, do you, gent? You gave me coin when I'd not a crust to eat for days. I owe you a bone reading."

And then I remembered him. He was a beggar – or had been. His lot had obviously improved, for his clothes were newer than mine. "Read my bones another day," I told him.

He laughed, "You said that last time."

I finished my drink, returned the cup, then repeated, "Another day," and walked off, slipping into the stream.

He fished me out again, hooking my elbow and pulling me back to the wagon. "Let me pay the debt, gent. What better have you to do tonight?"

I scanned him, thinking he could've found thievery more lucrative than begging. He emoted no danger though, nor did I detect any special power in him. The man, I concluded, was a fraud. So I agreed to have my fortune told. The experience might be amusing, I thought, and one thing he'd said was correct – I had nothing better to do.

He jabbered with the boy in Dray, then climbed into the wagon. "Come on up, gent. The owner's too drunk to care."

We arranged the kegs so we each had one to sit on, with a third between us for a table. From under his shirt he withdrew a leather pouch and handed it to me. The bones, he said, were inside, and I needed to hold them awhile. I expected him to ask about me, as fake seers are apt to do when setting up a mark, but he chatted about himself. He told me his name was Piduloc. I didn't tell him mine.

The boy brought us brandy at no charge. He and Piduloc murmured back and forth. I don't think they were previously acquainted. Their bond was a common language and the boy's courtesy stemmed, perhaps, from his native respect of a great wizard, for that's what Piduloc claimed to be. He told me he'd been brought to Tiarn by Jarl Renzwil, a cousin of Lord Sarum, before the last set of Games. His job was to use magic to alter the outcome so the Drays would win. When he failed, the Jarl not only abandoned him here, but took his left eye as punishment. "Warned the Jarl not to wager," he said, "predicted he'd lose," then grumbled, "royals don't like hearing the truth, gent."

As twilight faded, the boy lit a lantern, then refilled our cups, and Piduloc began his reading. The bones were chips of bone, carved into various shapes. He shook them between his palms like dice, then cast them onto the lid of the keg. One bounced off and landed by my foot.

"You're far from home," he said as he stretched to retrieve the chip. An easy guess. A man out alone rather than with his mates would more likely be from elsewhere. He hunched over the table-keg while he studied the lay of the other chips. "You have powerful enemies."

Does he say this to everyone? Perhaps, but his next comment drew my interest. "Most of your friends think you're dead."

I rose to the bait and nibbled. "Most?"

He looked up, tipping his head to square his one eye on me. "A few suspect you're alive. One knows for certain."

"Who?" I asked, swallowing the bait, and bait it was, for in order to respond, Piduloc had to cast the bones again – and only the first was free.

One hopence and another throw later, he told me the "who" was someone with power, someone I had known and respected in the past, someone who would reward me at some future date. Then he dangled the next lure. "You were sent here for a reason, gent. On purpose. If you try to go home ere your task is done, your enemies will capture you."

What was my purpose? After another hopence changed hands he told me my task would require great courage, but if I succeeded, many lives would be saved. "Thousands and thousands," he said, then added fresh bait, "you'll escape from your enemies, with help, if you know who to trust. Won't be easy, gent, to tell friend from foe."

And so it went. Each hopence bought a vague answer, with just enough substance to evoke a hint of truth, then he posed a new, tantalizing question, with just enough surety to raise the expectation of a firm answer, which another coin would buy. Piduloc was clever, and perceptive enough to choose alluring bait. I had two hopence left, and scores of doubts, when I stated I'd learned enough about my future. The question pending concerned my home – he never divined it was Evald, nor any specific place, other than not Tiarn – and how things had changed while I'd been gone.

It was dark by then. Moths had replaced bees and banged against the glass shield on the lantern, futile attempts of suicide. The boy had stopped calling to the trickle of passers-by, and sat with his back to a keg, his eyes closed. I wondered if he'd been born a slave, or had been sold by his parents to offset family debts, a common practice in Drayfed, or so their laws imply.

"You're not the least bit curious about home?" Piduloc tempted. "Not even about how your son is faring?"

I shifted my gaze to him and his wide-ass grin. Proving him a fake would also prove myself a fool. I gave him a hopence. "Tell me about my son."

He scattered the bone chips. "Your son misses you, gent. Prays every day for your return. Idolizes you, he does, and boasts of what a great man you are."

Is this not what every traveling father would want to hear? A skilled charlatan, Piduloc. His words had to be false. Yet I could detect no lie. Such a fool. I began to distrust my memory and weighed the possibility that my son could have, somehow, lived through that night in the cellar. A drop of sanity remained, however, so I asked if my son knew I was alive.

"No, gent." He shook his shaggy head. "Your son hopes you are, but doesn't know it. Listens to rumors about you and argues with his mother about leaving to go find you."

"His mother? Tell me how she's faring." I ceded my last coin, a small price to hear enough nonsense to convince myself of his knack at perjury.

"Hate to give you the news," he said after casting the bones. "She's taken up with an old friend of yours. Don't blame her, gent. Or him. They both think you're dead. And don't go rushing home. You've work here to do."

What more did I need? My partner, the mother of my son, is dead. Nothing can make me doubt that fact. Piduloc was a fake. I failed to detect his lies because he believed the rubbish he spouted. If I had risen immediately after hearing the proof and left him, I would not now be doubting that fact either. But he stood first, to fetch us more brandy, then tried to lure me into another reading, hinting he could forecast when it would be safe for me to go home.

"Your enemies are more powerful than you imagine," he warned. "You need my help to elude them."

"Maybe so," I said, "but I can't afford it."

"I'll give you all the readings you need, gent." We were both standing by then, he a span taller, but his size wasn't the source of my unease. His friendly tone carried a dash of what I'd heard often in my past – fear.

"And in exchange?" I asked, sure of the reply.

"Your services." He touched the leather patch over his missing eye. "A trade, gent. Your talents for mine." He had relayed the target with that touch, Jarl Renzwil, who may deserve to be someone's target, but not mine. Justice wasn't uppermost in my mind, however. I wanted to plumb the depth of the talent being offered.

My proof of fraud, solid only moments before, had dissolved into uncertainty. Was he a natural sensitive and had been discreetly picking my thoughts? Even if true, it wouldn't mean he had the skill to predict the future. And he could have simply seen me, as the Soehn Biehr, in the past, though I couldn't imagine where or when. "You know who I am?"

"Not who. What." He motioned to the keg lid where his divining bones lay. "I didn't tell you all they said."

"So I didn't receive what I paid for." I pinned a cold stare on him. "Correct?"

He unloaded his pockets, shoveling out coins, many more than he'd snared from me, which slipped between his fingers and clattered onto the wagon's floor. "Take them all."

I wish, now, that I had taken them, but I'd donned my former persona, and the Soehn Biehr would never scrabble after coins. Nor would insolence be tolerated. I glanced over at the boy who, awakened, was gaping up at us. "The part about my son and his mother ... True?"

"Maybe not," Piduloc recanted. Sensitives, especially poorly trained ones, are acutely susceptible to perceived aggression. I mentally projected hostility and he passed the test grandly, staggering back as if punched, and if it had ended there, I could have been reasonably sure everything he'd told me had been ideas or wishes stolen from my own mind. But he recanted again, crying out, "True! All I said, true," his arms raised as if to ward off another invisible blow. "But gent, don't kill her for it. She and your friend truly believe you're dead."

I was left with the same puzzle as before, fraud or seer? A little of both? "You're wrong about me," I said. "I'm not what you think. I'm not going to kill anybody."

"You're the one who's wrong." His arms lowered, and a grin returned, a fraction of its prior width. "You were sent here. And killing is what you're famous for. Get the wrong gent though and she won't be pleased."

The man was infuriating, with his dangling clues that led nowhere. "She who?" I asked, understanding how he could have enraged a jarl – lucky he lost only an eye.

"She." He knelt to collect his coins. "She who walks the ground by day and rides the wind at night. She who commands the sun and moon, who summons the storm, her eyes like lightning, her voice thunder." He babbled a litany of attributes that undoubtedly had more to do with Dray mythology than an actual woman. With his unkempt hair, and on all fours, he looked like a dog scrounging for table scraps. He sounded like a madman. "She who is dead and is living. She who is crowned by fire and cloaked by ice."

I can't recall every description. Some made me think of Sythene. "She who weeps for wolves and sleeps with bears." The symbol of the Massu family is a bear and Sythene's partner is Luka's foster son, an adopted bear. But Piduloc mentioned a host of animals, even fish and birds. "She who swims with salmon and flies with jays." I was about to give up on making sense of it and slip away while he was occupied, when he reared up. The lantern behind him sprayed a web of light through his tangle of hair.

"She," he continued, voice deepening into a rasp, "who sent you here, Me'acca."

Did he pull my name from my mind? Or was he possessed? I detected no alien force in him. The boy, frightened, leapt from the wagon and ducked beneath it, chain dragging after him then snapping taut, its limit reached. Perhaps I was supposed to be frightened as well. But I had lost interest. "Well," I said, "I should be going."

If possessed, Piduloc recovered quickly. "Wait," he called when I hopped down to the nearly deserted street. He crawled to the lip of the wagon and, kneeling there, flung more bait at me. "I can tell you things you need to know."

I walked away. He shouted after me, "That necklace won't protect you forever," turning me around to scan him once more.

Madman or seer? "Get rid of the necklace, gent, ere it betrays you! It hides you now. Not forever."

I again began walking, his shouts chasing me. "You need me, gent! Kill the wrong man and you won't get another chance! You need me! You won't know who to trust! Gent! They'll find you! You won't get home alive!"

There were more people on Martway than Fruit, but the crowds had evaporated, leaving the city's dregs – beggars, packs of drunken men, and street brothids hoping to attract occupants of the occasional carriage rolling by. I meandered to the bridge, stopped midway across and leaned against the railing. Lanterns, unevenly spaced along the span's rafters, were reflected darkly in the water below. I considered jumping. But knew my instincts would take over the moment I hit the water and I'd swim to shore. Are moths the same? When their wings ignite, do they flee the flame? Or plunge deeper into its heart?

Cyril had left a lamp burning in the dining hall. For me? I snuffed it before coming in here. No more moths will die tonight. Not in the dining hall anyway.

The kitchens feel strange. I feel strange. Drenched in sweat. Sticky with sorrow. I wish my partner was with another man. Wish my son had grown old enough to miss me. Thinking of the slave boy, I wonder how parents can sell their offspring. Did I sell mine? Sacrificed him. On the altar of politics. Not knowingly. Not on purpose. Does that matter? Stupid Fool. Father, I earned my name.

519, 8/19. I was sitting in the dining hall with others who had finished for the day. Cyril was doling out brew to us while women readied tables for evening meal, the same as every day of late. Sweat all night, get up, sweat over the ovens, sit in the dining hall, sweat and drink, then eat and sweat and drink more, then go to bed, and sweat. It's ungodly.

Today deviated from the usual monotony when Tlan, who was working the spit, poked his head through a window and announced, "Reverend Wessel's come." His use of Calec's title showed how opinions change in these kitchens.

Nearly everyone plowed outside. I took the opportunity to turn my chair and plop my feet onto the one Old Wix had vacated. Cyril doesn't like us to do this, but I was in an irreverent mood. Closing my eyes, I imagined myself lying naked in snow, an attempt to mentally cool my body, which I'd tried before, without success.

"Why didn't you go out to see Calec?" Mira asked, disrupting my concentration. She was standing by my feet.

"Why didn't you?"

"He weren't my friend." Hair had escaped from under her bonnet and clung to her neck like the dark roots of a fern. "Maybe Damut's with him."

"Is she?" I asked, sure Mira had peeked out a window.

"No." She unbuttoned the top buttons on her dress and fanned herself with the loose cloth. Trying to seduce me? She has already seduced Padder and Young Wix, sneaking from Filson's bed for trysts in the scullery. I've seen her with each of them, on nights when sleep eluded me, hardly a scandal in this pit of immorality, though secrecy itself can be more intoxicating than perfume. If the veil were lifted, the deeds made public, would Padder and Wix still want her? Mira isn't an ugly woman. Many years ago, I may have tried to seduce her. No, probably not. She would have intrigued me though, as she has here. She is, at times, amusing to spar with, but today my brain was too cooked to function. I couldn't guess the motive for her actions – and couldn't believe she had none.

Calec entered, changing the dynamics of the chat, if that's what Mira and I were having. He wore a yellow and red reverend's gown over pants and a shirt. Religion won over comfort, I suppose. Joy rang in his voice when he spied me, "So there you are, Sheever," yet he hesitated before walking past the empty tables toward mine.

I noticed a limp as he approached and asked if he'd injured himself. "Pony throw you?"

"No." His gaze lingered on Mira who had moved by my side. To give the impression she meant something to me? That's how he took it. His thoughts were clear as glass. He rubbed his hip. "Just getting old."

"Try sleeping in your bed instead of on the temple's floor." I could blame my harsh words on Mira's proximity and say her penchant for cruelty had been transmitted to me. No doubt she enjoyed seeing Calec's joy crumble. Yet whether she knew it or not, she was aiding my plans. I hoped Calec would view us a couple, hoped he'd be uneasy speaking around her. He had expected me to be alone, may have even asked Cyril to keep the others outside so we could talk privately. He wanted to snare me in his troubles. I wanted him gone.

He ignored my comment and started fresh, saying how well the garden was doing, how hard Damut had been working, how grateful all of them were for the help they'd received the past spring. He stated that the purpose of his visit was to invite us out to share the fruits of our labor, have a garden festival of sorts. "You'll come?"

I've lost the edge I once had. He was such a pitiful sight, sunburnt face and scrawny neck wet with sweat. His white hair, in thin damp clumps, looked like bird droppings on his head. "We've been busy," I hedged.

"Maybe for an evening," he suggested, "you could find time. Or on a free day."

"Maybe," I said, which is how we left it.

He limped back outside and soon everyone gushed in. They were all excited by the idea of a garden festival and talked of nothing else tonight, but it was just talk. No date was set, no plans agreed upon. Tomorrow, unless someone organizes these fools, enthusiasm will fade. In a week, Calec's festival will be forgotten.

519, 8/31. My prediction was wrong. Calec's invitation was not forgotten. The notion of a festival has been a daily topic, including arguments over who should go. People expected me to develop a plan. I didn't. Cyril took charge of the project and the problems. Our workload is higher than last spring, so he couldn't hand out free days as he did then. He solved this admirably by deciding we should go after work, which opened it up for anyone who wanted to go, even the scullery girls, who promised to stay up late and scrub pots when they returned.

Getting the use of a wagon (for the benefit of Old Wix and the children) became a snag because Jenner hasn't come up here lately. The restored friendship between him and Cyril must be more fragile than I thought, for Cyril balked at the idea of going down to ask him. Today, about noon, he pulled me from work and sent me down to do the asking.

Scattered clouds reduced the sun's heat to a simmer as I walked down to the stables. Jenner wasn't there and the stable hands wouldn't release a wagon without his approval. They also wanted his permission to go along.

I searched for him in the yards and ran across Col tethered to a rail of the pigsty. His mental state has improved, two other stockmen informed me. He now can feed himself and walk without help, which is why he was tied to the rail, for he has a tendency to walk aimlessly away and his mates had grown tired of chasing after him.

The stockmen suggested I look for Jenner in their quarters and that's where I found him, sitting outside the shack with Gim, drinking ale. Nothing in particular sparked a dash of mistrust. Gim is an ordinary-looking man, medium build, average intelligence. Muck on his boots grants him the smell of a man in charge of stockyards. When I came upon them today, Jenner was telling his story about Macon D'brae, and the smile Gim offered my intrusion showed his relief, a normal reaction if he'd heard the tale half as often I. Yet I wondered if Gim could be more than he seems. An agent of the Church? A spy couldn't find a better tool than Jenner, a virtual way station for gossip. I considered prying Jenner away, but that would provoke a spy's interest. So I stated why I had tracked him down. He granted use of a wagon, and asked Gim to go along.

The outing occurred, as planned, after work. Every man, woman and child in the kitchens was ready to go. I backed out at the last moment, citing as a reason that someone should stay to watch over things. Cyril agreed, even thanked me for volunteering, and no one would have doubted my reason – if Mira hadn't stated that she, too, would stay behind 'to keep Sheever company.' Her decision raised more than a few eyebrows, including mine.

What is she up to? Spending the evening with her shed no light on any plot. I drank ale while she stitched the seams of a dress she's making. Our conversation dealt with nothing of import. Maybe by staying behind she wanted to incite jealousy in one of her love interests, though she could easily make them jealous of each other. Maybe she didn't want to see Damut as the center of attention. But she heard about it. When everyone returned, the dining hall filled with praise of Damut and her garden. And Mira didn't shy from listening. I can't believe she has suddenly become a woman without ambition. But whatever game she's playing is on a different level than I'm accustomed to.

519, 9/3. I've been here eight years. As always on this date, my thoughts have lingered on when I first arrived, and why. Today differs slightly. The past year differed slightly. I question my perception of the truth.

I came here because I believed the memsa who sent me. I believed I could earn the Rite of Grace. This belief has not changed. What I have begun to question is how I am to earn the rite. By good deeds? The memsa told me to give half my wages to the poor, and I have done so. Have eight years of charity lightened my soul? Has my pride shrunk? Do I recall those I've slain and feel sorrow? Not hardly. Will I ever? Not likely. They deserved to die.

I can agree, in theory, that matters of life and death belong in the realm of gods. But if no god acts to enforce a code of justice, people must step in to do so. Why does this sound like something Juboe might say? Am I more like my father than I want to admit? The facts are I have committed murder, yet I can earn the Rite of Grace. How is the question. Not with good deeds. That was a ruse the memsa created, a feint to draw my attention from the true reason she sent me here. Oh, I'll continue to dole half my pay to the poor. I've already separated the wages I received today into theirs and mine. But if charity were the key to salvation, why send me here? Are Tiarn's beggars more needy than beggars in Eastland?

The memsa sent me here, not just to Tiarn, but to work in the High Lord's kitchens. Where to go was the clearest portion of what she told me. Why position me here? So I'll be in place when needed? To commit murder? Why not?

This premise stems from my encounter with Piduloc, a shaky foundation to be sure. I realize most of what he said was pulled from my own mind. But much of it makes sense. When he intuited what I was, what did he want from me? A dead body.

Why should a memsa be otherwise? The idea doesn't shock me. Not today. Eight years ago it would have. Maybe. I was sick of the paltry excuses people gave when they tried to solicit me. But no memsa would sanction a death without just cause. The vows of the Order forbid it, as I should know, since I swore those same vows. "Neither by act nor word shall I elicit harm upon another without due process of law." The due process is a path around this vow. It's also modified by the first and last tenets of the Codex Metapheni of Dynnas: "All things living have worth," and "All things living must die."

Every law, every vow, has a path around it. True, I broke my vows rather than waste time going around them. But a memsa wouldn't. And if the memsa at the way station had named a target and asked me to apply Metapheni's last tenet, I would have obeyed. So why didn't she? Was the target not solid eight years ago? The crime not yet committed? Have I been waiting here for another man to act, so I will be in a position to deliver punishment for his deed?

These have been my thoughts today. Drawn into the mix were my worries for Sythene, and I wondered – have I been sent here to eliminate her assassin? Not likely. The Dynnae protect her. Indeed, the most likely reason I can no longer sense her is the Dyns have created some way to shield her from even mental attack. I suppose a lowlander could have been groomed for an attempt on her life and I was sent here to cancel the threat before he had time to act. But that's a stretch of imagination. Odds are against it.

Toying with this notion, however, led me to a simple revelation. If I had been sent here to target a potential assassin, I would kill him, or her, without hesitation. No mercy. No concern for law. No alarm for my soul. Eight years I've been here, and I haven't changed a whit.

519, 9/14. Returned from the meadow early and rode out to the cemetery before coming here. It had occurred to me that chances are Gim is an ear for the Church and I wanted to warn Calec. A boast about Loric favoring Malison with rare powers might generate undue attention. I'm ashamed I had hadn't thought of the boy's peril sooner.

When I got there, Calec was dozing under the quince, Basal and Loren napping with him. Malison, sitting on the temple's stoop, rose to his feet. I expected him to go inside to avoid the temptation of speaking, but he stayed put and stared at me, his expression as clear as a verbal plea for help. I turned the horse and rode to the garden.

Damut was picking beans, face and hands tanned brown. She walked to the end of the row, basket under her arm, and frowned up at me. "Where you been all summer? With Mira?"

"Don't be silly," I said. It was then I elected to warn her rather than Calec. Dismounting, I briefed her on what had happened to Col. Most of it she'd heard from Baz and the other women who had filled her ears with gossip during last month's garden festival – and filled her head with the idea Mira and I had stayed behind to be together. I dispelled that myth before adding my suspicions about Gim.

"What's he to do with my boys?" she asked, "or with you not stopping by this whole summer?"

"Trust me on this," I pleaded. "It would be better if no one thinks you and your boys are special to me."

"Are we," she faltered, "special to you?"

"Yes," I told her. It was what she wanted to hear and in a way it's true. I don't want their deaths on my soul.

519, 9/31. A dark moon tonight. No illusions. Wondering who my target might be has been at the core of my thoughts this month. It slices into my mind when I'm working, slides beneath the surface when I'm talking to people, juts out again when I come into my room, pesters me until I drop into sleep, awakens with me each morning. Who?

High Lord Trivak is an obvious answer, but obvious answers are often wrong. The memsa's riddle is the only guide I have. "Serve the highest in the land," she told me, which can hardly be construed to mean Fesha Trivak should be a target. And if he were, why wait this long to trigger me? The same can be said for his son Prissen. No, I'm confident this reference was simply to place me here.

'Victors shall don new faces' relates to timing rather than possible targets. The only other person mentioned was the man 'who shall rule thy home.' Is he the target? Why? Because he will become the next Vic Chairman? That isn't enough to mark him. Because he's an Eshra priest who will become Chairman? Historically, most Vic Chairmen worked closely with the Church, Juboe being a notable exception. To have a priest overtly in charge of the Vic government might annoy memsen, but I doubt any would seek his death. The Dyns, yes. I could easily believe Luka would craft a plan to remove the priest from office, but not memsen.

Am I reaching this conclusion because I want it to be true? According to the riddle, the man who will rule my home will first save my life. Priest or no, the idea of killing him disturbs me. Doesn't seem ... courteous. Even more disturbing is the fact I so readily accepted the notion I've been sent here to kill anyone. Nothing in the riddle supports it. The closest reference to my being a soehn biehr was 'Ye shall taste what ye have given in thy craft and Pheto's door shall stand ajar.' This suggests I'll be the one who's poisoned, and will almost die from it. Unless the two parts have no connection. Most poisons can't harm me, though if someone tried to kill me in that manner, I would certainly taste it. This may be another clue about the time of my departure. Pheto's door ajar could mean I'll come close to dying, or it might refer to the Church and imply I must go through it to return home, which would fit with what I've already deduced.

Why have I sorted through the nonsense Piduloc told me and grabbed the idea of having a target? Do I miss being the Soehn Biehr? No. And yes. I don't miss the killing. I miss ... respect. Even as a child I was granted a measure of respect, as Juboe's son, as the son of a memsa, as someone close to Lord Haesyl. Being Soehn Biehr heightened the respect I received. There have always been those with higher status than I, but until I came here, I never endured life as a complete Nobody and, to be honest, I don't care for it. My pride refuses to accept my current position.

Even as I write this admission, my pride fights for dominance. I should struggle to reduce my baser instincts, to reject the lure of lethal actions. Some of Piduloc's words were false. But to ignore everything he said may be foolish. What harm in being prepared? I have the daekah the natals gave me. I remember thinking that with a gold piece I could buy my way home. An error, I think now. When the time comes, wealth, or lack of it, will account for nothing. Why not use the daekah to buy a few options?

If I'm going to believe Piduloc, I should get rid of my necklace. He said it would give me away. He also said it hid me. From the Church? Did Sythene give me more than a token to remember her by? Whatever the truth is, I'm not going to part with the necklace, proof I don't want to use Piduloc's ravings as a guide, but as an excuse. I should think twice before I again don the title of Poison Master.

519, 10/18. When I returned from the meadow today, Cyril was waiting for me in the back orchard. I had finished grooming the

Sheever's Journal, Diary of a Poison Master

horse Jenner lent me and as I walked up to the kitchens, I spied Cyril. He was standing by an apple tree on the second terrace, far enough from any window that he wouldn't be overheard, though I don't know if it was intentional. "Calec comed looking for you," he said. "I tolt him if you comed early, you might ride out to his place before you …" He scowled as he eyed me; I was filthy from road dust. "… wash up."

"Calec's determined to save my soul," I complained. "Can't rest with a kor-man lurking about. But I'm not ready to give up drinking."

Cyril swallowed my false account of Calec's motives. "Come on, Kor-man," he laughed, "I'll pour you a brew." He had more than Calec's visit to relay. Our free days are being cut to one a month. I expected this. Since Trivak announced his divorce, every family with a drop of royal blood and an unwed daughter has been flocking here. If the High Lord is smart, he'll make a match for Prissen before he picks a bride for himself. The cost of guests may pinch one's purse, but people vying to cozy up to a throne bring gifts. And the High Lord, not his son, is the greater catch. Prissen may never wear his father's crown.

There's little else to record. The weather's been dry, which made my stay at the meadow pleasant, but uneventful. I'm just as torn about what to do, if anything, with the daekah as when I left. Odd that when I was wealthy, I rarely thought about rationing coin. And when poor, there was nothing worthwhile I could afford. One gold coin, and I worry I might spend it unwisely. Might as well be poor.

519, 11/10. Calec dropped by. It was late afternoon and I should have been done for the day, but Kwint decided he wanted a wine sauce for the doves Padder had roasted, and Cyril gave the task to me. Bad enough to be cooking with Kwint and Cyril at my elbow, then Calec pops in. I told him I was busy and would be for a while, hinting that if he waited for me, he'd have to ride back to the cemetery after nightfall. Cyril, more polite than I, stopped chatting with Kwint and asked if anything was wrong with Damut and her boys.

"No," Calec insisted, "I just wanted to invite Sheever to come by on his next free day."

"I've already taken mine for the month," I lied. Cyril opened his mouth, as if about to correct me, then winked and let the lie pass unchallenged.

"Maybe next month?" Calec pursued.

"We've been so busy," Cyril cut in and began escorting Calec into the hall, "won't be no free days next month."

We have indeed been busy. And the shortening days make it seem we're even busier. It's dark when we sit to eat. Yet the mood here is anything but dour. Tongues wag nonstop with gossip, most of which originates with Kwint and the house staff who blab what they overhear in the palace. It's similar to a Game Year, but different. None of the other lords has come – nor do they intend to, if the chatter is correct – and though all three have sent family members, the difference is significant. Lords bring a host of officials with them, and many more guards than a niece, sister or daughter might warrant.

During Game Years swordsmen are at the fore. This year it's young girls. When Kwint hurries down to inform us of what's been requested, sweets, not meats, top his lists. Not that meats have been omitted. The surplus of girls has drawn a sizeable number of unwed men as well. The palace has become a marketplace for brides, and it throbs with gaiety – different than the fervor the Games bring. I've heard no racial slurs, nor rabid calls for knocking foreign heads. There have been, however, wagers placed on who may be Fesha Trivak's next wife.

None of us knows the players well enough to make guesses on a specific girl, so the bets are on which state she'll be from. Trivak's first and third wives were Mearan. His second hailed from Somer, which leads many to believe he'll choose a girl from either Drayfed or Verdina. That's where the heavier bets have been laid. Jenner, who claimed to be swamped with work, found time to rush in and put his coin on Verdina. No surprise. His love affair with everything Verdi has yet to wane.

I haven't wagered. I think Trivak will bide his time and choose no one, not now anyway. He already has an heir. Why hurry? If forced to pick, however, I'd say his next wife will be from Drayfed. The impression I've gotten from hearing years of gossip is Trivak, unlike Jenner, doesn't recall fondly his encounters with Macon D'brae.

As for Prissen, Old Wix ended any wagers on him by stating, "Has to be a Mearan girl for the boy's first wife. It's the law." I don't know if there is such a law, nor does anyone else here, but speculation ceased.

Personally, I prefer the type of energy resonating now over the hostility which bubbles up during the Games. But hearing about the people of import who have gathered here sharpens my dislike of being a Nobody. How I would love to be involved in brokering the deals being made.

519, 11/31. I chose today as my free day because I wanted to sleep in this morning – more accurately, I wanted to stay awake last night. Today is the anniversary of Sythene's birth and I'd hoped to focus on her last night, as I wish I had twenty-six years ago. My plans then, as now, didn't last.

Yesterday evening I was so tired I feared I'd fall asleep if I came in here. I walked up to Main Road, believing a stroll in the chill air would invigorate me.

Lanterns had been placed on the palace steps and along the pavement to the road. For whom? I crossed over to the dark side of the road and kept walking, but my curiosity had been pricked. Near the intersection with Natal Way, I stepped into Royal Wood. The old oaks provided excellent cover – and comfort. I settled among a snarl of thick roots, my seat cushioned by leaves, my back supported by a massive trunk. Though I'd walked too far and was closer to the Church, I still had a good view of the palace. The thrill of spying quickly ebbed. I dozed off.

The noise of carriages jarred me awake. A parade of them rolled by, each one stopping by the palace to unload a batch of Somebodies who sauntered up the lighted steps and went inside, a half moon adding a touch of silver to the scene. The people were too distant for me to see their faces, not that I would've recognized anyone. Young royals, I assumed, either returning from an excursion in the city or gathering for an event at the palace.

After the last of them had gone inside and the night regained its quiet, I stared at the moon, trying to retrieve my original plan and focus on Sythene. Yet she seemed as remote as the stars. The moon's bright and dark halves brought to mind the usual roster of opposites – good and evil, right and wrong, life and death, body and soul. Past and future. I felt out of step, in tune with neither one aspect nor the other. Lost in a grey void.

I lowered my gaze and spied a man crossing the road as I had done, choosing the dimmer side. But the moon betrayed him. I saw the sword at his hip, the glitter of metal studs on his leather tunic. A scar marred his forehead, warping an eyebrow, though it seemed to fit him, and I'd wager that whoever delivered the blow suffered worse from the clash than this man. The air about him was absolute. I was watching an assassin approach.

The white stag on his blazon – aglow in the moonlight – labeled him as a Verdi, which might explain why he was carrying rather than wearing his cape. The mild weather we've had this year must feel warm compared to the winter he left in Verdina. He walked past me to the intersection, then stopped and looked down Natal Way. That road runs smack into the Verdi Compound. I couldn't believe he'd target a Verdi natal, but I wished I had the ability to read his thoughts, for he stayed there quite a while, staring. Then he swung his cape over his shoulders, retraced a portion of his steps, and entered the Wood less than ten paces from me. Unlike me, he didn't seek a place to sit and doze. He spent the rest of the night standing. I spent it wondering how I could possibly slip away undetected. If he discovered me, the consequence was sure. This man was not the sort who dithers over the right or wrong use of his skill. A sense of purpose burned in him. I remembered how it felt to be caught up in a purpose larger than oneself, when guilt was a stranger. I envied him.

As the sky began to lighten, a man and woman came out of the palace. They descended the stairs at a normal pace, but at the bottom she hoisted the hem of her dress and ran to road, her cloak flaring open. She reminded me of the dichotomy of the moon – half girl, half woman. The closer she got, the more the woman half appeared to be illusion. Her green dress had wide bands of ermine at the bodice and hips to give a fuller impression of her immature shape. Yet her beauty was striking, black hair swept atop her head, strands of pearls looped through her curls.

The man, chasing after, soon caught her, and they laughed and chattered as they walked hand in hand toward the intersection. He was older than she – mid-twenties, I'd guess – and had blond hair. He wore blue satin pants and a matching doublet, lace at the collar and sleeves, a Dray fashion, which was the language they were speaking.

I had no reason to think these two were targets. Until the Stag near me stirred. To shout a warning would've been incredibly stupid. I remained silent as he slipped from the Wood onto the road. "Nena," he said, and the couple halted.

She proved to be fluent in Verdi, which was the tongue she and the Stag used. I couldn't understand a word. She showed no fear of him though. Indeed, she stamped a foot in anger. She pouted. She even wept, and the blond draped a consoling arm around her. None of it moved the Stag. Eventually, he escorted the couple back to the palace. No harm done.

I arose from my hiding spot and came down to the kitchens to warm up with tea, then went to the stables. Jenner welcomed an extra hand. While I helped him polish carriages, he gossiped and, when the time seemed ripe, I tossed the word "Nena" into his kettle of unfounded tales on the chance it was a name.

He grinned, for I had stumbled upon his favorite topic. "Wanena, you mean. She's the daughter of Macon D'brae."

"Could be," I said, and it would explain her fluency in both the Dray and Verdi tongues, and also her lack of fear if the Stag were her father's man. But why would Lord D'brae employ an assassin to watch over his daughter? To scare off unwanted suitors? Maybe. Especially if the Stag has a reputation, which I wouldn't doubt.

Jenner believes Wanena will be the High Lord's next wife. He figures she learned the dark arts from her Dray mother and will bewitch Fesha Trivak as her mother did Macon. But he fretted over the latest rumors. Apparently, Macon's eldest son is also here and opposes the match. "I've five coppers riding on her," Jenner confided. "Think I should change my bet?"

Wanena's dual heritage could make her a wise choice. And if she's the girl I saw, she's an attractive choice. But that doesn't mean she'll be chosen, witchcraft or no. I wouldn't blame her brother for trying to spoil the deal. If I were her brother, I would. "Never wager what you can't afford to lose," I told Jenner, advice I've never been able to live by. Nor will he, I suspect.

Sheever's Journal, Diary of a Poison Master

519, 12/3. Calec stopped by again, wanting to see me. The cooks were being paid, which always creates a disruption, so I led him out the north door to where he had left his pony. A dreary sky helped set the mood I wanted as I scolded him for coming. I thought rude treatment, rather than a warning, had more chance of keeping him away – and elicit fewer questions. "You'll get me booted out," I complained. He apologized, then proceeded to tell me his problems. Damn him.

Malison, it seems, wants out of his commitment. I asked if the boy had broken the conditions of baimyot. Calec said he has not. "But he prays for Loric to free him. Sheever, I need your help."

"If he's in baimyot," I said, "I can't talk to him." But that wasn't what Calec wanted from me. His plan is to bring Basal into the temple, teach both boys together and then, if Malison opts out, Basal could replace him. My task in this was to persuade Damut into surrendering another son. "She'll still have Loren," he said.

Convince her of that, I thought. "You should be the one to tell her," I said, and suggested he do it on the only day his religion allows him to speak with her – Gurn Four.

He nodded, as if agreeing. "But it would go better if you was there to help. She likes you, Sheever. And surely Gurn Four were a free day for everybody."

I laughed, "Maybe it should be, but it isn't. Gurn Five is the cooks' holiday." An utter mistake and he leapt on it, inviting me to come by after work on the fourth and sleep over.

"We'll be expecting you," he said. Damnation.

520, 1/1. Light fades to shadow. Darkness gives rise to light. Days blend. Time slips away, lost forever. One year ends, another begins. Cyril tacked a new almanac onto the wall. He'll lose a few more hairs this year. Filson will grow a few more. Change. I'm dizzy with excitement.

520, 1/4. I didn't go to Calec's today. These kitchens have been pushed to their limit preparing the royal banquet. By noon, when we shut down the ovens, I was too tired to walk out to the cemetery. Nor did I want to. Here I had stale gossip and free ale. There I would've faced Damut's temper and tears. What sort of choice was that? An easy one.

520, 1/5. I walked to the cemetery. I ate bidda before I left. My head was splitting. I tried to construct a worthy excuse on the way, but when Calec answered my knock, "Sorry, I'm late," was the best I could do.

He responded with a toothless grin. "Loric forgives."

We sat on the temple's cold stoop, door shut behind us, while we chatted. He hadn't mentioned his plan to Damut yesterday, and he blamed me. "I was waiting for you."

I suggested he soften her up with gifts before springing his ideas on her. He stated he'd given her a stove. "What more could she want?"

"The stove was for Malison," I said, which sounded as if Damut had sold her son for a stove, and perhaps she had. "If you want Basal, give her something else. Say, a cow."

"A cow! I don't have that sort of coin." He grumbled about how little he earns as a reverend, then blasted my ears with his opinion of Fesha Trivak who has 'forsaken Loric and taken up with godless foreigners.' He also ranted about the reverends at the Grand Temple. They treated him well when they wanted 'that girl Prissen killed' buried in his graveyard, but now they shun him. "They want to close this temple of mine. Close it! Can you believe that?"

I can. Calec doesn't turn a profit. And I sympathized, but I wasn't getting through to him. "Maybe you're rushing Malison too fast," I said, setting him up for the only weapon that might work on him – religion.

He muttered, "I have to rush the boy. Don't have time to go slow. If I was to die …"

"Reverend," I broke in, "only Loric knows how much time you have." I forced him to recall last year, when Malison came to the kitchens, and spun a fresh explanation. "Loric was speaking to you. Telling you to go slow. The boy needs to be in the world while he's growing."

That silenced him. I pushed the weapon to his heart and spoke of how his life could be if he released Malison from baimyot. "The cottage would be warmer, better for your health. You could teach both boys there, and Loren as well when he's old enough. Bring them to the temple each day to show them the Rites. But let them stay in the world."

He promised to pray on the matter. I didn't visit Damut. I couldn't have faced her.

520, 1/20. Fesha Trivak and Prissen left for Dartsport. No announcement has been made concerning a bride for either of them. They've grabbed the gifts and run. All bets are off.

520, 1/25. Rain and the High Lord's departure have emptied the palace of guests. Rumors abound, none worth recording. There's less work. Cyril offered the cooks a free day this week. He refused to give me four and he's right, it wouldn't be fair. But one day is of no use to me. Already Juboe nips at my mind. And the rains have just begun.

520, 2/7. For the past several evenings, I've been going into the city, nosing about in various apothecary shops, testing the competence of the owners. All of them stock common poisons. Nothing of value. I'm reluctant to ask for what I want. I want? Or Juboe wants? His voice torments me, urging me on a path

I'm not sure I want to tread, mocking my hesitation. How I hate him. Yet he may be correct.

What I want is a poison with the capacity to kill me. There aren't many. Mesinale would be best. I'm plotting escape, not suicide. But the outcome could be my death.

The plan. Arm a needle with mesinale. Seal it with wax. Plant the needle in the braided cloth of my necklace. If I find myself in an untenable position, I'll prick myself and induce a trance deep enough that I'll appear to be dead. My body will be discarded. I'll rouse from the trance. And rush to get the antidote. Possible? I have partial immunity to mesinale. I could last a week, maybe longer. But the beauty of mesinale is the searing pain it produces, handy when used on an adversary, not so handy when used on oneself. Could I function with my blood afire? It would be better to have the antidote with me. But my body would likely be stripped before it's dumped. I can't rely on having a cure on hand.

Flaws. What if I'm bound and can't reach the needle? No solution. What if the evidence, namely my body, is burned rather than dumped? No solution. What if I can't fool an Eshra priest? I'd still be trapped – and in agony. None of Juboe's tortures destroyed resistance as fast as mesinale can. Would I cut a deal to end the pain?

This plan is so flawed I can't believe I'm considering it. Am I? If caught, would I use mesinale on myself? Or kill my way out with it? No one need die. A victim could last the better part of a day, maybe two. There'd be time to fetch the antidote – and bargain for my release.

520, 2/16. My first attempt to purchase mesinale has failed. The apothecary I chose has the required knowledge, but lacks daring. He's an older man, with henna-tinted hair and sulfur-stained hands. When I visited his shop before, his much younger wife was tending the coin box. He seemed content to discuss various remedies with me, a potential customer. She nagged me to buy. Her sharp voice and pushy manner led me to believe he might understand why a man could decide to have a little poison on hand.

Tonight, I waited out in the evening drizzle while he finished with a client, then I stepped into his shop. He remembered me. As did she. "Bring any coin this time?" she shrilled. I flashed the daekah and avarice oiled her tongue. "What can we do you for?"

I asked him if we could speak privately. She hissed into his ear, then excused herself and hurried upstairs. A door squeaked open. I didn't hear it shut.

"Mate," the apo whispered, as if aware I knew his wife was listening, "want something personal, do you? A love potion maybe? Or a poultice to fortify your loins?"

Rather than answer, I surveyed his stock, the most precious stored in glass bottles on shelves behind his counting table. "You're on good terms with the Snakes."

"Good as any loyal Mearan can be," he dodged, though the proof lay in the exotic variety of his wares. He slipped behind the narrow table and faced me. "I trade with the Snakes so mates like you don't have to."

"And charge a fee," I added, "as you should." I placed the daekah on the table and rested a thumb on it. "What I want won't cost more than two silvers. The rest can be yours." A profit of eight silvers. Eight! Surely it should have been enough for him to find a little courage. But when I asked him to order a quarter dram of mesinale, his whispery voice dropped even lower. "Why you wanting demon's fire?" he questioned, calling the poison by its Vic name.

"You don't want to know," I whispered back at him. "A quarter dram. I'll pick it up tomorrow night." I removed my thumb from the coin, hoping greed might win over the fear I spied in his eyes.

349

"The Snakes know you're an honest man. They'll sell you a tiny pinch."

He shook his head. "Not of that they won't." I tried to convince him to at least attempt to purchase the mesinale, and got nowhere. That isn't exactly true. I got shoved out his door.

"Listen," he advised. "Don't go asking around for demon's fire. The Snakes don't sell it. Not to nobody, they don't. Not at no price. If they catch wind of you, mate, you'll get a spot of fire sure enough. But not how you'd be wanting it." Then he closed his door.

Option one. I still have the daekah. I could try another shop. Pick an apo with less knowledge. Only an idiot hires a fool to handle his business. Option two. Deal directly with the Snakes. The risk would be greater. There could be no errors. No blind attempt like tonight. The odds don't favor success. Option three. Choose another poison. Fine. But I'm stuck with the same problem. I want something that will cripple a man in an instant, yet can be reversed. Tincture of arsenic, which the apos have in abundance, won't do. Option four. Brew my own poison. That would rule out mesinale. There are other possibilities though. Finding the plants would be easy enough. But where do I distill an extract? In Trivak's kitchens? Not hardly.

Option five. Forget the whole matter. Sever myself from the past. Refuse to kill for any reason, including self-defense. This appeals to the part of me that prays for salvation, the shrinking part of my mind still free from Juboe. Can this part control the rest? It hasn't convinced me to store the daekah in my room. This month I've carried the coin in my pocket. Always with me. Always ready to be spent. The coin has gained a power of its own. It reminds me of what I once was, what I could be, what I could own. Today I am forty-three years old. I want to let go of the past. But the past won't let go of me.

520, 2/25. I smacked Helsa this morning. She was in my way. I didn't strike her hard. But everyone in the spare kitchen stopped and stared. Then Old Wix slipped out and a few moments later Cyril came by, wanting to chat with me, he said, and nudging me away from my station. The reason for the chat was obvious – and irritating. Other cooks hit the women here. Why am I held to a different standard?

Anger heated me as I trailed Cyril into the dining hall. A clutch of women was in there, mending clothes. He led me to a window. Rain drummed down outside. He cursed the weather, said it could drive anyone mad, then offered me a useless bottle of ophren. "Get some sleep."

"I don't want it," I grated, too loudly. Chairs scraped, and I knew the women were watching. "Cyril," I said in as normal a tone as I could, "I don't need more sleep."

"What's wrong then? I've not seen you this bad off."

What could I say? That I resent living in this hole with fools like him? That my father's voice is so fused in my mind I can't tell which thoughts are my own? That I savor the idea of killing every person in these kitchens? That I'm so full of rage I fear I may actually do it?

He grunted at my silence. "I should've given you them free days last month." Idiot. He blamed himself. "Well, take the rest of today free. And if you need this …" He again offered the ophren. "… just ask."

I spun away from him and walked out into the cold rain. Jenner wasn't in the stables. Drinking with Gim, no doubt. I saddled a horse anyway. His men didn't object. I had no destination. No purpose. I rode to the cemetery. The chimneys of both the cottage and the temple breathed smoke, evidence that Calec hasn't followed my advice. I rode to the eastern tip of the park, looped back and rode to the bridge. I didn't cross over into Tiarn. Too many temptations there. I took Natal Way to the arena, circled it, rode back to the bridge, out again to the eastern point, back again to the bridge, to the arena. I went nowhere.

I returned, soaked to the skin, during evening meal. The dining hall hushed as I squished past the tables. I came in here and had stripped off my tunic when a rap sounded. It was Baz, with a pot of hot tea and a plate of food. Why won't these people just leave me alone?

"You and me," she said, "is the sort that keeps secrets. Tell me what were wrong. You can trust me."

Not hardly. I took the tea and shut the door on her. My rage has no focus. I feel the impulse to destroy this room. Rip the wood off the bricks. Burn the plank with Tobb's name on it. Juboe laughs inside my head. He's the one I want to destroy, the one I want to kill. I can't shove him out. Can't hide from him with trances. He sabotages the inner worlds I create. He has become part of me. And I have become ... afraid.

520, 3/2. I'm calm. Totally. At peace with my future. A stay in the meadow deserves some of the credit. But not all. Before going, I bickered with Cyril. He wanted me to wait out a storm. "You'll be struck by lightning," he warned.

I next bickered with Jenner. Same argument. Late afternoon. Pounding rain. A wicked wind. No chance of getting far before nightfall. A sane man would stay put, leave the next morning. Opposition honed my determination – and my temper. Nothing short of death would have stopped me.

The gelding Jenner lent me jumped at every clap of thunder. At the bridge, a lightning flash startled him. He tossed me, then bolted east on Perimeter. I seethed as I trudged after him. Indeed, if the rain striking me had turned to steam, I would not have been surprised, so hot the rage in me. I found the beast near Cemetery Lane, trembling, unfit to withstand my wrath.

I rode to the temple and beat on the door until Calec opened it. I can't remember all the venom I spewed at him. Portions of the encounter that I do recall, if recorded here, might be mistaken as a civil chat, so I feel obligated to avow that I was not civil. He was though, standing in the doorway while I ranted, serene, as if draped in a holy mantle. I wanted to snap his neck.

I saw Malison by the candle-lit altar, his eyes wide. The boy understood how near the abyss I teetered. Calec understood nothing. Or so I deemed. I demanded to know what he had decided to do, whether to release Malison or commit Basal, or both. He said he was waiting for Loric to give him a sign. I told him he wouldn't recognize a sign if it were branded on his hand.

"If you truly believe in Loric," I challenged, trying to crack his smug faith and drag him into a quarrel, "why do you ignore the wife He sent you?"

"I don't ignore Damut," he countered smoothly. "She's in my prayers every day." He suggested I stable the horse and spend the night. "Damut will be glad to have you. And we can talk tomorrow. When you're in a less stormy mood."

Delay and pray were his tactics, and I realized he would win. He'd keep Malison hostage and steal Basal as well. Delay and pray. So simple. Damut had no weapons to combat him. Eventually, she'd have no sons. The injustice of it fanned my burning rage. I fished the daekah from my pocket, then seized his wrist. "Buy her a cow," I spat as I slapped the coin onto his palm. I left before he could respond – and before I could snatch the coin back.

The gelding again shied from the bridge. This time I dismounted and flipped my cape over the beast's eyes, then led him across and into the city. A sense of misfortune pervaded the deserted streets, of evil, leaching up from the ground to blend with the rain and bathe the city in decay. Doors and shutters were sealed against the odorous flood, as if mere wood could protect the people within. Fools. Tiarn is a city of the damned.

It was past sundown when I reached the gates, but they stood open, the guards too lazy or too fearful of the storm to tend their duties. The shanties beyond the city's walls lacked shutters and their lighted windows beckoned. A hopence would've bought me shelter for the night. Maybe I should have stopped. With a skittish horse, I didn't get much farther anyway, though I can't blame him. Darkness halted me. I couldn't see well enough to detect where the swollen river had merged with the road.

The storm lasted most of the night, then blew past. Between patches of cloud, stars emerged, bright and icy, melting in the glow of dawn. My rage had also melted. And Juboe was gone from my mind. I can't explain how or why, or say exactly when he vanished. He was simply gone. Because I gave the daekah to Calec? Maybe. Wealth is no sin, but that coin was a bane to me from the moment I touched it. I hope Calec doesn't fall prey to its curse.

I rode to the meadow without Juboe nagging me, without worrying how or if to buy a dab of poison. I felt numb. The meadow was more lake than field. But a strip of high ground offered enough grass to satisfy the gelding. Under a warm sun, I dropped into sleep, and slept more soundly than I have for weeks. No dreams. No tortured cries. No Juboe. I slept through the night and half the next day.

When I woke, I remained lying on the soggy ground, thinking. My mind seemed so clear, capable of grasping the breadth of eternity. This sensation, I should note, is not still with me. The peace it brought, however, is. I know why the memsa laced her predictions with riddles. I was like the gelding, afraid of the bridge, and she cloaked my sight of the future to shield me from fear. I tore off the cloak. I saw, or believed I saw, my fate, to become as Col and it terrified me. Not now. I don't know why. My fear is gone. I pray it won't return.

520, 3/11. My improved mood has rekindled rumors that I have a wife in Brithe. The cooks tease me. "All you needed was a girl!" Baz, despite my protests, is determined to match me with one of the women here so my humor will stay 'sweet.' Patience. This, too, shall fade.

520, 4/1. Malison dropped by this afternoon. I was working and didn't know he was here, when Cyril came in, asking, "Where did you get a gold piece to give Calec?"

I'm such a fool. Why hadn't I thought this through and covered my actions? I summoned a laugh and threw Cyril's question back at him. "Where would I get a gold piece?"

"That's what I were asking you!" He pulled me out into the hall and, as if tied to my apron, everyone else in the spare kitchen followed us to the dining room.

I heard Malison chattering before I saw him and his audience, a group of mostly women and children. The boy's tongue stilled for an instant when he spied me, then he blurted, "Sheever, we've got us a cow! And geese, too! With your gold piece!"

I never actually believed Calec would release him from baimyot. But he had. And the boy was there, blabbing everything he had witnessed on that stormy day last month. I had only one option. Denial. I tried to wound him gently, hinting he'd been dreaming rather than declaring him a liar. And wound it was, for he winced at my allegation, but the grit which helped him survive in these kitchens served him again, to my dismay.

"It's true," he avowed. "Ask Calec who gived him the coin. Calec will tell you who."

Padder volunteered to walk out to the cemetery and check the boy's story. Filson, not to be outdone by a competitor, also volunteered, as did Young Wix. Baz decided to go, contending the matter needed a woman's ear, and Mira agreed to go as well. Of course, I went along. Malison marched in front of us, silent, though little was said by anyone – thankfully, for I was busy devising a credible fabrication. Nobody would believe the truth.

Luck blessed me. We ran into Damut first. She was sweeping her stoop. She listened to Malison's tattle, then pinned her gaze on me. "Who do you say gived us the coin?"

"Your boy isn't a liar," I stated. "But I haven't been out here since the day we dug your garden. So I figure your boy is just mistaken. Maybe he dreamed it was me."

"What's the truth?" Padder asked.

Damut placed a hand on her son's head, then lied like a professional. "Truth is I've not seen Sheever's face since last year. So I guess he's right about my boy dreaming."

"No," Malison insisted. "Calec tolt you ..."

"Hush," she scolded, tapping his head. She smiled at us. "My husband's napping. I'll fetch him." When she opened her door, three geese swarmed out of the cottage. She swept them back inside, stepped in herself, then yanked Malison in with her and shut the door.

Calec came out, yawning and stretching. Filson posed the controversy. Calec responded, "Loric gived me the coin." Weaving fact with fantasy, he said he'd heard a thump on the temple door and, when he answered the knock, a gold piece fell into his hand. He deflected additional questions by inviting us to the stable to inspect the cow. The beast is brown, with a white face. Padder proclaimed it a fit animal.

On the trek back, the six of us walked more or less in a line across the road. I was on an end, Baz huffing beside me. Sunset painted the sky. Royal Wood, clad in spring green, rustled in a breeze. A fine evening for a stroll. But unease hovered around us like a cloud of midges. Then Wix voiced what the others were thinking, "Why would the boy make up that tale?"

"All children make up tales," Baz said. "How would Sheever here get his hands on gold? And if he did, he'd not give it to Calec." She flopped a big arm around my neck and tugged me close, jailing me in her yielding bulk. "Not Sheever. He'd buy us all a barrel of ale, he would!"

Though she nearly smothered me, the laughter her comment reaped cleared the air. Chatter switched to the cow itself, then expanded into the general wellbeing of the Wessel family. Mira uttered the only bitter note. "Damut," she twittered, "is a farmer's wife."

"Least she's a wife," Baz argued, "with a house of her own. And Calec, he were a reverend as well, don't forget."

What motivated Baz to defend not only me but Damut? I neither know nor care. I showed my appreciation, however, by buying her a pitcher of ale tonight. I have no remedy for my greater error. People here are stupid enough to believe gods drop coins into worthy hands. The fable is sure to fly off wagging tongues. But will Malison's version also sprout wings?

520, 4/6. I left the meadow early and paid the Wessels a brief visit. What a mess I've created. Damut's angry about having geese in her house. Calec refuses to release them outside untended, especially at night. She wants him to remove his family's trash from the stable so they can keep the geese there, and have a stall free for the pony that lost his spot to the cow. Calec refuses to part with his heirlooms.

My presence caused their running argument to flare. He threatened to move back into the temple. She told him to take the geese with him. I tried to forge a truce by offering to clean out the stable and sort through the items with Calec. "On my next free day." This satisfied him because it complimented his own tactics – delay. Waiting a month didn't sit well with her. She'd lived with these animals nearly a week and wanted action today. Impossible. The sun had already sunk from view and I had to leave then if I wanted to get back here at the usual time.

"Next month," I told her. "I promise."

520, 4/22. High Lord Trivak has returned. Prissen, according to the wags, has remained in Dartsport, charming a bevy of young ladies. Gossip about royals has curtailed the stories about Calec and his lucky gold piece.

520, 5/10. Meddling has its rewards. I pretended to go to the meadow as usual, leaving after work on the sixth, then I rode to the cemetery. Damut was sitting on her stoop, broom across her lap, a murderous look in her eyes. "You hungry?" she asked. "We're having roast goose tonight."

Calec was in fine humor. He'd solved everything, he said. Both the cow and the pony had roamed free the past weeks without problems. "Don't need to worry none on them till winter." The horse I brought was put in their stall. As for the geese, he had assigned Basal to herd them outside each day, and rigged a pen in the cottage to hold them at night. Loren, however, is walking now and into everything. Each morning he escapes his crib and sets the geese loose, so Damut wakes to chaos. Of the twelve originally bought, seven geese are still alive, and if I hadn't gone there as promised, I doubt any would be honking next month.

Calec is a master of delay. Nothing was solved. Not with the cow. Not with the geese. Not with the discord between him and Damut. Not with Malison. The boy spurned me the evening I arrived. When we sat to eat, he claimed not to be hungry and went outside. I slept under the quince so he could go in for the night.

Tension the next morning was sharp enough to cut bone. I coaxed Calec into unloading the stable. "Let's just see what's there." Damut ordered Malison to help us.

I'm not sure who was more glum, Calec or the boy. Their moods quickly lifted though. Every item we uncovered released memories for Calec and he shared stories of his family. "This were my dad's," he'd say, fondling an old shoe, then tell us a tidbit about a time long gone. Soon Malison was rooting into the heaps to shake loose another broken relic and asking, "What about this?" I let them chatter, while I methodically shifted the clutter from the stalls and spread it out on the grass.

Rusted axles, bent spades, clothes stinking of mildew, all had worth in Calec's eyes. There were hints of past wealth – a padded chair missing its hind legs, a vanity dresser suffering from dry rot. When Calec tired, I propped up the chair so he could sit out in the sun amid his treasures. He clapped his hands when I dragged out a mattress, feather stuffing matted and riddled with mice nests. "I were birthed on that bed!" He spoke fondly of his mother, then pointed to the area of the graveyard where she – and the rest of his ancestors – lay buried. Afterward I felt like tomb robber, pulling his family's property out into the light where it could be seen for what it was – rubbish.

About noon, Damut brought us bread and fresh butter. As we ate, she strutted along the stretches of trash like a warrior on a battlefield. "Most of this will burn," she stated and Calec, accepting defeat, didn't protest. He dozed in his chair during the afternoon, an old lord on a sagging throne, while Malison and I cleaned out his coffers.

I tried to start a conversation with the boy by asking if he intended to continue studying to become a reverend. "No," he muttered, "and I won't be no lying cook neither." So we worked in silence. His term in baimyot had taught him, if nothing else, how to be mute. In the last stall, we found a locked trunk. The leather straps had rotted so we pushed it outside.

Calec and Damut were arguing over when to burn the rubble. He, of course, wanted to wait until the next day. As if by magic, the bickering stopped and both of them came over to the trunk. "Were my granddad's" he said, then related a story about his grandparents, how in love they'd been, and how his grandfather had filled and locked the trunk after the death of his grandmother. He frowned at the brass padlock. "Buried the key with her, he did."

Curiosity enthralled me. I sent Damut to fetch a fork and, after bending a tine, I picked the lock. Calec laughed, "If I didn't know better, I'd think you was a thief." He got the honor of raising the lid. The scent of cedar gushed out, touching memories of my own and, in a small way, I understood how difficult the day had been for him. I, however, didn't want to be reminded of my past. I backed off and headed for the stable.

"Sheever," Calec called, "don't bring out more yet. Start a fire so we can clear some of this other first." No urge to delay. He'd fallen under the trunk's spell. His old hands reached in to lift a knitted shawl, the red wool preserved from rot by the cedar, and he tenderly draped the shawl around Damut's shoulders. "Suits you, it does, wife."

I moved twenty paces or so away. As I broke up the dresser for kindling, I watched them and Malison unload the trunk. The contents clearly had belonged to a Mearan woman with a little wealth: scarves, undergarments, aprons and dresses, most of the clothing red or black. Damut was as bewitched as Calec. A peaked riding cap, meant for a woman, fit Malison. Who cares about propriety? Red velvet with a curling black feather, the boy couldn't keep his fingers off the cap long enough to leave it on his head.

Basal plodded around the side of the cottage, leading Loren by the hand. "I've penned the geese," he said, then left his brother to run toward the trunk. "What's in it?" Damut blew a scarf his way before waving ribbons at Loren, luring the toddler into the ring of enchantment.

Fire is supposed to shield one from spells and, after I'd set the dresser aflame, I felt secure, as the Wessels reveled in their madness. Then I heard a thrum, like the cry of a lost soul, as Calec pulled out a lute. I had no resistance. "Do you play?" I asked, walking over.

Calec shook his head. "Never did." He offered the instrument to me. "Do you?"

I've owned far more expensive lutes. This one had only nine strings. Thick lacquer darkened what must have been the original color of its paint, Mearan red. A black hawk on its belly was barely discernible. In another life, I would have snubbed the thing. In this life, I cradled it my arms and hurried to the fire before my weakened knees forced me to sit. As I adjusted the brass tuning pegs, a jumble of songs clogged my mind, none of them with Mearan lyrics. I've played Vic songs – Juboe often made me entertain his friends – but those I sang in Universal. I tuned the lute so the notes would sound less foreign to a Mearan ear.

Malison strolled over in his new red cap. He placed another scrap of the dresser on the fire, as if that's why he'd come, then eyed me like a hungry cat.

"Want to learn to play?" I asked. Such is magic, he forgot I was a lying cook. He sat beside me and I transferred the lute to his lap. As I positioned his hands, I couldn't help thinking of teaching Sythene. Yet it's unfair to compare them. She had thousands of songs stashed in her memory and needed only the slightest instruction. He struggled with the basic chords and soon complained, "The strings hurt." Indeed. Callouses which once protected me had softened over the years. I, too, felt the strings. But for me, their bite caused a delicious pain. I craved more.

That evening Calec's young family gathered around while his heirlooms burned like a funeral pyre. I wanted to sing happy songs, but none surfaced, complete, in my memory. I sang of slain warriors and forsaken lovers, and even then had to hum through gaps, either forgetting the lyrics or unable to translate them fast enough. No one seemed to care.

"Where'd you learn so good?" Calec asked when I paused awhile, my fingertips sore.

"His minstrel father taught him," Damut teased.

I let her answer stand. And again, no one cared. After the Wessels had gone inside to bed, I reset the strings, tuning them as an Utte would. The pitch is slightly different, the chords slightly more difficult to achieve, but the sounds those small changes produce ... Utte music has a haunting quality, a bittersweet tone unmatched by any other. The moon hung pure and full in its web of stars. I played songs I had taught Sythene so long ago, then played ones she had taught me, tunes from a far more ancient time, of places and people forgotten except by her. If she could recall those ancient tunes surely she remembers me.

The next morning Damut came out, new shawl around her shoulders, with her milking stool and pail. The cow and the pony had wandered near the stable, as if knowing they belonged there. "Hold her for me?" Damut asked.

The cow is as docile as a pet. Patting its neck kept it still. Yet the stink of the beast didn't block the smell of cedar wafting from Damut's shawl and, while the rising sun cast shafts of light through trees beyond her garden, my thoughts drifted toward home.

"Heard strumming late in the night," Damut said as she rhythmically squirted milk into the pail. "Heard songs like them in Eastland. From Uttes. Did you learn them songs when you was traveling with Snakes? Is that who you're hiding from, Sheever? The Snakes?"

I didn't respond. She filled the pail, carried it and the stool back into the cottage, and didn't question me on the subject again. I don't owe her the truth. Indeed, I owe her nothing. She owes me. When I left today, all four stalls in the stable were usable and she had no geese in her house.

520, 9/3. I haven't written in months. Haven't wanted to record my actions. I can't let this date slip by, however, without a notation. As of today, I have been here nine years.

Now the journal is out of its box, the pen's wet, and I want to write more. Damnation. I knew this would happen.

The past summer has been the happiest I've had since coming to this rabbit hole. I spent my free days at the cemetery. I've been careful. People here still assume I ride to Brithe, or go moon-howling, or wherever they thought I went each month. None of them has had the urge to walk to the cemetery and nobody's died to prompt them. True, it's only a matter of time, but Calec, Damut and her boys know not to mention my visits. I can't believe I've accepted this rationale. I'm relying on children to keep secrets.

If my habits become known, so what? People will think I'm bedding Damut right under Calec's nose. I'll be teased and they'll be whispered about. No harm done.

Potential gossip isn't what worries me. Nor is it why I didn't write for months. I took the journal from its niche several times and put it back, unused, for the same reason I'm uneasy now. An odd sensation seeps from this journal. When I hold it, I feel as if I'm caught in a fold in time. As I pen these words, I sense another person reading them. Not Juboe. A living person. In another time, another place. I don't know when or where. More unsettling, I don't know who. Friend or foe?

I've already presumed I'll be arrested. Thus it's likely the person I sense is an Eshra priest, which makes it difficult, if not foolish, to continue writing. Yet the only option is to do what I did all summer – not write.

Words on paper are no longer in my control. Not true. I could destroy the journal. Burn it. The journal has helped me survive here. If I had never bought it, I'd be insane by now – assuming I'm not. I may destroy it later. For now, I could lie. Maybe I have already. Maybe I didn't visit the Wessels this past summer. How could a reader be sure? By asking them, that's how. Is that what I fear, having others dragged into my affairs? No, only an idiot would read this journal and believe any knowledge about me could be gleaned from the Wessels. Nor would they be useful hostages. I'd never compromise myself to save a family of Vics. Indeed, if I cared about the Wessels, I would've stayed out of their lives.

Last year Calec had a purpose, to teach Malison to be a reverend. This year the old man lazes in the sun, smoking his pipe and getting fat on Damut's pastries. I gave him the delusion Loric will extend his life until he's trained one of her sons to replace him. He's decided to delay death and wait for Loren to grow up. Malison hoped to be a cook like his father, then hoped to inherit Calec's spot at the temple, both respectable occupations. Now he longs to be a minstrel. The boy can't even hum in tune. Delusions. Damut has been hardest struck. She thinks I go there to see her. Last month she cornered me in the stable and poured out her heart, expecting me to do the same. Fool. I have no heart.

It was the lute that drew me to the cemetery each month. But I'm weary of the thing. I, too, have suffered from a delusion this summer. Music doesn't ease the weight of my soul. I need to fast, as I used to do on my free days. I need time alone. I need to remember who I am.

The summer has been pleasant. But it's over.

520, 9/27. Went to the meadow. Unable to fast. Ate every berry I found. Unable to focus. Damut and Malison kept jutting into my thoughts – with good reason, as I discovered when I returned. While I was gone, she sent the boy here. To check on me? If so, she was smart about it. The boy brought a batch of her butterhorns, supposedly to sell, though a kitchen is odd choice for a market. Cyril gave a hopence for the whole lot, 'to be kind,' or so Cyril told me this evening.

"How were they?" I asked. I'd arrived as the women were cleaning up after the meal and had dipped myself a bowl of tepid stew. He and Young Wix sat opposite me.

"They was good for a girl's work," Cyril said, "but not good as Wix here can bake." Liar. He and Wix thought I'd taught Damut to make the horns. They had plotted the conversation which advanced into an interrogation, with the aim to find out the ingredients for the cream filling.

"If you want her recipe," I said, "you'll have to hire her on as a cook." All three of us laughed at the idea. Cyril would never hire a female cook, as Damut well knows. By now, she also knows I deliberately did not visit her family this month. Nor will I the next.

Curious fact: tonight, I have not sensed that future person peering over my shoulder while I write. Maybe the path of my journal does end in flames.

521, 1/1. Autumn crawled by without my noting its passing. Nothing of import occurred. Once again, the date pushed me to wet a pen. A new year dawned this morning. A Game Year.

Already there's talk about who will win. No one thinks the Verdi team has a chance. On this date a year from now, the victors will have new faces. One more year to live.

521, 1/5. My free days began at noon yesterday. I considered going to the meadow, but Jenner came up to celebrate the holiday (the food's better here than in Fieldtown) and he brought Gim along, so I decided to linger awhile.

What I've written isn't a lie, not exactly. But I'm portraying myself falsely. I'll start anew.

My free days began at noon yesterday. It was rainy and cold outside. I wanted a reason to stay warm and dry. I waited around to be paid, then Jenner delivered the perfect excuse. I told myself that learning about Gim was more important than going to the meadow. Yet it didn't take long to be certain he is not an ear for the Church. I had time to saddle a horse and get out of the city before the gates closed. I opted to get drunk instead.

Free ale and fresh wages. A dice game was inevitable. Mira stood behind Filson, to bring him luck and keep his cup full. She did both laudably. I wasn't in the game, merely watching, keeping my own cup full. Padder joined in late, after Jenner (among others) had dropped out. Vraki tended his cup. She's one of Vraden's daughters and has been coupling with Padder since her father's death years ago. They're an odd match, at least in appearance. He's a big, handsome oaf. She inherited her father's looks – bushy eyebrows and a knot of a nose. Vraden had been a meat cook though, and Padder's friend, which may explain the pairing.

Anyway, Filson was winning and boasting about Mira being lucky. Padder, not a great wit when sober, was drunk and moody. "Lucky were she," he slurred after losing three plays in a row, "barren's more like it."

His comment led to a verbal battle between Vraki and Mira, each accusing the other of being less womanly, and each declaring her own feminine merits. Both used the number of children as proof, as if fertility alone gave a woman value. Mira disappointed me. The darts she threw lacked points. True, she had a son and a daughter, but both are dead. Vraki gave birth to a son two years ago and is fat with another child. To aim a finger at her belly and say she isn't fertile would be ludicrous. But Mira did just that. She must have realized her error, yet rather than expand on what constitutes a woman's worth, she stated that she, too, was with child. A lie.

Filson showed his delight by lifting his cup to praise her. He believed she'd outdone Vraki and, by association, he'd won over Padder, for surely he cared little about the prospects of fatherhood – he pays next to no interest in the other children he's sired.

Padder also took Mira at her word, but wasn't ready to lose. "Who's the father?"

An argument ensued, during which details of Mira's infidelities tumbled out, with more cooks than Padder and Young Wix claiming to have enjoyed her. These people never fail to astonish me. I doubt if any couple here has been strictly faithful to each other, not for long anyway. Yet suddenly that virtue became the only one with weight. Maybe too much ale had something to do with the rapid change in morals. Who knows. But Mira suffered for it. Filson beat her and when she ran from the room to escape him, he chased after her. Her cries echoed in the hallway. Then he returned and resumed his seat. And the dice game continued.

None of this is of import. I'm just idling the day away until it's dark enough to enter the city. Relieving my pocket of the beggar's share of my wages may mollify my guilt over not going to the meadow. Worth a try. There's little need to wait for sunset. It's so cold and grey out, I could go now. Unless another excuse arises.

521, 1/7. Never made it to the markets. I set out for them two days ago, shortly after my last entry, breaking my rule of waiting for sundown. Black clouds provided a comfortable twilight as I entered the city. I hadn't gone far when the clouds split, unleashing an icy torrent of rain.

A woman cloaked in a blanket hailed me from the doorway of a closed shop, "Ho, mate!"

I ducked under the overhang, joining her, before I realized she was a street brothid. She spread the blanket to give me a peek of her wares. She wore only an underdress beneath. "Just a hopence, mate." Her perfume, a lily scent, beguiled me. I asked if she had a room, thinking I could, if nothing else, warm up and wait out the rain. She wanted to couple in the doorway.

"I need a room," I said.

She frowned. "Cost you double."

Wind drove the rain into our faces as she led me back the way I'd come. She turned onto Bridge Street, a district notorious for harboring thieves and merchants who deal in smuggled goods. I'd frequented this area while working for the Kinship. The appeal of avoiding city taxes created an alliance between smugglers and Snakes. Greed, unfortunately, enticed some to stray from Kinship policy. I was brought in to assist an inquiry. A nasty affair. The Kinship gained a new Snake Master and I gained a host of enemies, many of whom might yet reside on Bridge Street.

I bowed my head when I followed Lily, as I dubbed the woman, into an inn. "Just me," she called – to the innkeep, I assumed. Her room was on the top floor. She knocked, and a girl of about eight or ten unbolted an inside lock and flung the door open. "Did you bring food?" the girl blurted, then spied me and jumped back.

"My sister," Lily informed me. Lie. The girl was her daughter. I shouldn't have been surprised. I suspected Lily was an illegal brothid thus likely to have a child or two.

"We'll eat soon," she told the girl, then pulled me into the room – a wretched place, cold and dim. That makes it sound worse than mine. It was not. Her room was larger by far, as was her bed. I was equating it with rooms I'd rented in the past, in my old life, and compared to them, hers was miserable. Rain pounding on the roof created a constant din. A candle burned atop a cheap vanity dresser, its bronze mirror supplying a dull double of the flame that bobbed from gusts breezing through a shuttered window.

The girl had sat on a stool by a small table. Lily spoke to her, too softly for me to hear, though she probably told her to leave, for the girl got up again. As she passed me, I handed her a copper. "Fetch us something to eat."

Her brown eyes were huge, like those of some night creature accustomed to darkness. "Enough for three?"

"At least," I said, and she scampered out.

Lily grunted, "Food's extra." She shed her blanket, peeled off the underdress and walked naked to the vanity. The sight of her aroused every aspect of my being – except my manhood. She gathered her wet hair and bound it at her nape with a scarf. "What you waiting for, mate?"

I unpinned my cape and let it drop to the floor, then moved behind her. The exquisite scent of her quickened my breath. I gazed at the reflection of her breasts, nipples pinched from cold. I wanted to caress her, but my hands, as if severed from my wrists, refused. A sense of foreboding crept into me. She turned to face me, and I glimpsed my own reflection, black hawk on my chest. I stepped back a pace.

"What's wrong?" she asked, then she, too, noticed the blazon on my tunic. "You weren't no trooper," she assessed. "What are you? Some sort of official?"

"Get dressed," I said. I went to my cape, but couldn't force myself to pick it up. I discerned a warming stove in the shadows and, going to it, knelt to examine the thing. Positioned on a slab of slate, the stove appeared to be usable, though coal ash in its grate was damp from rain running down the flue. A handful of dry twigs beside the stove's clawed feet, if lighted, wouldn't last long. "How much for heat?"

"What?" She had donned a frilly Dray-style camisole and knickers. Water dripped from her hair as she bent over me. "You weren't no list master, were you?" She gushed a series of lies, about how she'd lost her papers and so forth, then promised to service me for free.

"I'm not a list master," I said to hush her. "What does the innkeep charge for coal?"

"A hopence a bucket. Why?"

I gave her the coin. "Because I'm cold."

"I don't understand," she said. Nor did I. For a while I had the room to myself, and the chance to leave. I sat on a stool, rested my head against the wall, and wondered what I was doing. The answer eluded me then, but not now. I was trying to be someone else.

The girl returned before her mother. She put a warm kettle, cups, and two meat pies on the table. "That's all you got for a copper?" I asked.

She sniffed, "He took the rest for past due." In her faded pink dress, she looked the same as any girl from the kitchens, stringy hair, snotty nose, dirty socks on her feet. She glanced at my blazon, then stared at my face, her big eyes condemning me. "You going to arrest my mother?"

"Why would I do that?"

She shrugged. "'Cause you're mean."

"Sit down and eat," I grumbled.

She snatched a pie and bit into it before taking the remaining stool. I filled a cup. The tea was tepid and thin, no silth in it at all. The pies appeared to be stale. Had I received this sort of meal as the Soehn Biehr, the innkeep would have felt my displeasure.

I surrendered my seat when Lily returned and carried the coal bucket to the stove. While I kindled a fire, she and the girl whispered to each other, plotting, I supposed, about how to get rid of me. They eyed me like foxes as I cleaned my hands on my cape.

"Still raining," Lily said, which was obvious for the noise hadn't stopped. "Dark as well." She sucked a crumb from her finger. "You staying the night?" I asked the price. "Another copper?" she proposed, her tone implying she'd be willing to accept a lower fee.

I withdrew the coin from my pocket and placed it on the table. The girl faked a yawn as she stood. Within moments, she'd curled up on the floor near the stove, pretending to be asleep. I scanned her. She was wide awake.

Lily snuffed the candle before persuading me out of my wet clothes. She steered me to the bed. Again, the scent of her seduced my mind. Her breasts pressed against my chest, then she tugged on my necklace. "What's this?"

"A luck charm," I told her though I had no luck, as her hands plunged down and she discovered my limp condition. I am impotent. I'm certain now. I suspected it before, but wanted to prove myself wrong. Drink wasn't a factor. So I blamed Lily for being Mearan. I told her not to speak and imagined an Utte woman beside me. That evoked memories of my partner. My desire fled. I shifted away and onto my back. I blamed the rain for distracting me. I blamed my partner for dying. Lily snuggled against me. "It don't matter none, mate." Easy for her to say.

She fell asleep with her head on my shoulder. I gazed up at the darkness, listening to the rain. I sensed the girl rise. I figured she and Lily planned to rob me. Every coin with me, however, I'd intended to give away. An open scan let me perceive her stealthy creep toward the bed. But all she did was slip under the covers beside her mother.

I woke before either of them. The room was blessedly quiet. Pale light leaked between slats of the shutters. I got up and went to the window, wishing I had one in my room, and pushed open the shutters. Bridge Street is on the northern edge of the city with only an alley between it and the wall which Lily's room is higher than. The street curves to match a bend in the river so the view I received was more to the west than north. Clouds, blushed from dawn, hung low over Royal Wood, as if snagged by the bare branches and bleeding. Mist swirled over the river. In Evald, a water view is prized. The reverse is true in Tiarn. Lily's room was probably the cheapest in the inn. Like an Utte, I cherished the view. Like a Mearan, I pissed out into the morning air.

I retrieved my pants and pulled them on before tossing lumps of coal into the stove. Tea left in the kettle hadn't gained flavor overnight. I drank it to quench my thirst and glanced at the bed, mother and daughter under the blankets. Slipping away seemed the best course of action. I draped my still damp tunic over a stool and placed it near the stove to warm if not dry, then returned to the window. Many buildings in the area sport alternate modes of entry and the width of the sill hinted Lily's room was not an exception. I leaned out to see a ladder stretching from her window to the alley, convenient if eluding authorities.

When I straightened, I spied three carriages traveling the clear space between mist and cloud, all marked with the High Lord's insignia and escorted by a troop of riders. As I watched them cross the bridge, it occurred to me that Lily could've seen me crossing the day before and positioned herself to intercept me. Had my past caught up with me? Was she a relative of a former target? My suspicions seem irrational now, but not then. The foreboding I'd felt the night before struck anew and with such force my concerns rang true. Appalled by the ease with which I'd been snared, I clutched the window frame to steady myself.

The bridge burst into flame. Fiery timbers dropped into the water. Thick smoke billowed up. A dark army swarmed from the city and marched into the blaze, emerging unscathed on the far bank. I blinked. And the bridge was whole. A flock of geese flying over the river disappeared into the dawn-tinted clouds hugging Royal Park. Nausea gripped me. I retched up the tea, wondering if it had been laced with a poison I'd been unable to detect.

"You sick?"

I twisted around to see the girl. Before my eyes she grew into a woman. Glass beads adorned her hair. Her face was powdered, a trick aging brothids employ. Pain stabbed my chest and shot down my left arm. My legs melted. I lost my grip on the window frame and fell, banging my head on the sill. Either the girl or the woman rolled me onto my back. Actually, I saw them both, but it must have been the girl. The woman was an illusion. Their hands cradled my head. "Are you dying?" the woman asked. Or was it the girl?

I stared across the room at the door to the hall. Cold fear seized me as a man came through the door. Not the doorway. The door. Right through the wood. He was tall and well-built and transparent. His form became denser as he advanced, but my gaze was low. I saw knives sheathed in his boots. He apparently didn't see me lying in his path. He planted a foot in my chest and I cried out, so great the pain, as his essence ripped into me. I heard his thoughts, 'Damn you, Soehn Biehr, it didn't need to end this way.'

I vaguely recall being helped onto the bed. I drifted in and out of reality, in and out of dreams. I remember the phantom woman feeding me wine. Or was it the girl feeding me tea? "I sent a rider to fetch him," she said.

When I woke, rain drummed on the roof. Lily and her daughter were seated at the table, eating bread and cheese. I propped myself up on an elbow, then slid back down again, my head firm as a blighted potato. Lily glided over and sat on the bed. I asked if I'd slept the whole day.

"Mate, you cracked your head yesterday."

I told her I had to leave, and she helped me dress, shoving my boots onto my feet, a task I could not have accomplished alone. Weaker than water, I walked to the door, but was afraid to open it, afraid of what might await me on the other side. Fear forces cowards into odd choices. I left by way of the window, climbing down the slick rungs of the ladder while rain pelted me. Amazing that I reached the bottom without falling.

My absence had caused a stir. Cyril searched for me in the stables and spread such alarm that Jenner sent a rider to Calec's to look for me there, either above or below ground. Numerous theories were posed – I'd spouted wings and flown to Brithe; I'd found work as a cook in Tiarn – but Cyril convinced almost everyone that I'd been slain by a robber. The lump on my head gave credence to his guess, at least to the robbery part, and I considered playing along. But when he started his lecture about the dangers outside his kitchens, I pulled the remaining coins from my pocket. "You wasn't robbed?" Cyril blurted.

"Slipped and fell," I said, then concocted a tale about wandering around, dazed and lost, until I'd regained my wits today. Not far from the truth. I'm still a bit dazed. What caused the visions? I don't know, but the first one is easy to decode. The bridge will burn someday. An army will invade. The carriages leaving Royal Park imply the House of Trivak will fall. Someday. Doesn't mean I'll live to see it happen. Nor is it likely I'll see Lily's daughter as a woman, though she'll probably adopt her mother's profession. Surprise.

Only the third vision had personal content. The man knew me. Or knew of me, for I didn't recognize him. During the pulse of thought I received from him, I sensed regret. Of what? Being hired to kill me? The vision makes little sense. Why would he expect to find me there of all places? Nor can I fathom how he fits into the memsa's prophecy. Have I stumbled over an alternate line of fate?

521, 1/8. The carriages I saw may have been real. The High Lord left early on the 6th for Dartsport. Future invasion or no, maybe the House of Trivak won't fall. A pity.

Young Wix suggested I walk to the cemetery this evening. "So Calec won't be worried," he said, "and while you're there …" He wants Damut's butterhorn recipe, has wanted it since tasting them last year. Pride keeps him from going and asking her himself. He wants me to tease it out of her. I'm not the Soehn Biehr anymore. I don't get paid for doing another's dirty work.

On a different note, Mira claims she lost the child she was brooding. She blames Filson, but hasn't reaped much sympathy, not even from the women, while I've been showered with it. There's no justice here. True, she lied, but the beating she took injured her far worse than I've been. Her face is still swollen. All I have is a bump on my head.

521, 1/14. Onji came to the doorway of the spare kitchen, motioned me into the hall, then led me to the north door.

Malison was waiting outside in the rain. He refused to enter. "We was just wondering if you was alive or dead."

"So now you know," I said. Having Onji beside me saved me from questions I'm sure he wanted to ask. After an uneasy silence, I told him to go home and get dry, then I shut the door and went back to work.

521, 2/11. Returned from a damp stay in the meadow. Couldn't find wood dry enough to burn. It's been raining for more than a month. My room smells like a cellar. Haven't slept well. But Juboe's ghost hasn't tormented me. Small blessing.

521, 2/16. Today I am forty-four years old. Will this be my last birthday? Most likely. The idea of wasting the entire day in the kitchens sickened me. But I didn't want to be alone. I told Young Wix that if he made a batch of butterhorns, after work I'd take some to Damut and try to get her recipe. He wrapped five in oilskin to keep them dry, for it had been raining on and off all day.

"Tell her these are yours," he said, and I nodded, inferring I would abet his deception. I left the kitchens before sundown and intended to go to the cemetery. But as I walked through the fog, I thought of Lily, the odd visions I'd had, and when I reached the bridge, I crossed over.

Wall Alley was a swamp. I kicked muck from my boots before climbing the ladder. The shutters were fastened. I rapped repeatedly until, finally, the girl pushed them open. "It's you," she greeted me, with more wariness than warmth. "My mother's not here."

"I came to visit you," I lied. It was the room I wanted to visit. I gave her the butterhorns.

Lust filled her eyes as she peeked under the wrapping. "What do I have to do for them?"

"A favor," I said for lack of a specific request. Edging up a rung, I sat on the sill and produced my most harmless smile. "You going to invite me in?"

"I guess so," she mumbled, and I swung inside.

The butterhorns kept her distracted while I explored the room. I scanned everything, touched everything, especially the door to the hall – and detected nothing. I returned to the window and gazed out at the same sort of misty twilight I'd seen before the visions. The bridge didn't catch fire. I initiated a mild trance, trying to conjure a residue of the essence I'd perceived that day. A lonely ache filtered into me. Then the girl spoke. "You going to swoon today?" She was beside me, hand on my elbow, the obvious source of the sensation I'd received.

"No," I answered, wondering if she spent most evenings alone, "not today."

I let her guide me to a stool. She had eaten three of the butterhorns and, though she offered me the other two, when I declined, she devoured them as well. Caution gone, she mimicked her mother's flirty mannerisms, sucking crumbs from her fingers, teasing about the favor she owed me, hinting I'd get more if I gave more. "For a copper I could do a mate right." When I put a coin on the table, she sputtered a retraction.

"Too late," I laughed as I stood, but I headed for the window.

She trailed me, yammering, "You going? What about the copper, mate?"

"It's yours." I scrambled out the window, gripping the sill while I secured my footing on the ladder. Her hands grabbed my sleeves and she kissed me, her lips sweet from the pastries.

"I still owe you, mate. Come by again. Tomorrow maybe?"

"Sure," I said. Then she released me, and I climbed down the ladder and out of her life.

Wix must have been fretting the whole time I'd been away. He met me at the north door. "Well?" he demanded, "did you get Damut's recipe?"

I shook my head. "She won't tell nobody." Poor Wix. Pride has made him a fool.

521, 2/30. The sun broke free this afternoon. The moment I finished work, I took a chair out the west door, plunked its legs in the mud and sat, absorbing the bright warmth. Such a precious thing, sunlight. I shut my eyes and mentally recited a prayer of thanks. The rainy season is nearly over and I've remained sane. Have I banished Juboe for good?

Cyril came out, wanting to chat. He's worried about staffing, worried about whom he should name to be the next head cook. Filson, Padder and Young Wix have all learned to write well enough to tend the supply log and all three are pressuring him to decide among them. "You got me into this," he blamed. "Should've picked Filson from the start."

"So pick him now."

"It weren't so easy now. Don't you see? No matter who I pick, two of the three'll be sore. They'll gripe to their mates, get them sore, maybe some sore enough to …"

"Find work in Tiarn," I finished for him.

"It's a Game Year," he stated, which said it all.

I resealed my eyes, tipped my face toward the sun, and lied. "Heard Kwint gossiping. He said the High Lord planned to announce his new bride after the Games. Said Trivak might wait until Gurn Four. Said none of the lords would dare leave early like Macon D'brae did last time."

I enjoyed a moment of peace before Cyril caught on – not to my lie, to an excuse for a delay. "Wait till Gurn Four," he muttered, "nobody'd leave early." And so forth. Convincing himself the idea was his. Finally, he got up and went inside. And I went back to savoring the sunlight.

521, 3/5. Tobb and Grutin showed up this evening. Cyril hired them. He assigned Tobb to meats and Grutin to the spare kitchen. The only thing worse than the prospect of working with Grutin again is living with Tobb again. He's in bed now, snoring. His muddy boots tracked the floor. He stinks like a sewer. I feel invaded.

Grutin is sharing a room with Rebic and Lanerd, a room with space for four, but Tobb craved his old bed and Cyril gave it to him. I'll never convince the oaf to move out. "Missed our room," he said when he came through the doorway. "Dreamt of it every night." He stroked the plank with his name on it. "Not no place finer than here, mate." I wanted to retch.

He asked if I had missed him. I told him, "No."

He laughed, "Well, I missed you." He rubbed the stump of the finger I had cut from his hand, then dug into a filthy pocket. "When we was in Drayfed, I got you this." He tossed me the gift. "A wizard's tooth. Got it from a witch, I did. She weren't sure it would end a curse, but if you puts it under your pillow, it'll ward off new curses." The damn thing looked like a boar's tooth. I slid it under my pillow. Maybe it will ward off Tobb.

He and I didn't chat long. He didn't mention Cassie and I didn't ask. I don't want to know what happened to her. I'll create my own reality. Cassie met a man who agreed to marry her. An innkeeper perhaps. She left Tobb and is with a man who buys her shoes that fit her feet. I wonder how she spent my savings. On Tobb, most likely.

I glance up and see his bulk stretched over his cot. It's as though he never left. His beard gives the truth away. I doubt he shaved even once while he was gone. His chin is a disgusting tangle of hair and dried food. I hope Cyril forces him to bathe. His clothes should be burned.

"Dead tired, I am," he said before he fell asleep. A pity he isn't simply dead.

521, 3/6. Tobb entered as I was wetting my pen. He has a pitcher of ale. "Don't let me stop you from writing," he said as he refilled the cup I had brought in with me.

He's sitting on his bed, pitcher at his feet, holding his cup with both hands ... staring at me. When I looked up, he nodded at the container I'd bought for the journal. "Got yourself a tin box for it, eh," he said. "Still fit in the hiding spot I built?"

I told him it did, and it does, though I don't keep it there. I prefer the niche beside my bed. I'm not sure why I don't want to tell him where I store the journal. Lack of trust? If he wanted the damn thing, he could seize it from me now. Yet I know he won't. In my presence, I trust him. When he's with Grutin ... I'm not sure.

The two of them have been welcomed as if they were lost kin. No one seems to recall that they caused a girl's death when they fled from their debts. Selective memory. I should learn from these dolts I'm forced to live among. Tobb is the biggest dolt of all. I wonder what he thinks I'm writing. Does he think? I'm glad he's being quiet. I can pretend he isn't here.

He and Grutin weren't assigned chores today. Tobb slept most of the day. After evening meal, Cyril tapped a keg and everyone gathered to hear their adventures. The ale was free. I joined the adoring crowd long enough to down a cup or two. Grutin did the talking. Mira doted on him, pouring his brew, fussing with his hair, as if he were royalty. Filson didn't seem jealous. Nor did any of her other lovers. Tobb was unusually sedate, nodding from time to time, saying little while Grutin boasted of the purses they'd won and the foreign women they'd despoiled.

Tobb is still sedate. He's sitting there, tending his cup, watching me. I sense a difference in him. He's cleaner than I've ever seen him. But that's not it. Something inside has changed. I can't put a finger on what. He smiled when I looked up, but said nothing. I can't believe he didn't lure a woman in here. He could've easily done so. And why follow me in? Grutin's still out there, captivating the others. Considering Tobb's proclivity to consume brew until he vomits, why did he leave before the keg was drained? Maybe he'll go out again when his pitcher is empty. But he's had only a sip since he came in.

I paused to finish my cup. He stood to fill it again. Why is he waiting on me? His silence disturbs me. "You want something?" I asked.

"No, mate," he said. "Enjoy seeing you is all." I feel uncomfortable.

"You never done me wrong," he said. Selective memory in action. How do these people achieve it? "And you done good for Cassie." He wants to tell me about her. I sense the desire in him, but I know his ploy. He won't tell me unless I ask. It's a form of power, sparking curiosity then withholding information. I refuse to succumb. "Right good you done her," he said to prompt me once more. "Liked you, Cassie did." He's trying to make me feel guilty for not asking why she didn't return. I don't need to ask. He told me. Twice. Each time he said her name, I heard the answer in his voice. Cassie is dead.

He's saying, "Cyril tolt me you still go moon-howling." I'm not going to respond.

"You writing down Grutin's tales?" he asked.

"No." I shouldn't have spoken. It will only encourage him. If he wants to chat, why doesn't he go out with the others? There are plenty of people in the dining hall.

"It weren't like Grutin tells it," he said. "Them places he speaked of ... We was there and all, but it weren't fun like he makes it. And Grutin, he's lucky with dice, he is, but near everybody claimed he were cheating, and most of them purses was stole back from us. So we tooked to robbing. Weren't fun, robbing. Couldn't stay nowheres for long and when plague breaks out around Driden, we was chased from most towns. Folks don't want strangers passing by. We had to rob just to eat."

I asked him why, when things weren't going well, didn't he return to Tiarn. He's rubbing his beardless chin. The question was too difficult, I suppose, but if I remember correctly, the plague outbreak was more than two years ago.

"Cassie and Untha was gone," he's saying, "and Grutin, he keeped swearing things would get better." He's baiting me again. He used the word chierv, which translates into gone rather than dead, though dead is what he means. Why won't he just say it? Why does he want me to ask? Does he think I'll blame him for her death? "Cassie and Grutin never got along," he's saying. "And when Grutin finds she was holding out on us ..."

Tobb, why do you torture me? You say nothing and tell me everything. I hear the truth in your voice, see it in your eyes. I don't need the words. Grutin killed Cassie to steal the coins I gave her. I'm responsible for her death. He's waiting for me to finish writing. I don't want to stop, don't want him to speak, but I need to wet the pen.

"Sheever," he said when I lifted my hand, "it were you who gave her the coins, weren't it. They was yours." He has pierced my soul with his blade of guilt. I have no defense, no shield. The stupid ox has won. "It were good what you done for her," he's saying. "You always done good by her. And by me, mate." Is he trying to atone for what he's done to me? He stood and went to the door, but hasn't opened it. I have to look up.

Tobb left. These were his parting words: "Grutin and me, we swore an oath, we did. I can't never snitch on him. But Grutin, he knowed it were your coins Cassie had, and he figures you have more stashed in this room."

I told him I understood, and I do, finally. Tobb wasn't casting blame. He wanted to warn me without breaking his oath. He has more wits than I give him credit. He even hinted when Grutin will search this room – during my next moon-howling. I'll have time to move the journal.

I remember a children's story about a woman who lived in a forest. She'd tempt passing hunters into her cottage, but none who embraced her survived, for everything she touched withered and died. As a boy, I identified with the hunters. Tonight, I feel like that woman.

521, 3/9. I slipped out of the kitchens after work today. Tobb was tending the spit, roasting a boar for 'our fine' Hawk troopers. Game fever has already struck. I told him I was going into the city, then I walked to the cemetery. I wanted to warn Damut that Grutin has returned.

The family welcomed me as if I'd been away on a journey rather than snubbing them. Indeed, I felt like a bone tossed to a pack of hounds. Calec grabbed me first. He took me behind the stable to the paddock we'd started to enclose last summer. He and Malison completed the fence, or nearly so. "Don't got the gate right," Calec admitted, and the water trough leaks, but penning the cow and pony keeps them from Damut's garden, which makes his life easier.

"Loric's smiling on me again," he said, then told me that last autumn Wacha Leyourd's parents had stopped by to see her grave and paid him to pray for her soul. "A full silver, they gived me," he cackled and went on to say this year he'd sold five more prayers, "like in my granddad's day," to men who wanted a Mearan victory in the Games.

Malison had joined us by then and stood clutching the lute, obviously craving my attention and annoyed he wasn't getting it. "They only gave hopence," he stated.

"Hopence we'd not have," Calec admonished, "if Sheever hadn't turned our luck."

"Me?" The idea I had anything to do with his selling prayers surprised me, but he was determined to award me credit and traced his change in fortune, citing – it seemed – every instance our paths had crossed. He was rambling about the time we opened his grandfather's trunk when Damut came around the side of the cottage, drying her hands on a red apron.

"Sheever," she called, "something's wrong with the stove. Could you help me?"

I extracted myself from Calec and Malison, promising to return, and hurried to meet her. Certain she and I wouldn't have another chance to be alone, I gave her the news about Grutin as we walked back. "I doubt he'll bother you," I stressed, "but I thought you should know."

At the stoop, out of Calec's sight, she confessed that nothing was wrong with the stove. "I just wanted to tell you …" She took my hand. "… I'm happy you're here," she said, though her voice lacked joy. Each time I see her I'm aware it could be the last time, and so is she.

I stayed long enough to tune the lute and show Malison the chords again, and I listened while Basal prodded Loren into babbling silly words. I hate to record this, but Grutin probably is Loren's father. They have the same eyes.

Damut and Calec invited me to spend my free days there. I said I might which both of them knew meant I won't. I feel strongly about limiting my contact with their family. Not so strongly, however, that I prevented myself from borrowing a spade. Calec asked why I wanted it. I told him I planned to dig my own grave, and he laughed.

What I've dug is a grave for my journal. I'm in Royal Wood now, midway between the cemetery and the Dray Natal Compound. There's a sapling growing from the log I'm sitting on. I'll be able to recognize it and find this spot again. I don't like the idea of burying the journal, but it should be safe inside its box. I tossed a copper into the hole for luck.

I'll leave for the meadow when I finish work tomorrow. Tobb wants me to go the next morning so I won't be riding at night. Today he wanted me to wait for his boar to be done so he could escort me into Tiarn. "You should listen to me," he warned when I refused his offer of protection. "I know a thing or two about robbing." Scratching his jaw, he glanced around to be sure we were alone, then whispered, "and about killing as well."

I've grasped what has changed about him. He's joined the ranks of the damned.

521, 6/27. I have been searching for this place for months. Ferns grew up around the log, hiding it, and the trees leafed out. I must have walked past dozens of times, always with some burning thought I yearned to put in writing. Now that I've found the journal, my thoughts have cooled.

High Lord Trivak returned some time ago and we've been moderately busy ever since. There's talk about him choosing brides for himself and Prissen. Not sure if the gossip is true or merely an extension of the lie I fed Cyril months ago. True or not, among the working class, few care whom Trivak might marry. Though the Prelims are months away, chatter about the Games dominates most conversations. Cooks spend free hours watching the troopers spar, and each evening new odds are set and wagers altered over who will be the Mearan Champion.

Jenner, too, has been moderately busy. I donate as much time as I can to helping in the stables. He hasn't faltered on his promise of lending me a horse, but if there's one thing I learned from Juboe it's never take a sponsor for granted.

I've adapted to living with Tobb. When I lie awake, unable to sleep, his thunderous snores – which used to incite thoughts of murder – bring a sense of comfort. Insane, I know, and I can't explain why I react differently toward him. He's as oafish as ever.

My distaste for Grutin grows firmer each day and working in the same room with him grants me chances to torment him. I haven't harmed Grutin. Indeed, the pranks I played on him were so childish I'm embarrassed I did them. He, of course, pinned blame on me, but he blames me for all his woes, including the fact he's been stung by wasps countless times this spring.

"The Kor-man done it," he wails, as some portion of his body swells from a sting, "cursed me, he has." No one believes I can summon wasps to do my bidding. If I could, people reason, I would've done it to others, for I've certainly shown my temper on occasion. Thus Grutin handed me a perfect foil. No matter what he claims, no one will ever believe I'm at fault for his misfortunes. Despite the advantage, I stopped pulling tricks on him after the night I dreamed I crept into his room and slit his throat. The dream was so vivid, the next morning I thought I'd slain him – until he staggered into the spare kitchen, tardy, complaining I had somehow caused him to oversleep. He was stung on the neck that day. And his luck, even without my help, has remained poor.

Many of my dreams lately have been vivid. One I had two days ago, while at the meadow, motivated me to search for the journal this evening. I dreamed I was trapped inside the walls of a house. I could climb up and down, and crawl between floors and ceilings. It seemed I was trying to locate a passage that led into rooms I'd glimpse through cracks in the walls. I woke before I found a way out, or in, or whatever – still trapped, I mean.

The dream left me unsettled. But now that I've written it down, it seems more silly than dire. Recording my fears weakens their grip. I miss having my journal near. The year's more than half over. I doubt I'll see another spring. Is that a fear? Or a hope?

521, 7/10. I dreamed of Katre Haesyl last night. That, in itself, isn't surprising. Yesterday was his birthday and he was on my mind. In the dream he and I were in his sitting room where, in reality, I'd last seen him. He didn't look as he had then. He was old and gaunt, his skin like parchment. He wore a black gown beneath a white over-robe embroidered with gold thread. His shoulders seemed to sag under the weight of it. A simple gold band crowned his brow.

"Lord Lonntem tells me you've been working as a cook," he said. His lips cracked into a smile. "You were always clever, Me'acca. Even Dyn Massu thinks you're dead." It seemed so real, as if I were actually with him, yet a simple detail proved the dream false. He was standing and I was seated, a breach of protocol I'd never commit.

He turned away from me and toward the portrait of Daith Haesyl. "I always did what was expected of me. You did the opposite. Which of us was wiser?" Facing me again, he removed his signet ring and offered it. "Give this to my son. Help him do the unexpected."

"Both of your sons are dead," I told him, but it was as though I hadn't spoken. The ring vanished from his grasp and relief smoothed the weary pinch of his features.

"I'll see you in Pheto, Soehn Biehr," he said.

I woke to darkness. Had it not been for Tobb snoring, I may have believed myself already in Eshra's unholy realm. I got up and went out into the steamy night. The moon hovered above the western horizon, a slim crescent, nearly invisible. Tomorrow the moon will be completely dark. My dream was just a dream. Yet I can't shake my anxiety. I feel Katre needs me. And I'm too far away to help him.

521, 8/3. Pay day. I didn't want to be snared in a dice game and it was too early to go into the city, so I entered Royal Wood. I hadn't gone far when I heard someone behind me. It was Tobb. I confronted him, asking why he was following me. He claimed he wanted to protect me from thieves camping in the forest. There are men living in the Wood. I've stumbled upon several campsites, but Tobb's response was a lie. "You planning to rob me?" I asked him.

"Not of your pay," he muttered, then the truth spewed out. Grutin has heard the rumor that I gave Calec a gold piece. He's also seen me go into the Wood and has deduced I have a pot of gold buried in here. He coerced Tobb into finding out where. "I weren't going to steal it all," he swore, "just enough so Grutin, he'd not take it all." How does one counter such nonsense? I told him I didn't have any gold buried in the Wood.

"In the cemetery then?" he asked as though, if true, I'd tell him. "In a grave, maybe?"

"No, Tobb," I said. "I keep all my gold in Brithe."

"Oh." He nodded. "So it's safe."

"Safe," I agreed, then invited him to walk with me. He asked where I was going, and I told him, "Nowhere."

"It's too hot to walk about for no reason," he stated and headed back toward Main Road, which left me free to come out here and record what is not a revelation, namely, if Tobb had more wits, he'd be dangerous.

There's little else to say. The anxiety I felt last month is still with me, like a shadow, there but not a burden. If Katre had died, an emissary would have brought a copy of his will to Tiarn for the High Lord to approve, as required by the Cyntic Treaty. Surely some word of the event would trickle through the endless chatter about the Games and reach the kitchens. None has. So I'll assume Katre is well. No doubt he'll outlive me.

521, 8/32. I believe I've been discovered.

Yesterday morning Cyril was summoned to the palace. He returned about noon, gathered the cooks in the dining hall and told us we'd receive no more free days until after the Games. We all expected our days would soon be cut to one a month. But none at all? We've been busy, but not that busy. Plus staffing had always been left up to Cyril. This time he cited, "Orders."

"Who's orders?" Filson demanded.

Cyril stammered about having no choice before admitting he didn't know the name of the man who'd issued the orders. He uttered no lie, but the matter smelled none-the-less.

"I have four days owed to me," I said, for the month has been a lue-mout and I'd worked through. In fact, if I hadn't made a late trade with Rebic, I would've started my free days yesterday and missed hearing the new rules.

"You'll get them days after the Games," Cyril promised.

"I want them now," I insisted.

"If it was up to me, I'd give them days to you." Red-faced and flustered, he looked at the other cooks for help. They supported me. "Were his due," Padder expressed the consensus, "Not fair for him to have to wait."

Cyril whined, "It weren't me to blame. I got orders. And Kwint were tolt to count heads every day." It was then I felt a jolt, as if a fist had slammed into my gut.

"I quit," I stated and went for the door.

Cyril ran after me. "Sheever, don't do this." He grabbed my arm, halting me outside. "You'll get everybody quitting." The hot sun beat down on us. Sweat glistened on his scalp. "I can't lose you. You're my best sauce cook."

I searched his squinting eyes for a glint of betrayal. If a plot's afoot, he doesn't know it. "When Kwint takes his count, tell him I've quit. I'll be back in four days. You can rehire me, if you want." Leaving him – and my afternoon work unfinished – I scrambled down to the stables.

Jenner had already received his orders. No horses were to be lent to anyone without a pass. I suppose I could've forged one. Jenner can't read. But returning to the kitchens for paper and ink wasn't an option I cared to make. I wanted distance between me and the palace. Rather than go near it again, I cut through the stockyards, angling toward Perimeter. I saw Col – as if I needed a reminder of my fate – sitting on a dung heap, grinning, spittle on his chin. He laughed like a fool as I passed by.

I went east on Perimeter, then slipped into Royal Wood and circled back to position myself where I could watch the Church and palace. Trees filtered the sunlight and blocked any breeze. I roasted through the afternoon. People came and went. Strangers on mundane errands. The banality of it all might have calmed me – if my gaze hadn't drifted to the Saeween. Eshra's arena, dark and vile, like a black mold growing on the skin of the world. Yet oddly beautiful. The longer I stared at those walls, the more beautiful they appeared. Strong. Inviting. I felt the urge to cross the road, go closer, and lay my hands upon those walls. A passing carriage broke my line of sight. And restored my sanity. I did not stare at the Saeween again.

At dusk, lightning streaked overhead and thunder rumbled, though the sky was cloudless. Fog rolled in after dark, damp and stinking, chilling my body. Fetching my cape seemed too risky. Nor would it have helped. My soul had frozen. I shivered through the night.

My lack of courage shames me. Part of it stems from surprise. I thought I had until year's end. To be arrested now doesn't fit with the prophecy. My suspicions could be wrong. Yet I feel it in my core. The Church knows I work in the kitchens, knows I borrow a horse on my free days. The prophecy is unfolding. All these years I've prayed for this and now that it's happening, my impulse is to run. As if anyone could run from tomorrow.

When the fog began to brighten, I started walking. Slacking my thirst was my immediate concern. The few small streams I know of in the Wood are dry this time of year. I headed for the one sure source of water. I emerged from the trees above the cemetery. Sunrise gilded the horizon. A swath of fog had settled at the bottom of the sloping graveyard, veiling the temple and cottage, making it difficult to determine if the Wessels were awake. Yet I wouldn't get a better chance. Hearing no sounds of activity, I trotted down into the fog.

A dipper hung from a post by the spring, a post I had planted last summer. I reached for the dipper, then pulled back my hand. Does the Church employ sensitives who could sniff my residue on anything I've freshly touched? I crouched onto my elbows and knees, and slurped water like an animal. A thump startled me. I sprang to my feet.

Damut stood a few paces away. The bucket she'd brought to fill lay on the ground. "Sheever, you gave me a fright."

"You never saw me," I growled, then bolted, out of the mist, up the slope, into the trees. I pray I haven't endangered her. If I had a dram of valor, I'd return to the kitchens now and ensure her safety. But if my life can be measured in days not months, I want each of them.

I'd feel more confident if I had a viable plan. Those I devised in the past are worthless. All of them carried a common flaw, the assumption I'd have a portion of control. I won't, not at the beginning. The first move isn't mine. Or wasn't. The fact I wasn't arrested yesterday implies neither the High Lord nor his staff has been informed of me. No one in the palace would allow a poison master to remain as a cook. But food prepared in the base kitchens doesn't flow to the Church. The priests have nothing to fear. They want to contain me, which explains the orders Cyril and Jenner received, but they're in no hurry to nab me. Why?

Do they think I've escaped? If so, my return will baffle them. Will they snatch me quickly before I can elude them again? If I had alerted a target, I'd wait, let him imagine he'd been mistaken. Maybe I do have months to live. No. I'd never give a target that much time. A sixtnight, maybe, no longer. One thing certain, I can't go back early. I must make it appear I merely wanted the days I'd earned. Let the priests think I'm not aware of their discovery.

The notion the Church hasn't revealed my presence to the state authorities intrigues me. Maybe the priests don't want to share a soehn biehr with the High Lord. Are they so confident they'll be able to enlist my services? Am I sure I'll be able to resist? I wasn't sure yesterday. I'm calmer now. Calm enough to believe I'll refuse any offer, even if my life lies in the balance. Calm enough to feel tired and hungry. I have six hopence. Plus the copper I put in the hole months ago. I can buy a meal in the city tonight. At the moment, I need sleep more than food.

521, 9/1. Tiarn was crowded. No surprise. A high proportion of Drays. Swordsmen, which isn't surprising either, but they seemed more disciplined than the usual rabble who come for the Games. Dray troopers? That's my guess, though they weren't wearing ram blazons. I remember the rumors, years ago, about Trivak and the Dray Lord plotting to assassinate Ceither Tulley. Do they intend to lure him into a scuffle? If so, they should hang whoever conceived the idea. It's bound to evolve into a sticky affair.

I stayed in the city too long and foolishly spent all my coin, most of it on ale. Fog oozing off the river stunk of rot as it plugged the streets. I got lost trying to find the bridge. Had to wait for sunrise. Lost my way here as well. Ended up at the cemetery. The morning sun had burned off the fog and I saw Damut in her garden weeding a row of cabbage heads. A pity humanity isn't weeded, the sinners plucked out so healthy souls can thrive in peace. Why don't the gods tend what they've sown?

I settled down in a bed of bracken at the edge of the trees. A clump of widow's tears blooming in the graveyard released a soft fragrance. I couldn't keep my eyes open. Voices woke me about noon. Sitting up, I peered over the ferns. Calec was at the temple with two riders who wanted to buy prayers. More supplicants came during the afternoon, most on foot, in groups of two or three. Calec blessed them all and pocketed their coins. Good for him.

Toward evening, Malison began strumming the lute. The damn thing is out of tune again. He didn't notice, proof he doesn't have the ear to become a minstrel. I retract that. He's young. With practice ... No, he needs more than practice. The lute's tortured cries drove me away.

Finding the journal is easier when walking east to west, as I was when I originally picked this site. It's peaceful here. And reasonably safe. But there's no water.

393

521, 9/2. I headed for the cemetery at dusk yesterday with the aim to steal down to the spring after dark. The same eerie storm that followed sunset the past two days occurred again. Thunder and lightning with neither clouds nor rain. The storm had waned to an occasional rumble when I reached the graveyard. I kept myself hidden, for Damut was out among the graves, a dim figure in the twilight, pacing along the tree line, hissing my name and begging me to answer. She passed by without seeing me and I prayed she wouldn't meddle in my concerns. Her very presence, however, implied she already had.

"Come out," she demanded as she passed around again. "I know you've quit the kitchens." How did she know? Most likely, after she caught me at the spring the other morning, she sent Malison to the kitchens to check on me. Foolish woman.

"Come out," she sobbed. "We can hide you from the Snakes."

I doubt she and Calec could hide me from the Kinship. I'm certain they couldn't hide me from the Church. Yet the coward in me wanted to rush from the trees and go with her. Not to hide where I'd surely be found. But for a change of clothing and a few coins. It occurred to me when I was in Tiarn how easy it would be to disappear. Crowds pass in and out of the city gates each day. I'm confident I could blend well enough to slip away and never return.

I stand at a crossroad, perhaps the last in my life. I felt it in Tiarn. Felt it again – stronger – when Damut called to me, as she wept when I failed to reply. I could avoid the prophecy. At this late date, I could alter my path, bump my fate. The choice is yet mine. I could escape. I know it. But where would a new path lead? And who would bear the cost?

Damut surrendered to the darkness and stumbled down the slope. When I stepped from the trees, I saw Calec with a lantern meet her at the road and guide her into their cottage. He left the lantern on their stoop. Stars glittered overhead while I waited for them to be asleep.

Last night the moon was full. I ached to see it once more. Fog drifted in while I was quenching my thirst at the spring. I climbed the slope again and prayed the mist would stay in the hollow until moonrise. With all my soul, I prayed, to no avail. Fog closed in so thick I couldn't see my hands, let alone the moon. Yet I'm confident the moon did rise. Why can't I be confident Sythene exists in this world? Knowledge and faith. For some, they are one and the same. I wish they were for me. I have no proof Sythene is alive. Faith will have to be enough.

521, 9/3. It's past noon. Hot. I should be hungry, but my stomach is quiet. My mouth is dry, but content to wait.

A squirrel woke me this morning. The damned thing was perched in the sapling growing from the log I'm resting my back against. Screeching. A female, I assumed. When I lifted my gaze, she made an astounding leap onto the branch of a larger maple and sat there, waving her tail like a banner, flicking it from side to side. Within moments, she had attracted a male. She led him on a merry chase, jumping from limb to limb, tree to tree, racing around and around trunks, claws scratching the bark. Up. Down. Up again. When she allowed him to catch her, they mated. A charming, if brief, romance. I dubbed them Tobb and Cassie. Like their human counterparts, my presence didn't deter their courtship. For them, I was no more real than a ghost.

Perhaps it's foolish to notice and record the actions of the dumb creatures around me. It can't be more foolish than trying to devise a plan to outwit the Eshra priests. A prepared course of action is impossible. A dream I had some months ago, about being trapped inside the walls of a house, makes sense now. The house is my future. I can't plan a way out until I'm tugged in.

And I will be tugged in. I've chosen my path. Soon Cyril will lose his best sauce cook.

Maybe I won't need to outwit the priests. Maybe all I'll need is the courage to refuse them, deny them whatever they'll want from me.

A Mearan philosopher, Yorn Larrow, once wrote that every tale, when told its full length, ends in tragedy. He viewed death as an end. I do not. Sheever the cook is a dead man. Hardly a tragedy. Oh, I realize his body still breathes. I'm not yet an idiot like Col. But the cook is dead. As of today he lived exactly ten years. He died a moment ago. A painless death. I occupy his body now. I wield the pen. I'll bury his essence in the hole with this journal. A Mearan grave for a Mearan cook. Damut wept over his passing. No need for me to shed a tear.

This evening, his body will carry me to the kitchens. I'll pretend to be him and the fools there won't notice the difference. His body will withstand whatever tortures the priests put to it. I won't feel a damned thing. His body will ferry me home.

The future peers over my shoulder. I sense its presence more sharply than last year when it frightened the cook. If he were here, he'd panic and burn this journal. But he's gone. The future doesn't scare me. The Soehn Biehr is immune to fear.

Thus it begins.

Review Requested:

If you loved this book, would you please provide
a review at Amazon.com?